CW01208044

Copyright © 2020 G.A. Pickstock

First Edition 2020
Edge of Death

All rights reserved This book is a work of fiction. Names, characters, businesses, organizations, places, events and incidents either are the product of the author's imagination or are used fictitiously. And resemblance to actual persons, living or dead or actual events is entirely coincidental No part of this publication may be reproduced in any form, or by any means, electronic or mechanical, including photocopying, recording, or any information browsing, storage, or retrieval system, without permission in writing by the author.

Pickstock, G. A. — Edge of Death (River's Edge Mysteries Book 2)VGP Publishing. Paperback Edition.

ISBN: 978-0-9958379-6-6

Dedication

"Never give in—never, never, never, never, in nothing great or small, large or petty, never give in except to convictions of honour and good sense. Never yield to force; never yield to the apparently overwhelming might of the enemy."

Sir Winston Churchill

For my Family

My Mum and Dad, George and Muriel,

who will never get to read my work.

For my children Joseph, Matthew, Robert

and their better halves,

Rhonda, Krystal and Kristine.

For all of my grandchildren.

I love you all

Acknowledgements

I would like to express my sincere appreciation to all those who have aided and supported me in the writing and production of Edge of Death.

First, I wish to thank Christine Jarvis for her invaluable help in keeping me straight on punctuation and spelling. Christine is an award-winning author of a number of short stories and her latest novel,

A Duty of the Living

will be released soon.

Her expertise and encouragement throughout this whole process has done wonders for me.

A special thank you to Michelle Dunbar of Bolide Publishing - who went above and beyond in her efforts, using her expertise to provide me with an exhaustive and complete report on my work.

Michelle is a Developmental Editor at

https://bolidepublishing.com

And finally, I would like to acknowledge my wife and family for their support and encouragement during this process. Thank you for putting up with my late nights and constant pestering for feedback on design and plot and making coffee on demand. You are the best.

Edge

of

Death

By

G. A. Pickstock

1

BETWEEN THE HEARTBEAT OF peace and panic, Shinkwinn waited. The disused railway bridge had sat for decades, stretching across the highway in defiance of time. Iron guardrails that once protected traffic from errant objects falling to the roadway below had made reaching the hide easy. It had taken five minutes to slither into position, and now, with the heat of Indian summer radiating through the Ghillie suit, the sniper's concealment was complete.

Three hundred metres east, a blind bend in the highway would offer the first glimpse of Shinkwinn's quarry. The rifle, the latest version of the Airforce Texan Big Bore air gun, rested on its bipod. The experimental projectile, not yet loaded, had proven effective when tested and promised complete satisfaction. Time was an ally now, and that time would be short.

***

October was Harry Dalton's favourite month. It was a time of change. The humid, sweltering heat of summer gave way to the crisp nights and warm days of autumn. The trees gave up their greenery painting the forests with a rainbow of colour, giving Mother Nature her final coat of glory, before the defrocking of the cruel Ontario winter.

Harry especially loved his new Caddy. He'd paid cash for the Cadillac. It felt good to finally be able to do that. For most of his sixty-eight years, R. Harrison Dalton had lived by the golden rule: The man with the gold makes the rules. Consequently, when the dealership called him with the offer to return his eighty-thousand-dollar cheque and finance the vehicle at zero interest, he quickly responded that they should cash the cheque and shove their payment plan up their ass.

Harry had no filter. Throughout his life he'd always said precisely what was on his mind. Too bad if people got offended. Words were tools to get a job done. He never minced them. He said what he meant, and he meant what he said. Yet, he had a charm about him, and if one could look past his gruff exterior, then his humanity would emerge, and, quite possibly, one could understand what it was that made Harrison Dalton tick. Still, those who knew him well, knew also that he was two-faced. He used his words to manipulate and he was good at it.

Meeting Anne Lonsdale, a cyclonic romance and a private wedding, had changed his life. Harry Dalton had taken a ride on the carousel of love and snatched the brass ring. A brass ring that, to his amazement, was inlaid with a solid gold bank account. Harry had married into money and lots of it.

With Anne's money backing him, he was more at ease. There was a spring in his step, and even the employees thought he looked taller as Harry strode around in his black leather vest and suspenders; his thumbs hooked into them as if he owned the place, which of course he did. Things were different now. Now he didn't have to play the part of Mr. Congeniality.

Harry was finally free to do things his way. Anne's money gave him the power he'd craved, and now employees were easy to control. The euphoria he felt when he dangled money in front of them was unequalled. He loved that he could enhance someone's life by adding to their pay-packet or devastate that life by firing them.

It was a freedom short-lived. A series of bad deals placed the company in financial peril, a dilemma he dared not divulge to Anne. But Harry had a plan. He had tasted the power he craved, and this time he would win. Money was power, and Harry Dalton fed on it like a fly on shit.

The changing of the seasons meant renewal and new beginnings, and as he guided his new Caddy onto the highway, Harry reflected on the changes he was about to make.

When the local tire manufacturer had decided to close the Clarksville plant and lay off hundreds of workers, all the townsfolk could see was gloom and doom. Harry had smelled an opportunity and with a little bit of grit and what some would call 'titanium balls,' he had secured a contract to produce the same brand-name tires. The manufacturer, happy to be rid of labour disputes and local politics, agreed to the sale on the condition that Harry could guarantee on-time delivery.

He'd pulled it off and instead of massive layoffs, he had devised a plan whereby the employees became shareholders in the corporation. Dalton Tire & Rubber had prospered. The employee-partners in the company had prospered also, receiving thousands in annual dividends. Many of the original partners had retired with huge bonuses and healthy pensions, leaving room for the new generation of employees to share in the employee stock pool.

He'd devoted his life to this business and although some would say he was ruthless, the partnership had been a good one. He'd spent many long and arduous hours making sure that everything ran smoothly, and now it was time for his reward. He'd stepped on a lot of toes to get where he was, and he was about to step on a lot more.

At sixty-eight he was ready to retire, but not before he made one more big deal. Ahead, a ribbon of taillights snaked its way west along the Macdonald-Cartier Freeway, more commonly known as the 401. The golden glow of the setting sun hung just above the horizon, painting the mere wisps of clouds with a golden orange sheen as they merged into the blue-grey darkness of the clear autumn twilight. He was ready and if all went well, the trip to Toronto would take just over two hours.

Through his rear-view mirror, he watched Clarksville fade in the distance. He was in a game he knew was as dangerous as any war and if even a whiff of his plan was to leak, life, as he knew it, would end. Still, there was no way to be certain. To accomplish his goal, he had to trust the other side. It was a risk he had to take.

* * *

A pang of guilt swept over Emily James as she contemplated her garden. The weed-ridden flowerbeds had fallen dormant due to an early frost, and a large empty patch, near the gate, remained unplanted.

It wasn't her fault. She'd found an old leather purse buried in that spot. How it got there was a mystery. Turning the purse in at the police station should have allowed her to return to her chores, but meeting Detective Sergeant Colm O'Byrne changed all that. He had scrambled past a female constable almost knocking her down as he butted in front to serve Emily. His suit jacket hung open revealing a light blue dress shirt and black tie. The shirt was tight on his torso. A button had popped open, revealing a tiny tuft of chest hair as he leaned against the counter. When he spoke, she melted. His heavy Irish accent and the twinkle in his light blue eyes captured her and had never let go. And now they were a couple. Ignoring orders to "let it drop," they had solved the mystery of the leather purse. The owner, Kallita Prewitt, missing for twenty-five years and thought dead, had somehow resurrected and died again. But not before leaving a trail of murder in her wake.

With that behind the young couple, Emily now looked to their future, and as she surveyed her domain, she watched as a chipmunk rummaged through the leaves that had fallen from the maple tree at the back of her yard. Emily smiled at the small bundle of brown fluff bounding back and forth, making its way toward her. She knew what he wanted, and the small voice inside her chided her for failing to pick up a bag of peanuts.

She'd neglected her garden and her small family of furry friends. It was October, and snowy weather was just around the corner. The flower beds could keep until spring, but Mr. Chips couldn't. She would buy a large bag of peanuts today.

* * *

From the thirty-second floor of Toronto's Commerce Court building, Angelo Pellini gazed into the darkening sky of eastern Ontario. Sitting in the soft, yellow glow of a desk lamp, Angelo contemplated his hands. The callouses had almost vanished, but the scars remained, a constant reminder that flesh and machinery rarely got along. He flexed his fingers tightening them, repeatedly balling them into fists, loosening the joints to relieve his arthritis. Angelo was not a stranger to hard work, yet, at forty, the pain in his hands had become a dogged companion, reminding him daily of his roots. As he looked down at them, he marvelled that he no longer needed to use the tools. He had new tools now, and they did not require hard hands, at least not his.

His fingers drummed the desk beside the telephone as he considered his next move. It was a game of strategy, and he held the strongest pieces.

He was a solitary man, impeccably groomed with short, predominantly black hair, peppered with hints of grey and a close-cropped beard, that through some magic of genetics, bloomed forth with a tinge of red. His deep brown eyes were serious but friendly and his words, though velvet to the ear, held the hardness of steel tempered in the forge of experience.

Angelo had played well, maneuvering the pieces into place. The beauty of it was the ease with which he'd done it and the sheer surprise his opponent would feel when the coup de grâce finally came. As the sky darkened, he lifted the phone and made the call. From here he could almost see his future.

2

THE FIRST TIME EMILY walked through the doors to her new job, she almost pinched herself. Clarksville's new Emergency Dispatch Centre was a huge step up from her old workspace.

All-Comm Communications had held all the charm of a cell block with its row upon row of cubicles. The cloth-covered cubicles offered no privacy and as for absorbing sound, they didn't. The air, redolent of cheap perfume, sweat, stale coffee and silent farts, often gave her headaches—banging headaches, the kind that made her want to rip the eyes out of anyone who came near. Emily wasn't happy, and the image of her old boss lying dead in her Mercedes still haunted her dreams.

Here, security was much tighter, and as Emily stepped through the first of two doorways, she thought she was in a time machine. The heavy steel door closed behind her with a muffled thud, trapping her in a five by five cubicle, leaving her facing yet another heavy steel door. The air inside was fresh and cool and dead. That was the only way she could think of it. Sound, in the tiny enclosure, did not carry, and when she spoke to herself, as was her habit, the words evaporated into the walls. It was at this point she realized that she couldn't hear any noise from either side of the doors. She was alone with only the light in the ceiling for company. Startled by a loud click, Emily jumped, letting out a faint squeal. A green light flicked on beside the door handle. She pushed the door open and stepped into the future.

The dimly lit room gave Emily the sense of being in a military command centre, which in many respects it was. Large video screens monopolized the three adjacent walls opposite the doorway. Satellite images with red and yellow lines of text scrolled up and across some screens while another displayed live images of emergency services in action. A semi-circular array of workstations faced the screens, each separated by black partitions lined with three-inch conical foam for sound suppression. One station was vacant, and Emily supposed this would be her workspace. She heard the muffled voices of the emergency operators as they handled incoming calls, and despite the soundproofing, Emily was surprised that she could plainly hear the conversations. To her right and behind the workstations stood a glass-enclosed office where the shift supervisor monitored the room's activity. She knocked at the supervisor's door.

Lou Barret filled the doorframe and scanned Emily from head to toe. She scanned him back. He was a big man, taller than Colm and maybe forty pounds heavier. Her hand almost disappeared into the massive meat-hook he offered her to shake.

"I think you're going to fit right in here," he said, continuing to give her the once-over.

"Thank you," she said, "I have to ask, I'm surprised at the noise level in here, how do you manage to keep things straight with all this hubbub?"

Lou smiled, revealing a set of teeth that, in contrast to his coffee complexion, caused Emily to believe they were the whitest set of teeth she had ever seen. "Come with me. I'll show you the ropes."

He led Emily to the vacant workstation and said, "Have a seat. Now put the headset on." He clicked a button on an earpiece attached to his right ear.

The chaotic din in the room vanished the moment Emily donned her headset and, in an instant, she was alone with her own thoughts. None of the surrounding activity filtered through. She examined the computer screens in front of her. The left-hand screen showed a map of the call centre's area of coverage, while the middle display listed current calls and their status. The third display provided data about the current event. This screen sat blank for the moment.

"How's that?" Lou's voice boomed through the headset. She turned back to face him.

"Wow! That's amazing! I hardly know I'm in the same room."

"Yes, those headphone makes everyting irie," he said, slipping into his Jamaican patois. "We upgraded when we moved here. You wouldn't have liked it in the old location. Too much noise and no privacy. When a call come in here, we don't have to shout, and if it does get loud, you will probably never hear it. You're on your own but not alone. I monitor everything from my office, and if I need to, I can address any or all of you with the touch of a button. I love it. So, take a few minutes to get comfortable, and I'll be back in a minute."

Barret tapped his earpiece and walked back into his office, leaving Emily with her jaw open and a look of bewilderment as she slowly turned back to her station.

***

After a couple of weeks of training Emily was now flying solo, and so far, she had adapted very well to her new surroundings. She worked a four-shift system. It was an eight-day routine where she would work four ten-hour shifts and then have four days off. She had the best of both worlds, a well-paying job, affording her the ability to work fewer hours than she had at All-Comm, and the freedom to arrange her shifts to closely match Colm's work schedule. The newness of the job made everything that much more interesting. The best part was that she got to be a small part of Colm's world.

It was a quiet autumn evening in Clarksville, and as she checked the clock on the wall for the tenth time in as many minutes, she considered the possibility that this might be a long and boring shift. On the surface, this would be a positive sign, but boring was worse than busy. Despite her obsessive desire for order, Emily thrived on the excitement of handling the calls. Even the most benign gave her a jolt of adrenaline, and the possibility of sinking her teeth into a juicy mystery was right up her alley.

This facet of her personality surprised her. She'd always considered herself slightly introverted, a loner who kept to herself. For years it had been this way. She'd lived alone and minded her own business. She never got embroiled in discussions about politics or religion. She had her opinions, but they were private. And then she found that old purse and everything changed.

Emily's desire to return the purse to its rightful owner catapulted her into a twenty-five-year-old unsolved mystery resulting in a murderous trail of revenge and placing Emily in grave danger. Still, finding that old purse had awakened something in her, and she could not find a way to put it back to bed. The adventure revealed a skill she didn't know she had, and somewhere deep in the back of her mind, an old, unanswered question arose. Where is Gary, and why did he go away? It was a question long put aside, but not forgotten.

Her relationship with Colm, and her new position in the dispatch centre, ignited a belief in her. Maybe now she could get some answers. It was time to start her own investigation. It was time to find her brother.

* * *

Harry wanted a cigarette, and with one hand on the wheel of the powerful Cadillac, he glanced down from the road for just an instant as he stripped the cellophane wrapper from the stubborn package and in one fluid motion, deftly popped the smoke between his lips and lit it.

Rounding a curve in the road, the sun blinded him momentarily. He slapped at the visor to block the light. Blinking, his eyes tried to adjust to the brilliance of the setting sun, he finally recognized the railway overpass just a few meters ahead. As he entered the shadow of the bridge, he saw what looked like a white puff of smoke just before his windshield exploded, spidering into thousands of hairline cracks and blowing free of its enclosure. It was the last thing R. Harrison Dalton would ever see.

* * *

The .45 calibre missile coursed its way through the windshield changing direction upward, tearing into Harry's right cheek, ripping his flesh and splintering bone. His right eye exploded out of its socket, as the massive round continued its deadly journey. Ripping through his skull, the experimental bullet erupted out of the top of his head, showering the interior of the luxury sedan with his blood, brains, bone, and what little bit of hair Harry had left.

The car swerved left, careening off a concrete barrier. It flipped twice, ricocheting back across the two westbound lanes of traffic, sending two motorists spearing their way through the steel guard rails, smashing into the rock walls bordering the edge of the road. The Cadillac ground to a halt on its right side. Balancing at the edge of the highway, it leaned against the broken and twisted metal of the guardrail. A tidal wave of traffic swerved and skidded to a halt to avoid crashing into the crumpled grey hulk. Harry hung sideways in his seat harness. Blood dripped from the gash in his face, creating an ever-widening dark stain on the leather upholstery.

* * *

Mission accomplished, Shinkwinn gathered up the rifle, rolled sideways and slipped behind the steel guard walls of the trestle. The assassin slithered across the short expanse glancing only once at the carnage. Fascination with the commotion on the freeway was for others. The road would be closed for some time. There would be those who genuinely wanted to help, but the curious rubberneckers were little more than pond scum.

In the fading light, the darkened figure, barely a shadow in the tall grass of the open field, vanished as it reached the thick underbrush of the forested tree-line. Safely hidden now, Shinkwinn relaxed, shed the cumbersome suit and stowed it in the waiting SUV. Moments later, satisfied with the results, and as darkness loomed, the assassin guided the SUV through a field, and traversing a ditch, eased into the eastbound lane of the freeway as the congestion crawled past what looked for all the world as an ordinary traffic accident.

* * *

Although her experience so far had been limited to the odd bar fight and a few domestic call outs, Emily secretly dreaded the time she might have to deal with a serious call. She glanced at the wall clock. One more minute and she could take her break. She had almost removed her headset when her screen sprang to life. A red call icon flashed impatiently.

As she hit the answer button, she noticed the other operators had become extremely busy also.

"Police, Fire, Ambulance. How can I direct your call?" she asked.

"Yeah, I'd say send all three." The voice was unusually calm. Most of the calls she had handled had sounded frantic, yet she could sense no stress in this caller's voice.

"May I have your name?" She clicked an icon to open a report.

"I'm out here on the 401, and there's been a terrible accident. It looks pretty bad." The caller's voice remained flat and unemotional.

"The police are on their way. I need your name. Where are you exactly?"

"Just send help — 401, just east of the old railway bridge."

Emily's display showed No Caller ID. "Please verify your number for me in case we get disconnected."

She heard what sounded like a chuckle, followed by, "As if." The voice chuckled again. "Just send the cops and an ambulance. I've done my part." The chuckle morphed into a laugh. "Now it's your turn."

The line went dead. Frustrated, she turned to Lou for help.

"I just got this call. There's been an accident, but the caller hung up before I could get any information."

Lou Barret looked up from his screen and nodded at Emily. He motioned for her to look at the main screens on the wall. "Have a look, we've had ten calls in the last two minutes. They're all the same. Cops have been dispatched."

Emily turned to the monitors. The large screens showed a series of maps and satellite images of the centre's service area. Active incidents were marked with red icons. Ions blinked at her, pointing to a spot a few kilometres west of town and according to the satellite image, it was indeed just east of a disused railway overpass. Blue, orange and green icons showed the GPS locations of first responders as they approached the site.

Emily's hypnotic attention to the scene in front of her promptly broke as a penetrating beep sounded in her headset. Another call flashed on her monitor.

"Police, Fire, Ambulance. How may I direct your call?" Emily had to force herself to ignore the chaos on the screens as now the video feed from the police dash-cam appeared on the big screens.

"I think something's wrong with my mom." A small squeaky voice said. "She's asleep and won't wake up."

Emily snapped to attention. The phone number of the caller appeared on the screen, and she secured the address as 21 Simcoe Street. "What's your name, honey?"

"Sammi—Samantha," the voice replied.

"Ok Sammi, stay with me, hon. Is your mom breathing?"

"I — I don't know. I can't tell."

"That's ok, honey, how old are you?"

"Five."

"Are there any other adults in the house?"

"No, just my mommy." The little girl began to sob.

"Don't cry, honey, I'll stay on the phone with you. Help is on the way. You need to be brave. Can you do that?"

"I'll try..." Sammi's voice trailed off.

"Sammi, are you there?" There was no response. *Oh God,*

something's wrong at that house.

She kept trying to talk to the child as she watched the icons on her screen. They moved interminably slowly, raising Emily's anxiety even higher. The seconds dragged on, and more calls came in, each one automatically directed to the next operator. It was as if the accident had caused an avalanche of emergencies throughout the area. At this rate, they'd have to dispatch from the satellite detachments sooner than later. She stayed on the line, willing Sammi to answer her.

"Sammi, honey, please answer me. Are you there? Can You hear me?" Still nothing as Emily watched the GPS icon creep toward the Simcoe Street address. Through her headset, she could hear sirens as the ambulance approached Sammi's location. She kept trying to engage the child as the sirens grew louder. "Sammi, help is almost there. Can you hear me, dear?" From somewhere deep inside the home, Emily could hear a small weak voice.

"I …hear … them …" and then the line went dead. The responders were on scene, but more than that, she could not tell, and she would not learn of the status of this call until and unless she could get the information out of Colm.

One of the rules of the job was don't get personally involved, but how do you do that when it's a child in distress? How do you turn your emotions and feelings off like a switch? This was the first time Emily had experienced such an emotional call, and her heart raced as she worried about little Sammi. Was she hurt? Sick? What? She had to know. She glanced around. Lou was busy handling a call. She looked at the monitors. No calls pending, good! Everyone else was occupied. *Do I dare call Colm? I have to know.* She pulled her cell phone from her purse and tapped Colm's icon.

G. A. PICKSTOCK

3

CONSTABLE KRIS MARTIN LIKED this truck. The Chevy Tahoe could go almost anywhere. Facing the traffic jam ahead of them, Kris fantasized about dropping the rig into four-wheel and driving over the blocked roadway. The thought, brief though it was, made him smile. Instead, he and his partner spent the next fifteen minutes weaving in and around the traffic clogging the westbound arteries of the 401. The lights and sirens had little effect. There was no room to move, and as vehicles edged over to allow the SUV to pass, his frustration meter crept higher and higher.

"I hate this section of the highway," he said to his partner. "It's a god-damned bottleneck. Always has been. How are we supposed to get through this?" It was a rhetorical question. Concrete barriers on the left, guard rails and an eight-foot ditch followed up by a twenty-foot wall of rock on the right, made it impossible for traffic to make room for the police car. "Jesus! I swear there's more accidents on this stretch of the 401 than any other spot in the whole province, and it's always us that gets the call."

Chrysti McNeil looked over at her partner and grinned. "We go through this every time we have to attend an accident, and it doesn't matter where it is. You hate the paperwork."

Kris fought hard to conceal his true feelings. He'd much rather be busting the head of some lowlife than ferreting out what happened to some road jockey who was too stupid to keep it between the lines with the shiny side up. Traffic accidents took hours to sort out, and the paperwork was monumental. He shook his head as they approached the scene. She was right, but it wasn't just the paperwork. More to the point, after twenty years of service in the Ontario Provincial Police, Kris figured he would be done with traffic accidents. But the top brass at headquarters in Orillia had long and unforgiving memories, and a ten-year-old black spot on his record continued to plague his advancement within the ranks.

When Staff Sergeant Dan Clifford was murdered in the back corner of the detachment parking lot, Kris thought perhaps this would be his opportunity for promotion. A promotion that by seniority alone should have placed him in command of the Clarksville detachment. When Colm O'Byrne, a young Irish Detective Sergeant and a relative newcomer to the force, replaced Clifford as interim commander, Kris almost went ballistic. He kept his anger in check around his superiors, but with his peers, he wasn't as reserved. Many of Kris's fellow officers shared his resentment of Colm's rise to command, fuelling Kris's ire, and leading to several uncensored tirades around the detachment bullpen. Chrysti had seen his act, and she knew sitting in a patrol car playing traffic cop to a bunch of idiot drivers would not sit well with Kris, and because of it, she was in for a stressful shift.

"Ah, shit! Look at that would ya," Kris complained.

The sun had dropped to the horizon, and the sky lit up bright red. Tomorrow would be a sunny day, but it would be dark soon, and from what the police officers could see, it would be a long night. Two vehicles had pierced the guardrail. The twisted front end of a black SUV sat wedged between the bottom of the grassy ditch and limestone rock wall. Its front wheels hanging a foot off the ground, the front bumper and driver's side fender jammed into the cliffside. Glass from broken headlights and windshields littered the wet, soggy grass of the ditch. A red minivan had narrowly missed hitting the rear end of the SUV but still wound up on its side. The roof of the van had twisted and bent sideways leaning to the left side like a lopsided layer cake. The rear cargo door, sprung open by the impact, teetered on one hinge. The van had rolled at least once, causing what looked like a week's groceries to spill into the ditch. The occupants sat quietly against the side of the rock wall, slightly bruised and scratched up but relatively uninjured, albeit badly shaken up. Turning his attention to the Cadillac leaning precariously against the guardrail, Kris surmised that such was not the story there. As he pulled up behind the car, Kris saw what looked like blood spattered on the rear window.

"Christ, we're gonna be here all night. So much for going home in an hour. You better call it in. We're gonna need the duty Sergeant, and if they haven't already, you better roll the paramedics."

Chrysti keyed the button on her microphone. "6Juliet506, roll the duty Sergeant to this location, and we're gonna need an ambulance."

Kris positioned the Tahoe across the highway to block any movement of traffic. Stepping out of the vehicle, he turned to his partner and nodded toward the ditch and the crash survivors.

"You deal with them. I'll deal with Mario Andretti in the Cadillac."

Chrysti nodded in agreement, happy to be out of Kris's firing line. As long as she was busy elsewhere, she wouldn't have to hear him bitch. She gathered the first-aid kit from the trunk of the cruiser and walked over to the two motorists sitting by the base of the rock-cut.

As he approached the front of the Cadillac, Kris gazed westward into the setting sun. The railway bridge stood black against the sky, casting a large shadow over the scene. The constable circled the car looking for the driver and any occupants. As he moved around to the front of the vehicle, he stopped at the guardrail and peered inside. The broken windshield and the darkness of the shadow made it difficult, but from what he saw, he knew instantly, they had a fatality.

"Dammit!" he said to himself. "Chrysti, call in a 750 will ya. We're gonna need the coroner. Shut this fuckin' highway down. This is gonna take all night."

G. A. PICKSTOCK

4

DETECTIVE SERGEANT COLM O'BYRNE stared out the passenger side window of the command cruiser. It seemed familiar and odd at the same time. Familiar because he always drove on the left back in Ireland and odd because traffic in the opposite lane was going in the same direction. Odder still, Colm and Constable Jennifer Stroud were alone on this stretch of road. The accident had forced them to take a circuitous route, driving west along secondary roads to access the highway at the next interchange. They'd travelled ten kilometres out of their way, and now they were speeding the wrong way in the westbound lane heading for a scene for which Colm wasn't prepared.

He hadn't attended an accident since he'd left Ireland. He was rusty, and he knew it. Thankfully, he had Jen with him and Kris Martin. Although not what Colm would call a friend, Kris was an experienced constable with more years under his belt than he. A fact Kris reminded Colm of daily.

* * *

Six years with the Garda in Ireland, his tenure as a Guard had reached a standstill. A Sergeant in command of the local Garda Station, he had progressed as far as he could in his hometown. While having a pint in the pub, he met Kendra Jacobs, a vacationing cop from Ontario, who encouraged him to look into opportunities with the OPP. He did so, and a year later, he found himself posted in Clarksville with the rank of Detective Sergeant.

After the murder of his commanding officer, headquarters appointed Colm as interim commander of the detachment; a decision that irked a lot of the rank and file, not the least of which was Kris Martin.

"So, tell me what's up with Kris Martin? He seems to have a hair across his arse where I'm concerned."

"What can I say?" Jen replied. "He hates the fact that he wasn't made detachment commander. He thinks he should have got the job ahead of you." She glanced over at Colm to gauge his reaction.

"Well, now, how does he suppose that's going to work since I outrank him? And what's that all about anyway? He's got twenty-plus years on the force. How is it he's not a Sergeant or better by now?"

"With Kris's record, he might never get his stripes."

"Oh, and why is that?" He turned toward Jen who was looking at him. "Eyes on the road, please."

Jen quickly faced forward, smiling at the rebuke. "Kris fouled up a bunch of years ago and arrested the wrong guy on a bunch of charges. Turns out, the guy was innocent, but the perp spent a couple of months in lockup for assaulting Kris." Jen could finally see lights in the distance and began to slow down.

"Ok, so he arrested the wrong guy. It happens. That's no reason to lose his chance at advancement. Is it?"

"Ordinarily not, but apparently during the arrest, the perp … er ah … suspect had knocked Kris to the ground cracking his skull. He was out of commission for quite a while. As the story goes, once Kris finally got back to work, his case started to fall apart—" she stopped herself.

"Fall apart? How?"

"Maybe I shouldn't say. After all, nothing was ever proven." She sneaked a quick glance in Colm's direction.

"Ok now you have to spill it, I can't let that go, what wasn't proven?"

Jen slowed the cruiser to a crawl and pulled to a halt a few meters short of the accident scene. "From what I hear, it was a case of Kris placing the guy in his sights, and then looking for a crime to pin on him. Kris obtained a warrant to search the guy's property. He subsequently found some pretty damning evidence in the trunk of an old car in the garage. It would have convicted him but for the timing of the discovery. The suspect was in jail when Kris apparently found the smoking gun, so to speak. I'm not sure what it was that he found, but it turned out that there was no way the suspect could have placed it there."

"How's that?"

"Well, again, this is just hear-say, the guy couldn't have placed the evidence in the car. Turns out he'd bought the vehicle from a dealer out west, and the car was in transit when the suspect was arrested, so, he couldn't have put the *evidence*,"—she held up two fingers on each hand to make quotation marks— "in the car. Kris swore he had the guy dead to rights, but the guy's lawyer got the evidence thrown out and cast a lot of suspicion on how it might have wound up in the back of that car."

"That's quite a story. So, who was the perp?"

"Oh, you're gonna love this. You know Roy Prewitt?"

"Yeah, what, was it him?"

"No, it was his brother, Alan."

Colm's eyes widened. "The same Alan Prewitt that disappeared the night we caught Kallita at Roy's house?"

"Yes, sir! The same Alan Prewitt who everyone thinks is dead. Kris had him pegged as the doer for over a month before he arrested him. When he tried to put the cuffs on him, Prewitt knocked him down and put him out of commission for weeks. They held him without bail for assaulting a police officer, but when the business with the bogus evidence came to light, they dropped all of the charges, even the assault charge. Kris was livid but I reckon he was lucky. If they'd have been able to prove he planted that evidence, odds are he'd have gone to jail. He'd have lost his job for sure. Instead, the best he'll ever do is Senior Constable, and it eats at him every day. Martin has a real hate-on for the whole Prewitt family, but even more so for the system that's keeping him down."

Colm shook his head. Sometimes good people do bad things, he thought, as he surveyed the scene before him. Police cars and ambulances crisscrossed the accident scene. Lights flashed, and police officers and paramedics scurried around tending to the accident victims. This highway would be shut down for hours. A black and white SUV stood parked under the railway bridge. Kris Martin leaned against the side of the vehicle, talking to Chrysti McNeil.

Jen interrupted his contemplation, "You'd do well to step lightly around him, Colm. Others have tangled with him and regretted it."

"Good advice, but I can handle Kris Martin. Don't worry, I've dealt with worse." I think.

Kris Martin didn't hide his disdain for his new commander.

"O'Byrne, ya might know. I ask for a Sergeant, and they send you." He turned his back on Colm and started toward the wreckage.

"You asked for a duty sergeant, and I'm it tonight. Besides, you forget, I run the show these days," Colm shot back.

"Yeah, well, you might better have stayed home for all the use you'll be." Martin eyed Jen and snapped, "See that mess over there?"—He pointed at the pile of traffic blocking the roadway— "Make yourself useful and help those guys get traffic turned around," he ordered.

Jen looked at Colm for direction. Clenching his jaw, and turning back to face Jen, Colm raised his eyebrows and canted his head back toward their police cruiser.

"Go sit in the car, Jen, I'll deal with this."

Jen nodded and retreated to the car.

"No! I don't think so," Martin snapped back at her. "Get over there and do as I say. We have a fatality here, and I'm in charge. Got me?"

Colm chafed at the rebuff. The Irish in him wouldn't let it go. Moving in close to the Senior Constable, Colm drew him aside.

"See now Kris, that's where you and I have a wee bit of a problem. I know you think you should be running the show. What you're forgetting is that I,"—he turned his right hand inward, tapping himself in the chest—"am in command, and I won't have you undermining my authority. It's your accident scene, sure, and I won't interfere, but you answer to me until such times as Orillia appoints a full-time commander. Now, tell me what the bloody hell is going on here."

He turned to Jen. "Go back to the car. I'll be with you shortly."

Turning back to Kris Martin, he locked eyes with the six-foot-four Senior Constable.

"Now, put your willy back in your trousers, and let's get this mess cleared up."

5

EMILY SLOWED TO A crawl as she neared the house at 21 Simcoe Street. It was an older home, tired and dirty, and the grounds around the outside were unkempt and overgrown. Whoever lived here had no pride of ownership, and Emily imagined what it must be like inside.

It was late, and Colm hadn't returned any of her calls, which meant that he was busy.

"Probably that accident on the 401," she said to the empty seat next to her.

Emily had a habit of thinking out loud. It frustrated Colm. Her thinking out loud always triggered a response from him and many times, he had no idea what she was talking about.

A police car sat outside, which meant they were still examining the scene. Emily saw a light from what she guessed might be the kitchen window. Back home in Blind River, a small town on the north shore of Lake Huron, she had lived in a house very similar to this one. They were so much alike that for a moment, her mind was transported back. She envisioned herself standing beside her mom drying dishes; the memory jogging more questions in her mind. Questions of another mystery from long ago.

She itched to get inside. She needed to know what had happened here and if Sammi was all right. Getting involved was wrong, but her curiosity trumped logic, and the urge to know more was strong.

"Damn," she sighed. "I guess I'll have to interrogate Colm when he gets home." Thoughts of how she would get him to talk made her smile as she drove away.

* * *

It was 2:30 in the morning when Colm finally clocked out for the night. As he slipped behind the wheel of his Mini Cooper, he replayed the events of the evening in his mind. With one lane open, westbound traffic was moving again, albeit slowly. The coroner had not wanted to move the body. He'd told Colm that he had an odd feeling about something, but would not comment further until he could inspect the vehicle in daylight. Kris Martin was furious as it meant he had to remain on call while his crew secured the scene and directed traffic all night. Martin's consternation fell on deaf ears as Colm got back into his cruiser. Closing the door on the red-faced senior constable, he smiled, relishing the moment.

"Maybe next time you won't be such an arsehole," Colm mumbled.

"What was that?" Jen asked as she started the cruiser.

"Huh? Oh, nothing, just thinking out loud."

Colm debated whether to go to Emily's or perhaps spend what was left of his night in his own apartment. She'll be pissed if I don't come home. Home, I've finally started calling Emily's place home. The thought made him contemplate just how far their relationship had progressed. It was true that when he first laid eyes on her, something inside him clicked. His memory of that day was still fresh. He had watched on the security monitors as she entered the detachment.

Petite, five-foot-two with a slim figure, she'd floated across the parking lot, almost fairy-like in a navy blue and white print dress. The sun glimmered off her long, auburn hair as the wind blew it about her face. Emily James was possibly the most beautiful girl he'd ever seen. He wasted no time in butting in front of Jen Stroud to attend to her. He grinned as he recalled his first impression. She had brought an old purse into the detachment and wanted him to find the owner. That meeting had developed into a full-blown romance, advancing to the point where he rarely spent any time in his own place. He thought hard for a moment and finally decided that he should at least visit the apartment where he was paying to store his meagre belongings. Risking the wrath of one fiery redhead, he swung the Cooper into the roadway and drove to the place he used to call home.

* * *

Sure enough, Emily was miffed, and Colm sensed from his early morning phone call that he was in deep crap with her.

"Three times. I left you a message three times, and not one response." Emily's voice held the harsh edge of a teacher scolding a child for not doing his homework.

"But Em, it was really late and—"

"And you couldn't come home? You couldn't even call." It was more of an accusation than a question.

"I—I didn't want to disturb you—it was—"

"Will I see you at all today?" Emily's icy tone told Colm all he needed to know.

"Yes, but I have to go to work first." There was only silence from the other end, and after a prolonged and awkward pause, he asked, "Em, you still there?"

"Yes, I'm here." Her voice had softened slightly. "Fine. I'll see you later."

He knew it wasn't fine as he put the phone away and surveyed his apartment. It had been home for the past fifteen months, but it held no real importance to him. The only thing of value was his big screen TV and the sound system. He had a computer, but it was an old one and extremely slow. He couldn't remember the last time he'd used it. The furnishings had been there when he moved in, and although well worn, they served his needs well enough. The landlord had offered to remove them, but Colm had insisted that they stay. He could use the furniture and save his money. Now he wondered whether it was time to move on. It was evident that Emily considered their relationship as more than casual, and he felt the same way. Neither had discussed the future, but it was inevitable the subject should come up. Maybe now was the time.

G. A. PICKSTOCK

6

DOCTOR BOB GENTRY ROLLED up behind the lone cruiser parked at the side of the road. As he walked over to the car, he observed the two constables inside sleeping. The driver sat with his cheek pressed firmly against the door's window, a thin trail of drool leaked from the corner of his gaping mouth. The other, a rather bulky fellow with a bent nose, leaned with his head back against the headrest. He too slept with his mouth wide open.

Gentry thought about leaving them to it, but what fun would that be? Standing just enough behind the slumbering duo so as not to be seen, he rapped loudly at the passenger-side window. Both of the officers jumped in their seats at the disruption.

"You guys nice and comfy?" Gentry asked half joking.

"Just trying to stay warm Doc. It gets cold at night. It is October you know." The burly cop rolled down his window and squidged around to see the coroner better.

"Yeah, I get it. It won't be long before the ghosts and goblins will be banging on our doors. Speaking of ghosts, how's your charge doing?" Gentry gestured over to the wreckage at the side of the road.

"Hasn't moved a muscle all night," the officer quipped.

It was light enough now for him to examine the body efficiently. He had not wanted to move it before he could get a clear sense of the effects of the devastating impact. It had been a savage crash causing severe damage to the driver's head, but something seemed wrong. He'd attended many accidents, some, far more gruesome than this one. Still, he couldn't put his finger on it, but there was something that didn't feel right. Even now, in the light of day, the thought still nagged at him, however, he could not isolate it in his mind.

He stood at the front of the Cadillac and peered through the gaping hole where the windshield used to be. Glass littered the interior, save for one small section just in front of the driver's body. The body still hung at a grotesque angle held in place by the shoulder strap of the vehicle's seat belt.

Gentry pulled his camera from his car and set about taking pictures of the wreckage and the body. He had requested that an ambulance attend the scene and he could see it approach as he snapped away with his camera. Once he was satisfied with the number of photos, he walked back over to the cruiser.

"You can get a wrecker out here to move the car. I'm pretty sure you'll be able to open this lane in about an hour."

"How you gonna get him out of there?" the burly constable inquired. Gentry looked over at the wreck. The ambulance had just pulled alongside. Two medics had disembarked and were now perusing the scene.

"That, my dear fellow, is a question only you and those two young fellas over there"—he pointed at the two medics—"can answer. The crash has done all the hard work for you. I'm sure you'll figure it out. The sooner you get this done the sooner you can all get out of here."

Gentry supervised the men removing the body, making sure that whatever needed to remain intact did so, and that nothing was added that might affect his report. At this point, this death was the result of a traffic accident, but it wouldn't do to have some foreign material influence his diagnoses.

"Hey Doc! You might want to have a look at this."

7

COLM PULLED IN BEHIND Emily's Mustang and sat for a moment. Wiping his sweaty hands on his trousers, he scanned up and down the sidewalk. Why am I so nervous? He was twelve again and had just been caught nicking candy from Mrs. Conner's sweet shop. She'd said he had to tell his parents, and she must hear from them by five, or she'd call the Garda. Scared witless, he stammered his way through his confession, but not before delaying it as long as he could. It was like that now, but why? He was twenty-seven for God's sake. Why should he be afraid of a five-foot-two red-head who said she loved him? But he was. Her opinion of him meant everything, and displeasing her bothered him tremendously. He knew the scolding would continue. He expected it, but for some reason, he wasn't ready to face it. She was lovely, and he loved her, but she had a way of making him feel guilty, even when he wasn't. Perhaps it was the Catholic in him. After all, Catholics are raised on guilt. His mother and their parish priest thrived on using it to their advantage. He looked for a reason to delay, wishing old Mrs. Johnston was out watering her garden. She loved to talk and took every opportunity to extract or impart some juicy tidbit of gossip. Sadly, this was not to be. He switched off the car and stepped out. He would face the music, whatever that was, and then they would kiss, and it would all be over. He hoped.

In the far front corner of the living room, Emily sat in her reading corner, legs tucked up under her, a book rested on the arm of an old easy chair large enough for both of them to sit in. It didn't match anything else in the room, but Emily loved the chair. It was the only thing she had brought from home when she moved to Clarksville. It was her corner where she would squirrel herself away and read, listen to music or gaze out the window and lose herself in thought.

As Colm entered, she appeared to be totally engrossed in the text. He lingered in the tiny entryway and watched as she read. She had to have heard the door open, although she hadn't acknowledged it, and she hadn't looked up, which meant he was still on the shit list.

"Good morning," he said, euphemistically throwing his hat in the ring.

Emily checked her watch. "Well, I guess technically, it's still morning." She raised her eyes from the book, closed it and set it on the table beside her chair. "You took your time."

"I told you I had to go back to the detachment. I was only there an hour. C'mon Em, are you going to keep me in the doghouse all day? I'm sorry, I should have called you, but it was late and well—"

Emily shot him a look. He'd seen it before, and he knew he was done for. It was anger, but it was hurt as well, and he sensed he was in a losing battle. He decided to change lanes.

"What do you think about me moving in?" Colm sat across from her trying to gauge her reaction.

"What do you mean, move in? You're already in!" she said.

"No, I mean all the way, I'll give up my apartment. I only have a few things there anyway. Most of my gear is here already, so it wouldn't take much and well, I don't need the extra expense of renting an apartment I don't use. So what do you think? Can I move in permanently?"

She tried not to smile, but Colm sensed that he'd taken the right path. The smile was there, but it was her eyes that told the story. The fiery anger and disappointment transformed to delight, and then she was his again. Colm had his Emily back, and he knew he had won. He placed his hands on his knees and leaned forward, "I can do it today. I'll hand in my notice and move out right away."

"Okay," she said. "But I need you to do something for me first." She patted his knees and stood, moving past him, wafting him with the hem of her skirt.

Puppy dog obedient, he followed her into the kitchen. He wrapped his arms around her waist and snuggled her neck from behind. She tipped her head sideways, allowing him better access.

"Sure, n what would that be now?" He whispered through his kisses.

She spun to face him, and tilted her head to look him in the eyes, "I want you to tell me what happened to Sammi." She stood on tiptoe and gave him a quick peck on the lips, broke free of his embrace and darted back into the living room.

*　*　*

"Sammi is in hospital. She's grand, but the doctors are keeping her for observation."

Emily rested her elbows on the kitchen table. She had made breakfast while Colm had looked into the 911 call. "So, what's wrong with her?" she asked as she swallowed a bite of her bacon and tomato sandwich. "Uhm, and what's up with her mum?"

"As far as I know, nothing, but mum, ah now, she's not too grand. Children's services will be having a chat with her. It seems she got into some stuff she shouldn't have, and when the medics found her, she was totally wasted. She's currently sleeping it off in the hospital." Colm finished eating and gulped the last of his coffee. Wiping his mouth with a napkin, he said, "I have a feeling Sammi might not be going home anytime soon. Anyway, that's the story. Now, am I forgiven or am I still in the doghouse?"

"I'm still mad that you didn't call me, but ok, you can move in if you want." She lifted their plates from the table and set them in the sink. "I'd still like to know what's going to happen to that little girl."

"Do you think that's wise? Sure, you're not supposed to be getting involved with the victims or the families. It's against the rules, and God knows, I know it better than anyone. I see it every day just about. Believe me, Em, you can't do it."

Colm searched Emily's face for some sign that he had reached her. He knew that if she allowed herself to get too close, it would cause trouble in more ways than one. She nodded that she understood, but it did nothing to allay Colm's concern that she might not heed his words.

"I mean it Em, don't get involved, love. You've no idea what you're opening yourself up to."

"What will happen to her mother?" Emily asked.

"When the doctor says she's fit to leave, she can go home. Technically, she hasn't committed any crime. We didn't find any drugs or the like. She was just legless, and we don't know how she got that way. So she'll be free to go. In fact, she'll likely be gone by now. Still, Child Welfare won't release Sammi to her until they've done an investigation."

Emily's mood brightened at this revelation. Coming around the table, she bent low in front of Colm and kissed him. "Thank you, I know I shouldn't get involved, but that little girl sounded so alone and frightened. I'm glad she's ok. I hope things will work out for them both." She smiled, kissed him again this time longer and more deeply than the first. "You can move in anytime," she whispered. "Go get the rest of your stuff. I have errands to run before work."

She had errands to run, but not the shopping kind. They were the kind that Colm wouldn't approve. Her first stop would be the hospital.

* * *

The hospital had recently undergone a multi-million-dollar renovation, albeit not without controversy. Many thought the money had been squandered on updated waiting rooms and administrative offices, instead of upgrading the level of service and equipment needed to run an efficient and progressive healthcare facility.

Emily had heard the arguments and had experienced first-hand some of the points of contention. The waiting areas had indeed been expanded at the expense of additional beds and treatment rooms. On the surface, at least, the level of service had fallen. Still, as she stepped off the elevator into the pediatric ward on the second floor, the transformation became clear. A lot of money had been spent here.

Directly in front of her, a sleek modern reception counter, curved outward, spanning the distance between two corridors set at a ninety-degree angle to each other, offering the staff a clear view in either direction. Bright orange floor tiles dazzled in the light from an expansive east-facing glass wall. Cartoon characters, animals and familiar figures, gamboled along the walls through floral and foliage patterns telling stories of great adventures complete, with fairies and pirate ships.

The ward looked more like a fantasyland than a hospital. Not an inch of white space had escaped the artist's brush. In the centre of the waiting area stood a play gym where a few small children laughed and giggled as they climbed and slid around. To the sides, cloth-covered chairs in blue and green and yellow offered a place for the parents to sit and talk. And further still, to the left of the elevator, a small quiet room stood in subdued lighting, offering a place of solitude for the families of children who might be suffering more serious conditions. This was a place of light and delight but also held a serious undertone.

Two staff members dressed in pale blue uniforms busied themselves behind the reception desk. Emily stepped up to the counter and set a large pink Teddy-bear on top. The nurse, a tall brown-haired man, who, according to his nametag, was called John, looked up from a chart he was studying. He had a kind face and Emily placed him in his mid-thirties.

"Yes, miss, how can I help you?"

"Can you tell me what room Sammi Saunders is in, please?"

The nurse checked his chart. "She's in room 202. Are you a relative?"

"No, just a good friend, although she does call me Auntie Emily," she lied.

He hesitated as he turned to look down the corridor in the direction of Sammi's room. It was empty save for a lone figure walking away from them.

"I'm sorry, I can't let you in until visiting hours. You can come back after 3 PM if you like."

"Are you sure I can't see her? Just for a minute," Emily flashed the sweetest smile she could muster. "I promise I won't stay long. I have to go to work this afternoon, and well, I must give this to her" — She lifted the Teddy-bear — "It's her favourite." She lied again, shooting the nurse another engaging smile. *If Colm was here, he'd kill me.*

He gave a furtive look down the corridor once again. It was empty now, and the ward was quiet. He grinned and stepped back from his station. Taking one last look around, he said, "Please understand, I'm not allowed to break the rules but well" — he turned to his companion behind the counter – – "Isn't it time for our break?" He didn't wait for an answer. Turning back to Emily, he winked and said, "I'm sorry I have to take my break now. I can't let you go in, you'll have to come back later." Spinning on his heels, he tapped his partner on the shoulder, and the pair disappeared through a doorway, leaving her standing at the counter alone.

Seconds later, Emily stood outside the door to room 202. Something wasn't right. She scanned the corridor. All the room doors were held open by magnetic holdbacks that only released in the event of a fire. *Why is this door closed?* Grasping the lever handle, she turned the latch and pushed the door inward. Only one of the beds was occupied. She saw the silhouette of someone standing beside the child's bed. He wore a dark hoodie and blue jeans and had his hand over Sammi's mouth.

"Hey! What are you doing to her?" Emily pushed the door aside, slamming it into the wall. She sprinted to the side of Sammi's bed, shrieking, "Leave her alone! What are you doing?" She grabbed at his hand and pulled him away. "Who the hell are you?" He froze for a second, his face ashen and white, the tendons in his neck pulsed. The fear in his eyes turned to contempt as he swung his arm wildly. He caught Emily under the chin sending her sprawling across the bed next to Sammi's. The bedrail jammed into her side, knocking the wind out of her. When she regained her footing, she saw the man flee through the door. She checked on Sammi. She was breathing, but her eyes were closed. "Sammi, Sammi honey, are you ok?" Sammi didn't respond. She lay motionless, her breathing shallow and laboured.

Emily darted for the corridor screaming, "Help! Please, someone, get a doctor in here! Sammi won't wake up!"

8

READING THE RIOT ACT to junior officers wasn't anything new to Colm, but this was different. The chip on Kris Martin's shoulder was a big one, and Colm had to find a way to knock it off without starting a mutiny. Martin was senior to him in every way but one, rank. He had more than twenty years on the force, and despite his blemished past, he knew the job. But that was where his seniority ended. His disdain for Colm's position showed plainly. The report he'd delivered was vague and incomplete and lacking in detail. As detachment commander, Colm could not allow Martin's attitude to go unchecked.

The surly constable sat across from Colm, arms crossed and leaning back in his chair. He let out a heavy sigh and demanded, "Why am I here? I got shit to do."

Martin's aggressive posture did not phase Colm. The man had stepped out of line. Colm could not afford to let go unchallenged. To his mind, Kris Martin was a lazy, self-aggrandizing, arrogant man. He believed by sheer longevity alone that he deserved the respect of his peers.

"You know, Kris, nothing would please me more than to turn the reins over and let you run this zoo. I'd much rather be investigating crimes than administering to a bunch of whiny, out-of-shape donut eaters with chips on their shoulders."

Martin's mouth curled into a half-smile. "Then why not—"

"No, don't speak," said Colm. "There's more. You're pissed off. I get that. You think you've been wronged by the system. Maybe. It's not for me to say, but as long as I'm in command here, you'll bloody-well follow orders and comport yourself accordingly. You don't like me. I get that too. I'm not here to be liked. I'm here to do a job, and I'm not going to let you interfere with that."

Colm had two reports lying on his desk, one of which was Martin's.

"This report—" he tapped the paper lying on his desk— "doesn't line up with Bob Gentry's initial findings."

"How's that?" Martin leaned forward in his seat, trying to see the Coroner's paperwork. "It was a car accident, pure and simple. Dead guy in a Cadillac end of story. What else could it be?"

Colm turned the Coroner's preliminary report around and pushed it across the desktop. "Take a look for yourself. That's not definitive, but he thinks there's foul play involved."

Martin lifted the report and read for a moment. "Gentry's full of it. He's an old man who sees murder at every turn. I'm telling you, this guy—" he sifted through the pages— "who the hell was the driver anyway—" he stopped talking as his eyes lit upon the driver's identification. "Oh shit! Harrison Dalton! You gotta be kidding me! How did I miss that?"

"What do you mean, miss, miss what?" Colm wondered at the constable's reaction. "Who's Harrison Dalton?" he asked.

Martin shook his head. "I don't know how it escaped me. I should have known by the car. Damn, where was my head at?" He stared at the paperwork in his hand. "This says he was shot, but how?"

Colm took the report back from the constable. "What do you mean, you should have known, and who the hell is Harrison Dalton?"

"Trust you not to know," Martin sneered. "Harrison Dalton is – was the largest employer in this town. Does the name Dalton Tire and Rubber ring any bells for you? That was his Caddy, I should have recognized it. With that gold grill, it's hard to miss. It was pretty bashed up and it was getting dark. Maybe that's why it never registered." Martin leaned back in his chair, crossing his arms again.

"Dalton Tire? You mean he's the owner?" Colm had heard of the company, and knew a bit of its history, but had never met the owner. He had crossed paths with a few of the employees over his tenure. He had actually put one of them in prison. Mark Taylor was serving time for the attempted murder of the now-deceased Kallita Prewitt. Mark had worked at the factory along with a couple of other suspects in the Prewitt case. He thought for a moment longer as the two policemen sat in silence.

"Ahm—" Martin opened his mouth to speak, but Colm cut him off.

"Bob Gentry believes he was shot. Half the man's head is missing. He says the wound has all the earmarks of a gunshot." He waited for a reaction from Martin. He didn't get one. Martin stared back at him with a 'what do you want from me,' look on his face. "How is it that you had all night at the scene, and you couldn't mention the victim's injuries in your report? Hell, you didn't even identify the driver. Did you even run his plates?"

Martin shrugged his shoulders. "Well, I don't know what to tell you. If Gentry says he was shot – ok, then I guess that's up to the detectives to figure out. Oh wait, we don't have any detectives cuz the one we did have, is running this looney bin. Go figure!" Martin's demeanour darkened. He stood, placed both hands on the desk and leaned into Colm, his six-foot-four frame towering over him, the pupils of his steel-grey eyes closed to pinpoints. "Guess it's all up to you now—eh, Boss. Can I go?"

Colm raised himself from his chair, drawing level and narrowing the gap between them. He could feel the man's breath on his face, "Aye, I'm done with you. You can go." He waved toward the door. *Sure, n, don't let it hit you in the arse on your way out. Feckin eeejit.* He picked up the phone and made the call he'd wanted to make for months.

* * *

Anne Dalton wiped her arm across her forehead as she gazed across the nine acres she called home. The temperature was unseasonably hot, and she'd worked up a sweat in the garden. Yard work never ended on this property and in her mind, she was the only one who cared that it got done. She could hire a gardener, but what fun would that be? If she did it herself, she could save the thousands in wages and make Harry's life more miserable with the constant digs to his ego and nagging about his laziness around the house. A house that she had paid for, a house he lived and ruled in, and for the life of her, she could never reconcile why she had allowed that to happen.

After the death of their parents, Anne and her sister, Amelia, were left alone in a world they knew little about. With millions held in trust accounts, the women enjoyed a carefree life, travelling and living well. The idea of husbands and family never entered their minds. And then came Australia, the Gold Coast, and Harrison Dalton.

The rest of that vacation found Anne spending more and more time with the charming Mr. Dalton and spending less time with her sister. It was true. Harrison was in Australia on business. He owned a tire factory, supplying tires for many of the major automakers, and was looking to secure a contract in Brisbane. He was a little rough around the edges, but Anne believed he had a good heart, and when he spoke of his business, his passion for his employees and their work shone through. The more enamoured of Harrison Anne became, the more Amelia disliked the man. Amelia flatly refused to speak to her sister. Cutting their vacation short, Amelia flew home ahead of Anne.

Amelia's unwillingness to accept Harrison drove a wedge between the sisters, and when Anne finally announced they were getting married, Amelia walked out of her life. Their estrangement devastated Anne, and her attempts to reconcile met with indifference. Anne sadly gave up and chalked it up to jealousy. Harrison Dalton had changed everything, at least where Anne was concerned. She gave herself to him, mind, body, and bank account. It took two years before she realized her error.

It wasn't until she'd received an invitation to Amelia's wedding four years later that the sisters reconciled. By then, Anne's marriage was beyond hope, and she desperately needed someone to confide in. The years that followed found them devising many plans to extricate Anne from the death grip Harrison had on her. Divorce was an option, but not a good one. Every time she thought about the prenuptial agreement, she cringed at her naiveté. Harrison had gifted her ten percent of his stock in the company, but Anne had loaned him millions to help keep it afloat. Loans that were held in non-performing debt. Divorce was decidedly not an option. It appeared as though Harrison would have to die before Anne could be free.

The Daltons hadn't slept in the same room for almost nine years. Harrison's charm had long ago tarnished to where Anne loathed his presence. They never touched, and the very thought of the man laying his bony fingers on her made her shiver with disgust. Thankfully, the union had produced no children. Anne had wanted kids in the beginning, but when Harrison's true colours became apparent, she soon put an end to that possibility. There was no way in hell she would rely on him for support, especially with kids involved. The early years had found him lacking in the fidelity department, and she would have divorced him then but for the money she had invested in him. Depression and despair gave way to resignation. More than once, she had considered suicide, but what good would that do? He'd end up with everything, and in the end, he'd be the winner. She'd even explored the possibility of putting a hit on her husband. She'd gotten as far as getting a name when Harrison approached her with a substantial cheque repaying a long overdue loan. Fearful that he'd somehow gotten wind of her thinking, she abandoned the idea and cancelled what could have been a deadly and devastating meeting.

If nothing else, Harrison Dalton was a salesman, he could sell ice to an Eskimo, and water to a drowning man, and for a while, Anne believed his pitch. She'd financed more than one failed project, and now after thirteen years, Harrison finally had a winner, but not before Anne had loaned him almost every dime she had. There was still a bit left. She could live comfortably, but nothing like the life she should have had. Harrison had seen to that. They'd had big dreams in the beginning. He was a businessman without a backer, and she was a lonely woman without a man, but she had the one thing he didn't—money.

From the seat of her lawn tractor, Anne watched a dust cloud winding its way toward her property. The cloud subsided, and a black puddle-jumper of a car pulled into her driveway.

* * *

Notifying next of kin was the worst part of being a policeman. Colm could delegate it to someone else, but in this case, that someone would be Kris Martin, and he couldn't trust him to handle the task with dignity. You never knew what to expect from the family. He'd encountered it all, tears, hysteria, anger, disbelief, but the one he couldn't get his head around was indifference. Indifference was not natural. He'd even seen outright joy at a family member's death, but apathy didn't make sense, and when he saw it, alarm bells rang. This time it would be doubly hard for him because of the suspicious nature of Dalton's demise. He had little to go on other than Bob Gentry's report. An investigation was in order, but this had to come first.

He pulled into the paved driveway of the Dalton home. To the side of the property, he saw a woman driving a lawn tractor pulling a small trailer laden with branches and twigs. He estimated her to be in her late fifties. She wore a large green floppy hat, a red and white plaid jack-shirt and blue jeans. As she pulled up alongside the Mini Cooper, Colm stepped out and showed her his badge.

She switched off the tractor, removed a pair of dark sunglasses, glanced at the badge, then up at Colm. Anne Dalton had a look of resignation as if she'd been expecting him.

"Detective Sergeant, eh? What's he done this time?" Her long, silver hair curtained her age-worn face. She had the air of a woman who had seen it all and possibly done most of it as well. She stepped off the tractor, cocking one leg over as if dismounting a horse.

"It's a beast of a thing, but it gets the job done." She eyed the detective. "So, tell me, why are you here?"

She was tall, almost as tall as he was, and Colm thought he could detect a slight British accent. If he had to guess, he'd have placed her from the London area, maybe Oxford or Swindon. However, it was plain she'd been in Canada for a long time. She moved with the agility of someone half her age. Her demeanour put him off balance, and he had to think for a moment before responding.

"Mrs. Dalton, may we go inside. I have some news for you. You may want to sit."

She shook her head. "Anything you need to tell me you can say right here. I've heard it all before. Hell, I've probably said it myself once or twice. Let me save you some bother. It's my husband, isn't it?" She reached into the trailer, pulled out a rake and began raking leaves from the lawn.

"Yes," Colm replied. "But I don't think you understand. You see he—"

"Listen, Irish, he didn't call me last night. No surprise there. He's away on business, and if I know anything, he got shit-faced and needs me to bail him out. Well, he can rot for all I care. What did he do anyway?"

Colm struggled to keep his composure. She wasn't listening. He placed his hand on the rake and lifted it from her, setting it against the trailer. She turned to challenge him.

"Mrs. Dalton, I'm a detective with the OPP. They don't send detectives to tell wives their husbands are drunk." He spied a lawn chair on the front porch. "Please, let's have a seat." He gestured to the chair.

Anne Dalton's countenance became unreadable as Colm led her to the chair and insisted that she sit. "Mrs. Dalton, I'm here to tell you that Mr. Dalton, Harrison Dalton, died last night." He paused to let the words sink in. "There was an accident on the 401. I'm sorry, but your husband's car was involved, and he was declared dead at the scene."

The silence that followed almost deafened Colm: No tears, no crying, no sobs of anguish, nothing. He stared into the widow's eyes. The sparkle was gone replaced by a flat coldness fixed on a spot somewhere in the heavens.

Her gaze finally rested back on Colm, still flat and emotionless. "I'm sorry, detective. How? I mean, what happened? Are you sure it was Harry? How could this be? He's in Toronto." She pulled a cell phone from her jeans and began dialling his number. Colm put his hand on the phone and gently took it from her.

"We're sure it's Harrison, Mrs. Dalton. Please, is there anyone else at home? You really shouldn't be alone right now."

She shook her head, finally managing to conjure up some tears. "No, there's no one. I'll be fine. My sister lives in Pickering, I'll call her. I'm sure she'll come down. You said it was an accident. Where?"

"Yes, ma'am, he was in an accident. On the 401 just west of town, near the old railway bridge. Do you know it?"

She nodded, "Yes, I know where you mean. It's a bad corner—been a lotta accidents there."

"Yes, ma'am, listen, I need to ask you, why was your husband going to Toronto?"

"Why? Is it important?"

The tears had dried up, Colm noticed. "We investigate all accidents, Mrs. Dalton. Just trying to get some sense of what was happening." Alarm bells were ringing. *Is she truly upset or just trying to get me to go away?* He decided to leave it for the moment. He needed more information, and until he could see Bob Gentry, this interrogation would have to keep. He pulled a business card from his pocket. "This is not the right time, but I do need to ask you some questions. I'll be in touch soon. Meanwhile, if there is anything you need—call me—one more thing, perhaps you'll give me your sister's number in case I need to get in touch."

She nodded, "It's on my phone. Amelia Lonsdale, look in my contacts."

Colm copied the number to his phone and dismissed himself.

* * *

As she watched the Mini Cooper back out of the driveway, a cold realization flooded over her. Harry's death changed everything. Had she reacted properly? She suspected the few tears she'd shed hadn't impressed the detective. The news should have caused an emotional reaction, but she couldn't muster anything. She'd reached deep into her memory, conjuring up thoughts of her dead parents to produce any tears at all. Then they collided with the image of Harry and cancelled out any emotion she could manage. She was numb to Harry's death. He could wait. After all, where was he going now? No, she had things to organize, and before this news reached the wrong ears, she had to have her ducks aligned. There was no guilt, no repressed anger, just a cold realization it was over. Was the struggle worth it? And what would replace it now he was gone? What would she do next?

The empty coldness warmed, and when she thought the detective could no longer see her, she broke out into a wide grin. Picking up her phone, she called the one person who would know what her next move should be.

"Hello, Ames, I need you down here ASAP. Harry is dead—that's right, I said the asshole is dead. We need to get busy."

* * *

Colm backed out of the driveway and glanced back at Anne as he pulled away. "She's got a feckin' smile on her face! Now isn't that just grand? Her old fella's lyin' cold on a slab, and she's grinnin' from ear to ear. Well now, I reckon we'll have to look into this." *Jaysus! I'm talkin' to meself, God I'm turnin' into Emily.*

9

EMILY RAN INTO THE hallway just in time to see Sammi's attacker disappear through the door to the stairwell. She chased after him. The man's footsteps thumped on the steps heading down the single flight of stairs, followed by the crashing sound of the emergency exit door. A blinding flash of daylight flooded the space as the door flung open. She was too late. When she finally reached the exit, the intruder was gone. There was no sign of the man anywhere. Rubbing her chin, Emily returned to Sammi's room. Her jaw throbbed. The intruder was gone, but she had seen enough in the hospital room. She believed she could describe him.

Nurse John stood in the doorway. "I knew I shouldn't have let you in."

"Well, technically, you didn't," Emily retorted, still rubbing her chin. She sensed an iciness in him that wasn't there before. "And if you hadn't taken your break"— she made a sign of quotation marks with her fingers— "who knows what might have happened to Sammi? By the way, I'm fine, thanks for asking. Is she ok?" She attempted to look past nurse John straining to see through the open doorway. A team of medical staff hovered over the child obliterating her view, and Emily could only guess what might be happening.

He looked at the mark on her chin and nodded. "It's gonna leave a bruise, but you'll be fine. It's a long way from your heart."

"What about Sammi? How is she?"

"Sammi will be fine. She's awake and talking, just a bit frightened. Now, if you don't mind, please go into the waiting room and take a seat. The police are on their way, and I'm sure they are going to want to speak to you."

Emily thought better of arguing. Besides, she had to figure out how to explain this to Colm. She reached for her purse and realized it was still in Sammi's room.

"I need my purse, please," she said. "May I go in and get it? It's right there on the bed." She pointed at the bed next to Sammi's.

"I can't let you in there. Stay here. I'll get it."

Emily watched as John went inside to retrieve her purse. She could see Sammi now. The little girl was sitting up, and a doctor was listening to her chest. Sammi seemed more confused than frightened, her eyes darted all over the place. She squirmed around, pulling the covers up to her chin as though trying to get comfortable. The nurses kept telling her to be still, and everything was all right. Nurse John picked up Emily's purse and returned it to her.

"Are you sure she's ok? She seems somewhat dazed to me,"

* * *

Colm spun around in his chair as the intercom buzzed. "You have calls on lines one, two and three, Sarge," a voice from the front desk announced.

"Grand, three at once. Who's who?" he asked.

"Kendra Jacobs on one, Bob Gentry on two and Emily on three."

"Tell Emily I'll call back. Ask Gentry to hang on, please." He stabbed the button for line one. The conversation lasted all of two minutes, and as Colm disconnected, he could see that lines two and three were still blinking. He pushed the button for line two. "Next," he said into the mouthpiece.

"Colm, I need to see you in the morgue. There is something here you need to see." The urgency in Gentry's voice was unexpected.

"Can it wait, Bob? I've got a lot going on, and I have a meeting I can't put off."

"No, I'm afraid it can't. You need to see this, and it's time-sensitive. Five minutes that's all I need." Gentry hung up, and Colm stood still holding a dead phone. Line three beckoned to him with a relentless red flash. He jammed his finger down on the button.

"Emily love, it's not a good time, can I call you back?"

"I need your help." Emily managed to squeak out her response. She hadn't known what to say, but the few moments on hold had allowed her to formulate a plan. "I'm at the hospital, and there's been an incident. Can you come?"

Colm sensed Emily's incident was somehow self-inflicted. "I have appointments that will take most of the afternoon. Besides, aren't you working today?"

"Yes, I go in at three," she said. "But I need you to come here as soon as you can. It's important."

Colm searched for a reason to dissuade her. Whatever it was couldn't be that serious. "Are you hurt?" He asked. "Is something wrong that I need to know about? Why are you even at the hosp—" Then it hit him. Sammi. "You've been to see Sammi. Haven't you?"

"Colm, I need you here, please. I have to go. The cops are here now. Get here as quick as you can."

Colm wanted this day to end, and if he had his way, at least two of his problems would be solved.

G. A. PICKSTOCK

10

IT WAS SERENDIPITY THAT the Clarksville morgue resided in the basement of the Clarksville General Hospital. Colm would keep his appointment with Gentry, and then quickly bounce up to deal with Emily's dilemma.

He entered through the side entrance, descended the flight of stairs into the basement, stepped into a wide, dimly lit corridor and turned to his left. This part of the hospital had seen no improvement during the renovation process. The grey walls hadn't had a fresh coat of paint in years, and in the subdued yellow light of the fluorescent fixtures, they were what Colm often referred to as baby-shite green. It was a disgusting colour worthy of the moniker and always imparted a feeling of hopelessness to him. He disliked the place, but his attendance here was unavoidable. Large metal-framed carts dotted the hallway. Parked like buses in front of various rooms and offices, they contained everything from bed linens to towels, gowns and medical equipment. From somewhere in the depths of this dungeon-like atmosphere, the distinctive aroma of cafeteria food assailed Colm's nostrils. It permeated the corridor getting stronger as he ventured deeper into the maze of hallways and ante-rooms.

He proceeded down the corridor, eventually arriving at a set of steel grey double doors. A brass name-plate announced the room in large black letters.

- MORGUE -

Authorized Personnel Only

Colm pushed at the handle and walked in. The frigid air hit him, and the heavy aroma of formaldehyde and isopropyl alcohol immediately replaced the stale odour of the cafeteria. In the centre stood a stainless-steel table. The naked body of a man rested on top. Bob Gentry stood on the opposite side from Colm and raised his head as he entered.

"Is that our victim?" Colm asked, grabbing a mask from a shelf near the door.

Gentry grinned at the policeman. "You don't need that," he said, "this guy had nothing catching."

Colm shook his head. "Nah, it's not that. It's the smell. How do you keep your breakfast down in this place? It's horrid."

Gentry laughed. "That won't help; besides, you get used to it. Ten minutes from now, you won't even notice it. You know, if it didn't smell this way, I'd think I was in the wrong place. Oh, and yes, this is our accident victim. Colm O'Byrne, say hello to the venerable and very dead Harrison Dalton."

Colm moved to the side of the table. It wasn't the first time he'd been here, but this was an experience he didn't think he would ever get used to. Compared to the hallway, this room was antiseptic. The room was ablaze with light, the floors were pristine, and the walls gleamed white. One wall held a series of steel compartments where the bodies were kept refrigerated until released to relatives or to a mortuary for burial.

"So, this is the famous tire man." Colm gazed down at the body of the man who, as local lore had it, saved the town by buying the tire plant saving the jobs of hundreds, if not thousands of people, assuming you counted the spin-off trade that might have folded had the factory gone under.

His chest was flayed open like the covers of a book. The man's ribcage was gone, and a strange emptiness remained where his lungs and heart had once been. His organs sat in steel dishes at the foot of the table.

"So, Bob, what has you all worked up about this guy? Your report said something about him being shot, but Kris Martin insists this was an accident pure and simple. His words, not mine." He looked up from the body waiting for Gentry to respond.

Without a word, Gentry reached across the table and turned Dalton's head toward Colm. The detective fixed his gaze on the disfigured face of the dead man and grimaced. "It's nasty, I'll say that much but so what? What is it, I'm supposed to see?"

"Look closely at the wound." Gentry turned the head further to allow Colm a better view.

Colm looked for a long moment and finally shook his head. "I'm sorry, Bob, I guess I'm blind or something. I don't see what you're getting at."

"I wondered if you would. You see, something nagged at me all last night. And then again this morning when we picked up the body. His right eye is gone. Part of his face is literally blown away, and well, as you can plainly see, the top of his head is missing."

Colm shook his head again.

"Don't you see? This isn't normal for a traffic accident. He had airbags in the car. Six of 'em, and they all deployed. This guy should have survived. Hell, an egg would have survived this crash. No sir, these injuries—" he waved his hands around Dalton's head— "happened prior to the crash, and I can prove it."

Colm stepped back from the table, trying to digest what Gentry had just told him. "Prove it. How? What makes you say this was more than an accident?"

"The only injury to this guy is the head injury. Not a single broken bone, not even a fracture. None of the internal organs is damaged except for his lungs. The irony here is, he had cancer. I doubt he knew, or if he did, he didn't care. The point is, the only damage to this guy is the head trauma."

"Isn't that enough?" Colm asked.

"Look again." Gentry pointed to Dalton's head. "See here, just under the eye where his cheekbone should be?" He didn't wait for Colm to answer. "It's a hole, not a cut or laceration, but a hole. A bullet hole."

Colm moved in closer to see what Gentry was pointing out.

"Now look, his right eye is gone, blown out from the inside not gouged out as you might expect from debris or trauma from impact. And then the top of his head is missing, again, blown out at the back. No, sir, this guy was shot. I'd stake my reputation on it." Gentry straightened up and removed his gloves. "He was shot. As sure as I'm standing here, this man was shot. And from the damage, I'd say the bullet was not something I've ever seen before."

"Why do you say that?" Colm asked.

"The wound. Something about it isn't right. I haven't figured that out yet, but I will." Colm turned away from the body, scratching his head. He removed his mask and tossed it in a waste can. "Bob, you seem awfully sure about this. I was there last night. There was a lot of damage to that car, and there were other vehicles involved. Witness statements all point to him losing control of the vehicle. And we searched every inch of the car. If there'd been a bullet there, we would have found it."

Gentry countered, "No, sir! He was shot. There's a bullet somewhere."

"If you're right, then we have a murderer out there. I'm going to need something more to go on. From the witness statements, no one heard or saw anything that remotely resembled shots or a gun going off. There's nothing to indicate anything other than an accident. Martin thinks this guy fell asleep at the wheel. Isn't that possible?"

Gentry motioned for Colm to follow him. "Come into my office, I think I have something that will convince you."

Unlike his lab, Gentry's office was a mess. Stacks of files and half-empty coffee cups littered his desktop. Gentry cleared a stack of files from a chair and motioned for Colm to sit. He reached across the desktop and grabbed a set of photos.

"Here," he said as he handed the photos to Colm. "Look at these. Check out the windshield." He leaned against the edge of his desk.

Colm sat and studied the pictures. The Cadillac was on its side, and the body of Harrison Dalton hung in the seat. The windshield, what was left of it, was leaning inward toward the interior of the car. The next photo was a close-up of the remaining glass. Colm saw a quarter-sized circular opening surrounded by dozen or more fine cracks spreading out like fingers from the edge of the circle, spider-webbing the glass in all directions. At that moment, Colm knew Gentry was right. This was the remains of a bullet hole. A large calibre bullet hole at that. He looked up from his seat to see Gentry sporting the biggest shit-eating grin he'd ever seen.

"I told you I could prove it."

11

EMILY HAD GREAT RESPECT for police officers, but Constable McNeil was interrogating her as though she were a suspect instead of a witness. She had taken everything Emily had told her and twisted her words in an attempt to incriminate her.

"You say you're a 911 operator, is that right?" Constable Chrysti McNeil's five-foot-six frame towered over Emily as she sat in one of the waiting room chairs. The constable crowded her. Invading her space so that she had to shift her feet to prevent them from being stepped on. As a result, Emily found herself sitting sideways, twisting herself to the right to look up at the constable. From this position, Emily could clearly see the constable's gun-belt and holster. The retaining snap on the holster was undone. Emily noted the procedural violation. If necessary, she would put it to use.

"Yes, that's what I told you," Emily replied.

"So, do you make a habit of checking up on the people who call for help?"

"No, not at—"

"So, it's only young girls you hunt for, is that it?"

"No, what—I told you, I just wanted to know if she was ok. Listen, can you step back just a bit?"

"You're fine just as you are. Yeah, you said that. But you have no connection to her, right?"

"Well, no but—"

"And you say some guy was attacking her, right?" McNeil edged in, her shins inches from the seat cushion

"Yes, he had his hand over her mouth. I think he was trying—"

"Yeah, smother her, yeah, you said that. With his hand, not a pillow. Sounds a little off to me." The elevator bell sounded, causing Emily to break eye contact. "What about the teddy bear? Where did that come from?"

"Teddy bear? Really! Where do you think it came from?"

"That's an expensive toy, do you always buy expensive toys for kids you don't know?"

Emily had stopped listening. Her attention was diverted, and her heart jumped when she saw Colm appear from the elevator. She'd had enough of being berated by this woman.

"Huh, what? Uhm no! Was that actually a question? You know what? I've got nothing more to say to you. Why don't you go do your job, and find the guy who attacked Sammi?" Emily tried to stand, but McNeil placed her hand firmly on Emily's shoulder, preventing her.

"I'm not done with you."

Emily pushed back hard enough to make the constable step backward. Colm had arrived. She was damned sure she wasn't going to deal with this arrogant cop any longer. She pushed her way to her feet.

McNeil pressed on, unaware that Colm was standing behind her. "I am doing my job, and right now, I'm looking at the only person who we can be sure entered that room. So why don't you sit back down, and tell me what really happened?"

Emily stepped to her left, smoothed her skirt, flicked her hair back over her shoulders, and cast her eyes toward Colm.

Talking past the constable, she said, "I'm done with you. I've told you what happened. If that's not enough for you, then I can't help you."

She brushed past the policewoman. Emily's flint-hard eyes bored into Colm. He'd arrived too late. She didn't know why and at this point, she didn't care. Besides, explaining why she was here to Colm was going to be hard enough, and in her mind, the best defence was to go on the offence.

"How do you get anything done with people like this working for you? I've told my story to her three times, and she still doesn't get it. She thinks I attacked Sammi. I can't help it if she's too obtuse to understand. You talk to her. Tell her she's barking up the wrong tree."

She turned back to the constable, pointed at Colm and asked, "Do you know who this is?"

McNeil replied, "Yes, of course, I do."

Emily turned back to Colm. "You tell her. Maybe she'll believe you."

She marched to the elevator. Glaring daggers at both the police officers, she pressed the down button. Moments later, the elevator doors slid open, and she disappeared inside, leaving Colm standing in the middle of the waiting area with a dumbfounded look on his face. She had one more stop to make before going to work.

* * *

"You'd better sit down, and tell me what just happened here," said Colm.

The constable sat, her face flushed with embarrassment and confusion. She told Colm the story Emily had told her and insisted that she was doing her job.

"She was pretty pissed. Why did you question her as though she were a suspect? I heard that last bit of that, and well, you came off pretty arrogant. Is she a suspect?" Colm asked.

"Well, sir, I have to think everyone is a suspect, and if I have reason to think someone might be lying, then it's my job to challenge that. Right?"

Colm listened to McNeil's account of the incident and deduced that her tone and manner could stand some improvement. He had to agree up to a point. McNeil was new on the force, and so he had to allow her some latitude. From what he'd heard, he knew she was parroting the example of someone else, someone, very senior to her, someone, with many years on the job.

"Where's Kris Martin?" He asked.

"Down the hall interviewing the nurses and the doctor. Room 202." McNeil sat with her eyes downcast, her complexion finally returning to normal. She held her hands in her lap, fingers interlaced, and Colm thought for a moment that she was praying. She'd messed up, and Colm suspected that Martin had put her up to it.

"I want you to go back to the detachment and write up your report. Stay there until I get back." Colm dismissed the constable and stood to go find Kris Martin.

"But what about Kris, how will he…"

"Don't you worry about him. I'll deal with him. Just go back and wait for me."

"I just have one question, if I may?" McNeil looked up for the first time. "Why did she talk to you the way she did? Does she know you?"

"I guess you could say that." He flashed a wry grin. "She's my girlfriend. And oh yeah, secure your weapon." He pointed to the unfastened snap on her holster. "Sure, it wouldn't do to have that thing fall out of its holster now, would it?"

McNeil quickly secured her weapon and watched, mouth agape, as Colm walked down the corridor.

12

EMILY HEARD THE INCESSANT ring of the doorbell emanating from deep inside the home. It wasn't the familiar ding dong of her own doorbell, but more like a school bell that only ceased when she stopped pressing the button. Surely, Sammi's mother must have heard it. Yet there was no answer.

She was about to try the side door, when she noticed through the screen, that the interior door was slightly ajar. She tried the handle on the screen door. It wouldn't budge.

"Damn, it's locked." Emily rang the bell again, pressing the button for what seemed like a full minute. Still no one answered. She yanked at the screen door handle again, harder this time, and the it popped open. She gave the inner door a tentative push, allowed her eyes to adjust to the dimly lit room beyond, and called out, "Hello, anybody home?"

No one answered. The aroma of fresh-baked bread reached her nostrils and Emily thought perhaps Sammi's mom was in the kitchen. She called again, "Hello, can you hear me?"

Had it not been for the clutter and the furnishings, Emily could have been standing in her childhood home. She picked her way through the living room, dodging boxes and bags of clothing, careful not to step in anything that might squish beneath her feet. The kitchen fared a little better. Where the living room was a pigsty, the kitchen merely looked lived-in. It was empty save for a table covered with a clean, white tablecloth. Two wooden chairs sat neatly at either end of the table. An empty cardboard box sat in the middle of the table.

Two fresh loaves of bread, still in their loaf pans, sat atop the stove. A green tea-towel hung from the oven handle. Emily moved to the oven, careful not to touch anything. She felt the top of one loaf. *Still warm, someone must be home.*

Moving deeper into the house she wound her way down an L-shaped hallway, and found herself in what would have been her old room had she been at home up north. Only this wasn't her old room and she wasn't up north.

* * *

The empty pit in Chrysti's stomach made her want to flee. The pin-drop silence in the conference room unnerved her as she studied the three people sitting opposite her. Her eyes flicked from one to the other without making contact with either. Her mind raced, she had never been in this room, and she wondered why she had been called here. *Could this be about grilling Colm's girlfriend? Surely not, I did everything by the book.*

Colm sat in front of her with Jen Stroud to his right. Another woman, who Chrysti did not know, sat on his left. Resting her sweaty palms on her knees to keep them from vibrating, Chrysti caught a slight movement to her right. She turned to see Kris Martin take the seat next to her. Arms crossed, with a *why are you wasting my time* scowl on his face, he pushed his chair away from the table, putting himself out of Chrysti's peripheral vision.

Chrysti set her gaze on the newcomer. She was a fifty-something woman, and although dressed in civilian clothes, a navy-blue blazer over a crisp white blouse, she was the only one in the room to make eye contact with her. Chrysti knew, without question, this woman outranked everyone in the place.

"Before we begin," said Colm. "I want to introduce you to Staff Sergeant Kendra Jacobs. Kendra has twenty-eight years with the OPP. For the past few years, she has been stationed in Orillia. I met Kendra a couple of years ago in Ireland, and if it were not for her, I would not have joined the force."

"Shoulda left him in Ireland," Martin muttered to himself.

"What was that, Kris?" Colm shot back.

Kris looked up, startled that he'd been heard, "Huh, ah nothing, it's ok."

"Didn't sound like nothing, Kris, we all heard you. I'd mind my tongue, if I were you," he shot him a *shut up and be quiet* look. "As of oh-eight-hundred tomorrow, Staff Sergeant Jacobs will be Clarksville's new detachment commander."

Martin's face reddened. He dropped his chin to his chest, eyes cast downward, and began rubbing at an imaginary spot on his uniform.

"What's up, Kris, you spill some coffee or something?" Colm asked.

"Huh? Somethin' like that," Martin muttered.

Colm turned to Kendra and offered his hand, which she shook.

"I'm happy to turn the reins over to you, Staff Sergeant." He fired a sardonic look at Martin. "It's been a long time coming."

Chrysti rolled her seat to the left a little, angling herself toward Kris as he continued to fiddle with his uniform. The redness in his face faded, but she knew this would not sit well with him. Months of sitting in a patrol car listening to his bitching about Colm and headquarters had told her all she needed to know about how he might react. It was bad enough that Colm had been given the job of commander, even if it was temporary, but to have it go to a total stranger, who was chum's with the Irishman and a woman to boot, well, she could only wait for the volcano to erupt. And she was certain it would.

Jacobs rose from her seat, turned to Colm and said, "Thanks, Colm, I'm happy to be here. This will be a huge change for me, and I hope we can make the transition as seamless as possible. My appointment here will necessitate some changes." She paused for a moment to let the news sink in. "First, Acting Staff Sergeant O'Byrne will return to his original post as Detective Sergeant, sorry, Colm."

Colm raised his hands in mock surrender. "Not to worry, I'm grand, so I am. You're welcome to it." He shot a wry look at Kris Martin.

"Next," Jacobs continued, "Constable Jennifer Stroud is promoted to Detective Constable, which brings me to you." She fixed her eyes on Chrysti.

"Whoa, wait a second," Martin interrupted. "What about me? Why am I here?"

"Kris, right?"

Martin nodded.

"I thought so." She lifted a file folder off the table. "This is your personnel file. I will need to see you in private before we continue this."

Jacobs' eyes riveted themselves to Martin's, daring him to challenge her. Kris didn't disappoint her.

"So, if we need to talk in private, why am I here? This is a total waste of my time." He sprang from his seat flipping his chair backwards. "I don't need this crap!" He started for the door.

"Just a minute, Constable! Pick up that chair and sit your ass back down. Get this straight. I don't suffer prima donnas or crybabies. I will not tolerate any insubordination, and when I give an order, I expect it to be carried out."

Kris picked up his chair and sat. Jacobs gave Colm a knowing look then turned her attention back to Kris. In a quiet voice, she directed her words to the Senior Constable.

"I said, I want this to be seamless, and I mean it. You're here as a courtesy to Colm. He requested you be included in this meeting. Frankly, I would have made you wait along with the rest of the detachment, but now I understand. I don't know where you get your attitude from, but I can assure you it won't be tolerated under my command. Understand?"

Kris said nothing.

"Understand!"

"Yes, I understand, but—"

"No buts, Constable, be in my office at eight AM on the dot. Dismissed!"

Martin rose, carefully moving the chair back into place as he excused himself. In one last attempt to show his contempt, he tried to slam the door as he left the room, but the best he could muster was a sudden swish of air as the hydraulics of the door closer took control.

Jacobs turned her attention back to Chrysti.

"Constable McNeil."

Chrysti wanted to leave the room. She was a deer in the headlights, and, after what just happened, she vibrated from head to toe. She squeaked out a diminutive, "Yes sir—er ma'am."

"I've looked at your personnel file, and I think we should change things up for you. With Constable Stroud's new rank, we have an opening on the command staff. Colm thinks you'd be a good candidate to take her place. It's not a promotion as such, but it is a lateral move that will put you in line for something better in the future. What do you say?"

Chrysti sat, mouth open, her eyes darted around the room. The thrumming of her blood as it pulsed through her veins drowned out the sound of her breathing, and, as the adrenaline rush, of moments before, left her body, she became mentally and physically exhausted.

Finally, fixing her gaze on the OPP crest hanging on the wall, she said, "I need to pee, may I be excused?"

G. A. PICKSTOCK

13

"**EMERGENCY, FIRE, POLICE, HOW** may I direct your call?" Emily cringed at the sound of Lou's voice.

"Lou, Lou, it's Emily, I need help here."

"Emily, you're late! Where the hell are you and why are you calling on this line? You should know better."

Lou began a trace to see where she was.

"I'm at 21 Simcoe Street, and I need the police and an ambulance. Please, Lou, hurry! A woman has been shot, she's still alive but barely, and there's blood everywhere."

Lou hit the appropriate buttons, and the dispatch went forth. "Ok, help is on its way. What the hell is going on? I need to speak to you, call me back on the private line."

* * *

The conversation with Lou hadn't gone well. Colm was not going to be pleased with her, and this time, Emily didn't think she could wiggle her way out of it. She stepped over to the constable guarding the door.

"Is she going to make it?" asked Emily.

"It's touch and go. I don't think so there's' ope. She lost a lotta blood, and from what I saw, the wound was' orrific," he said, in a thick French-Canadian accent. Constable Harold Papineau ran his fingers underneath his collar. He had a rash on his neck, and the itch was unbearably distracting.

Emily noticed the young cop's discomfort and asked, "Are you ok? That rash looks nasty. Maybe you should have it looked at."

"It's the uniform, he itches like crazy. I think I'm allergic, maybe." He kept rubbing at the spot on the side of his neck. "Me, I'm going to need a statement from you."

"Of course," Emily replied, thinking she really didn't want to tell her story twice. "Do you know Colm O'Byrne?"

"Oui, yes ma'am, he is my boss." The constable gave her a puzzled look.

"Maybe you should call him. He is my boyfriend. He will probably want to talk to me." She winced at the thought of another grilling like she'd just experienced.

"Oui, but I still need a statement. He will demand a report from me so, please, tell me what 'appened 'ere."

* * *

Come on, Colm, what's taking you so long? Emily twisted her hair around her fingers as she watched from the periphery. Lou had not been happy with her tardiness. He told her to take the rest of the day off, without pay. She could return to work on her next scheduled shift. On the bright side, she would not return to work for another five days, leaving her free to investigate what had happened here. She was desperate to get back inside the house, but the crime scene tape was up, and Colm had been here for over an hour, neglecting her the whole time. He finally emerged from inside, but instead of approaching Emily, he stopped to talk to Constable Papineau.

"Oh, so now he's gotta talk to this guy." She fumed to herself, twisting her hair tighter.

Colm kept glancing over in her direction as the young officer gave his report. The window was down, but she could only hear wisps of the conversation, and could not get any sense of Colm's demeanour. She was desperate to go back inside. Emily was convinced that whoever attacked Sammi was behind this.

Finally, Colm strode over to the car and jumped in the passenger side.

"I've been watching you," he said. "Sure, I can see it in your eyes, and no, you are not to interfere. It's a police matter, and I can't have you poking about in this."

Emily smiled. "But—"

"But, nothing, Em. I mean it. Short of giving a statement, you have to let us do our job."

"I think I can identify the guy who did this," she argued. "And I have time on my hands, I can do a bit of poking around. I promise I won't get in the way." She turned to him and reached for his hand. He waved her off.

"No, no, no! You can't use your magic on me this time. I already went too far with the 911 call and now look." He shook his head.

"But see, if you hadn't done that and I hadn't come to the hospital when I did, Sammi might be dead now. And I wouldn't have found her mother in time." She pleaded with him, her eyes glistening almost to the point of tears.

"True, but I'm sorry to say you weren't in time, love. Sammi's mom didn't make it. She was DOA. I'm sorry."

Emily's face paled, and now the tears gushed forth. "If I'd only been a little sooner getting here, maybe—"

"Maybe you'd be dead, too. Don't you see? Whoever did this is dangerous. Anyone who would try to kill a child is pure evil, and not someone an amateur should tackle. No love, I want you as far away from this as possible."

She heard the words come from his lips, but he was speaking to deaf ears. This had just become very personal to her, and her focus was on her next move.

G. A. PICKSTOCK

14

KENDRA JACOBS SURVEYED HER new office. It was functional and clean, but the air was stale and smelled of man. The room needed some greenery. She would buy some plants over the next week or so.

A box of Colm's personal effects sat on the floor near the door. The call to the Saunders residence had interrupted his move, thus preventing him from helping Kendra settle into her new digs.

She'd met Colm in Ireland while visiting an old friend who had just retired from the Garda. She couldn't have known two years later she would be Colm's commanding officer. Kendra liked Colm and had followed his progress within the force. He was a good detective and was wasting his talents sitting behind a desk. Dealing with the daily scatology of the office made no sense. A replacement for Dan Clifford was long overdue, and the suspicious death of Harrison Dalton forced the need for Colm to return to his old post, thus hastening Kendra's arrival.

Conversely, Kendra was a good administrator. Having grown through the ranks, she knew the trials her constables faced. She also knew the internal politics and gamesmanship that existed. She hadn't officially taken over, and she'd seen some of it here already, which made her think. *There's no point in waiting until tomorrow.* She stepped out into the hallway in search of Kris Martin.

* * *

The partially covered body of Nicole Saunders occupied Bob Gentry's examination table. Gentry was about to open her chest when Colm walked in.

"Oh, good! I'm glad you're here. I took plenty of pictures, but now that you're here, you can see for yourself." He set his scalpel back on the instrument tray and beckoned Colm to join him.

"Take a look here." Gentry pointed to a hole about the size of a nickel. Colm had seen gunshot wounds before. This one didn't look all that different. Ruby red bruising surrounded the dark red, almost black, centre of the wound.

"So, what am I looking at here, Bob? Is there something special about this?"

"Yes, there is, but before I show you, look at this." Gentry reached across the woman's body and lifted her to show Colm an exit wound the size of a grapefruit.

"It's an amazing, great hole sure, I'll give you that, la. Nothing I haven't seen before. So, what's so different?"

"Look closer," the pathologist said. "Tell me what else you see."

"A great gaping hole in her back and a wee one in the front. Ok, so the bullet expanded on impact. Nothing unusual, like." He examined the exit wound and then had Bob lower the woman so he could see the entry wound again.

The bullet had entered just under her right breast. Colm was about to give up when he saw it. The wound had a faint grey ring around it. He gave Gentry an inquisitive look.

Gentry shrugged his shoulders. "I don't know yet, but from what I can tell, it tracks straight through the wound path. We have the same discolouring on the exit. Oh, and what you don't know is, I found this same discolouration on our friend, Harrison Dalton."

"Let me see if I've got this," Colm said. "You're saying I have two murders, and the same killer did both?"

"It would seem so. But there is something I haven't figured out yet. I've sent samples to Toronto for Forensics to analyze. We're just not set up for it here. It will take a while. My guess is a couple of days at least."

Colm scratched the top of his head. "This woman was shot. This we know for certain, but there's no bullet anywhere. Sure, there must be, unless the killer retrieved it. How likely is that?"

Colm stepped away from the table and found a stool. "When Emily found her, she was still alive, yet with all that damage, how could she survive that shot?"

"I'll know more when I get her open, but from what I can see, she could have hung on for a while, but she was done for. There was no way she would have lived." Gentry picked up his scalpel and held it up for Colm to see. "You gonna stick around for this?"

"No, ta, I'll wait for the movie. Let me know what you find."

* * *

Emily watched from a safe distance as the police cruiser drove out of sight. Waiting five more minutes to be sure they weren't doubling back, a tactic Colm told her they did quite often if they believed a suspect might be hiding out, she approached the house and checked the front door. Yellow crime scene tape covered the front entry.

"Not this way, I wonder…" Emily's home up north had a cellar with an exterior entry door. She moved to the back of the house to investigate.

Her heart leapt when she discovered this house had a similar entrance. A set of concrete steps led down to the cellar door, bordered on both sides by cinder-block retaining walls rising above the ground. The knee-high walls delineated the space around the stairwell, creating a resting place for disused flowerpots and rusty garden tools. She descended the steps and tried the latch. The door wouldn't budge.

"Damn, it's locked."

She remembered her parents used to hide a key outside in case either of the kids might lock themselves out.

"If I were a key, where would I hide? Hmm…"

She searched everything she could find, lifting flowerpots, looking under discarded boards and garden items, checking for nails or hooks secreted away in some inconspicuous corner. Finally, giving up in frustration, Emily sat on the edge of the wall. She wanted to get inside, but attacking the front was risky, and this was the only other way in, short of smashing a window, which she wouldn't do. Resigned to try another day, she rose from her spot, her arm accidentally brushing against a large terracotta flowerpot containing a half-dead geranium. It fell, leaving a trail of dirt and bits of broken flowerpot down the steps.

"Damn!" As she picked up the broken pieces of pottery, she saw something brassy in the dirt. It couldn't be, she thought. She brushed away the dirt.

"A key! Right on!" Emily snatched it up, discarding the pottery, and tried it in the lock.

With a satisfying snick, the lock slid open, and she was in. She opened the door just wide enough to see inside. The light from a basement window cast a single beam across the floor. Dust particles danced and drifted in the air as a slight gust entered through the opening. She stepped inside and closed the door. Allowing her eyes to adjust, she glanced around the cellar. It was damp and musty and smelled of a dead rat. In the grey dark of the room, she could see boxes stacked upon each other, the bottom ones had fallen prey to water damage. Dusty strings of spider-webs crisscrossed the room. She spread them aside with her left hand as she moved deeper into the basement. A wooden shelf, set against the far wall, held dozens of jars of god-knows-what, covered in cobwebs and crusty dust.

Flakes of grey paint lifted at the edges of the cracks in the concrete floor. It was plain that this house had issues with flooding and damp. She saw what looked like a tide mark on the walls, a thin wavy line of white limestone leaching out from the concrete, separating the dark grey blocks at the bottom from those lighter in colour above. A thick, crusty film covered the floor, and with each step, Emily felt years of accumulated dust and damp break beneath her feet. Reaching the stairs, she looked up. At the top, a closed-door barred her way, and she could only hope that it wasn't locked. The basement door up north had a hook on it to keep it shut. When she was in the kitchen earlier, she'd seen the door but hadn't noticed how it was secured.

The steps creaked as she climbed the disused staircase. She turned the knob and breathed a sigh of relief. It opened with a squeak, and she was in. She could still smell the bread. Moving through to the bedroom where she'd found Nicole, Emily stepped in, mindful not to tread in the blood staining the floor. She went directly to the dresser and began her search. She had no idea what she was looking for, but there was something amiss in this house.

Why would anyone want to kill Nicole? More to the point, what possible threat could Sammi hold that her life would be in danger? Advancing through the house, Emily dug into everything she could find. The police had searched, but they left a lot of paperwork and mail behind. Emily found a photo album under one of the beds and a folder with more photos and tax returns. Either the police missed them or didn't think they were relevant. Gathering the papers and pictures, Emily sat at the kitchen table. The aroma of the bread beckoned to her, tempting her to dig in. That would be a no-no, she thought as she looked over at the stove. To her astonishment, the bread was gone. Emily shook her head in the realization the cops who'd secured the property had taken it. *Evidence? Not!*

For the briefest of moments, she felt she was not alone. Fearing the police had returned, she stuffed the papers and photos into the cardboard box, still sitting in the centre of the table and sped down the cellar stairs. Safely back in her car, she headed for home, the box of paperwork sitting safely beside her on the front seat.

* * *

Bubbles of rust dotted the faded black paint of the old van, its windows tinted so darkly that peering inside was almost impossible. The front license plate hung askew fastened by a single bolt, and its mismatched wheels and tires spoke of neglect and abuse. In any town, anywhere, the van wouldn't receive more than a cursory glance, but when Emily saw it turn the corner five-hundred metres behind her, the hair at the back of her neck stood up. She'd seen the van before, but she couldn't place it.

G. A. PICKSTOCK

15

TWO AND A HALF hours after Colm's visit, a haggard and distraught Anne Dalton opened her front door, and let her sister in.

"You look like hell, Anne! My God, I'm so sorry for you." Amelia reached out to hug her older sister.

"Sorry? Hell, don't be sorry for me," she said, pulling herself free of her sister's embrace. "Help me find that asshole's will. I've been searching for hours, and I can't find the G-D thing. Without it, I'm screwed." Anne shut the door behind her sister and led her to the office.

A grey-bearded chain smoker prone to wearing blue jeans, a checkered or striped shirt overlaid with a sleeveless black leather vest and red suspenders, often gave the impression that Harrison Dalton was more biker than businessman. On the contrary, he abhorred clutter, and despite his habit of allowing ashtrays to fill to capacity and beyond, everything else had to be correct and in place.

His home office reflected this, and although it could barely qualify as a cubby-hole, it held two filing cabinets neatly placed against the wall adjacent to the doorway, allowing just enough room for a small desk, positioned opposite under the window. A beat-up leather office chair, old, but still functional, ate up the remaining space allowing enough room to maneuver without having to stand. To the left of the desk on the adjacent wall, a built-in bookcase shelved dozens of reference manuals, catalogues and trade binders, books on business and the stock market, interspersed with a couple of novels. He had one shelf dedicated to his trophies: an award for

Businessman of the Year, a couple of track and field awards from high school, and a die-cast model of a Rolls Royce Silver Cloud. All neatly kept, with the books arranged symmetrically. The overpowering stench of stale tobacco and cigarette ash contradicted Harrison's obsession with tidiness. The odour hit Amelia the moment she entered the space.

"Oh, Jesus! That's disgusting!" She pointed to a large ceramic ashtray, overflowing with cigarette butts, and perched precariously on the edge of the desk.

"I know, I suppose I've become immune to it over the years. I tried to get him to quit, but I was flogging a dead horse, and well, I just quit caring. I'd have ended it long ago if I hadn't loaned the asshole so much money. I rue the day I met the man, and that's the truth." She turned her attention to the file cabinets.

Anne was in the process of searching the file cabinets when her sister arrived. In the grey light from the window, she pulled open the second drawer of a file cabinet and pointed to the one beside it.

"The last time I saw it, it was in a blue folder. You check that cabinet, and I'll finish this one."

"Are you sure it's here?" Amelia asked. "You know his lawyer probably has a copy, why not just call him?"

"It's not the will, I care about. What I need is his proxy for his shares of the company. It's in the same folder, and I need that to vote on his behalf." She waved to her sister to keep looking.

"Yes, but he's dead. I don't understand. Why do you need his proxy?" Amelia pulled open the top drawer and immediately closed it. She leaned forward over the cabinet, turning her head to face her sister. "You're looking for a will you can easily get a copy of, but it's more important to find this proxy." She slumped into the old leather chair and gave her sister a quizzical look. "I'm missing something, what is it?"

Anne leaned against the side of the desk with her back to the window. The light from outside cast her into a dark silhouette. Her hair shimmered at the edges creating a silver halo around her face. "I need the proxy to gain control of the company. It's that simple."

Amelia squinted at her sister, trying to see her face in the poor lighting. "You'd better explain that one to me. I would think as his spouse, everything he had would be yours."

"It's all too complicated for words. Last year Harry came to me for money again. He needed to make payroll, and his receivables were too high, and his cashflow too low. He asked me to lend him the money. It was supposed to be short-term, but I was fed up with his constant mismanagement of the finances, and because I only hold ten percent of the shares, I don't have any control. So I forced him to sign an irrevocable voting proxy. I was going to use it to vote him off the board if he ever got into trouble again. I never used it, you understand, but according to an agreement with the employee stockholder association, if Harry ever becomes incapacitated or dies, they get interim voting control of the company until the will is probated. That could take years, especially if Canada Revenue gets involved, and I just know they will. The company is worth millions, and there is no way I'm going to leave a bunch of uneducated blue-collars in charge. This proxy supersedes that provision and gives me control of the company and my investment. I have a lot of money tied up in that plant, and I intend to get it back. Whatever it takes. Now, help me find that damned folder." She stepped back up to the file cabinet and began pulling folders from the drawers.

"It has to be here somewhere."

Amelia remained seated for the moment. She had learned over the years of Anne's propensity to help her husband, and for that reason, her opinion of the great Harrison Dalton scored very low on her Richter Scale. She considered him slightly above an amoeba on the evolutionary chart, a Neanderthal at best, a man whose opinion of women was to keep them barefoot and pregnant at all times. Well, he hadn't managed to get her sister pregnant, but he had almost drained her trust fund to the point of being shoeless. His death would not be mourned by either of them, of this, Amelia was quite sure. If this paper was that important to her sister and her future, then they would tear the house apart to find it.

* * *

Emily bit at her nails as she looked up from the photo album and gazed out the window. The black van had followed her. Now, it was just sitting there, parked in the playground at the end of the street. Should she call Colm, and have a cruiser take a look? The events of the day had her rattled, and she couldn't shake the disquiet deep in her soul.

Colm would be home soon, and she had more to deal with than an old black van. She had a lot of explaining to do. Not the least of which was her possession of the photo album and other papers she'd procured. There were many questions demanding answers. One, resurrected by recent events, had nagged her most of her life. It was time for answers.

Stuffing the photo album down the side of her seat cushion, she grabbed her phone and made a call. The line answered on the second ring.

"Hello, mom, I need to ask you a question."

* * *

Kris Martin set his coffee down on his workstation. Light from the wall of windows filtered through fighting the overhead LED fixtures for dominance, a battle it would lose as the day wore on. The room housed several T-shaped computer stations, each one with its antiseptic, white surface mounted on black metal frames with corners sharp enough to make you swear every time you bumped a knee or accidentally smacked a hand against them. At the far end of the room, the wall housed a bank of bright red gun lockers used to store firearms while interviewing suspects and witnesses. Martin had seen this rule violated many times. He smiled as he considered that he was probably the worst offender.

If there was one thing bad about police work, it was the mountains of paperwork involved. Every incident had to be backed up in writing, and God help you if you pulled your gun in public, the paperwork would stagger a medieval bible scribe. Kris sat at his computer like an author with writer's block, staring at the cursor. He knew what to write, but his anger wouldn't allow him to concentrate. He looked around the room and spied Stan Worthington working in his corner.

"A woman, a fuckin' woman! Of all the dumbest fucking things, it's just bullshit, pure and simple," Martin ranted.

"Huh, what's that?" Stan removed a set of earbuds from his ears. He was a veteran, matching Kris Martin year for year in longevity in the force. Content to be a senior constable, Stan worked his shifts, did his job, and was counting down his days to retirement. He had a cushy little gig lined up for when he pulled the pin, and he had no intention of screwing it up by pissing in anybody's cornflakes. So, when Kris Martin and his buddies started bitching, Stan kept his head down and his mouth shut. Today, he was a captive audience, lifting his head to a distraction he hadn't quite heard.

"I didn't catch what you said Kris, what's bullshit?"

"A fucking woman. That's what! We're getting a new commander, and it's a fucking slash. Jesus Christ, I've been here too long." Martin spun his chair around, launching himself upward, slamming the back of his chair into the desk behind him. He stomped over to Stan's desk, planted his hands on his desktop and leaned forward, invading Stan's personal space. "It's not official 'til tomorrow, but our new commander is a god-damned female, and my guess is she's a real ball-buster. What's more, Paddy O'fuckin-shamrock still out-fuckin' ranks me—us!"

Stan was about to speak when a movement at the doorway caught his eye. A thin smile formed on Stan's lips. He wasn't fond of Martin. He and his cronies had a way about them that he considered detrimental to good police work. In his mind, Martin was lazy, and not above bending the rules a little when it suited his purpose. He knew firsthand of Martin's history, and he knew to keep well clear. His smile widened as Kris continued.

"What the hell are you smiling at? There's nothing funny about this. A woman boss? Shit man! What do you think?"

Stan glanced past Martin and nodded.

"He knows enough to keep his opinions to himself. The sign of a wise man."

Martin spun around to see Kendra Jacobs standing in the doorway.

G. A. PICKSTOCK

16

DALTON TIRE AND RUBBER occupied a thousand acres of Clarksville's industrial park. If not for the savvy dealings of Harrison himself, it would have been one of the largest contributors to the tax base of the community. In the late 80s, he negotiated a forty-year property tax exemption in return for purchasing the tire plant, taking a huge step in saving the local economy. He also guaranteed to expand the plant and create new jobs.

The expansion had massive effects on the local housing market and commercial trades, resulting in a level of prosperity Clarksville had not seen in many decades. In 1999, Harrison Dalton received the Clarksville Town Council's Businessman of the Year award.

Then came the fall of 2008: the economy nose-dived and along with it many of Dalton Tire's purchase orders simply vanished. The business still maintained a decent bottom line but nothing like what the boom years had enjoyed.

The signs of decline around the plant were evident as Colm pulled past the abandoned security gate. The once almost impenetrable barrier now stood open, monitored only by a security camera and a disused intercom. A large white sign instructed in bold red lettering "Visitors—Please Report to Main Reception" and a left-facing arrow pointed the way.

Colm parked and proceeded to the main offices. The office receptionist met him at the door. Dressed in a powder blue sweater and blue jeans, arms straight down in front of her, her slender fingers interlaced with her palms facing downward, she radiated friendliness. Colm could tell at once she had no idea how devastatingly pretty she truly was. The name tag hanging from the lanyard around her neck said, Isobel.

"My name is Isobel, you must be the ah—inspector from the police, yes?" She asked in a noticeable French accent.

Struck by this girl's magnetic aura, Colm had to remind himself he was in love with another beautiful woman. In an awkward attempt to regain his composure, and somewhat surprised by her accent, he managed to say, "Your name tag uses the Scottish spelling of your name. Yet, you are obviously French."

"Oui, yes sir, my father, he is from Scotland, and my mother is born in Quebec. My mother she chose my name. My father, he wrote it on the registry of the birth. So, I am Isobel." Her smile was radiant as she lifted her name tag as if to verify the fact. "And you are Irish, yes?"

"Detective Sergeant O'Byrne, fresh off the boat, so I am. I'm here to see your plant manager. I have an appointment."

"Oui, yes sir, please follow me." Isobel turned and led Colm down a long hallway, passing several open office doors. The door at the end of the corridor was closed. She knocked once and entered. "Mr. Roberts, Inspector O'Byrne is here for you," she said as she ushered Colm into the office.

Jim Roberts stood in front of a massive rosewood desk, behind which stood a matching credenza and bookcase. The windowless room, illuminated by indirect lighting mounted on the walls, presented a subdued work environment. A few steps away sat a large rosewood coffee table bracketed by two armchairs upholstered in black leather. Framed photos of race-cars adorned the walls adjacent to the desk. The figure of a man decked out in a racing jumpsuit standing beside the race-car was familiar to Colm. He'd seen that face before. Jim took a seat in one of the armchairs and beckoned Colm to sit in the other.

Isobel turned, bumping against him. She blushed as they passed. "Puis-je vous chercher de l'eau, ou peut-être un café?" Her blush deepened. "Oh, I'm sorry. I mean, may I get you some water or perhaps a coffee?"

Colm blushed slightly as well, taking in the scent of the pretty blonde. "Oui, café s'il vous plait, noir, un sucre," he responded, surprising her with his French.

Her face beamed with delight. "Comme c'est merveilleux, vous parlez français?"

Colm grinned. "Juste un peu, only a little. Just enough to get by and probably more than I need to get in trouble. If it's all the same to you, let's stick to English."

Jim Roberts cleared his throat. "Ahem, if you two are about finished, Isobel, two coffees, please, just as the detective has requested, thank you." He dismissed her and said, "It's been a while. How can I help you?"

It surprised Colm to see Jim Roberts in the manager's office. They had met previously during his investigation of the Kallita Prewitt case. For a short time, Jim was a suspect in that case, and now here he was cropping up again. Colm got to the point.

"I think by now you have heard that your boss died last night."

It was not the reaction he was expecting. Jim Roberts' face drained of all colour, and for a moment, he thought the man might collapse where he sat. "I'm sorry, I thought his wife would have told you by now. She was informed earlier this morning. Jaysus, man, are you going to be okay?"

Roberts appeared to be having a hard time breathing. He slumped sideways, holding himself up with his right arm. Colm sprang from his seat and lifted the man's shoulders, pulling him back to a sitting position. Jim stared blankly at Colm, his breathing shallow and laboured. Isobel came in with the coffee and Colm barked at her to call 911.

"No, no, I'm ok," Jim sputtered, struggling to catch his breath. "I'll be fine," he said, the colour returning to his face. As his breathing became more regular, Colm released the man's shoulders and backed away from him, watching Roberts for signs of a relapse.

"Are you sure?"

Isobel placed the coffee on the table and retreated. She glanced at Colm with a questioning stare.

"I think I've given your boss some bad news, but it looks like he'll recover. We're grand, thank you." He dismissed her and turned back to Jim Roberts. "Are you sure you're okay?"

Roberts nodded and sipped his coffee. "I'm fine. How? Where? Dead! I just don't believe it. I just talked to Harry yesterday afternoon. I was expecting a call from him any minute. And no, Anne Dalton didn't call me. But then, that shouldn't come as a huge surprise." He took another swallow of his coffee.

Colm reached for his own coffee and took a sip, allowing the comment to pass for the moment. "I wasn't aware that you were the manager here. The last time we spoke, I got the impression you were a mechanic."

Roberts placed his mug on the table. "I am a mechanic. I've worked on cars all my life. I guess you could say it's in my blood. My dad was a mechanic, and a racer like me, and my gramps was a mechanic as well. Cars and working on cars is all we know. Most people don't know I have a BA in business management also. Mechanics do ok, but I make a lot more money here than I could in a garage."

Colm leaned back and took another slug of coffee. "So then, how long have you worked here?"

"I started on the line as a foreman in '99, Harry hired me on the spot. Took one look at my resumé and never even asked me any questions. But then that's the way he hired everyone, so I guess there's nothing special there. From there, I worked my way up, department manager, plant manager, and when Ted Savage resigned about a year ago, Harry promoted me. Savage had only lasted about six months when I got the nod."

"Why was that?" Colm's eyebrows raised at the news.

"Harry's thinking was all messed up. He figured by bringing in an outsider, the guy would have no ties to anyone in the plant. Therefore, he would be able to manage without any bias to one side or the other. The trouble is, Savage was a buffoon. He knew nothing of the business, and no one here respected him. Even Isobel didn't like him and believe me, Isobel likes everyone. She's the sweetest girl on two feet, but Savage rubbed her the wrong way—" he took another gulp of coffee—"take it from me, that's one French Canadian you don't want to piss off."

Roberts' chest seemed to swell as he settled back in his seat, a broad smile crossing his face. Colm couldn't decide if it was some kind of fatherly pride or if there was more to it.

"Promoting me to GM was totally against character for him, but the ESA put the pressure on him. They wanted one of their own in charge, and I guess I was their pick."

"ESA, what's that?"

"Employee Stockholder Association. The employees own twenty-five percent of this company. The association administers those shares, ensuring that the dividends from the stocks are distributed accordingly. All the employees here have a stake in the company. The ESA elects one member to sit on the board of directors. We have a direct influence on how this company runs, and so far it has worked well. Our annual bonuses run into the thousands and sometimes into five figures. If you have seniority here, you earn a larger share of the pool."

Colm decided it was time to get down to the dirt of the matter, "You said you're not surprised Mrs. Dalton didn't call you. Why?"

"She's a bitch," Roberts said without hesitation. "She owns part of this company, and yet never sets foot in here. When she does come in, she's all business. No small-talk. It doesn't matter who it is or how hard we try, she simply isn't friendly. I don't know what will happen now that Harry is dead. This is all too much to think about right now. Harry—dead, damn!"

Colm reached into his inside pocket and removed his cell phone. He should have been recording this conversation, but because of Jim's adverse reaction to the news, he had forgotten to do so. He tapped on the recording app, and placing the phone on the desk he said, "I hope you don't mind, I'd like our conversation on the record from here on. I should have done this earlier."

"I've nothing to hide, Detective. Record away." Roberts sat back and finished his coffee.

* * *

"What can you tell me about the man himself? Was he a decent boss, or was he difficult to work for?" Colm settled back in his chair and sipped on his coffee.

"I guess that depends on who you're asking. Harry Dalton is— was —an enigma. I take it you never met him."

Colm shook his head. "No, I'd heard of the company sure, but then I've only been here a year and a half and let's face it, my days generally don't revolve around tires. If you get my drift, no pun intended."

Roberts smiled. "No, I suppose not. Well, Harry didn't have many friends. I'd say he didn't have any. He knew a lot of people, and he knew quite a few in business. If there was anyone he could call a friend, it would be Barry."

"Barry, Barry, who?" Colm asked, placing his empty cup on the desk.

"Barry Blackmore, he's a land developer here in town, probably the largest in the region."

Colm had heard the name before, but couldn't recall where or why.

"So, you say he had few, if any, friends. Ok then, how did he get along with the workers?"

"Harry was blue-collar all the way. But he was double-minded, and that made him unpopular." Jim saw the confusion in Colm's face. "Harry had a habit of making a decision, and ten minutes later changing it. He allowed himself to be lobbied by anyone. He would listen to people, and if they made sense, then he was inclined to go along with what they wanted. It wasn't the guys on the line that did this, but they were the ones affected. Let me give you an example. One of the department supervisors felt he could save the company money by buying supplies from a certain vendor. I won't go into detail, but he went to Harry for a decision and walked away happy. A day later, a different supervisor who worked the night shift in the same department, and who by the way didn't like that supplier, lobbied Harry to use the original supplier. Harry changed his mind without notifying the first supervisor. It created a ton of confusion and resulted in double ordering materials, which created an overstock situation. Returning one of the orders would have cost us tens of thousands. Instead, we kept both orders, depleting our liquid cash, and placing us in serious overdraft. We got past it, but Harry was like that all the time. He hired guys to do jobs they couldn't do, and fired guys who happened to piss him off, despite their capability to do a good job. Honestly, I don't know how I've lasted this long. I really don't know how the business has done as well as it has. We always pay bonuses, and the bottom line looks good. But I'll tell you now, it has nothing to do with management style. Harrison Dalton had only one thing going for him, and that was a huge set of brass balls. He wasn't afraid of a challenge."

Colm lifted his coffee mug forgetting it was empty. "Would you like another?" Jim asked.

"I'm grand, thanks anyway, force of habit, I guess. Tell me, so he had no real friends to speak of, how about enemies?"

"Oh, he pissed a lot of people off. Hell, there's a dozen in this factory I can name who'd happily piss on his grave. Quite a few in fact, and I can think of at least six or seven who left here with huge chips on their shoulders, and some of them rightly so."

"I'll need a list," Colm said.

"A list? Why?" Roberts leaned forward, his eyes narrowed, and the lines in his forehead deepened. "You know, in all the confusion earlier, you never told me how he died. What's going on?"

The cordial atmosphere became noticeably less so as the two eyed each other. Colm contemplated his next move. Should he tell him the truth? He knew Jim Roberts, and he knew the man held secrets. He was no stranger to lying, and he was good at it. Placing him on the defensive at this point might be the only real alternative. Letting him think it was little more than an accident wouldn't work. *No, go for the throat, Colm old son. See what happens.*

"Harrison Dalton died last night as a result of a gunshot wound. Now, you can give me the list voluntarily, or I'll get a warrant. Up to you."

Roberts hung his head, hiding his face in his hands. He sat for a long moment rubbing his eyes, taking deep breaths. He let out a deep sigh and looked up at the detective. In that moment, Colm sensed that Jim Roberts felt a profound loss.

"I'm sorry there is no easy way to say it. I'm afraid Harrison was murdered."

"Yes, thank you, Detective, I'm sorry, it's just such a shock. I had no idea. When you said he was dead, I figured it was an accident or maybe a heart attack or something. The guy wasn't in good shape, and he smoked like a chimney. I'll get you your list. In fact, I'll give you copies of their files."

"I'll give you a few seconds to get your head around all this," Colm said. "Maybe that coffee wouldn't be such a bad idea."

Roberts pressed a button on his phone. A second later, Isobel's voice answered, "Yes, sir."

"Could you bring us both a refill please, Isobel, and then I have some files I want you to pull for me." He ended the call without waiting for a reply.

***

Moments later, Isobel appeared with the coffee, and shortly after, returned with a stack of file folders. She gave them to Jim Roberts, who immediately passed them over to Colm. The name on the top file read Ted Savage.

"Tell me, this Ted Savage fella, why did he give up his position here?"

"I said he resigned, but the reality is, he was fired. He was useless as a manager. Harry should never have hired him. He deserved to go, but I kinda felt sorry for him when it happened."

"How's that?" Colm asked.

"He was useless. He didn't get along well with anyone. Take a look around this place. It's not a suit and tie operation. The only guys who wear suits are the outside reps, the sales guys. But we're all blue jeans and golf shirts in here. In the plant, it's all cover-alls." Roberts made a motion with his hands, spreading them in a waving motion from head to toe. "At any given moment, we might have to go into the plant."

Colm's eyes narrowed, "How's that?" He asked.

Jim Roberts grinned at the detective. "I'd take you back and show you, but I'm afraid you're not dressed for it. Suffice to say, we make tires here, detective, and it's a dirty business."

"I still don't get it, what has that got to do with Ted Savage?"

"He insisted that everyone in management, right down to shop foremen, wear business attire. Despite what any of us could say or do, he insisted. So we did. The next day, Harry walked in wearing his blue jeans and suspenders, took one look at us and laughed his ass off. That ended the dress code bullshit, but it didn't stop there. In fact, it all started when he first got here. Management 101, we called it. Savage got it in his head to interview everyone in the plant. Can you imagine? This plant employs over four hundred people. We have three hundred or more on the line, another forty or fifty support staff, a couple of dozen outside reps and thirty managers and shift bosses. That lunatic wanted to interview everyone. He tried for a week, starting with the night shift. Ten-minute interviews, where he had them fill out a questionnaire stating their goals in life. Where do you see yourself in five years and crap like that? It was a joke, and when Harry got wind of him wasting their time and costing the plant money in lost production, he went ballistic. He almost fired the dumbass on the spot. I don't know what stopped him. It was like that all the time, and it wasn't long before Ted became the joke. Like I said, no one liked him. Still, I had to feel sorry for the guy when he finally went."

Colm looked up from the files. He'd been sifting through them as Jim spoke, and he'd seen some familiar names. "How's that?" He asked.

"Well, two weeks before Ted's exodus from here, he got married to a girl he'd been dating. She'd moved here from Toronto. Gave up her job and everything. Ted made good money here, and I guess they figured they could make it on his salary alone, at least for a while. So, she moves down, and they get married. They bugger off to lost wages, Las Vegas, for a honeymoon, and when they get back, he's called into a meeting with Harry's lawyer and accountant. Thirty minutes later, Savage storms out of the office with a banker's box full of his stuff swearing he'll get even with the prick. Oh, and yeah, true to form, Harry is nowhere to be seen. Typical Harrison Dalton style, hire them by all means, Harry's the hero, but fire? No way! He hides away somewhere and lets someone else do it."

* * *

Roberts had no windows in his office, but he did have access to the plant's extensive surveillance system. The room seemed somehow smaller than before, and now as he watched the detective meander his way back to the exit, his mind scrambled for answers. The thought of Harry lying on a slab in the morgue made him shudder. The news had knocked him for a loop, something had gone terribly wrong. Roberts replayed the interview in his mind, and now feared he'd said too much. The list he'd given Colm had one name Jim wished he could have omitted. His hand hovered above the phone. He had to do something. Snatching up the receiver, he dialled an outside line.

"We need to talk. You know where," Jim dropped the phone back into its cradle. *God, I hope this isn't what I think it is.*

G. A. PICKSTOCK

17

STANDING OUTSIDE HIS NEW commander's office like some school kid waiting to see the principal, Kris Martin checked his watch. The hands of the Omega timepiece seemed frozen in place, barely creeping toward the top of the hour. His shift would end shortly, but not, he suspected, in time to escape what was to come.

It wasn't the reprimand, he could handle that. He'd had more than his share of those. No, it was the loss of face. Being chastised by a woman for being himself would cost him credibility within his little group of six. It was just wrong. Wrong on so many levels. How could he be expected to kowtow to a woman? His mind scrambled for a way out. Some excuse to release himself from the grip of the torture he knew was coming. He rechecked his watch. Five o'clock could not come fast enough.

New brooms sweep clean. First, Colm, and now, this woman for sure was going to be a problem. Martin had to do something, but first, he had to endure the reading of the riot act. He rechecked his watch.

"Five bells. Well, I guess I'm done for the day," he said to the empty hallway.

"Not so fast, Constable. We need to talk. Now!" Kendra Jacobs held her office door open for him and saw his reluctance. "Now, Constable Martin, we need to get some things straight."

***

"Take a seat, Constable," said Jacobs as she took her place behind her desk.

Martin sat, leaned back in his chair and folded his arms, waiting for the inevitable verbal berating he knew was coming.

"Your behaviour in the common room is unacceptable. I heard what you said. It was insulting and demeaning and sexist and downright disrespectful." She paused, allowing her words to linger in his mind.

"Do you think what you said in there is new, that I've never heard it before?"

Martin opened his mouth, but all he could utter was, "Uhm—"

"Uhm, that's all you can say," she snapped. "I've dealt with your kind my whole career. I know you hate that I'm a woman and I'm in charge. That's tuff! News flash, Constable—the boys club days are over. I am in charge, and that's not going to change simply because you don't like it. I don't care how long you've been on the force. Your seniority holds no gravity here. I don't care how old you are, who you are, whether you're black, brown, grey, or polka dot, man, woman or ferret. If you disrespect me again, if I hear even one syllable of that kind of talk from you again, it will go on your annual performance report, and I think you know what that's all about."

She lifted the file folder sitting on her desk and removed a document.

"I was going to wait until tomorrow to do this, but there is no point in delaying. This comes directly from Orillia. After reading your file and witnessing your actions here today, I will go on record as agreeing with this." She handed the paper to Martin. "Read it," she ordered.

Martin sat, stone still, the document hovered in front of him as Jacobs held it for him. He stared at the paper. He'd wanted a change. He wanted nothing more than to see O'Byrne pushed out of the command chair, but this wasn't at all what he'd expected. Another change was coming, and it was only inches away. The ominous document fluttered in his new boss's hand, and all he wanted to do was leave. This was unfair. He was a kid again back in school, and the slash was scolding him like she was a high-school principal.

Jacobs waved the page in his face. "Well, take it!" She leaned forward, pushing the document into his hands.

With trembling fingers, Kris unfolded the page and read it. Kendra had never seen a man's face glow incandescent before. For a moment, she thought Kris Martin was going to burst a vein. His face turned the most strawberry red she'd ever seen, and a large purple vein pulsed wildly up the side of his neck. He raised himself halfway out of his chair and immediately slumped back again. He crumpled the paper into a ball and bounced it off the desk, striking Kendra in the chin.

"This is a joke. Kaladar? Really? You're going to send me to Kaladar? After twenty years with this outfit, fifteen of them right here in this detachment, you're going to move me to Kaladar? I don't believe it." He was standing now and beginning to pace.

"Constable Martin, please sit down." Kendra Jacobs' tone became less adversarial. "As I said, I had no input into this decision, but I do agree that your experience and talents are needed in that detachment."

Kris sat as ordered but kept his gaze turned away from the new commander. He contemplated his shoes as he listened to what she had to say. When she finished, he looked up and said, "This is total bullshit! I've put my time in, I've paid my dues. Ok, I screwed up ten years ago, but I paid for that, and now you're going to move me to clod-hopper Ontario. Why?"

"You're needed there," Kendra said. "Besides, it's not that far away. It's only forty minutes from here. Be happy you didn't get posted to Hearst. I hear they need people there as well."

"Six of one and half-dozen of the other, the cost to move me is the same. You still have to pay for the move. It just doesn't make sense. Nobody with twenty years gets posted unless it's requested or for a promotion. At least I won't have to worry about dissing you again."

Jacobs shook her head. "No, Kris, you're wrong. You forget something. You won't be moving, at least not at the expense of the OPP."

"Huh, what?"

"Well, Kris, I think you've forgotten, Kaladar is under our jurisdiction. You'll be working there, but your posting is still Clarksville. You're not moving your house unless, of course, it's something you want to do on your own. You won't qualify for moving expenses. Oh, and I will still be your boss."

* * *

In the year and a half Colm had been in Clarksville, Kris Martin had dominated the roster. He commanded more respect than Dan Clifford had. Clifford had kept his distance with the troops, thus making it easier for him to deal with them objectively. Despite the ultimate revelation of his collusion in the Prewitt case, he was well-liked and respected. Kris Martin was the godfather in the detachment, the go-to guy when you needed something. If you had issues, he was the guy who could get things done.

Consequently, no one crossed him, which allowed him to rack up points. Favours, he would call in as it suited him. Good turns that might not be easy to oblige. He got what he wanted, when he wanted it, earning him the not too loudly spoken moniker of "Don Martini." He'd heard it whispered, many times, it made him smile, giving him a sense of empowerment. And why not? In his mind, he deserved the promotion to detachment commander. This new revelation had him in knots, and he would not sit still for it.

When he heard the news, Colm almost felt sorry for the man. The events of the past twenty-four hours had changed everything. Relegating Kris Martin to a northern satellite office in the middle of nowhere was tantamount to sending him to the Arctic Circle to monitor the annual snowfall. With only three constables in that office, plagued with every nuisance and domestic call going, the closest thing to excitement might be arresting a bunch of drunks getting thrown out of a bar on a Saturday night. Still, as Senior Constable, he would, in effect, be an acting sergeant placing him in command. Colm smiled at that thought. Maybe he wasn't so sorry for him, after all. *Fair play to ya Kris, I hope you have a grand time.*

18

JEREMIAH BANNISTER CURSED IN pain as the van's steering wheel tore free of his grip, spinning wildly around and smacking the back of his hand. It was the second time the front wheels had dropped into a crater in the disused roadway, each time with painful results. He made slow progress as he struggled to keep the van from veering off into oblivion.

As he rounded a bend in the road, the sight of the dilapidated farmhouse sent a wave of relief over the gunsmith. He took a cursory glance around as he turned into the driveway. An old rusty gate, hanging on one hinge, leaned against the shrubbery at the side of the entrance. The path, two wagon ruts divided in the middle by knee-high grass, wound its way to the rundown old porch. In its day, the old house would have been called stately, but now it fell far short of the title, with its paint-peeled white siding and green-trimmed shuttered windows, some of which had missing louvres. The window glass was still intact, but the windows hadn't seen soapy water in decades. A lone lightbulb dangled on two wires from the porch ceiling, the dim light declaring to visitors that the house still lived.

Jeremiah drew near the porch and leaned on the horn. There wasn't supposed to be anyone home. Still, he didn't want any surprises and confronting unsuspecting occupants and or their dogs were not on his list of favourites. He had left the first delivery on the porch as instructed without incident. He expected nothing different this time.

He retrieved the parcel and approached the front door. As with the rest of the house, the door's dark green paint peeled away in large flakes. The blackened brass hardware with its old corrosion-encrusted letter slot and mechanical doorbell and ornate butterfly thumb-turn spoke of an era long ended. He set the crate down on the floor in front of the doorway and spun the butterfly handle. As with the first delivery, the bell rang loudly enough for him to hear it. Delivery made, Jeremiah Bannister climbed back into his van and drove away, satisfied that the contents of the package could not be traced back to him.

* * *

In a dark control room, a series of signals flashed across the computer monitor. The operator stabbed at a button on the control panel, and four images appeared on the screen. He watched as the driver, a skinny old farmer, placed a package near the front door. He rang the doorbell and returned to his van. Moments later, the operator made a phone call. A garbled voice answered.

"Your item has arrived," he said. There was no response from the other end, just the deadened air of the phone disconnecting, and a quick flicker on the screen as the images vanished.

19

OUT OF THE THREE stacks of papers now piled on the kitchen table, Emily held a single letter in her hand. The stacks were sorted into tax returns, bills and bank statements, and personal correspondence had revealed little until she found the message from a local law firm. The letter raised questions. Yet, none of the paperwork in the three piles offered any insight.

"There must be more," she thought aloud. "But where?"

"More what?" Colm's voice boomed behind her.

Startled, Emily jumped, almost falling off her chair. "Colm, oh crap! You scared the life out of me! What, where—I didn't expect you home for—what time is it?" She checked her watch, realizing that time had slipped away on her. She'd had no intention of showing Colm the paperwork, at least not yet. After his admonitions to step away from the investigation, she knew he wouldn't react well at her violating a police crime scene. But the toothpaste was out of the tube now, and she scrambled to straighten herself up, trying to gather the papers together, hoping that Colm wouldn't ask about them. It was a useless effort, and she gave up as quickly as she began.

"What's all this?" He asked as he picked up one of the tax forms.

She moved in close to him, placing her right hand softly on his chest. "Don't get upset," she whispered. "I went back in and found these papers. You guys didn't do a great job of searching that house. There's all kinds of stuff like this in there."

Colm said nothing, moving around her to the opposite side of the table. Emily watched as he fingered through the piles of papers, sifting through bank records and bills, some with "Overdue" and "Final Notice" stamped over them. His hand came to rest on the lawyer's letter, and as he picked it up, Emily saw her opening. If she could get him interested in the contents of that letter, she might avoid the impending battle.

She didn't know why, but the Irish knew precisely how to deliver a good telling-off. Maybe it was genetic, an evolutionary result of thousands of years of turmoil in a country so green and lush it inspired magical tales of fairies, leprechauns, and pots of gold. Yet, Ireland and its people had suffered so much terror and struggle. How anyone could emerge unscarred was anyone's guess. It was why the stereotypical Irishman was a hard-drinking, hard-fighting man with an impish sense of humour and a short temper.

This was not her Colm. Her Colm was a gentleman, slow to anger but firm and unafraid. He liked his beer but rarely allowed it to get the better of him, and Emily knew his feelings for her were strong. Disappointing him was wrong, but she had her own set of values, and she could not look away and ignore the situation in which she now found herself.

"You need to read that," she said as he unfolded the letter. "It raises a lot of questions."

Colm pulled out a chair and sat. He smoothed the letter out on the table-top and read.

The letter read:

Law Offices of Davis & Leonard LLP - 543 Market Street North - Clarksville - Ontario.

RE: Acct.# 2498675AG24367 – Tax Arrears - 4234 Dalton Road, Greater Clarksville, Ontario

July 5, 2016

NOTICE! SALE OF PROPERTY FOR TAXES OWED

Dear MS Saunders,

I have been engaged by my client, the Town of Greater Clarksville, hereinafter known as Petitioner. The Petitioner states that the property identified above and as outlined and described in schedule-A- attached, is in default of property taxes owed. The amount in arrears is $42,039.19.

Payment of this amount must be made by July 20, 2016, According to the Ontario Property Statute, if payment is not received by the aforementioned date, the following actions will apply:

- the property will be listed on the next tax sale.
- the property will be advertised in local newspapers and on our website.
- said advertisement will appear for one week only, immediately following the deadline.
- Clarksville will notify any mortgage holders of the sale.
- after the property sale, anyone registered on title except for provincial or federal liens loses their interest in said property.

Conduct yourself accordingly. Failure to remit the full amount will result in the above intended action.

Sincerely ...

* * *

It had been a hell of a day, and Colm was exhausted. He hadn't the energy to fight with Emily about her breaking into the Saunders' home. They had talked for over an hour. Despite being miffed with her for violating the crime scene, he was just as angry with himself for missing vital evidence. As he unbuttoned his uniform, he caught his reflection in the dresser mirror. The tired face looking back at him reflected his mood. His eyes were hollow and dark with a faint trace of thin lines fanning away from the corners. It was not the face of a twenty-seven-year-old detective in the prime of his career. He felt older, but he hoped that would change. Now that Kendra Jacobs was in charge, he could finally get back into his routine. One thing was sure, Kris Martin was no longer his problem.

The image in the mirror reinforced his need for sleep, but his mind would not allow it. He hadn't expected a connection between the two murders, but the tax letter changed his thinking. He could not ignore the questions arising from this new revelation.

Nicole Saunders lived in a modest area of town. Simcoe Street was hardly Knob Hill. Homes there averaged under two hundred thousand on a good day. So how did it happen that this woman, who appeared unable to bang two nickels together, owned prime industrial land in the heart of Clarksville's industrial park? And why, assuming this was true, would she not sell it for its value instead of accumulating such serious tax arrears? Judging by all her overdue bills, she could certainly use the money.

It makes no sense, he thought as he stepped into the shower. Ten minutes later, Colm emerged from the sauna-like enclosure, his pale Irish skin lobster-red. Wrapping a towel around his waist, he flipped the switch for the light leaving the fan running to exhaust the steam. As he dried himself off, the sight of the king-sized bed beckoned to him. Succumbing to its charms, the day's tension ebbed away as he flopped onto the soft duvet. *She who must be obeyed won't like you placing your wet backside on the bed. Ah, but it feels so grand, so it does.* His eyes snapped shut, and Colm was out for the night.

* * *

"Tell the truth and shame the devil, it's because I fell asleep and got your duvet all damp and wrinkled, so I did."

Emily scowled at him. "I don't care about the duvet. It's your side that got wet. You live with it."

Colm placed two coffees on the table. "So why are you so surly this morning? All you've done is grunt at me." The toaster clicked, and two cinnamon raisin bagels popped up. He gingerly retrieved them from the appliance and set them on a plate. "Butter or cream cheese?" he asked, hoping to get a civil response.

"You know what I like, and I'm not surly." Emily pulled a chair out from the table. It caught the leg of the one beside it and sent it crashing to the floor. Colm turned his head far enough to see Emily struggling with the chairs and quickly turned away, hiding the grin on his face.

"Pure shite. I don't know how you can stomach the stuff. Cream cheese, yuck, baby vomit if you ask me." He took a large dollop and slathered it on her bagel. Still grinning, he applied a liberal helping of butter to his own bagel and turned in time to watch his sweetheart get control of her chair.

"Nobody's asking you," she retorted, pushing the offending chair back into place.

The couple sat across from each other and ate in silence. As if on cue, each looked at the other and spoke.

"It's not shi…"

"Why are you…"

"I think we just had our first fight," Colm said, taking the last bite of his bagel. Emily blushed and bit her bottom lip. "You do that a lot as well."

"Do what?" asked Emily.

"Bite your lip. You do it all the time when you're nervous or stressed about something. You even do it when you're excited."

"I do not." Emily snatched his plate away, gathered up her own and placed them in the sink. "And this wasn't a fight. If we'd been fighting, believe me, you'd know it."

"Oh, yes, you do, darling. You'd never be a good poker player. Everyone would know your tell after the second hand. So, tell me, what's in your craw."

Colm leaned back and took a large gulp of his coffee. He believed her about the fighting aspect. Emily's femininity belied her courage. She was all woman, a real girl's girl, but she was a fighter, and God help anyone who got on her wrong side. She liked gentlemen. Manners were important to her, and she rarely tolerated profanity except for Colm's occasional slips of the tongue. Still, his cuss words came out all Irish, and although they held the same context as the real expletive, they held little of the vulgarity associated with them. She wasn't a prude by anyone's imagination. Emily had heard it all working in call centres.

Her timing might not be perfect, and her impulsive nature grated on him, but Colm had to marvel at her determination and tenacity to get things done. She was almost obsessive about order, which was evidenced in the way she had her home arranged. Everything had a place, and everything was in its place. Even Colm knew where he stood, and Emily's reaction to his recent sojourn to his own apartment was clear evidence of the fact. She was a force and with that came a redheaded temper. She'd unleashed it more than once during their short romance, thankfully, not on him.

"I don't have anything in my craw, thank you very much, I just don't see why I can't help you with the Saunders case. You know I can do it, and I have the next five days off." She placed a pod in her Keurig and hit the power button. "How long do you think it would have taken you to find that letter if I hadn't gone in there?"

Colm turned to her and offered his mug for her to refill. "We might never have found it. But I don't know if it's relevant. The woman owed taxes, so what? I'll look into it, but I can't see how her owing money to the town has any bearing on her murder. I'm more concerned about the how and who of it. Once we know those answers, the why will reveal itself."

Emily returned to her seat, setting Colm's coffee in front of him.

"Maybe so, but don't you think Sammi deserves answers? What will become of her? She's just a child, and now she has no mum, and from what I saw at the house, it doesn't look like there's a dad anywhere. Why not let me follow up on that? I can canvas neighbours and do some digging. It wouldn't interfere with your investigation, and I can report anything I find to you right away."

Colm pondered this for a moment. He trusted Emily more than some of his fellow officers. His first impulse was to refuse and warn her away from investigating. He knew she wouldn't listen. She hadn't done so far, and, like it or not, she was hip-deep in this investigation. The balls were back in the air, and his juggling act was about to begin once more. Only this time, he had the woman he loved stuck between two murder investigations and his new boss.

"It's against my better judgement, sure, if you promise to stay away from anything dangerous and concentrate on the background for Sammi, then I'll cover for you with Kendra." He lifted his coffee, tested the temperature of the mug with his tongue, and blew on it before taking a sip.

"Who's Kendra?"

Colm set his mug down. "My new boss," he said, dabbing his mouth with a napkin. "She starts today." As he checked the time, a big cheesy grin crossed his face at the thought of Kris Martin driving north to his new digs. *Kris should be about halfway there by now.* "With all the excitement, I never got to tell you, and then I—well, you know the rest."

"Is this the same Kendra who you met in Ireland?" she asked.

"Aye, the very one, sure. She's a good cop, and I'm thinking she'll make a grand boss. She already solved one of the biggest pains in my backside, and I get to go back to wearing a suit. Which reminds me, I've got to get a move on, I have a quick meeting with Kendra this morning, and then I need to make some visits. Please promise me you'll stay out of trouble and don't go back to that house."

He grabbed his phone from the table, kissed Emily twice and dashed out the door. Emily followed him and watched as he backed out of the driveway. She lingered a moment as the Mini-Cooper stopped at the corner to make a turn. Her breath caught in her throat as Colm's car disappeared behind a tall hedge at the intersection. She hadn't noticed it until she lost sight of Colm, but the black van from yesterday idled in the playground parking lot at the end of her road. She was sure it was the same one. It had to be. *How many dumpy old black vans with wonky license plates can there be?* A chill ran up her back, and the hair on her neck bristled. With a quick shiver, she snatched a light jacket from a coat-hook and stepped through the door, setting off toward the playground.

G. A. PICKSTOCK

20

CLARKSVILLE'S TOWN HALL WAS the centerpiece of the small town's market square. The building had served the town and surrounding counties for over a century and a half. It was the centre of taxation for property owners in the area, and with amalgamation, it now serviced many hundreds of square miles of outlying counties and townships.

The main reception area held a semi-hexagonal counter stretching across the full width of the building, separating the public space from the central bank of offices behind. A small half-gate controlled by an electric lock split the counter at the centre, allowing access to the offices. Positioned behind the split counters sat four old wooden desks, relics salvaged from an old school. Secretaries and clerks sat working at computer terminals, shuffling papers and talking on phones. Beyond the counter, the central office corridor stretched the full length of the building, dividing it down the middle. Colm could see the light from the rear entry windows at the end of the hallway. Just to the right of the hallway entrance, a large vault door stood open. It was a newer vault installed to replace the original safe that had outlived its use. The new vault had a much larger capacity, and despite the world's penchant to become paperless, the need for physical records still trumped the desire to save trees.

Colm heard a soft curse come from a silver-haired woman in her late fifties as she knocked her thigh against her desk. She extricated her rotund and more than ample frame from her chair and winced in pain as she hobbled to the counter.

"Can I help you?" she asked. A bead of sweat formed at her temple, and for a moment Colm thought the old girl might pass out. It was evident that she'd been a desk-jockey for quite some time. She was breathing hard, and standing was difficult for her. Colm scanned the rest of the room to see if anyone would come to assist the poor woman.

"Well," she said again. "How can I help you?"

Colm showed her his badge and said, "I'm investigating an incident that happened on Simcoe Street yesterday. I need to talk to someone in your tax records department."

"I see," she puffed, giving the badge a cursory glance. "Well, I don't know—" She looked around the room as if searching for someone. "Jack isn't here right now, and I'm not sure when he'll be back." She turned to make her way back to her chair, holding tightly to the edge of the counter as she transited back across the short expanse to her desk, letting go only when she could steady herself on the side of the old wooden workspace.

"Is there anyone else who can help me?" Colm called after her, somewhat nonplussed at the woman's sudden retreat.

"Perhaps I can help."

The voice came from a man in a grey suit. His jacket was open, revealing a rumpled white shirt, and a loosely knotted, red and blue striped tie with the top shirt button undone.

"Hi, I'm Cal Jenkins, the deputy clerk. I'm afraid you must forgive Rita. She can be a little abrupt, and she—well, let's say she's not doing too well. As I said, maybe I can help."

Jenkins ushered Colm through the half-gate into an office at the far end of the corridor. A horseshoe-shaped computer work-station dominated the small room with just enough space behind it for its occupant and a filing cabinet with a small laser printer sitting on top. The high ceiling gave the office a sense of spaciousness it didn't deserve, and a single-pane window spanned the width of the back wall stretching from the wainscoting to the ceiling. It was a grey day in October, and the light from the window cast the deputy clerk into silhouette as he strode around the narrow passage to the opposite side of the desk. Jenkins indicated the vacant chair for Colm to sit. Once seated, Colm retrieved the tax letter from his inside pocket and handed it to the clerk.

"I'm investigating the murder of Nicole Saunders, and we came across this letter. Can you tell me if these arrears were paid, and if so, by whom?"

Cal Jenkins studied the letter, taking much longer than needed to read the document. He flipped the paper from front to back as though something was missing. The lines in his forehead deepened. He nodded, then handed it back to Colm. Cal Jenkins' hand trembled slightly as he reached for his computer mouse. A long silence followed as the deputy clerk searched his computer terminal. A few clicks later, Jenkins turned his attention from his computer monitor to Colm. Jenkins' voice caught in his throat as he spoke.

"The short—ahem"—he cleared his throat— "answer is yes. The taxes are paid. However, I'm bound by privacy laws that prevent me from telling you who paid them."

"Perhaps you didn't understand me," Colm responded. "I'm investigating a murder. This information might be vital to solving this case."

"Might be, detective, but I'm sorry, the information is confidential. Without a warrant, I can't give you any more information." Jenkins regained his composure as he sat back and crossed his arms. "It's a privacy issue."

It wasn't true. Colm knew the information wasn't private, nor did he need a warrant to get it. The Land Registry Office would have a record of the property transfer, and anyone, with the appropriate fee, could obtain the information. Still, Jenkins wouldn't budge, which raised a question in Colm's mind. *What doesn't he want me to know?*

"Mr. Jenkins, I can get the information," Colm smiled, "I'm sure you know that. I hoped you'd be kind enough to provide it and save me the bother." As Colm stood to leave, he said, "You know as well as I do, all I have to do is check with the Land Registry Office. They will provide me with all I need to know. Or will they?" Colm locked eyes with the clerk. "Perhaps I should get that warrant after all."

Cal Jenkins' face paled at Colm's last statement, it was as if someone had let the air out of his body. *Bang on boyo! You're hiding something, and I'm going to find out what it is.* Colm turned on his heels and left Jenkins sitting behind his desk.

* * *

Half an hour later, Colm walked out of the Land Registry Office with all the information he needed. The land in question was a six-acre parcel with one disused building erected on the property. It was located at the corner of Dalton Road and County Road 7, which, as it turned out, was right on the north-west corner of Dalton Tire's existing property. Nicole Saunders was the registered owner and no, she had not paid the taxes, and so the property was listed for sale according to the terms of the letter. A numbered company had purchased the property bidding a final price of seventy-four-thousand dollars for it. The amount far exceeded the taxes owed, but there would be no surplus left for Nicole. After the local government got their share, and the lawyers, auction brokers, real estate fees and land transfer taxes were paid, the whole works added up to a zero balance. Nicole Saunders had lost it all, and as far as Colm could see, she'd never had a chance. He also knew what Cal Jenkins was trying to hide. *It's a small town, Cal old son. Secrets don't stay secret long. Reckon I'll get that warrant.*

* * *

The church at the end of the street was a recent addition to the neighbourhood. Only two years old, it boasted a large congregation and had opened a private school on the premises. From Emily's living-room window, she could see the back edge of the parking lot and the children's playground. The brisk, cold air caught Emily's breath as she made her way down the street. The black van idled in the parking lot of the church playground on the opposite side of the T-shaped intersection. She guessed whoever was inside the van was trying to keep warm. She pulled her jacket tighter around herself as the wind gusted, blowing up her skirt and making her wish she'd put on a pair of jeans. But then she hadn't intended to go out either.

Emily approached the tall hedge at the end of her street and ducked behind it, concealing herself from view. Only thirty metres away, she peered through a gap in the bushes.

She couldn't see anyone through the front windshield, and the side window facing in her direction was tinted so dark there was no hope of getting a peek.

"You're the broad from the hospital." A thick, gravelly voice emanated from behind her sending shivers up Emily's spine. The hair on her neck was standing up again. The cold penetrated deep inside her, causing her bladder to scream for release. Emily clenched, stiffening up as a hand gripped her shoulder, preventing her from turning around.

"Don't move. Stay right like that," the voice commanded. "You need to keep your nose out of other people's business."

The hand forced Emily into the wet mud and grass at the base of the hedge. His breath reeked of stale coffee and cigarettes as he leaned in closer to her. Close in her ear, he growled, "Leave it be, bitch, or next time I won't be so nice." She lost control of her bladder as the man shoved her the rest of the way to the ground. Facedown and frightened, Emily lay there waiting for the next assault to occur.

Moments later, she turned, tentatively looking for her assailant. She was alone. No one had seen what happened. Raising herself from the filthy wet ground, she glanced through the hedge at the parking lot. Muddied, soaked in her own urine and shaking more from the cold than fear, she stepped onto the street in time to see the van's taillights turn a corner.

* * *

Amelia Lonsdale sat cross-legged on the floor. They'd almost wrecked the house, searching everywhere, they'd even pulled the panelling in the garage off the walls, thinking the man was paranoid enough to hide it where no one might look. Amelia was back where they'd started. Neither file cabinet had produced the proxy they searched for, nor had any of Harrison's books and binders once carefully stored away on the now-empty bookshelves. The desk drawers sat scattered atop the desk, removed from their homes to allow scrutiny of the space within, but still nothing.

Alone for the first time in this office, Amelia tried to put herself into the mind of a man she barely knew. Harrison Dalton was no fool. If that proxy existed, he had hidden it well. The thought that Harry may have destroyed it crossed her mind, but she dismissed it. Had Anne demanded to see it at any point, he would have to produce it. She was the fairy-godmother to his fairy-tale life, and without her money, he was toast. That proxy had to be here, but where?

Anne appeared with coffee for them. Amelia reached up to grasp the edge of the desk, leaning on it to help herself up. Her hand slipped, knocking against a wooden floral appliqué. She thought she had broken the hand-carved rose. She inspected the damage and realized it wasn't broken. The rose had turned slightly from its original position. Amelia twisted the flower back into place and almost left it alone when a thought crossed her mind. It couldn't be? Closer inspection revealed the carving was designed to turn. Amelia twisted the flower, and it came to rest with the stem at nine o'clock. Nothing happened. She rotated it back and forth with no result. On her third attempt, Amelia gave the rose petals a firm push, and the flower clicked and moved inward. The full side panel of the desk fell open, revealing a cavity deep enough to hold two ledgers and a blue file folder. They could have searched for years and not found it.

21

THEY CALLED IT GOD'S Country, all green, and lush, and wild. But not today, today it was grey, and the trees were barren. Naked branches stretched forth, reaching skyward as if begging the gods for forgiveness at their inability to remain clothed while cloaking their feet in the warm comfort of the kaleidoscopic carpet of greens and reds, mixed with yellow and orange.

Kris Martin could see quite well from his new digs, but the view from his office was anything but scenic. All he could see was an empty asphalt parking lot, three flagpoles, the detachment sign, two lanes of highway and bush. Miles and miles of bush. Somewhere out there, animals foraged for food and stored away nuts and berries for the winter as if building up their bank accounts. Martin had been doing the same thing.

Putting bad guys behind bars meant that sometimes you had to colour outside the lines. He knew where the lines were, and which ones he could stray across. He, and his crew of six like-minded cops had made a lot of money colouring outside the edge. They'd put a lot of bad guys behind bars, most deserved it, some didn't. The group didn't care. The lines were like speed limits. Speed limits were just suggestions as to how fast you can go. If you exceeded those limits, and Martin and his cronies caught you, you paid a fine. And that's where the lines blurred for Kris Martin and his six-pack.

Clarksville OPP patrolled fifty kilometres of the 401 highway. This fact alone gave Martin's crew a more than a hundred kilometres of east-west autonomy. Theirs was a hunting party, and the prey was any motorist who lived outside Clarksville's jurisdiction. Fighting a traffic ticket could result in extreme inconvenience and costly fines.

With the aid of CPIC—the Canadian Police Information Centre—they could run license plates and determine the best pigeons to hunt. It was on these the six-pack painted huge bulls-eyes. The threat of massive fines and lengthy suspensions of driving privileges would cripple many of these drivers, opening the door to "off the books" penalties. For over a decade, Kris Martin and his crew had squirrelled boxes of money away for the proverbial rainy day.

* * *

It hadn't always been that way. In the early years, Constable Kris Martin believed in the creed: To Serve and Protect. It was a calling. Keeping the peace and working for the good of society was a noble thing, and he truly believed he could make a difference. He was a good cop, and as he grew in experience, he'd become respected. His peers turned to him for guidance and leadership. Frequently assigned to him for training, the younger cops, the rookies, learned from him. He enjoyed the recognition, and it fed his ego.

But the paradigm had shifted, and change was the one thing Kris Martin resisted. He liked the status quo. Evolving attitudes within the old guard were creating upheavals within the ranks. Increasingly, female officers were deployed in the field, and it wasn't long before Kris rode with a female partner. He had no choice. Kris had to accept it, but it wasn't right. Not right by any standard, and that's when his attitude changed. He'd been happy until then. The boys club atmosphere was his refuge, and his alpha role within the ranks made him feel invincible. Then the Prewitt episode had happened changing his outlook forever.

* * *

It was a ten-year-old cancer that grew and festered in his mind. Martin was convinced that Prewitt was stealing outboard motors from local marinas, but he had no proof. He'd been watching Prewitt for months, but could never catch him in the act. Yet, the man always had a used motor for sale, which only served to deepen his suspicion.

His chance to nail him came after receiving what turned out to be lousy intelligence. On a cold January morning, Martin and his partner served an arrest warrant on Prewitt. As Martin attempted to handcuff him, Prewitt resisted, knocking Martin to the ground and fracturing his skull. He spent eight weeks in the hospital. Prewitt remained in custody until Martin was fit to testify. By then, however, the case had fallen apart.

Desperate to make the charges stick, Martin planted evidence in the trunk of an old car. It would have worked, but for the fact that at the time of the arrest, the vehicle was three-thousand miles away in British Columbia. It was a mistake, but the deed had been done. Prewitt walked free, having received an eight-week slap on the wrist for the resisting charge. Martin's culpability couldn't be proved. Still, the doubt surrounding that event served as the prelude to the rest of Martin's career.

* * *

From that point forward, Kris Martin's favour spiralled down. He was a senior constable and would remain so for the rest of his career. A man only months away from promotion and possibly a glorious future with the OPP, he was now little more than a pawn on a chessboard: expendable, usable, but not nearly as useful as his potential. He was still policing, but now he was picking his battles, and the winning side didn't always wear a blue uniform.

Martin had plans, plans that could not be achieved on a cop's salary alone. So, with a little skim here and a little grab there, he and his crew had created their own pension plan. With twenty-four and a half years under his belt, he could retire in six months, take an early pension and with a fat, offshore bank account, he and his missus would fade into the mist. The Islands called loudly to him. There was one more facet to his plan, and if all went well, he'd be there soon.

* * *

But all was not going well. Kaladar was not part of his game plan. If Kaladar wasn't the backside of the world, it was right next door. Sitting for the first time at his desk and seeing the view from his dust encrusted window, Kris Martin vowed to escape his fate. He had business back in Clarksville, and no woman commander would keep him from doing it. He reached for the phone on his desk and then thought better. It wouldn't do to use this phone. He pulled his cell phone from his shirt pocket and cursed. "Shit! No service!"

"Excuse me." Constable Brianna Jones stood in the office doorway. "Is something wrong, sir?"

Kris Martin looked up from his desk. "Huh? No, I can't get any signal on my cell."

"Yeah, I know we're in a dead spot here," the young constable smiled at her new boss. "You won't get service unless you go to the top of the hill." She pointed up the highway to the intersection where Highway 7 and 41 met at the bottom of two hills. The detachment offices sat right in the swale. "Use the landline. No one here cares if you use the phone for personal business. We all do it." She gave him a knowing wink and walked away.

"Yeah, right," Kris said to the empty doorway. *But not for this, not today, not ever.*

* * *

It wasn't much of a hill. Nine metres, barely thirty feet, made all the difference. Kris Martin sat in his patrol cruiser and stabbed the speed dial button on his cell phone. He had three bars here, yet in his office, he could get no signal at all, solidifying once more the eternal hell he'd been cast into. How anyone could look around this emptiness and call it God's Country baffled him beyond belief. He'd been here for three hours, and that was three hours too long. A familiar voice answered on the fifth ring, and without hesitation, Kris Martin spoke one word.

"Meltdown!"

* * *

Emily fought back her tears. She wasn't a crier, but she wanted to cry. Her shoulder throbbed, and her knees hurt, but that wasn't why. When she told Colm what had happened, his countenance changed. The soft, angular lines of his chin hardened. His dimple deepened as he clenched his teeth. It worried her, but it was his eyes that troubled her more. Colm's bright orbs were red and had sunk into their sockets, creating puffy grey circles under them. Emily sensed he'd been crying. She hadn't seen it. He'd hidden it from her. Colm was angry and sad, but there was more, and then it hit her. Colm O'Byrne was afraid. The man she loved, the one she intended to marry, was frightened.

She sat in her reading chair watching Colm and two other policemen scour the area down by the hedge. The incident had left her with two scraped knees and a nasty bruise on her shoulder. Colm was pointing in the direction the van had gone, upon which the two constables returned to their police car and set off in the same direction. Moments later, Colm stepped through the door.

"Nothing, there's nothing there, except mud and a few smudged footprints. And you didn't see who it was?"

Colm asked as he gave her a once-over, "Are you hurt?"

"I'm fine," She replied.

Emily wore a pair of faded blue jeans with holes torn in the knees. It was a fashion statement Colm could never get his head around. Why anyone would pay top dollar for torn clothing baffled him, but these jeans had cost Emily over a hundred dollars, and every time she wore them, he had to smile. Only he wasn't laughing now. The rips in her clothing couldn't hide the scrapes to her knees. The V-neck on her white pullover hung to one side, revealing a trace of the black and blue bruise on her shoulder. Colm promised himself whoever did this would pay, and there'd be more than bruises involved. This was personal now, and his anger was pushing the cop in him into the background.

"What made you think confronting the guy in the van was a wise move?"

"I'm not sure the van had anything to do with it," Emily responded.

"It must have and don't change the subject. Confrontation isn't smart," he rubbed the back of his neck with his left hand. He was getting all knotted up again. He dropped to his knees in front of her and took her hands in his. "How can I protect you if you take risks like this?"

"You don't have to protect me," she said, pulling her hands free and crossing her arms. "I'm a big girl. I can take care of myself." Her bottom lip disappeared. She looked away and then back at him.

Colm closed his eyes and shook his head. He heard himself saying it, and he knew he was wrong, but for whatever reason, his tongue had a mind of its own.

"I suppose peeing your pants and gettin' all banged up is taking care of yourself, is it?"

Emily shot an ice-melting look at him. "Screw you!" She jumped up from her chair, pushing him backward and knocking him off balance. "Move your car! I've got things to do, and you've got a killer to catch." She grabbed her coat and purse and stormed through the door.

* * *

Colm remained rooted to the seat of his car and watched as Emily drove away. Her impulsive nature worried him. She hadn't thought her actions through, and that annoyed him. More to the point, it scared him. Emily had said, "If we're having a fight, you'll know it." He wondered if this was it. If so, it was as close to a fight as he wanted to get. He put the car in gear and chased after her.

G. A. PICKSTOCK

22

ANNE'S FACE BEAMED AS she waved a document in the air. "Got it! I knew it was in here," she said. "I can't believe that son-of-a-bitch had a secret compartment in that desk."

Amelia listened without comment as she inspected the remaining papers. Harrison's will and the proxy were there as expected, but there was more. As she scanned each one, her eyes dropped on a name.

"Who's this Barry guy?" she asked. "Barry Blackmore, that name shows up a lot. They look like contracts, offers to purchase and such."

Anne turned her attention to the paperwork her sister was reading. "Barry Blackmore is a real estate developer here in town. He helped Harry buy a lot of the land the plant owns, and he built most of the expansion project. Why, what have you got there?"

"It looks like an offer to buy a parcel of land—no, wait a sec, it's a proposal to purchase for taxes owed." Amelia turned the document around for Anne to read. "Did you know about this? According to the date, this is recent."

Anne scanned the paper and thought for a moment. "You know, Harry asked me about this. He wanted me to help him finance the purchase of a small piece of land right next to the tire plant. I said no. I told him I wasn't giving him any more money. Besides, this land—" she tossed the paper back onto the pile—"is too small to do anything with. So, I said no."

Amelia listened and nodded while continuing to dig through the papers. She agreed with Anne's refusal to fund another of Harrison's deals. Harrison had used her sister as his private piggy bank for far too long. And judging by the document, the small piece of land could do nothing to improve the future of the plant. Anne was right to refuse. She pulled another sheaf of pages stapled together into a booklet, out from the pile. The cover page read: Blackmore/Dalton Holdings LLC - Urban Reclamation Proposal. She handed it to her sister.

Anne read the complete document twice before turning it back over to Amelia. When she finished reading, Amelia laid the papers down on the table. Neither of them could speak. The contents of the brief before them once revealed, would have a nuclear impact on the entire region. The sisters sat silent, their eyes riveted on each other.

"Do you think it's true?" Amelia finally broke the silence.

"I don't know. Harry hasn't been—wasn't always forthcoming with his business affairs but this—" she pushed at the papers on the table—"this is crazy. If it is true, and Blackmore has his finger in the pie, he'd be slicing a big chunk off for himself."

"How do we find out?"

"We make a call, that's how. But not before I have a meeting with the Board of Directors at the plant." Anne lifted her phone and called a number. "Isobel, I need to speak with Jim. Please put me through right now!"

* * *

The air in the conference room reeked of stale tobacco. Anne could only guess that due to her husband's predilection for smoking, he had abandoned any concern for others as to the effects of second-hand smoke, and had instead, blatantly defied the health and safety laws banning smoking in the workplace. A violation of which held fines of up to fifty-thousand for first-time offenders. None of this seemed to matter to Harry. He liked to smoke, and if he could find even one compatriot in the room, he would light up and never quit. Today this would change. Harry was gone, and the conference table was noticeably devoid of ashtrays. The air conditioning was on in an impotent effort to scrub the offensive scent from the room. It was uncomfortable, but Anne wore a thick sweater in preparation for the cold temperature. She would endure, much to the chagrin of the rest of the board.

"Jesus! It's bloody cold in here, Anne. Can we at least turn off the AC?" Jim Roberts hugged his arms across his chest, rubbing his shoulders to warm up.

Anne sat in Harry's usual spot at the head of the table. A stack of papers sat neatly in front of her. "Quit moaning, Jim, and have a seat. Before the others get here, I have something I need to discuss with you." She motioned to the seat directly to her left. A moment later, Amelia walked in, also clad in a heavy, wool sweater. She took the chair to Anne's right, facing Jim across the conference table. Anne turned her attention back to Jim.

"This is my sister, Amelia Lonsdale. Amelia is here in an advisory capacity today, she is a paralegal, and I have asked her here as a witness to this meeting."

"Wow!" Jim said, leaning back in his chair. His arms were still folded, more to keep warm than anything else. "So what gives? Why the sudden need for a meeting?"

"Harry's dead, but then you know that," she said coldly. Anne pulled the proxy from the top of the stack and slid it across to Jim. "I am executing this proxy according to the conditions of our Corporate Bylaws and rules of incorporation."

Jim picked up the document and read it aloud:

"TO THE BOARD OF DIRECTORS AND MANAGEMENT OF DALTON TIRE AND RUBBER LLC.

I, Harrison Dalton, hereby appoint and empower Anne Dalton as proxy fully authorized to represent me, cast votes, make proposals and sign all the necessary documents in my name in accordance with my instructions written here-below, at Any and All Board and Director's meetings of Dalton Tire and Rubber LLC that will be held at the address of 4300 Dalton Road in the town of Clarksville, Ontario.

A) SCOPE OF THE POWER OF REPRESENTATION..."

The proxy read on, giving Anne full control over Harrison's voting privileges and shares in the company.

Jim dropped the paper. It fluttered and skidded its way across the table, coming to rest in front of Amelia. She immediately picked it up and placed it back on the stack of papers.

Jim stood and walked around the table to a bookcase where a collection of corporate volumes and binders resided. He reached for a binder.

"I'm not sure that document is worth the paper it's printed on. I think you'll find we have a prior agreement in place, and it will nullify your so-called proxy." He placed the binder in front of Anne and opened it to a page. "Read that."

Anne looked it over and said, "I'm not getting into a pissing war with you over this, Jim. Harry's dead, I have his will and his proxy. The proxy gives me control of his voting shares. All of which are mine as of the date of his death. It might take a month to iron out the legalities, but the end of it is, I own this company. I control it. I'm your boss as of now." She stood to face Jim, daring him to disagree. The door to the room opened, and one of the plant managers poked his head inside. Anne turned and snapped, "Give us two more minutes. Please!"

She turned back to Jim, and in a subdued voice, she said, "You can fight me or join me but know this—" she reached in the pile of papers and pulled out another document and handed it to Jim—"Harry died owing me millions. This company owes that money, and I hold the demand note. Get on board with me now, or I will call this note. Decide. You have thirty seconds."

Jim slumped into his seat. Leaning on the table, his left hand cradling his mouth and chin, he contemplated the papers on the table. At last, he looked up at his new boss and said, "You win. What is it you want me to do?"

"Business as usual," Anne said, "at least for now. Now get the rest in here so we can inform them there's a new sheriff in town and she wears a skirt," she said, smiling. "I have an appointment at one." Anne checked her watch as if to say, Get a move on.

* * *

It took less than an hour to learn 19570722 Ontario LLC was a holding company based in Toronto. There was only one director, and his name was Angelo Pellini. The company description stated it was an investment company. It had been newly formed within the past two months and had no quantifiable financial records that Colm could find. Angelo Pellini, according to the Internet, was a self-made entrepreneur who had amassed a considerable fortune in the construction business. Beyond that, there wasn't much more about him.

This business and the man behind it was a virtually empty shell, yet for some reason, he and it had procured six acres of prime industrial real estate in Clarksville. The price paid was a steal, and it raised questions in Colm's mind. Why? Why would an obscure little start-up business in Toronto buy a piece of land too small to build on? Why buy it in Clarksville? And why now?

It seemed to Colm that the logical purchaser should have been Harry Dalton. Was this a power play? Was Angelo Pellini so shrewd a player in the land game as to be able to suss out a minuscule parcel of land in an obscure little town? And what if he was, did it naturally follow that Dalton would buy that property at an inflated price merely to complete a land-based jigsaw puzzle? There had to be more to it. And what of Nicole Saunders? How did this factor into her murder? She could not pay the taxes. She could have sold the property at a reasonable profit and walked away with a tidy sum in her pocket. So why didn't she? But the biggest question loomed over him, who killed Harry Dalton and why? Colm believed all of this was tied together. He needed to find the thread. Once he did, he knew if he pulled at it hard enough, the whole story would unravel.

G. A. PICKSTOCK

23

JIM ROBERTS FIGURED MEETING in plain sight was the best way to have a clandestine meeting. They were just two friends having a coffee together. Tod's Coffee Corner was just such a place, and today it was crazy busy making it easy for the pair to blend into the background. Ted Savage picked the sprinkles off a donut.

"Why'd ya have to get me one of these? You know I hate sprinkles. Jeeze, a plain donut would have been fine with me." At thirty-seven, Ted was in good shape. His 165-pound muscular frame showed no fat. Ordinarily, he shunned sugar. His only real weakness was the occasional plain donut. These were the best in town. Still, he limited himself to only one.

"Shut up and eat. Quit your whining," Jim said. Then in a lower voice, he leaned in toward his cousin and said, "Harry's dead."

The news didn't faze his cousin. Ted scraped the last of the sprinkles off his donut and stuffed half in his mouth. Mumbling the words through a full mouth, he said, "So where does that leave us?"

"I'm not sure, with Harry out of the picture, maybe it leaves us nowhere. The deal might not go through now. Anne Dalton took control of the company. Hell, I don't know if she even knows about Harry's plans."

Ted finished his donut washing it down with a large swallow of coffee. "Yeah, well, all I know is, somebody promised us a lotta money to keep shtum. That somebody is gonna pay one way or the other."

Jim stared past Ted at a poster hanging from the ceiling. It read "Send A Kid to Camp," and for a moment, that's just where he wished he could send his cousin.

"What can I do about it? This wasn't supposed to go down like this, and you know it."

"Shit happens. We've held up our end. So far, but that can all change." Ted shrugged his shoulders and wiped his lips with a napkin. "I want my money. I got expenses, you know."

Jim had told his cousin there was a lot of money in it for him, but nothing was guaranteed. If everything worked as it should, they would see a substantial payday, worth hundreds of thousands. A lot had to happen just right. Harry Dalton had concealed his plans well, but not well enough. In truth, serendipity had played a large part in Jim's learning of Harry's plan. His first reaction was anger, but after some reflection, Jim realized that Harry's subterfuge could work to his own benefit. Harry was smart, but Jim was no fool. He'd spotted a weakness in the plan and decided to exploit it. Still, he needed Ted's cooperation, and so he had to keep the fish on the hook.

"You'll get it soon, just be sure you keep a low profile. We don't need any unnecessary attention. If you know what I mean. The fewer questions asked, the better. I'll call you in a day or two." Jim stood to leave, but Ted grabbed his jacket, pulling him back into his seat.

"How soon? Let me remind you cousin, we're not playing video games here. If shit goes wrong, we can't just hit restart."

"Ok I get it, but you need to get this, shit's already gone wrong and raising a couple a hundred K isn't easy. There's a new wrinkle now, and I don't know how it's all going to pan out. Just be patient." The lie slid from Jim's lips as if it were gospel. *But then, it wasn't all a lie, was it? Things had changed and now getting at any money would be difficult if not impossible.* Jim arched his back to relieve a cramp in his side and glanced around the restaurant. "Shit!"

Ted turned to look in the direction of Jim's gaze. "What? What's shit?"

Jim diverted his eyes back to his cousin. "My nosey neighbour and her boyfriend are sitting on the other side of the shop. Damn. The last thing I need is for them to see me with you."

"I don't understand. What's the big deal?" Ted scanned the area behind him to see who Jim was talking about. "So what if we're seen together. Big deal."

Jim scrunched down in his seat, attempting to make himself smaller. Thankfully, his younger cousin had broad shoulders. He thought for a moment. There was no way he could tell Ted about the list. He'd find out soon enough, but for now, Ted had to stay in the dark.

"The boyfriend is a cop, and he's already been nosing around out at the plant. I don't need him connecting me to you. Listen—" Jim grabbed Ted's forearm— "Just keep a low profile for a few days like I asked, OK?"

"Why—"

Jim cut him off. "Just do it! OK?"

Ted nodded and broke free of Jim's grip. He grasped the edge of the table, swung his legs around sideways, accidentally rising into the path of a passing patron. He tripped her. She fell and dumped her tray-load of coffee and pastries all over the next table. The chain reaction that followed had people scrambling for napkins and towels as Ted stood dumbfounded at his clumsiness. Jim turned away, directing his gaze out the window to obscure his identity. His plain-sight clandestine meeting had become all too public. *Low profile. Shit!*

* * *

The call from Bob Gentry came just as Colm parked beside Emily's Mustang at Tod's Coffee Corner.

"Please tell me you have something," said Colm as he stepped out of his car. He waved at Emily through the window of the coffee shop. She had two cups on the table, and as he walked toward her, he pointed to the phone and mouthed, Bob Gentry. He sat down.

"The results are in from forensics."

"Is there anything significant? What can you tell me?"

"You need to see this. How soon 'til you get here?"

"We'll be there in ten." He grabbed Emily's hand, pulling her from her seat, "C'mon, we've gotta scamper."

"But—our coffee. We—"

"It'll have to wait—" Colm stopped short as a commotion on the opposite side of the restaurant caught his attention. The couple stood and watched as a young girl was body-checked into a table, sending food and beverages sailing through the air. In the middle of it stood a man in his mid-thirties and seated to his right was someone both Colm and Emily recognized.

Jim Roberts had turned his face to the window, but the reflection in the glass was unmistakable.

"Looks like Jim is in a bit of a tiswas. I wonder who that is with him. Anyway, Bob Gentry has info for us," Colm said, shrugging off the distraction. "We need to see him now."

Emily grabbed her handbag, slugged down one last gulp of her coffee and followed Colm to his car.

As Colm wheeled the Mini out of the parking lot, Emily gathered herself together, rearranging herself to get comfortable. Colm glanced at her knees. The scrapes visible through the tears in her jeans sent a shiver up his back. Biting his tongue, he turned his attention to the road. The silence hung in the air like a fog.

"Why am I coming to this meeting? I mean, it has nothing to do with me, does it?"

Colm thought for a moment, organizing his words. He'd already put his feet in his mouth and extracting them might be a tricky job.

With his eyes focused on the road, he said, "I'm sorry. I shouldn't have spoken to you like I did. I understand that you think I don't need to protect you. But I love you. When something bad happens to you, it happens to me. In my world, men look after their women. If that sounds sexist to you, then so be it. I am who I am."

He glanced over to gauge her reaction. Emily stared forward, and Colm could almost hear the gears grinding in her mind.

He continued, "So, why are we going to see Bob, together? Because from here on, we are a team. I don't know how I'm going to square it with Kendra, but I will find a way."

Emily didn't respond as she allowed his words to sink in. A few moments later, Colm swung the Mini into the hospital parking lot, taking advantage of a small area right beside the door to the back entrance. Colm opened Emily's door for her and offered his hand to help her out. She took it and stepped out of the car. Much to his chagrin, there was nothing in Emily's expression to indicate forgiveness. Her face was all business, and he wondered if he'd ever get out of the doghouse. They walked to the morgue in silence.

* * *

Emily had never been to the morgue. She'd seen many pictures on TV and had an image in her mind of what to expect. But this was different. It surprised her that the place was so clean and antiseptic. And where were the bodies? She'd expected a half-naked body lying on a table, chest splayed open like a gutted fish, and a towel covering the genitals. This was a small room with a counter to the left and a single steel table in the centre. Unlike an operating theatre, the table had a sink at one end and troughs running down either side. The counter held various lab instruments, a microscope, beakers and test-tubes, and a large cylindrical container with the letters "LN2" printed on the side.

Emily had met Bob Gentry once before when she discovered her old boss's body in the parking lot at All-Comm. The wizened old man with his bald head and tufts of white hair on either side stood at the counter. Realizing their presence, he looked up and smiled.

"Colm, Emily, good! Come in, come in." Gentry motioned for them to come over to the counter. He was leafing through a report housed in a manila folder. "I want you to see something." Gentry closed the folder and beckoned the couple to follow him. He led them into a small room next to the main examination room. And there they were.

Emily let out a sharp gasp as she stepped into the brilliantly lit room. The naked bodies of Harrison Dalton and Nicole Saunders rested upon two steel tables. There were no towels placed in strategic locations. Nicole had her chest splayed open, and Emily could see this had also been Harrison's fate, albeit he'd been stapled back together. Emily's stomach fluttered as she ventured further into the room. Gentry watched from the side, mildly amused at the young woman's reaction.

"Your first corpse?" He asked.

Emily gagged, fighting back the urge to vomit. As cold and antiseptic as the room was, she could still detect an aroma of decay, and the sweet, sickly scent caused her head to spin. Swallowing hard, she replied, "Not like this, this is so—so—cold." She shuddered as she spoke. "I found Nicole's body, and that was bad enough. But this—well, this is just—"

Gentry interjected, "It's just not what you see on TV, is it? What can I say? Art doesn't always imitate life. And then there's the smell—" he shot a glance at Colm— "I'm surprised your boyfriend hasn't put a mask on yet. I don't notice it myself. It kind of grows on you after a while."

Emily smiled and crinkled her nose, "I wasn't going to say anything, but between the odour and the image I almost threw up."

"Are you two about finished?" Colm interrupted. "What did you have to tell me, Bob?"

Gentry's face turned serious. He motioned the couple closer to Nicole's body. Gentry had the woman's torso spread open, revealing an empty cavity where her organs had once been. The sight of this young woman's body in such a state reminded Emily of home. This time of year was hunting season back home, and the sight of eviscerated deer and moose carcasses was commonplace. Still, this was a human being, and the proximity to such a vision caused her stomach to knot even tighter. Gentry pointed to the wound on Nicole's right side.

"You see here," he circled the wound with a gloved finger. "This discolouration had me baffled. I had a theory but wasn't sure until I received the report from Toronto. This discolouration is frostbite. It's safe to say that someone shot both of our friends here with a frozen bullet. And judging by the wound tracks…"

Colm had stopped listening. Gentry's explanation had triggered a memory, and now Colm's brain was trying to piece it together. "How frozen?"

"Way below zero. I think your bullet was super frozen. Maybe even down to LN2 levels."

"LN2, what's that?" Colm asked.

"Liquid Nitrogen."

And there it was. Colm had seen it. Twice. Once at Nicole's murder scene, and again somewhere else. But where? "How easy is it to get liquid nitrogen? I mean, it's not something you can pick up at the corner store, is it?"

Gentry smiled at the young detective. "Easier than you think. LN2 is commonly available. It can be obtained from any company that provides oxygen or other such gases. You know, welding suppliers and the like. I guess it would depend on your needs. It's dangerous to handle, but not if you take the proper precautions. But wait, there's more." He directed their attention to the larger wound inside the cavity. "You see this? This is the exit wound. Notice the surrounding discolouration."

"Aye, more frostbite," Colm said.

"Correct," said Gentry, "but look closer. There is a silvery substance present also."

Colm raised his eyebrows. "I don't understand."

"It had me baffled also. Since the accident on the highway, I've had a nagging feeling I was missing something. At first, I thought I had it nailed when I realized Dalton had been shot. But there is more. It wasn't until I opened Miss Saunders that I found it. I've confirmed the silvery substance is mercury. These two were killed with bullets made from mercury. Come with me. I want to show you something."

Gentry ushered Colm and Emily back into the main room. He walked over to the canister on the counter and unscrewed the lid. A grey-white fog cascaded out the top and down the sides of the container. "This is liquid nitrogen," he said.

Gentry picked up a small brown bottle labelled Hg-80 and removed the lid. "This is mercury." He placed a small glass container inside a large beaker and poured the mercury into the smaller bowl. Then he took the LN2 canister and filled the beaker to the level of the small container. Within seconds the mercury had frozen. Gentry grinned at his science students.

"That's not the end," he said. "There's more." He produced a small metal plate from a drawer and placed it on the counter. With a pair of tongs, he lifted the mercury and set it on the plate. The fog surrounded the metal, and the plate frosted up within seconds. Gentry took his finger and pushed at the mercury sending it skidding across the plate.

Emily and Colm gawked in amazement. "How cold is that?" Emily asked.

"Minus one-ninety-five Celsius," Gentry replied.

"I don't understand," said Colm. "Something that cold would freeze, stick to whatever it touched. Just like sticking your tongue on a frozen pipe. Isn't that so?"

Gentry nodded and shook his head at the same time. "You've got the right idea, but there is a scientific principle in play here. Look, watch this." He filled the large beaker to the top with liquid nitrogen. The liquid bubbled and steamed like boiling water for a few seconds, finally settling as the temperature of the glass dropped to that of the nitrogen. Once it calmed, Gentry held up two fingers on his right hand and immediately dipped them into the nitrogen. He removed them and held them for the couple to see.

"It's called the Leidenfrost effect. It's a physical phenomenon in which a liquid, in near contact with a mass significantly hotter than the liquid's boiling point, produces an insulating vapour layer keeping that liquid from boiling rapidly. Or, in this case, for a short while, freezing the mass. As long as I take my fingers out quickly, there's no danger of injury."

Gentry believed the mercury would take approximately two minutes to thaw at room temperature, longer if the receptacle it was housed in was also at the temperature of LN2.

Colm asked, "The canister you have there, how long will it last? I mean, if it boils off at such a low temperature, how do you keep it in liquid form?"

Gentry pointed to the canister on the counter. "This is a dewar. It is insulated to preserve the liquid, much like a vacuum bottle only better. A dewar like this one will last about four weeks, longer if I keep it in a cold environment. Laboratory grade Dewars aren't cheap. A good one will cost over a thousand dollars. It won't last forever, so the shelf life is short, shorter still if you don't have the proper dewar."

Armed with this information, Colm and Emily made for the exit. Gentry followed them to the door.

"One more thing, Colm, whoever did this had to have used a very high-power rifle."

Colm turned back. "Oh? Why?"

"The entry wound," said Gentry. "I'm no ballistics expert, and what I know about guns I could write in the palm of my hand, but there is no mercury near the entry wound on the woman or on Dalton. In fact, I couldn't find any mercury on him, but considering the damage done, that's not surprising. Still, when you consider the friction involved and the time from muzzle to target, not to mention the propellant, then the bullet had to be travelling at high velocity, maybe a thousand feet per second at the point of impact. Believe me. You won't have anything to go on as far as ballistics are concerned, but you are looking for a firearm capable of very high velocities. I'd bet money on it."

* * *

On the drive back to pick up Emily's car, Colm brought her up to date on his findings. They stopped to have the coffee they'd missed earlier. An hour later, they were still sitting in the coffee shop nursing yet another cup of coffee. Colm thought his teeth were floating, and he excused himself to go and settle the matter.

When he returned, Emily said, "We don't have any suspects, do we?" She sipped at her coffee and gazed out the window. She hadn't quite forgiven

Colm yet. Not making eye contact was her way of delaying the inevitable. *Just make him squirm a little longer. Then let him back in.*

Colm warmed his hands around his coffee mug, twisting it back and forth as he contemplated the rich, black, liquid steaming up from the cup.

"I have one or two candidates, but no one I can move on yet."

Emily's eyes snapped back to Colm. "Oh! Who?"

Colm continued to contemplate his drink. *Two can play at this game.*

"Well, I haven't discounted Anne Dalton yet. Sure, she stands to inherit the tire company, yeah? And then there's this Angelo Pellini fella. I don't know how he fits in with all this, but he's in it somehow. I'm positive. Then there're a few from the plant that might have some motive as well. So, we have suspects."

"You mentioned Angelo Pellini in the car. You said he bought Nicole's land. There must be a good reason for that. So, ok, what about Nicole's killer and the guy who attacked Sammi and me?" Emily asked.

"Well, I'm not sure, but there is a connection between Nicole's and the Dalton murder. Both of them were shot, and it seems as though the killer is the same person. At least the method is the same, and Pellini's involvement with the land deal puts him in it. We need to talk to him. A trip to the big city might be in order. We have more questions than answers, sure. Not the least of which is who makes frozen bullets?"

G. A. PICKSTOCK

24

COLM TURNED FROM THE paperwork and gazed out the window. The afternoon sun spilled through, warming him, belying the outside temperature. Colder days were coming, and it wouldn't be long before they'd be turning the clocks back an hour. Emily poked her head in from the kitchen.

"Are we on or off duty?" she asked, waving a couple of beer bottles at him.

"Sure, if you twist my arm, we could be off duty," Colm smiled as he reached to accept the brew. "We've a lot to go over here, and I think we need to set a plan of action. I've been checking the files Jim Roberts gave me. I'm not sure yet just how to approach this. In any event, we have some people we need to interview."

Emily handed him a beer and stood, waiting.

"What?" he said.

"You're in my seat."

"Aye, 'tis a grand seat, so 'tis. Very comfy."

"Well, I'd like it back," Emily challenged, one hand on her left hip and the other holding her beer.

"You would, would you? Well now, there's room here for both of us." He laughed as he reached out and grabbed Emily's left hand, pulling her into the chair. She tumbled in beside him, almost dropping her beer.

"Hey! Be careful, you almost made me spill my beer."

"Now, that would be a crime. In Ireland spilling beer is a mortal sin.

It'd be ten Hail Marys and five Our Fathers for that, so it would."

Emily giggled as she snuggled in beside Colm.

"What have you got there?"

"Jim Roberts gave me a bunch of employee files. They're all people who might have a grudge against Harrison Dalton. I've done some checking on them and have eliminated all but three. Of the three, remaining, two are unlikely."

Of the dozen employee files Jim Roberts had given him, five had moved on to other employment almost immediately following their departure from Dalton Tire. Two had passed away, and two more had retired, taking their pensions. He didn't consider these as potential suspects.

"Here's the odd bit. Mark Taylor tops the list." Colm tapped the file on the top of his stack.

"Mark Taylor? Who? The same Mark Taylor from the Prewitt case?" Emily's eyebrows stretched upward in disbelief.

"I know it's crazy. Taylor is in prison. He couldn't have done it. Still, he had good reason according to this file, and it's not inconceivable that he had a hand in this despite being in prison. But that's not all, check this out." Colm lifted another file from the stack and placed it in Emily's lap.

"Alan Prewitt!" Emily couldn't believe what she was seeing. "What is it with this town? Everything bad that happens seems to involve these people. Next, you'll be telling me Kallita Prewitt isn't dead and that she's a suspect. Although, I'd be tempted to believe that one." Emily rubbed her neck, remembering the spot where Kallita had injected her with a paralyzing drug. She continued, "Alan Prewitt is dead."

"Aye," Colm had to agree. "I tripped over his body. I saw it with my own eyes. But you saw it too. His body disappeared, and we've never been able to find any trace of it. His brothers think he was dragged off by wolves, but there's no evidence to suggest that. As far as the OPP is concerned, Alan Prewitt is a missing person."

Emily thought for a moment. "OK, so if Alan Prewitt is still alive, why would he kill Harrison Dalton?"

"According to his file, Alan Prewitt liked fishing more than making tires. For years he ran a part-time fishing charter. Because Alan was a shift worker, he could take guests fishing at hours that didn't conflict with work. My guess is, he made good money at it. I did a bit of research. Charter captains can earn up to seven or eight hundred dollars a day. Not hard to understand why he'd go fishing really, but not conducive to a good work ethic. Still,"—Colm flipped the file open on Emily's lap—"Prewitt's attendance record looks good. However, the write-up on his dismissal sheet says he took the day off without permission. That was enough for Dalton to fire him. Jim Roberts told me Dalton went ballistic when he learned Prewitt had taken the day off to take a charter. Harrison didn't like it when his staff could make more money in one day than he paid in a week. Dalton took an immediate dislike to Prewitt and fired him the next day. Prewitt made a huge scene and promised to get even in front of witnesses."

"So, who's number three on the list?" Emily reached for the last file folder.

"The former general manager, Ted Savage," Colm handed the file over. "According to Jim, Savage had the best motive of all to want revenge. If it's true, what Dalton did was pretty dirty. Savage is number one at this point."

"What's next?" Emily drained the last of her beer. "When do we question Savage?"

"Soon, but first, I have to talk to Kendra. I don't want anything messing up this investigation. If you are going to be part of it, I have to find a way to make it official."

* * *

Colm tapped the end button on his phone and turned to Emily. "Congratulations!" he said. "Welcome to the OPP, Auxiliary Constable James."

Emily looked up in astonishment. "That quick? How did you do that?"

Colm grinned, "I know people," he said. "It's not official yet. Kendra has to wait for approval from Orillia, but that won't be a problem. We can pick up your badge in the morning. The rest can wait until the approval is official."

"Rest, what rest?" Emily asked.

Colm flashed a wide grin. "You'll see. In the meantime, we need to check on Sammi, and I need to interview Ted Savage. Just do me one favour."

"What's that?"

"Try not to get into trouble."

25

EMILY SWALLOWED HARD AS the elevator doors slid open to the pediatric ward. Nurse John had his back to her and had not turned around despite the annunciating "ding" of the elevator. She had hoped he would not be on duty. Their last encounter hadn't ended well, and Emily would rather not revisit the episode. Taking a deep breath, she stepped forward and strode up to the counter.

"Remember me?" Emily asked.

John turned at the sound of Emily's voice. His face soured.

"How could I forget? You had the whole ward up in arms. I would have thought you'd be in jail or something after that fiasco." John lifted a clipboard from a rack mounted behind the counter. "Dare I ask, what can I do for you?"

Emily flashed the badge Colm had given her from the detachment. "No, not in jail. In fact quite the opposite," she said, grinning.

John looked at the badge and failed to notice the auxiliary portion of the identifier. "You're a cop? Why the hell didn't you say so last time you were here?"

"You didn't ask and besides everything happened so quickly," Emily was only half lying. "I'm here to see Sammi," she said. "And this time it's official." The badge gave her a sense of authority, and she found herself liking the feeling.

John's face softened as he rubbed at the stubble on his chin. "I'm afraid Sammi's not here. She was discharged this morning."

Emily frowned. Hearing this caused her stomach to clench. Sammi had no one local who could have signed her out, and she was far too young to be allowed to leave alone. Someone had to have taken her.

"Who? Who took her out? I need a name."

John put his clipboard away and turned to the computer terminal at the end of the counter. A few keystrokes later, he looked up from the monitor and said, "Sammi was discharged by Dr. Patel at 09:30 this morning. She was released into the custody of her father, a Mr. A. Pellini."

"Her father!" Emily gasped. "As far as we knew, Sammi had no father, at least none in this town."

John tapped a few more keys and turned the monitor for Emily to see. The screen showed an image of a driver's license bearing the name Angelo Pellini. The address was a street in Pickering.

"You had to have more than this to release the child into his care. How did you determine Mr. Pellini was her father?" Emily was biting at her lower lip, and she winced slightly as she bit a little too hard.

John didn't flinch. "Miss James, we are not incompetent here. We had no choice. The child was well enough to leave, and according to Dr. Patel, Mr. Pellini had guardianship. I had nothing to do with this. It was all handled at the admin level. All I know is Dr. Patel turned Sammi over to Mr. Pellini, and they left here hand in hand. The child did not seem nervous at all. In fact, she seemed quite happy."

This news had Emily's mind reeling. Unsure what to do next, she asked, "Is there any way you can print me a copy of the discharge papers and a copy of that license? I need to follow up on this."

John hesitated, "I—I don't know if I should. I mean this is all confidential. I could get into a lot of hot water here."

Emily pushed back, "Look, Sammi's mom was murdered. I'm only looking out for the child's best interests here. All I want to do is check out the dad and make sure Sammi is safe. However, if you force me, I will get a warrant."

John relented, "Ok, ok, but it didn't come from me. All right?"

Moments later Emily had the documents in her hand.

"Thank you, John, you've been a big help," Emily said, flashing him a warm smile as she stepped into the elevator. "Your secret is safe with me."

Emboldened by Emily's smile, John asked, "Would you like to get a coffee sometime?"

Emily turned back to the nurse and said, "That would be nice, but I don't think my boyfriend would approve."

John opened his mouth to reply, but the doors to the elevator closed before he could utter a word.

* * *

Emily stared at the copy of Angelo Pellini's driver's license. The grainy, black and white image, made worse by the copying process, showed a man in his early to mid-forties, dark hair and a full beard. Although she'd never seen the man, something about his features seemed faintly familiar. Pellini had appeared unannounced, presented documents proving his guardianship of Sammi, and just as quickly scooped the child up and departed.

The elevator doors parted, and Emily made her way to the exit. She tugged at the zipper on her jacket to close out the damp air. Stuffing the paper into her purse, she moved off the concrete sidewalk and started for her car. As she turned past a high stone wall separating the parking area from the hospital entry, Emily stopped in her tracks and gasped. The black van was parked beside her Mustang with its engine running. Before she could retreat into the hospital, Emily felt the iron grip on her already bruised shoulder.

"Owe, hey, that hurts!"

"Shut up and keep walking! Don't turn around." It was the same gravelly voice she'd heard the day before. "You don't learn. Well, this time, maybe you'll get the message."

The side door of the van slid open. Gravel Voice shoved Emily forward. She fell onto the floor of the truck, knocking the wind out of her. The door slammed shut, leaving her in total darkness. Emily remained quiet, trying to catch her breath and listened to the noises around her. She could hear someone breathing but could see nothing.

"Who are you? Why are you doing this?" Emily squeaked.

"Shut up and be quiet, and maybe I'll let you live."

Emily's heartbeat quickened, her limbs shuddered and trembled, her breath came in gulps as she sucked the foul, stale air of the van deep into her lungs. Bile rose in her throat. She wanted to retch but was afraid she would lose all control, and control was what she needed to hold onto now. For the first time in her life, Emily was genuinely terrified

G. A. PICKSTOCK

26

THE SIGN ABOVE THE door read: JB Gunworks - Jeremiah Bannister - Proprietor. An old building in desperate need of renovation, the gun shop stood alone at the eastern edge of town. Its limestone walls and old cedar framing had escaped the wrecking ball only because of its historical significance. People rarely noticed its existence, and Jeremiah liked it that way. He had his own clientele, and walk-in trade was infrequent.

The jangle of an antique brass bell announced Colm's arrival, and the door's ancient hinges creaked as it swung inward. The long narrow shop consisted of two rooms divided by an interior wall running the length of the building. Colm stood in what he suspected was the reception area. An extended counter stretched the length of the narrow room, dividing it down the middle, creating a space just ample enough for two individuals to pass one another. An archway in the dividing wall led into the shop beyond. The aroma of gun oil and cleaning solvent reached Colm's nostrils, and for a moment, he thought he had stepped back into the old west. The bell jangled again as Colm closed the door. Jeremiah Bannister emerged through the arch, wiping his hands on an oily rag.

"Can I help you?"

On the surface, Jeremiah was a hick, a redneck with long, salt-and-pepper hair and hillbilly beard. A pair of brown coveralls complete with suspenders engulfed his skinny, five-foot-eleven frame. From his point of view, Colm failed to understand how this man's gnarled and weathered hands could ever be those of an artist. Yet, Colm had been assured the man was an artist, at least where guns and ammunition were concerned. People who knew

Jeremiah well considered him a Rembrandt. His work would never hang in a museum. No one would ever look at his masterpieces and marvel at the intricacies of his touch or the meticulous effort he poured into the work. In truth, Jeremiah's masterpieces, when finished, looked no different from any of their counterparts. Yet, many appreciated and benefitted from the results of his efforts. And that was the essence of his art. Sadly, should he fall prey to the Grim Reaper, his talent would not survive him.

"I hope so." Colm reached into his inside pocket and produced his badge. "My name is Detective Sergeant Colm O'Byrne. I'm investigating an incident that occurred a couple of days ago, and your name came up during my inquiry."

Jeremiah cocked his head to the side, his nose crinkled, and his brow furrowed. Through squinted eyes, he said, "Oh, how so?"

"I'm told you're an expert on bullet making."

"I reload bullets if that's what you mean." Jeremiah leaned against his counter, both hands firmly gripping the edge of the countertop. "There is a difference."

"Perhaps you'd like to elaborate."

"Well, reloading is taking a spent cartridge and doing exactly as the word implies, reloading it. Kinda like recycling. We refurbish the brass, put in new powder and lead and create a new bullet. It's something many shooters do, especially competition shooters. But hunters reload as well," said Jeremiah. "Making ammunition implies beginning from scratch, and that would mean manufacturing from raw material."

"I see, so, what do you do here? The sign says gun works, but I don't see any guns around here."

Jeremiah stroked his beard and paused before answering. "The sign says Gunworks, not Gun Shop. I'm a gunsmith. I don't sell guns, I fix 'em."

"And the ammunition?" Colm persisted.

Jeremiah moved to the end of the counter and lifted a short section of the top. "It will be easier to show you. Come on in Detective, I'll show you my setup and try to help any way I can."

Jeremiah's workshop was almost an exact duplicate of the reception area minus the counter. An oil-stained wooden workbench stretched across the front wall of the shop. To his right, a series of shelves spanned the distance from the archway to the bench. The floor to ceiling units housed volumes of gun catalogues, books on ballistics and other trade-related journals. Boxes of parts and pieces, as well as canisters of gunpowder, filled the shelving to capacity. Against the opposite wall, a metal cutting lathe and milling machine dominated the space. A large brick fireplace monopolized the back wall.

Jeremiah indicated an old wooden kitchen chair and said, "Have a seat. Why don't you tell me what you want to know?"

"If I knew what I wanted to know, I wouldn't be here." He smiled at the gunsmith. "I'm not unfamiliar with firearms, but let's face it, I don't use mine very often, and when I do, I don't pay for my ammunition. Still, I know that bullets are pricey, so I'm guessing that reloading is a way to keep the cost down."

Jeremiah had taken up residence in a tattered old armchair situated kitty-corner to Colm and in front of the fireplace. He looked up at the detective; his beard bristled as he grinned.

"Yeah, you could say that. Ammo ain't cheap depending what you shoot. Most recreational shooters stick to twenty-twos. You can buy a brick of them cheap."

"A brick?"

"Yeah, a case lot, usually five hundred rounds per box, although some run up to fifteen hundred. They can cost fifty bucks or more dependin' on the number of rounds and brand. Cheaper than centerfire cartridges, that's for sure, a lot cheaper. And before you ask, no, you don't reload twenty-twos. You can, but it ain't worth it. Centerfire cartridges, on the other hand, are a different fish. A box of twenty can run upwards of fifty bucks, more for premium ammo. That gets expensive. So, lots of shooters will save their spent brass and reload the cartridges. Hell, I have one customer, bought a box of 308 shells ten years ago, hunts every year, and hasn't bought another box of ammo since. Reloads all the time."

"How hard is it to reload a bullet?"

"Cartridge," Jeremiah corrected. "Here, let me show you." He stood and motioned Colm toward the workbench. "Those cast-iron monsters mounted to the bench"—he waved his hand across some iron and steel contraptions mounted to the edge of the workspace—"are called reloaders."

Jeremiah stopped in front of what Colm could only describe as a very heavy "C" clamp bolted to the top of the bench. Jeremiah grasped the handle attached to it and cranked it up and down. A steel rod moved upward and back again as he did so.

"This is a reloading press, they come in different types depending upon the kind of reloading you wish to do." He pointed to another at the far end of the bench. "That one is for shotgun shells and has five stations. This one is a single-stage press and this one"— he tapped the next one in line — "is a progressive. Single-stage means exactly what its name implies. For each stage in the process, one crank of the handle performs one function. The progressive, on the other hand, means that every time you crank the handle at least three operations take place. Here, I'll show you."

Jeremiah moved to the progressive machine.

"First, we take an empty casing and place it in the holder. Crank the handle, and the casing is elevated into the resizing die. At the same time, the old primer is ejected."

Colm watched as the brass casing rose into a steel enclosure, and a small silver button dropped out the bottom of the holder. When Jeremiah pulled the lever back, the casing emerged, and the holder turned to the next stage. Jeremiah then placed another casing into the next space in the holder.

"This unit can reload three cartridges at a time," Jeremiah continued. "Each time I pull the handle, another function is accomplished. This time, not only will it resize and replace the primer, but the right amount of powder will be measured into the preceding casing. Next comes the bullet."

Jeremiah reached into a box and pulled out a lead bullet. He placed it in the open end of the first casing and cranked the handle. A completed cartridge was ejected on the next upward crank. He handed it to Colm for inspection.

"Seems pretty easy," said Colm.

"It is easy. Anyone who can read can do it. All you have to do is pay attention to what you're doing. There is some risk, but for the most part, it ain't rocket science."

"What about the bullet?" Asked Colm. "How do you get those?"

"You buy them in bulk." Jeremiah pointed to a shelf behind Colm. "I keep thousands of rounds here, all different calibres. That's the cheapest way, but if you're into accuracy, then that's where things get technical."

Colm's ears perked up. "Oh, how so?"

Jeremiah pointed to a series of trophies sitting on a high shelf. "I compete in many shooting events, but the one I'm most proud of is this one."

He reached up and lifted a plaque from the shelf and handed it to Colm. The plaque had a gold medal with a saucer-sized target mounted beside it. Dead centre of the target was a pencil-thin hole.

"I won this at a shoot in Germany. If you look closely at the target, you can see three distinct crowns at the edge of the hole. Kinda like a very tight cloverleaf. I put all three rounds through the same hole at two hundred metres." Jeremiah's face beamed with pride. "I made all my own ammo for this one."

Colm was impressed. This target was proof positive that Jeremiah knew his business, and now more questions flooded his mind.

"With this kind of accuracy, would you consider yourself to be a sniper?"

Jeremiah laughed. "Hell no! I'm just good at target shooting. What I am is a gunsmith. I make regular production rifles accurate, but sniper accurate? That takes more than technology. That takes training as well. I can make the round, and I do. I've made target grade rounds for hundreds, maybe even thousands of customers. Usually ten or twenty at a time, but sniper? No, not me. There's more to it than that. The cartridge is important, but if the gun is shit, then you've wasted your time and money. No, to make a round super-accurate, you need a combination of precision equipment and top-notch ammo. The real magic happens over there." Jeremiah pointed to the lathe. "Give me your firearm, and I'll make it sing," he said.

Jeremiah's enthusiasm for his craft was undeniable. Colm believed him. "Let's get back to the bullet," he said. "How would you make a specialty bullet?"

"Specialty? I don't understand."

"If I asked you to make me something unique, say something out of the ordinary, could you do it?"

It was hard to detect through Jeremiah's facial hair, but Colm thought he could see the gunsmith's countenance change.

"What did you have in mind?"

Jeremiah turned away from him and began cleaning his bench. It was in disarray, but the man was diverting his attention away from the question. Jeremiah was talking, but his enthusiasm had vanished. He pressed on cautiously.

"For instance, if I needed something accurate but hard to identify afterward, how would I— could I do that?"

Jeremiah turned back to face the detective. "How accurate?"

Colm thought for a moment. Dalton's Cadillac had come to rest a mere twenty metres away from the railway bridge. Working on the premise that a sniper had assassinated the businessman, then it stood to reason that the bridge would have been the preferred location for the sniper's hide.

"I'm not sure, let's say sixty metres, maybe eighty."

"That's easy. Use a shotgun. No ballistics. That is unless the shooter uses a rifled barrel or choke and a slug, but if he uses plain old shot then, no ballistics. Even a rifled slug through a smooth bore wouldn't tell you anything. You might be able to match the spent casing to the action of the gun, but even that's a long shot. Nope, you want to make it hard to detect. Use a shotgun." Jeremiah returned to cleaning his bench.

Colm rubbed his chin, frustrated at the gunsmith's answer. *Of course, a shotgun, but I want something more from you.* "You said you made your own bullets to win this trophy. How?"

Jeremiah stopped fussing. "Let's sit, and I'll explain it to you. I make—no, I fine-tune the round. There's no point in remaking something that already exists. So, I simply adjust it to make it better. I cast my own bullets to a precise size, weight, and shape. Then I measure the powder to obtain the best ignition and pressures, thus, giving me the desired muzzle velocity. The brass is sized and trimmed to microscopic specifications. Everything, including the firearm, is tuned to its utmost ability. Combine all that with countless hours of practice and thousands of rounds of shooting and the result is"— he waved his hands at the trophy shelf — "self-evident."

It was a process that took many hours of practice and experimentation. Colm got that. He also understood that Jeremiah Bannister was better than most when it came to making custom ammunition.

"So, is it safe to say that you sell this ammunition?"

"Absolutely not! I do not sell guns or ammo. There's too much government bullshit that goes along with that, too many regulations and far too much paperwork. I fine-tune firearms, and I'm damn good at it. I can take any hunting rifle, within reason, and make it match-grade ready. As for ammo, I do my own, and if a customer wants some specialty rounds, they bring me the makings. I put it all together and charge for my time. No muss, no fuss, no paperwork. And most of all, it's legal."

Jeremiah had lowered his guard, he was offering a lot of unsolicited information, but Colm sensed much of it as a smokescreen. This man was making money somehow and fixing firearms was probably only part of it.

"Ok, can we go back to my original question about the special bullet? You mentioned a shotgun, but I want to know about accuracy as well and, correct me if I'm wrong, a shotgun simply isn't very accurate at long range. I want to know, other than a shotgun, could you make a bullet or projectile that would be both accurate and impossible to trace once fired?"

Jeremiah sat silent for a long moment, his eyes skittered around the room, never resting for more than a second on any one item. Colm knew the man was searching for an answer, and he sensed, as he had moments before, that he had hit a nerve with the old gunsmith.

"What? Are you talking about a disappearing bullet? Like James Bond kinda thing? You're dreaming," he chuckled. "That's fairy tale stuff, science fiction." Jeremiah finally locked eyes with the detective.

"Come on, Mr. Bannister, you know what I'm talking about. I find it hard to believe that a man with your experience hasn't thought of this and perhaps experimented with it."

Jeremiah's chin stiffened, forcing his lips into a thoughtful frown. "Sure, I've considered it. But why? What would be the point? The only reason for such a thing would be to hide evidence of a crime. What's this all about anyway? Why all the interest in specialty ammo? You think maybe I made such a bullet?"

"I'm simply asking a question. When you cast a bullet, how is it done?"

Jeremiah pointed to a small iron pot hanging from an iron hook in the fireplace. It dangled over a propane burner.

"When I cast bullets, I do it there. I melt lead in the pot and then pour it into moulds. Once they cool, I size them and trim them to shape and weight. It's not rocket science. Nothing I do is rocket science. Like I said, if you can read, you can do it. To do it well takes time, practice and attention to detail. In other words—artistry! Everything I do is conventional in nature. I have no idea how I would go about making an untraceable bullet. I can tell you others have tried and failed. Some have tried using ice, but that just isn't practical."

Now we're getting somewhere. "And why would that be?"

"Well, for one thing, ice melts, and it don't have the density of lead. It will fracture under the pressures exerted on it from the powder igniting. Contrary to what many think, modern gunpowder does not explode, Detective, it burns at a furious rate. This builds up immense pressure inside the casing, thus forcing the projectile outward and away from the source. Ice melts and the pressures cause it to fracture. It is science, physics actually, but again, not rocket science. It simply isn't feasible. Now, if you'll excuse me, I have work to do, and this ain't gettin' it done."

Colm insisted. He knew what material he was thinking of, but he wanted Jeremiah to mention it. "Can't you think of any other material other than ice?"

"Not off the top of my head. Frankly, I haven't given it any thought. Why would I? Now please, I have to get back to work."

Jeremiah led Colm back through to the public side of the shop and escorted him to the door. "Have a good day, Detective."

Colm reached into his pocket and produced his business card. Handing it to the gunsmith, he said, "Think on it for a while. I'm sure someone with your knowledge might be able to solve this riddle." He shot Jeremiah a knowing look and stepped through the door.

* * *

Jeremiah watched as Colm pulled away from the curb. He knew what Colm was getting at, and he knew that Colm knew that he knew. His thoughts raced back to the moment…

The challenge had arrived by email. 'Make me a round as accurate and deadly as any you have ever made and make it vanish.'

Disappearing bullets weren't new. Ice crystals didn't cut it.

He'd made projectiles from glass, having moulded them himself in a furnace and shaped them in moulds of his own design. They worked, and although they didn't disappear, they disintegrated, making ballistic tests inconclusive, but then, any shotgun round could manage that. Still, his instructions were clear. These rounds had to vanish. Why didn't matter. He didn't want to know the answer. What a customer did with his work was none of Jeremiah's business.

He had found a solution. His years of study and knowledge rose to the surface to create his masterpiece. As he returned to his workshop, he glanced at his fireplace. The cast-iron furnace had sat quiet and cold. Instead, there had been only the vapour from a laboratory-grade dewar of liquid nitrogen. The staggeringly cold liquid had held a dozen projectiles so deadly they could kill on their own, but when moulded into .45 calibre bullets would be doubly deadly.

The job was done. The delivery had been made and payment received. With luck, the detective would never know.

G. A. PICKSTOCK

27

TED SAVAGE STOOD ON his balcony overlooking the Clarksville River, contemplating his next move. Jim was pissed, and he didn't care. Harry Dalton was an asshole. He deserved to die. Why should he care if the old fart bought it on the highway? Jim wasn't about it, but that was too bad. He'd given Ted a job to do, and he'd done it.

Now Jim wanted him to keep out of sight with his mouth shut. Ted understood why, but meanwhile, he had to live, and that required money. Harry Dalton had cost him everything, his job, his wife, his home, self-respect, everything. So Harry was dead. Good! And good riddance! All that was left to do now was get paid and disappear. That last bit would be easy. Money was the problem. Ted stepped back inside, closed the balcony door, grabbed his coat, and stepped out of his apartment.

* * *

Colm stood at the elevator and watched as the man locked his door. He recognized him immediately. He could have been any construction worker leaving for work. His olive green peacoat hung open at the front, revealing a plaid work-shirt. The shirt was untucked and draped loosely over the man's dirty blue jeans. His battered leather work-boots were untied and scuffed the floor as he walked. The laces dangled from the eyelets and dragged at his feet, threatening to trip him with every step.

Reaching into his inner pocket to withdraw his badge, Colm said, "You're the guy from the coffee shop. The one who knocked that girl over and caused all that ruckus." He held the badge up for Ted Savage to see. "You are Ted Savage, are you not?"

Savage stopped short, giving the badge a quick glance. "What? You're kidding, right? They called the cops and a detective no less. Come on, I said I'd pay for any damages. This can't be real."

Colm grinned, "No, I'm not here about that. You are Ted Savage, yes?"

"Yeah," Ted said. "What's this about?"

"I'd rather not talk in the hall, Mr. Savage? Perhaps we can go back inside." Colm took a step in the direction of Savage's apartment.

"First, you can tell me what this is about."

Savage stepped sideways blocking Colm's path; his feet planted shoulder-width apart he squared his chest to the detective. Colm recognized the posture of a man preparing to go on the offensive. He smiled, he had dealt with men like Savage many times back in Ireland, and he could see the tension rising in Savage's face.

"Ah, now Mr. Savage, you don't want to be going all bulldog on me now. Sure, all I want is to ask you a few questions, and I'm thinking it would be best if we talk in private now."

Savage gave him a puppy-dog cock of his head as if to ask, what's it all about?

Colm pressed on, "Look, all I want to do is talk. Does the name Harrison Dalton hold any meaning for you?" Colm watched intently as Savage digested his words.

"He was my boss, why?"

"Not in the hallway. Now, we can go back into your apartment, or do I ask you to come down to the station? Your choice." Colm shot him a make-up-your-mind stare and pointed to Savage's locked door.

The indecision in Savage's eyes told Colm the man was nervous about going into his apartment. His suspicions were confirmed when Savage said, "I don't know what this is about, and frankly, I don't care. Harrison Dalton was a two-faced asshole. He caused me nothing but grief. Now, if you don't mind, I have shit to do." He stepped forward, brushing Colm's shoulder out of the way.

Colm's first instinct was to reach out and subdue the man, but he had no cause to arrest him, and if the man had no desire to talk, he could not force him—yet. He stepped aside, allowing Savage to pass.

As the elevator doors slid shut, Savage glared back at him, a defiant grin crossed his face. Colm grinned back. *Round one to you Mr. Savage, fair play to you. Next time, it's my turn.*

* * *

The absence of light in the van was almost absolute. Emily laid in silence, her back pressed against the cold, steel side of the truck. With every lurch and bounce the van made, a metal support rib jammed into her aching shoulder, sending new spasms of pain throughout her left side. As her eyes adjusted to the darkness, she saw a faint circular glow of red in the upper corner. She recognized it instantly as an infra-red illuminator. She knew at once that a camera was watching her every move. She had not been bound, and the silence in the van was broken only by the deep-throated growl of a bad exhaust pipe and the steady thrum of the tires on pavement. The foul stench of exhaust fumes assailed her nostrils, making her sick to her stomach.

Emily knew she was alone. Yet, someone was driving the van, and if the red glow was indeed a camera, then it followed that she was being watched.

"Who are you? Why are you doing this?" Emily's voice cracked as she spoke. There was no response. It appeared as though silence was the only dish on the menu, and so she concentrated on sounds around her. Her head throbbed. Dizziness overcame her, and she fought back the urge to vomit. The engine's exhaust did its job robbing Emily of her consciousness. Somewhere in the darkened space encapsulating her, everything went silent, and Emily closed her eyes and slipped into oblivion.

* * *

The hammering in her head drove Emily back to consciousness. Opening her eyes, the light blinded her for a moment, and she immediately threw up. She had no idea how long she'd been unconscious. Gradually, she raised herself to a sitting position and tried to open her eyes once more, this time allowing the light to creep its way in, in the hope of retaining what might be left of her breakfast.

The van was gone. Emily sat in tall grass at the side of an old dirt road. Behind her was only scrub brush and forest. Across the road, a field of scrub and waist-high thorny ash bushes protected a scattering of small saplings. The sun hung above a distant tree-line and was the only indicator Emily had of which direction she might be facing and which way the road might lead. Nevertheless, she had no concept of where Clarksville might be.

Gathering her composure, Emily surveyed her immediate surroundings. Rising to her feet, she stepped into the roadway. Walking away from the sun, and, she hoped, toward safety. She'd gone only a few feet when she happened upon her handbag, its contents half spilled out on the ground. She scrambled to pick it up. Gathering her belongings, she realized her cellphone was gone. A mild panic overcame her when she found the copy of Pellini's license. A note had been scribbled across it. NEXT TIME YOU DIE!

28

THEY CALLED IT THE Hunter's Moon. The bright orange orb rising in the east lit up the sky like a second sunset. The moon cast its light, bathing her surroundings in its warm glow as if to encompass the crater-filled roadway, welcoming it into its own moonscape. Emily thanked the Moon gods for it, lest she missed the outline of the old rusty gate. It hung at an angle from a bent hinge and was all but obliterated by tall grass and weeds.

Considering that the road she'd just walked was full of holes large enough to swallow Colm's Mini, the light by which she found her way seemed fitting. The sight of the gate was a welcome relief.

The rusty old barrier rested unevenly against an equally dilapidated fence and had it not been for the gate, anyone driving past might not see the driveway for all the overgrowth around it. Knee-high grass grew in the centre of two ruts, and although the path looked derelict, Emily saw what she thought were fresh tire marks.

Encouraged by this, Emily proceeded up the winding pathway. Rounding a slight bend and exiting a grove of trees, she was rewarded with the vision of the old farmhouse. On the porch, the light from a single dim bulb beckoned her forward.

* * *

Real-time monitoring of video cameras had become big business in the security industry, and Enzo Grassi's small company had exploded overnight. A shortage of qualified operators had him doing the work of three and was proving more hectic than he'd imagined. His eyes scanned the myriad of images flashing across the screens in front of him, and as he worked to prioritize each occurrence, the lone image of a young woman knocking at the old farmhouse door failed to catch his eye. It didn't help that out of sheer frustration and annoyance, Enzo had muted the audio alerts opting instead to trust his visual acuity to recognize alarms as they occurred.

Enzo's eyes finally fell on the image of the farmhouse door. It stood wide open, and emanating from within the house, he saw light flooding through the entrance. Worse yet, he saw a shadow moving back and forth. To his horror, more than an hour had elapsed since the alarm had occurred.

Right-clicking on the image brought up the client account information. The dryness in Enzo's mouth dissipated as he let out a sigh of relief. The account, although still active, had a temporary "no action" order assigned to it. Enzo had dodged a bullet, but what he saw nagged at him, and so, he made the call. His client didn't answer. Having failed to contact his client, he clicked the button for the next number.

"OPP dispatch."

"I'd like to report a burglary in progress…"

* * *

Constable Harold Papineau eased his cruiser up the winding wagon path. He could think of it no other way. Only a hay wagon could maneuver its way through here without ripping up the weeds and scrub that had overgrown the centre of the driveway. Papineau grimaced at the sounds of his police car bottoming out on the rutted driveway. He eased the car along in the hope that he would not damage it, cringing at each bounce as he felt and heard it obliterating the vegetation, ripping it from mother earth as he drove over it.

The car's headlights pierced through the darkening gloom as it approached the house. From inside his cruiser, Harold saw the figure of a young woman standing on the porch. The light from the open doorway placed the woman in silhouette. The constable didn't exit immediately. Rubbing at the irritating rash on his neck, he surveyed the area before stepping out of his cruiser. As he exited the police car, Papineau, right hand on the grip of his sidearm, shone his flashlight and swept the figure standing on the porch.

"Place your 'ands where I can see them," Papineau ordered as he brought the beam up to Emily's face. He recognized her immediately. "Merde! You are Miss James, oui?"

Emily stepped forward, closer to the edge of the porch step. Papineau could see plainly that she was indeed Colm's girlfriend.

"What are you doing here?"

"Papineau! Am I glad to see you. You need to call Colm now!"

* * *

They sat at an old wooden table in the centre of the farmhouse kitchen. The electricity was working, but the old house hadn't been lived in for a long time. The taps didn't work, and there were no appliances of any kind in the kitchen. The only furnishing in the whole house was the table, three chairs and a half-dozen cardboard boxes stacked in the corner.

Colm listened in silence as Emily recounted the events of the day. Each word cementing itself in his mind, steadily building an image of the ordeal his wife-to-be had endured. As the video in his head played repeatedly, Colm's mind drifted, and Emily's words became part of the background along with the sounds of Papineau and two other constables who were busy searching the house and grounds. The space around him was vivid and real and yet, Colm felt as though he was out of it, drifting above it all, floating through the scene like a ghost in some horror flick.

"…and that's about it. The next thing I knew, Harold had my clothes off, and we were making hot, sweaty love right here on this table." Emily finished her story, glaring at the distant look on Colm's face.

"You haven't heard a word I've said," Emily snapped.

Colm didn't respond. She waved a hand in front of his face. "Hello, is there anybody in there? Are you listening?"

"Huh, yeah, sorry, yeah, every word, you and Harold on the table, grand." Colm rose from his seat and crossed to the boxes stacked in the corner. He'd been staring at a box resting on the top of the pile. He picked up the container and held it in his hands, turning it over and back.

Without hesitation, Colm turned to Constable Papineau and said, "You lot are here for the night. This place just became a crime scene. Let no one in this house tonight. I'll have the SIU team here at oh six hundred to relieve you." He turned to Emily. "C'mon, hot-n-sweaty, we've got work to do."

"We do?"

Colm was already halfway out the door. "Sure, we've got to find out who owns this place so I can get a warrant."

"Why, what is that?" asked Emily, pointing at the box.

Colm turned the box for Emily to see.

The plain white label in bold black letters read Hg - 80.

29

KENDRA JACOBS HUNCHED OVER her desk, rubbing her temples. The headache she wanted desperately to go away wasn't in her head. However, it was under her command. It was a headache she could do without and now Colm was demanding, not requesting, demanding an SIU team to attend some obscure farmhouse in the middle of nowhere. To top it off, he wanted to trek off to the big city in search of a person of interest. She understood that it was personal for him, but it was a request Kendra had to deny. She had plenty of contacts in Toronto, any of whom could be trusted to find and interrogate this mystery man named Angelo Pellini. She raised her head from her hands to look at her Detective Sergeant.

"I'm sorry Colm, I simply can't spare you right now. Martin's UA, and it seems six of his cronies are also."

Kris Martin hadn't reported for duty. He was AWOL along with six other constables who, for the past forty-eight hours, had not been heard from. They had, in fact, been off duty, but now they were beyond late for work. Officially listed as UA, unauthorized absence, none of them had called in sick, and no one was answering his phone. Aside from the sudden frantic scramble to fill vacant shifts, Kendra had to expend valuable resources to track down the truant constables. A trip to Toronto for her best investigator was totally out of the question.

"Who is this guy anyway?" Kendra asked.

"He's a person of interest in the Saunders case," Colm replied. "He signed Sammi out of the hospital, and we think he might have had something to do with Emily's abduction. According to the hospital staff, Pellini says he's the child's father, but we've found nothing to indicate there ever was a father in her life. And, by the way, he might be connected to the Dalton case. Pellini bought some land abutting the plant property. I don't know yet how that fits in, but I have to think it does. His turning up to collect Sammi and whisk her away tells me he's connected to all of this. There are too many coincidences. It all smells bad to me, Dalton, Saunders, the tire company, land deals, no, Pellini is in it up to his arse, and I'm going to find out how it all connects."

Kendra shook her head. "I get it. I really do, but I just can't let you go with all this other crap going on. You need to find my missing cops and soon."

"I'll find your wayward cops, but someone has to talk to Pellini and the sooner the better. I'm worried about Sammi and Emily is beside herself."

Kendra's face brightened as a thought flashed into her head. "What if Emily went to Toronto to interview Pellini? I'll team her up with Mac Somers. Mac is an excellent detective. We worked together for a couple of years. Mac is one of the best, and I'm sure Emily will fit right in. They can question Pellini, and Emily can report back. If there is anything there, then we'll bring the SOB in and take it from there. How's that?"

* * *

Colm hadn't liked Kendra's idea. He wanted Emily close by and playing truant officer to a bunch of cry-baby cops did not sit well with him. Still, he couldn't argue with Kendra's logic, and Emily was tough. Tough enough to handle the likes of Pellini, especially if she had an experienced investigator with her. Emily, on the other hand, couldn't wait to leave. Standing in the driveway, Emily's kiss still lingered on his lips as he watched the Mustang disappear around the corner. It seemed to Colm that she was in her car and westbound before he'd finished telling her the plan.

* * *

With all that she'd been through, Emily should have been exhausted. She hadn't slept in almost thirty hours, aside from a half-hour catnap on the way back into town. Unconscious for much of the time, Emily hadn't realized how far the black van had taken her. She thanked her lucky stars that it hadn't been worse. As Colm had observed, despite her ordeal, Emily wasn't too worse for wear, and now had gained her second wind. With her new mobile phone in her purse, she eased the Mustang into the westbound lane of the 401 and headed to what many called the Big Smoke. Emily knew it better as Hogtown. Either way, Toronto was a big city, and it had been ages since she'd been there.

Unbeknownst to Colm, Emily had two reasons to be excited. Interrogating Angelo Pellini topped the list, but a phone call home to her mom had revealed that her dad was in a small town just east of Toronto. He was buying a new boat for his charter business and had planned on travelling to Clarksville to surprise her. If she timed it right, she could meet him in Whitby and have a long-overdue visit.

"That would be fantastic!" Emily almost crawled through the phone to hug her mom.

"Dad wants to see you. He's anxious to talk about—you know—"

"Gary," Emily finished her mom's sentence.

"Yes—Gary, listen, go easy on him," Mom said. "It's been a long time, and he still has scars. You don't know what hap…" Emily's mom began to cry. Through stifled sobs, she said, "He loves you Em, just remember that, and go easy. I have to go, sweetheart…"

The line went silent, and as Emily put her phone down, her mother's sobs persisted in her mind.

She was twelve when Gary left home. He'd always been rebellious. With her dad away most on the lake boats for months at a time, her mother had difficulty dealing with Gary's transition into adulthood. More than once he'd been escorted home by the police; always for a minor infraction, but still, he lived on the edge, and that tended to get him in trouble. He and Emily had been close, but the difference in their ages made it difficult for them to socialize outside the home. Gary had always had a mysterious side, and Emily knew he was keeping secrets from her. Try as she might, she could never find out what they were. Then one day, he was gone, and in the weeks and months to follow, her parents systematically removed all vestige of his existence. They never spoke of him, and even family photos of him slowly disappeared. It was a secret long held from Emily, but it was a secret she intended to learn. Whatever had happened, those many years ago still held a great deal of pain for her parents. This time, Emily would not be denied, this time, she would make her father talk.

G. A. PICKSTOCK

30

HE'D CHOSEN THE LAKE Grill because the food was excellent, and it was only a couple of blocks from the marina where his new boat was being fitted out. It was a small restaurant, and as it was mid-morning, the breakfast crowd had moved on, giving Gerald the dining room to himself.

Gerald James dwarfed the thin bent-framed chair in which he sat. It was stout enough, but it still creaked under his large frame as he shifted around to see his daughter pass through the door. The sight of Emily brought a tear to his eye. It had been more than a few years since he'd seen her, and it surprised him at how she'd changed. A woman stood before him. This was not the little girl he'd sent off to university, and the look on her face told him she had more than ice-cream and pony rides on her mind. Even so, her broad smile reassured him that this would be a good reunion.

Forty years on the lake freighters, twenty-eight of them as a Captain of one of the largest ships in the seaway, had turned Gerald Ambrose James into a man accustomed to getting his own way. Full-grown men with as much experience as he followed his orders without question. Yet, where his daughter was concerned, he was a pushover. Emily could ask anything of him, and he would find a way to oblige. Anything, with one exception, an exception that had driven a wedge between them for many years. An exception, which from her expression this time, he would have to acquiesce.

He stood, arms stretched wide to envelop his pride and joy as she melted into his chest. They hugged each other for a long moment. As Gerald lifted his face from kissing the top of his daughter's head, he spied the wait-staff watching them. A wave of self-consciousness overcame him, and he gently separated himself from Emily.

Gerald James was an even-tempered man, not prone to public displays of emotion. Time and distance had robbed him of his daughter's presence, and he found himself awkwardly searching for the right words.

"Let me look at you. God, your mother, wouldn't recognize you. You're all grown up," he said. "Come on, let's sit down. It seems we're putting on a show." He nodded in the direction of the counter and cast his gaze directly at the waitress, "Two coffees, please."

The waitress nodded back and grabbed a carafe and two mugs.

* * *

They had crammed seven years into less than two hours by the time Emily broached the subject. The restaurant had become steadily busier as lunch-time approached.

"Dad, you can't keep deflecting the subject. I'm not twelve anymore, and I'm not leaving here without an answer. You have to tell me what happened to Gary."

Emily knew the signs. Her dad had remained calm, but she could see in the redness forming under his eyes that he was struggling to hold his temper. She was immediately thankful that the restaurant had become so busy. She'd asked her mother many times only to see her retreat within herself and become melancholy. Emily pushed harder.

"Why, Dad? Why is it so hard to talk about? What happened to Gary?" Her voice rose loud enough for the next table to fall silent.

Gerald shot the occupants of the table a 'mind your own business' stare and turned back to his daughter and growled, "Suffice to say, as far as this family is concerned, he's dead and gone."

"I can't accept that," Emily shot back. "You've been holding something back for years. What secret could be so devastating that it must be held forever? I want to know what happened to my brother."

Gerald James bowed his head, his hands balled into fists, and for a moment, Emily thought she had pushed her father too hard. Fearful that he might lose it in the middle of a now crowded dining room, she thought seriously of letting the subject drop. Whatever it was that troubled her dad so profoundly that he would bury it and keep it from her for so long perhaps was not something she should know. Resigning herself to failure, she gathered her things and pushed back from the table.

"If you refuse to tell me, then there's nothing more to say. I have an appointment in Toronto, and I have to get going. Give mom a hug for me when you get home," Emily said, rising to leave.

"Wait!" Gerald said. "Sit down. If it means that much to you…" his voice faltered. "I'll tell you—maybe it is time you knew."

* * *

"I blame myself, really," said Gerald. "Gary was a good boy, but he had a wild side." He flashed his daughter a sheepish grin. "Most lads do. Something you'll learn about if you don't already know. Anyway, my being away so much didn't help, and as Gary got older, he became harder to control. You were just a young girl. You probably didn't see some of the issues we faced with him. Remember, he was thirteen when you were born. It was a shock to all of us."

"How so?"

"Well, we thought we were done having kids. Mum and I tried for ages after Gary was born and—" Gerald stopped to gather his thoughts— "I'm not real comfortable talking about this with you."

"I'm a big girl, daddy. I know about stuff." Emily grinned. "Even stuff about boys."

Gerald had to admit, his little girl had indeed grown up, but talking about relationship issues was not easy for him, and he especially didn't want to confide in his own daughter. Catching the eye of their server, he motioned for a refill of their coffee.

With a steaming fresh cup of courage in front of him, Gerald sucked in a deep gulp of air and continued.

"Like I said, after we had Gary, we tried to have a baby right away. I was on the lakes for almost eight months out of the year, so we tried to plan it so that I'd be home for a few months to help mom with the new baby. It was all supposed to be very scientific. It never happened and after a while we stopped trying. Twelve years later, oops! You come along. Gary was a teenager with all the raging hormones that come with that. I'm still on the boats, and your mom has to cope with a newborn and an adolescent. Gary helped, and in fact, he fell in love with you. I'm afraid we came to rely on him too much and then…"

Her dad's eyes became misty and swollen, "Well, he started staying out late. Sometimes he wouldn't come home for days. He wound up getting into trouble with the cops. More than once he was brought home in a cruiser. I was tired of it. We put up with his antics for a long time. Mostly because of my job; he did after all, help out around the house. But then it happened. The cops arrested him and charged him. He never came home after that. Blind River is a small town. Everyone knew, and it's taken years to live it down."

"Knew what—dad—what did he do?"

Gerald shook his head. "Suffice to say it was serious enough to keep him in prison for many years. You have to understand, Emily, we tried, we tried so hard to keep him out of trouble. But trouble always found him. It was killing us inside. I'm not proud of it, but for our own sanity and your welfare, we had to let him go."

Tears streamed down Emily's cheeks as she tried to digest her father's story. "Y-you just abandoned him. Why?"

"It wasn't like that. Gary was found guilty and went to prison. He was ten hours away. We couldn't even visit him and with me on the water for months on end, it was doubly impossible. Then one day, about eight years ago, he shows up at the house. He barely spoke to your mum. He just walked into his old room, packed up his belongings and asked her for a few sticks of furniture for his apartment. He had a woman with him. They loaded everything in a pickup truck and drove away. Not so much as a kiss my ass."

Gerald's eyes hardened, his tears had dried up with the recollection of that day. "It was at that moment that we knew; we no longer had a son. We put every memory of him away."

"Where did he go? Do you know where he is?"

Gerald shook his head. "I have no idea."

"Why did he go to prison?"

Her father leaned forward across the table and took his daughter's hands in his own. He looked deeply into her eyes and said, "I love you more than life itself. There isn't anything I wouldn't do for you, you must believe that. The memories you have of Gary are good ones and for that reason alone, I will not tell you. You can look for him until the cows come home. You won't find him."

31

IT WAS THE CLOSEST thing to a castle Emily had ever seen, albeit undoubtedly a lot smaller than the real thing. The two-story dwelling boasted hand-hewn limestone brickwork forming two semi-octagonal towers capped with conical roofs tiled in black slate. The turrets bordered the centre façade that jutted forward, showcasing a massive bespoke oak door complete with wrought iron furniture and period hardware.

The house was custom right down to the interlocking brick paving encompassing the Trevi-style fountain in the centre of the front courtyard. At first glance, Emily was impressed by its grandeur. However, as Mac pulled the Crown Vic into the south end of the U-shaped drive, Emily glimpsed the two-car garage located to the side of the property. Although it was done in the same stonework, she thought it was a shame that the garage looked like an afterthought, certainly not something that had been part of the original concept.

"Would you believe he dropped over four million for this place?" Mac said as she slid out from behind the wheel. "I checked it out before you arrived."

For some reason, Emily had expected Mac to be a man. After her recent close encounters, Emily had been nervous about teaming up with a male counterpart. When Mac Somers proved to be a petite brunette in a form-fitting business suit, Emily breathed a sigh of relief, mentally thanking Kendra for her insight.

"Well, it is Toronto, after all. House prices are crazy here," Emily replied.

"Emily, we're in Pickering for God's sake, four million-plus, that's a four and six zeros behind it. Shit, my house is twice the size of this one, and I bet it cost less than that stupid looking fountain." Mac stepped up to the front door and rang the bell.

* * *

They stepped into a cavernous foyer bathed in natural light from an octagonal skylight high above. In the centre, a grand staircase descended from the second-story landing, flaring out to either side as it reached the main floor. The deep golden hue of the solid oak steps and railings stood in stark contrast to the brilliance of the white marble floors.

Emily's gaze wandered to the landing, fully expecting to see an old vintage clock at the top of the stairs. There was no clock. However, there was a man dressed in tan slacks and a navy-blue golf shirt. He descended the steps quickly, reaching out to shake hands. His short black hair didn't quite match his full, neatly trimmed beard. The facial hair was an infusion of red and brown, and upon close scrutiny, Emily spotted more than a few grey hairs. Angelo Pellini was fit and trim, and his pearl white teeth flashed a brilliant smile from behind his whiskers.

"Four point eight," Pellini said to the detectives.

"Huh? What, four point eight?" Mac responded.

"Four point eight million," Pellini replied. "You're wondering what all this costs. Everybody does, I shouldn't be embarrassed if I were you. It's quite natural to wonder."

His accent was almost too posh for Emily to accept. Yet, there was something in his voice, and for some reason, Emily could not disengage herself from Pellini's deep brown eyes.

"You understand, I'm not bragging. It's just one of those things that I find constantly preoccupies any conversation. So, I like to get the damnable issue out of the way at the outset. That way, we can progress onward, and all are satisfied that I, and the bank, have deep pockets."

"Don't you want to know who we are?" Mac asked somewhat disarmed by Pellini's aloof behaviour.

Pellini broke his gaze from Emily and turned to Somers. "Judging by your mode of transportation, I should imagine you are the Police, correct?" He didn't wait for a response. "I suppose I should ask to see your credentials, but let's dispense with that, shall we? We all know who we are and why you are here. It has to do with Samantha, does it not? Now, please let us retire to the living room. We can talk there."

He led them into a carpeted room dominated by a white leather sectional sofa and a glass-topped coffee table. Two complimenting chairs in black leather sat opposite the couch. Emily took note of a small antique bookcase positioned against one wall and, for a moment, she thought there was something oddly familiar about the piece. Its presence in the room didn't fit the decor, but that wasn't it, there was something else. The thought dropped from her mind as their host spoke.

"Samantha's upstairs playing with her sister," Pellini said, taking up residence on the sprawling sectional. He motioned to the two empty chairs, "Please make yourself comfortable."

"Sister?" asked Emily. "How can she have a sister? She was Nicole's only child."

"True, Nicole only had one child, but I'm Samantha's father," Pellini smiled. "Rebecca is Samantha's half-sister." He paused, waiting for the penny to drop.

Emily jumped in. "Sammi's father, yes, that's why we're here. Detective Constable Somers and I are investigating the validity of that statement. From what we've been able to ascertain, there is no record of Sammi's father on file in Clarksville."

Pellini rose from the sofa and moved to the bookcase. Opening a panel in the upper left corner, he revealed a small secretary desktop behind which resided a series of pigeonholes. Pellini withdrew two sheets of paper from an envelope and retook his position on the couch.

"I need you to understand one thing. I have nothing but the best of intentions for Samantha. She is my daughter, as these documents will attest. When I became aware of her situation, I acted immediately, and I will cooperate with you in every way possible." As Pellini handed the documents over to Mac Somers, he noticed Emily focussed on the bookcase. "I know it doesn't fit the room. It's an old piece of furniture and not valuable at all, but it is all I have from my mother. She gave it to me many years ago, and it has a lot of sentimental value."

Emily fixed her gaze back on Pellini. The nagging little tickle in the recesses of her mind would not let up, and the longer she remained in Pellini's presence, the more it persisted. Whatever it was, something about this man was interfering in her quest for information. Giving herself a mental shake to clear the distraction, she said, "I can't help but think I've seen one like it, but for the life of me, I can't remember where."

"I believe they're quite ubiquitous, I'm sure they were mass-produced, certainly not unique at all. My parents did not come from wealth and could afford very little. I keep it as a reminder of my roots, and whenever I become too full of myself, I open the desk and think back to the days of my youth. Which isn't so long ago you understand, but still, sometimes I need reminding that everything wasn't always thus," he spread his arms as if to encompass the palatial lifestyle he now enjoyed.

Mac Somers gave the papers a cursory glance and handed them over to Emily. The documents, the registration of Sammi's birth naming Angelo Pellini as the father and the second document, a DNA certificate confirming Pellini's paternity of the female child Samantha Saunders, put paid to any question of Pellini's claim to the child and certainly seemed to give him authority to collect Sammi from the hospital. There were other questions, however, and Emily wanted answers.

"By the way, the hospital has copies of these documents. I had to provide them before they would release Samantha to my custody," Pellini said.

"Please understand Mr. Pellini, we were concerned for the child's welfare. We had to follow up regardless of anything the hospital had to tell us. Sammi's mother was murdered. I'm sure you can understand our interest here."

Emily handed the forms back across the coffee table, and Pellini reached out to accept them. It was the first time Emily noticed the man's hands. "Do you mind telling us what you do for a living?" She allowed her eyes to survey the room taking in the totality of her surroundings. "As you have openly stated, you have deep pockets."

Pellini folded the pages and set them neatly on the table. Settling back into the deep recesses of the sofa's back cushions, he said, "Let's see, how can I explain it? I suppose one might describe me as an investor, a financier. Yes, that would sum it up. I'm a mover of money."

"Judging by this house, you move a lot of it," quipped Mac.

"I suppose I do," replied Pellini, smiling at the dig.

"Those aren't the hands of an executive," said Emily. "Those scars aren't from paper cuts and the callouses didn't come from banging away at a keyboard or from dialling a phone. They're the hands of a man accustomed to hard work. If you don't mind me asking, how did you lose the finger?" Emily indicated the ring finger on his left hand. She hadn't noticed it until she'd handed him the papers, but it was plain to see that he was missing the top of the digit down to the first knuckle.

Pellini raised his left hand and spread his fingers apart, recalling the memory. "It was a stupid accident at a ridiculous time in my life," he grinned as he considered his hand. "I suppose you could say this was a turning point in my life. The result of too much flesh contacting too much steel revolving at too high a speed." Pellini flexed his fingers, repeatedly balling them into a fist. "Can't feel a thing in that finger," he said, allowing the formality in his voice to waver.

"A turning point, how so?" asked Mac.

Pellini's face darkened, "It was at that precise moment that I determined to start working smart instead of hard. I won't go into how, but I managed to cobble together enough money to buy an interest in some property in the harbour district. The profits I earned from the sale enabled me to make some other investments," he pondered his hands again. "Among other things, I have a background in construction and experience as a land developer—"

Emily interrupted, "Is that why you purchased Nicole's property out from under her? I have to say, that's a pretty cold thing to do to the mother of your child. From what we've learnt, Nicole could have sold that land at a profit and put that money to good use."

Pellini leaned forward, his face reddening behind his whiskers. "Nicole was a waste of skin, an addict who allowed herself to be dragged down by any guy with enough scratch to get her to her next fix. Don't talk to me about putting her money to good use," Pellini scowled, abandoning all of his previous airs of decorum. "She allowed that property to fall into the hands of the taxman, and I bought it. I did it to secure a future for my daughter. Yes, that property is valuable, but you have no idea just how valuable it became once I bought it. I—" he stopped himself in mid-thought. "Just suffice to say, if things go as planned, Samantha will have a very bright future. As for Nicole, I hope she rots in hell."

* * *

Pellini's words echoed loudly in the minds of the two detectives. He leaned back in the cushions, his body sagging like a deflated blow-up doll. The redness in his face waned, and his eyes dilated.

Regaining his composure, Pellini broke the pregnant silence permeating the room. "Now if there is nothing else, Detectives, I have other things I must attend to. Is there anything else I can help you with?"

"As a matter of fact—"

"Only one thing," Emily cut Mac off before she could ask her next question. "We need to see for ourselves that Sammi is safe and healthy."

"I can assure you, Samantha is extremely well and completely safe. However, I understand you have a job to do," Pellini replied. "I'll have my housekeeper bring her down."

Pellini lifted a phone from an end table, and moments later, Sammi and a slightly older Rebecca scampered into the room, scrambled up onto the couch, bracketing their father. He wrapped his arms around them, cradling each girl into his sides. "She's quite well and happy as you can see," he said, his gaze riveted on Emily.

The moment was not lost on her, and the message in his eyes confirmed her suspicion. Despite the happy family façade, his outburst had revealed something that Emily suspected he wanted to remain hidden. There was far more to Angelo Pellini than she could have anticipated, and the niggle in the back of her neck was well-founded. She had had an epiphany and the realization that Pellini recognized this worried her.

On the ride home, Emily had time to ponder the events of the day. Something continued to nag at her brain. Throughout the ride home, the thought kept coming back, over and over, and each time she could not jog the information loose. She needed help. Emily finally surrendered. She knew precisely who to call.

"Clarksville OPP."

"Detective Constable Jen Stroud, please," said Emily. A moment later, she heard Jen's voice.

"DC Jenifer Stroud here, who is this?"

"Jen, it's Emily. I need a favour."

32

"THEY'VE GONE DARK," COLM said as he hefted a canvas bag full of cellphones onto Kendra's desk. "I've had officers attend all of their homes and usual haunts, and this is all we can find of any of them." Colm dumped the bag allowing more than a dozen phones to spill out across the desk.

"All of the phones are active and have working sim cards. We were supposed to find them. They were laid out in plain view on the kitchen counters of their homes." Colm plopped himself down into the chair opposite his new boss. "It's like they were raptured," Colm said.

"What do you mean, raptured?" Kendra asked as she attempted to access the phones trying to determine which was which.

"My mum used to talk about it. You know, people would be there one moment and gone the next. She called it the Rapture. God comes and takes the righteous and leaves the damned." Colm stroked his chin as he considered what he'd just said.

"Bloody hell, no way Kris Martin was righteous, so, something else is afoot here," said Kendra as she kept tapping at the phones. "They couldn't have vanished without some trace. Are you telling me there is no trail whatsoever?"

"Sure, you can try all you like to get into them, they're iPhones and they're all locked. And no, no trace. Wherever they went, they went together, and they travelled with little more than the clothes on their back. They left everything behind right down to their undies. We've checked everything, bank accounts, credit cards, airlines, taxis, car rentals, no one has seen or heard from them, and I find that hard to fathom. Let's face it, Clarksville isn't that big. You can't fart in this town that someone doesn't hear it. All seven of them are gone, and they took their wives and families with them. They left everything behind, but someone knows something, and I will get to the bottom of it. I just don't think it will be soon. By the looks of it, they don't want to be found, which raises a bigger question. What the hell have they been up to?"

* * *

"Enjoy your trip, Mr. Christopher. If you need anything or run into any snags, all you need to do is call the number on the rental agreement."

The agent behind the counter flashed a broad smile as he watched his latest clients file out the door to the waiting RVs. October was a slow month and renting seven A Class motor homes all at once was unheard of. As all of his RVs had been winterized, the agent had to scramble to get them ready on short notice, but the client was insistent and willing to pay a premium for the inconvenience. Looking a gift horse in the mouth at this time of year was just stupid. Besides, the guy paid for the whole works on a Platinum credit card, and that was money in the bank. To top it off, Mr. Christopher and his entourage were, in fact, doing him a favour. By dropping the motor homes in BC, he was effectively getting the rolling stock out of his inventory, and thereby reducing his monthly admin fees from the leasing company. In seven heavenly days, the seven behemoth RVs would become someone else's problem. Following Christopher to the door, he closed and locked it from the inside, all the while, grinning and waving them a fond farewell.

* * *

Kendra stacked all the cellphones back into the canvas bag. Frowning, she looked at her senior detective and said, "What have you dragged me into here, Colm? A few short days ago, I was blissfully happy sitting behind my desk in Orillia. Coming here was supposed to be a bird course, an easy gig. So far, you've handed me two murders, and a delinquent and insubordinate senior constable, who, along with six of his buddies, has evidently vanished from the planet."

Her shoulders sagged under the stress making Colm wonder if Kendra had regrets. He tried to lighten the mood. "Sure 'n you'd be bored stiff if you hadn't taken this job, so you would," he grinned, hoping she might smile back. "I'll find them. I promise I—"

"No, you've done your bit," she said, still frowning. "These men are under my command. I'll deal with them from here on. You have other work to do. Which reminds me— " Kendra picked up a sheet of paper from her desk— "the judge signed your warrant." Kendra handed him the paper and gave Colm a "dismissed" wave as she picked up her phone.

The disappearance of any police officer was a serious business. Seven missing cops would send the situation nuclear. Kendra knew Orillia would employ every resource to find them. Two minutes after she hung up the phone, every police agency in the country received a "BOLO" for seven male constables and accompanying family members, possibly travelling as a group. It was a poor description, but it was all Kendra could provide. At least they had photos of the wayward cops, and because they were cops, Kendra knew every blue uniform would *be on the lookout*.

Even so, she held little hope that these men would surface any time soon. They were, after all, experienced police officers, and if indeed they were up to no good, then they had an advantage they would use to its maximum potential. Knowing this, Kendra focused on Colm's question: What have these men been up to, and why disappear now?

G. A. PICKSTOCK

33

HOMEWARD BOUND, AMELIA MERGED into the westbound lane of the 401. Her job was done, and two days in Clarksville had been all she could endure. She had accomplished her task, helped her sister locate the vital documents, thus ensuring what she hoped would be a smooth transition of power. The train had been derailed, but only for a moment and now back on track, progress could be made. Still, there was a glitch in the plan. Someone had leaked, and the thought of discovery made her stomach flutter. All Anne had to do was make the right choice, and to Amelia's way of thinking, the decision was simple.

She hadn't wanted to come to Clarksville. Aside from the dislike of her sister's husband, she had a more profound reason to hate this area, one far more costly than she could have imagined. This stretch of the 401 was a speed trap, and as the principal director of a successful corporation, Amelia had travelled this highway hundreds of times. More than once, she had found herself in the crosshairs of Clarksville's road warriors, and it seemed as though it was always the same cop that pulled her over. Admittedly, Amelia had a lead foot. She liked to drive fast, as evidenced by the car she drove. The Audi R8 was indeed a fast car. More to the point, however, it was also an expensive car. Something which Amelia came to regret.

Three months before Harry died, she'd been stopped for speeding, again. Only this time, she wasn't supposed to be behind the wheel. Amelia's license had been suspended for one year. Nevertheless, she still needed to travel for business and so, had risked driving even though if caught again, she might face jail time.

She recognized the cop immediately as he swaggered over to the vehicle with an 'I've got you' this time grin on his face. Amelia hated that face. It was the kind that no matter how she tried to envision it, she just wanted to punch it; over and over again until that supercilious grin vanished into a putrid puddle of blood, torn flesh and mangled bits of bone. Still, she knew he had her number this time, and she knew from bitter experience Constable Kris Martin would make her pay.

She squirmed in her seat, her teeth grinding as she thought of that price. Martin had found the land prospectus. Amelia had left the folder in open sight on the passenger seat of her sports car. They'd been in the middle of negotiating her get out of jail free deal when the arrogant bastard spotted it.

"What's this," he said, picking up the file folder and flipping it open.

"Nothing that concerns you," Amelia shot back.

"We'll see," said Kris as he began reading. He sifted through the pages for a long time then said, "Wait here, I'll be right back."

Amelia watched as Kris returned to his cruiser. Through her side mirror, she could see he was making a phone call. Ten minutes later, Martin emerged from the cop car and handed the prospectus back to Amelia.

"I'm afraid the price of freedom just went up," he said.

That was three months ago, and now Amelia not only had a free pass to drive the 401, at least in the Clarksville corridor, she also had an unwanted and undeserving business partner. One who would if allowed, be a thorn in her side for a long time. There was a bright side. Having a crooked cop in your toolbox wasn't all bad, and he had proven useful when she required some specialty work. Kris Martin was a tool undoubtedly, a costly tool, but a tool, nonetheless. Her plan was in full throttle, and like tools that had outlived their usefulness, Kris and his six-pack of nuts and bolts would soon find themselves on a shelf from which they could not jump down.

***

Barry Blackmore shivered as he leaned against the rail of his office balcony. The crisp scent of autumn, mingled with the spray from the waterfall cascading beneath his perch, penetrated deep into his lungs, reviving his wits and driving the cobwebs from his thoughts. He needed a clear head for what he was about to do, and the chaotic serenity of the waterfall was just the prescription he needed.

The balcony, once used as a service platform for a long-disused waterwheel, extended over the waterfall and served now as Barry's solitary place of refuge. The Blackmore family had, in essence, built Clarksville, and had, at one time, been the largest employer in the area. Beginning with a small furniture factory located at the edge of town on the Clarksville River at the head of the waterfalls, the factory grew in reputation, and Blackmore furniture gained favour worldwide. As the company grew, so did the Blackmore ambition giving rise to Blackmore Holdings and Property Solutions. The company swallowed up available land, immediately building residential housing for the workers in the factory. With a captive workforce paying a goodly portion of their earnings back to the company in the form of rent, the Blackmore family prospered even more.

Closing the factory had hit the community hard, causing the Blackmore name, once held in high esteem, to become synonymous with betrayal. Many in the town felt cheated, and the animosity persisted for years. Being "Blackmored" meant you'd been screwed over, and it wasn't until Barry helped Harrison Dalton save the tire plant, thereby reviving the local workforce and, in turn, the economy, that resentment gave way to forgetfulness and eventually, forgiveness. With the Blackmore legacy approaching its bicentenary, Blackmore Holdings stood on the precipice of its most ambitious and potentially most profitable venture.

Harrison Dalton's death was a contingency they hadn't anticipated, and now success weighed heavily on the actions of Harry's widow. Anne Dalton had arrived, and he had to find some way to persuade her to honour Harry's commitment. Barry stepped back inside to welcome his new business partner.

"My sincere condolences Anne, please come in and sit," Barry offered his hand, ushering her to a chair. "Harry was a dear friend."

Anne Dalton sat stern-faced. "Harry had no friends," she said. "Only people he tolerated, and only those who could further his ambitions. So drop the bullshit." She reached into her bag and removed a file folder. Retrieving a document, Anne dropped it on the desk in front of Barry and asked, "What the hell is Blackmore/Dalton Holdings LLC?"

* * *

The board meeting dragged into its second hour with Anne fielding dozens of questions, most of which pertained to the future of Dalton Tire, and how current positions within management and supervisory staff might be affected. Truthfully, all she could do was reassure them that, for the foreseeable future, there would be no change in the daily operations of the plant. Notwithstanding Harry's death, the company still had business to do and orders to fill. As the meeting digressed into a doom and gloom speculation of the future, Anne decided to put a halt to it.

"Gentlemen!" Anne interrupted the quarrelling, "It's time we all got back to work. As I said, no major changes. I don't know how I can say it more plainly. However, if you'd be happier with me making changes—I can accommodate you."

Six men sat in silence as they considered the message from the stone-faced woman at the head of the table. One by one, they rose from their seats and made their way out of the room. Jim Roberts remained.

"I don't think you made any friends here today," he said, pushing his chair back into place. "These men are understandably concerned, what with the current financial position of the company."

Anne stood and moved her own chair back into position. "They should be concerned, Jim. They have a lot to answer for. From the short time I've had to survey the books and the operation of this company, I'd say there's a lot of deadwood, and not all of it floating out in the plant. So, Mr. General Manager, here's something you need to consider; this place is hemorrhaging money. Find a way to fix it, 'cause the bank of Dalton is closed for business. Oh, and by the way, if that means cutting staff, then so be it, but be sure you cut the high-priced deadwood as well as the low-hanging branches."

* * *

Anne surveyed Harry's sparsely furnished office. If not for the massive L-shaped desk the cavernous office would seem empty. Sitting in Harry's chair, she contemplated the rays of light spearing their way through the narrow windows. There were four of them stretching from floor to ceiling. Two on one wall and two on the adjacent wall behind her. The beams battled each other in a desperate contest of wills creating a ballet of glints and flashes as they struggled to claim the dust in the stale, tobacco-laden air. She'd been in this room many times and hadn't realized how cold and empty it was.

Decisions were made here, decisions that affected the lives of hundreds. For better or worse, this decision had fallen on her, and as she deliberated her choices, she realized the only advisors she had were the windows, and they were busy battling over dust.

34

AS CAL JENKINS ENTERED the reception area of the Town Hall offices, the chatter and hubbub typically present at this time of day fell silent, causing him to stop and survey the room. One by one, the office staff cast their eyes back to their work as Jenkins' eyes met their own. Rita shuffled her way to the gated counter and opened the gate.

"What?" said Cal as he scanned the faces in the room.

"The cops are in your office," said Rita. "One of them is that young detective who was here the other day and another in uniform. They have a warrant to search your office and your computer. I'm sorry, Mr. Jenkins, I had to let them in."

Jenkins felt the blood rush to his face. Sweat trickled down his armpits, and as he gazed upon the office staff, he opened his mouth to speak, but nothing came forth. Unable to manufacture enough saliva to talk, he nodded. Patting Rita on her arm, Jenkins slipped past the nervous secretary and headed toward his office.

Colm met Jenkins at the door, preventing his entry.

"I'm sorry, Mr. Jenkins, I'm afraid you can't come in just now." Colm handed Jenkins a copy of the warrant. "We're conducting a search of this office and your computer for information as outlined in here. Please don't leave the building. It may be necessary to talk to you."

Cal Jenkins took the paper, and with shaking hands, he turned away. The words on the page blurred as his eyes fell on his name combined with WARRANT TO SEARCH AND SEIZE... The remaining characters on the document morphed into Cyrillic text as the harder he stared at it, the less he comprehended. Jenkins retreated to the staff lunchroom and slumped into one of the plastic cafeteria chairs.

He had no concept of how much time had elapsed, but the appearance of Colm in the lunchroom doorway shocked Jenkins back into the moment.

"Mr. Jenkins, if you'd like to join us in your office, I have some questions for you," Colm said, gesturing for the man to stand.

"Do—do I need a lawyer?" he croaked as he levered himself off his chair.

Colm caught the heavy scent of Jenkins' body odour as he stepped aside to allow the clerk to pass. He could see the man was worried, and with what they had discovered, he was right to be concerned.

"Sure now that depends. Have you been up to something you'd be needing a lawyer for?"

Jenkins stopped short at the sight of Jen Stroud occupying his chair, busily tapping away at his computer.

Jenkins sat, taking one of the two chairs reserved for visitors. His gaze firmly locked on the detective constable pecking away at his computer. He opened his mouth to speak…Colm raised his hand to interrupt the clerk.

"I'll ask the questions, Mr. Jenkins. The last time we spoke you lied to me. You said you were bound by the privacy laws not to reveal information regarding the sale of the Saunders property. That was a lie. You wasted my time, but that's fine because it was not only a lie, it was a mistake. Don't lie to me again. You won't like the result."

Colm turned his attention to Jen Stroud.

"Have you got what you need, Jen?"

"Yes, most of it anyway, I still have more to search," she said.

Colm lifted a folder from the desk and flipped it open. Studying the contents, he said, "What can you tell me about the Cayman National Bank?"

Ashen-faced, Jenkins stammered, "H-how did you—"

"We have our sources. More to the point Cal old son—may I call you Cal? I think by now we should be on a first-name basis, don't you? You can call me Detective."

Jenkins nodded, his mind straining to reconcile how his secret had been exposed.

Colm repeated, "More to the point, that's not the kind of thing you can hide, and well, you of all people should know better than to use your work computer for personal business. It seems working for the town pays well, Mr. Jenkins. Perhaps you'd like to explain."

Colm didn't wait for Cal to respond. "I don't care about you, Cal, I want to know where the money came from, and what you had to do to get it. After all, a quarter-million-dollars is a lot of dosh. Even high-priced bureaucrats such as yourself don't make that much money, do they?"

Jenkins cast his gaze down to his shoes and shook his head. "No, not in this town anyway. We don't make nearly enough," he grumbled, trying to regain his composure. Straightening up in his chair, he asked, "I don't know if I should say anything. What happens if I don't?"

Colm grinned, "Jail," he said. "Look, I have enough right here to charge you with fraud. All I have to do is keep digging. We'll find more, we always do. You can't explain this money easily, but what you can do is tell us where it came from. Either way, it's gone. Forget any idea you might have about keeping it. That just ain't gonna happen."

"What? No way! That's my money, you can't just seize it without cause."

"Oh, but we can boyo, sure, if we don't, Canada Revenue will. It's my bet they've never been told about this money, yeah?" Colm leaned forward in his seat, getting close enough to feel Jenkins' breath. "You've only one chance to walk away from this. Tell me where that money came from and why?"

Jenkins' upper body trembled. He clutched at his shoulders, and with a shaky voice, he said, "Look under the bottom drawer of my desk. There's an envelope taped to it."

Jen pulled the drawer out and dumped the contents. She removed the envelope and handed it to Colm.

"What's this?"

Still shaking, Jenkins responded, "I received that a month ago. You can see from the paper, it's the original statement from the Cayman National Bank in my name. Right after I got that, I got a phone call telling me I would get the password to that account if and when the Saunders property went up for a tax sale. I don't know who sent the letter or who called. All I know is the property was so far in arrears that complying didn't seem out of line, and a quarter million for doing something that was bound to happen anyway, well shit, who wouldn't take that deal?"

"Then what?" Colm asked, sitting back and taking in the yarn.

"Then nothing! The property sold but no password. I got a nasty phone call saying the wrong party won the bid. Hell, I didn't know who was supposed to win. All I had to do was make sure it hit the auction. I did that, but it all went sour. I've been scared shitless ever since. Then the Saunders chick got killed, and I knew it was just a matter of time. And here you are. Sorry, I don't know any more than that." Jenkins let his arms drop to his side, and with a huge sigh, he added, "One thing I did find out, however, rumour has it there's a monstrous land deal afoot. I don't know who's involved, but there's been a lot of applications for zoning and easement changes made to the OMB. That's the Ontario Municipal Board, in case you didn't know."

Jenkins sat back, folding his arms and smiled for the first time. He'd just told the detective something he didn't already know. It irked Colm that the clerk had got one over him.

"How do I know you don't have the password for this account? You've already told me it's your money." Colm asked, waving the paper at Jenkins.

"Because according to that paper, it is my money. All I need is the password. Still, I'm not as stupid as you think I am. If I'd have gotten that password, I'd have transferred that money, and I sure as shit wouldn't be sitting here, that's why!"

Colm had to grin. The man's logic made sense in spite of his newly found bravado. "So, you say you don't know anything about this so-called land deal?"

"Nope, now if you are going to charge me, do it, otherwise, I have work to do."

Colm rubbed his chin as he thought. It had been a ruse to get the clerk to talk, and it had worked but not in the way he'd hoped. He had learned about the bank account quite by accident when Jen found an image of the bank statement on the computer hard drive. Had Jenkins not been so foolish as to save a scanned copy, Colm would be none the wiser. Still, he didn't have enough to charge the man, and even if he did, a good lawyer would win at trial.

"You're grand for now. As for work, you'll need a new computer.

We'll be taking this one with us. Jen, let's pack up and go."

Jenkins stood, allowing Jen Stroud to pass by carrying the computer case. He moved to his desk and sat listening as the police officers trudged down the hallway then turned to look out the window. Momentarily, the two cops came into view as they got in their cruiser. Jenkins looked down on the OPP officers, and as they pulled away from the curb, his lips curled into a thin smile. *Poor bastards, you have no idea.*

* * *

As they pulled away from the curb, Jen shot a sardonic grin at her frowning boss. "It bothers you, doesn't it?"

"What?"

"That he got one up on you. That bugs you. I can see it in your face."

Colm's lips curled into a sneer. "Let him have his little victory. Sure, guys like that make me crazy. They tend to be little tyrants, stuck in a rut with no way out. He thought he'd found an easy exit, but he probably won't survive another week in that job. It's my guess the money in the Cayman account is long gone, and the poor bugger was never going to see a penny of it. More's the pity, because when Canada Revenue gets wind of that Cayman account, our Mr. Jenkins is after gettin' a world of grief. One up? It won't last long. Cal Jenkins did himself no favours by keeping his mouth shut and allowing that property to go to auction. He made a big mistake there, so he did."

Jen waited for Colm's expression to change into a satisfied smile. To his credit, his countenance remained stoic and thoughtful. He'd had a job to do, and now she could tell he was planning his next move.

G. A. PICKSTOCK

35

THE VIEW FROM THE front window hadn't changed. The playground at the end of the street still stretched away terminating at a line of bushes shielding the neighbouring back yards from the raucous activities of the private school's play area. Almost every house on the street had a maple tree in the front yard, and only a few of them still clung to their foliage in a last desperate struggle to fight off the coming winter. Across the street, old man Palmer busied himself putting up Christmas lights around a Blue Spruce tree next to his front steps. He had a step ladder precariously perched on the edge of his porch, and Colm watched as the old man extended himself beyond safe limits to wrap a string of lights around the top. *That poor sod will break his neck, climbing that ladder.* He watched a little longer as a frustrated Palmer finally tossed the light string around the treetop. *Mission accomplished, fair play.*

"We're no closer to figuring this business out," Colm said, fixing his attention on a chipmunk as it scampered up the tree in their own front yard. "Mr. Chips is back, by the way."

"Excuse me, sorry, I didn't hear you I had the mixer going," Emily appeared in the kitchen doorway, her face smudged with flour. "I'm making brownies, what did you say?"

"I said, we're no closer to figuring this thing out. All we've got are two dead bodies and a bunch of rumours about who's doing what." Colm flopped into Emily's big chair, the furrows in his brow, revealing his frustration.

"That's not entirely true," Emily said, wiping her hands on a tea-towel. "The way I see it, Angelo Pellini is in this up to his butt. He bought that land out on Dalton Road, and if I believe him, and I do, that little piece of the puzzle just became very valuable. Put that together with what you learnt from Jenkins, and it doesn't take a genius to figure out this so-called land deal involves Dalton Tire or at least, the land around it."

"Yeah, I had that much figured, sure, but why kill the old bastard? And why Nicole Saunders? Her land was going up for auction regardless. We need to find out who's behind the land deal. Maybe then we can put the pieces together. That reminds me, I have to take another crack at Ted Savage, I don't know how yet, but he has something to do with this."

"There is something—" Emily bit at her lower lip—"I need a favour."

"Favour, now why would you be needin' a favour? Sure, wouldn't I do anything for you? Favour indeed, what is it you want, it's yours if I can afford it." Colm grinned, lifting himself out of the big chair and taking her into his arms.

Emily hugged him, breathing in his scent, she allowed her body to nestle into him, and for a moment, the distraction of their closeness caused her to hesitate. "I need help," she whispered. "I want to find my brother, and I think I have a lead on his whereabouts."

* * *

The brownies were good, but they weren't enough to keep Colm home for long. He decided not to engage Ted Savage directly. The former manager's reluctance to talk to him voluntarily had Colm wondering what it was that Savage was hiding. There had to be something. Savage was very active on social media, with dozens of friends spread all over the world. Some were closer to home, and one, in particular, might know the ex-manager better than most.

The whirlwind marriage of Ted Savage to his Toronto sweetheart resulted in a quick divorce only weeks later. Colm had to be sure, so he checked court records and confirmed that Mrs. Caroline Cuthbertson-Savage had indeed filed for an annulment of the marriage because she was intoxicated at the time and therefore unable to give consent. Since the wedding took place in Las Vegas, and since it had been less than a month since the nuptials, the judge granted the decree of annulment and wished the unhappy couple a nice life. *Who better to talk to than a former wife, who might have an axe to grind?*

Sure'n, I know just the girl for the job. Colm picked up the phone and called Emily.

* * *

CC's Footwear & Leather Boutique occupied the rear addition to a century-old building that had, at one time, served as a saddlery, and despite its low rent location, this was no bargain-basement boutique. The upscale shop held all the trappings of an establishment designed to separate its clientele from their money. Emily fully expected to be met by an impeccably dressed personal sales attendant, offering her a glass of champagne. Instead, two sharp electronic beeps sounded as she stepped through the shop door onto a raised landing.

What the boutique lacked in square footage, it made up for in elegance. Two steps down, she found herself in the main sales area. The muted earth tones of the cloth and panelled furniture occupying the centre of the room matched perfectly with the alternating light and dark walnut chevroned floorboards. Emily readily surmised that this shop was all about personal service. CC had sacrificed precious retail space to accommodate her clients in luxurious comfort and style. The only hint of commerce being the snug alcoves set into the sidewalls, each subtly backlit with LED lighting, created a cozy home for the leather goods and footwear on display. It was clearly a place where women of affluence could enjoy a few moments of divine retail therapy, and men avoided at all costs. Emily wondered why she hadn't visited this shop until now.

The chevrons pointed ahead, beckoning her forward, welcoming her into a comfortable atmosphere perfumed with the scent of new leather.

She noted the absence of a sales counter. A small vanity-styled desk served as the single point of sale for any transactions. A blonde shop attendant, Emily pegged to be in her mid-thirties, busied herself at a small tablet and keyboard. She wore a pair of tortoise-shell spectacles, perched forward on her nose, creating a matronly appearance that belied the woman's stunning good looks. As Emily approached, she looked up over her glasses.

"I'll be right with you," she said without lifting her head. "I swear, these damned screens get smaller and smaller. I can barely see anything with these specs."

"That's ok, take your time, I'm in no rush. I'm looking for Caroline Cuthbertson. I understand she works here."

"That's right," said the blonde, lifting her gaze and removing her glasses to get a better look at who was asking. "Who are you?"

"My name is Emily James. Are you Caroline?"

"It depends. Who's asking and why?"

Before she could respond, the woman said, "James, I've heard that name before. Aren't you the one involved in that turmoil with that lunatic woman who killed all those people a few months ago? Her name was James, right?"

Emily blushed at the recognition. She had lived and worked in Clarksville for four years, and despite the publicity surrounding the Prewitt case, she'd been able to keep a low profile.

"Guilty as charged. I'm surprised you remember my name. I didn't think it had been publicized at all. In fact, I had insisted that the police keep me out of it."

"I didn't read your name anywhere, but this is a small town, and people talk." She held out her hand to Emily.

Emily shook hands, saying, "Yes, I guess they must." *I'm hoping you're no different.*

"Yes, I'm Caroline, please, call me CC, believe me, I know. I'd barely lived here a week, and it seemed the whole town knew who I was and all about my troubles. So, what can I do for you?" She tapped the keyboard one last time, saying, "This will have to keep, for now; I'm guessing you're not here to buy shoes."

Emily retrieved her badge from her purse and presented it to the shopkeeper. "I'm working with the police on a matter concerning the Dalton Tire company. I understand you know Ted Savage."

* * *

For almost two hundred years, Clarksville's business centre dominated a short stretch of what used to be one of Ontario's main highways. As the town grew, shops and businesses expanded. Like the root system of a great oak, buildings extended their reach to the north and south of the corridor. These roots spawned roots of their own creating alleyways and backstreets. Attracted by more affordable rents, many boutiques and small businesses occupied the rear sections of buildings that fronted on the main street. In some cases, customers were allowed to patronize the other company without having to circumnavigate the street.

Ted Savage entered the principal office of Clarksville Cruise Vacations and, with a friendly nod to the clerk behind the desk, indicated he would like to pass through to CC's Footwear & Leather Boutique. Recognizing Ted from previous visits, the clerk acknowledged his request with a warm smile, cocking her head in the direction of the doorway leading to the back section. A small sign read CC's Footwear Rear Entrance.

As Savage opened the door, he heard the distant beep of the alarm keypad as it announced his arrival. The warning alerted shop staff anytime an entry door opened. Making his way down a long, darkened corridor, lit only by the ambient light of the sales floor and the green glow of the exit light at the far end, Savage took care not to disturb the overloaded shelving bordering both sides. He expected Caroline to appear at the opposite end. She always checked the passageway when she heard the door open. This time, however, Caroline failed to appear. He was about to step out into the sales area when he heard his name. He stopped, slipped into a shallow alcove at the mouth of the passageway and waited. Hidden from view, he froze in place, listening to the conversation between the proprietor and her customer.

* * *

CC shook her head and laughed, "Yeah I guess you could say I know him. I was married to the man for all of two minutes."

"Wow! That long. I guess it didn't work out," said Emily with a slight chuckle as she lifted a tan coloured handbag from a small display next to the desk.

As Emily examined the bag, CC said, "That's Italian leather, it's a Gucci knock off, but it's really nicely made and only a fraction of the cost."

"I can see it's well-made, I'll have to put it on my Christmas list," said Emily with an admiring smile. "You were saying?"

"Saying?" CC asked, crinkling her nose. "Oh! Yes, Ted and I—two minutes, well, more like two weeks."

"Two weeks, how long had you known each other," asked Emily?

"A while, we dated for about six months, and when he took the job with Dalton, we thought he'd found the job of a lifetime. He asked me to move here. That's when Ted started getting serious. He was living here already, and the long-distance thing seemed silly so, I moved down here. A week later we went to Vegas. I guess you could say we did it backwards. We had the honeymoon first, and on the last night there, we both got wasted and woke up married to each other the next day. When we got back, Dalton fired Ted. We were devastated."

"Why, what happened? Did Ted do something wrong?"

CC shrugged, "I don't know. His cousin said it was because he took time off, but there had to be more."

"Ah yes," said Emily remembering what Colm had told her. "He works in sales, right?"

"Ha! That's a laugh, sales? Well, I guess you could call it that, after all, he runs the show now. Jim fired Ted and then took his job. Some cousin," CC's face flushed. "I never understood that part. Ted was Jim's boss, but Jim fired Ted. I get it, I just don't know how you do that to family."

"It couldn't be just for taking a holiday," said Emily, "there had to be another reason."

"It wouldn't have been the first time, believe me. If you ask around and I did, it was a common occurrence at Dalton, but the real truth was Ted couldn't do the job. He knew nothing about the tire business and to top it off, he's an anal-retentive ass. He took a college course in business administration and wound up over his head in a job he knew nothing about. He's not a bad man, but everyone hated him there. Harry Dalton had no respect for him, and Jim told me that the guys in the plant used to put his picture on a dartboard in the lunchroom. They'd each throw five bucks in the pot and the first to poke his eyes out won. No one respected him, and if it hadn't been for Jim, he never would have been hired in the first place."

Emily listened intently, digesting the fact that Jim Roberts was Savage's cousin. Colm couldn't know this, or he'd have told her.

"So, why did you guys split? It's not like you didn't know each other."

CC pointed to the settee in the centre of the sales floor.

"Let's have a seat," she said, "this might take a while."

Emily followed CC. As she stepped past a dimly lit alcove landing, Emily asked, "What's back there?"

CC flashed a cursory glance over her shoulder, "Oh, just some storage and the back entrance from the front of the shop."

"The back from the front?" Emily raised an eyebrow.

"Yeah, sounds odd, right? It's my back door, but it leads to the front of this building. There's a travel agency in the front. So really it's my back door and the back door"—she pointed to the door through which Emily had entered—"is my front door."

"Ok, I get it," Emily said, thankful for the chance to sit. "So, where were we?"

"I thought I knew Ted," replied CC. "When we lived in Toronto, he was a different man. He had his audio-visual business and seemed happy doing that, but the money wasn't steady, and that made him moody. I should have seen the signs sooner. Not long after Ted started at the plant, he changed. I never did figure it out."

"Changed how?"

CC's chin quivered as she recalled the memory.

"Ted hardly ever touched alcohol. He couldn't handle booze. Except for that one night in Vegas, I don't think I'd ever seen him drunk. After he lost his job, he hit the booze a lot and started making crazy threats about getting even. It scared me, enough to know I wasn't going to spend my life walking on eggshells around a man who might become violent. My mother did it. I vowed I never would."

"You say Ted became violent. How, exactly?"

CC's lips tightened, "He never became violent. What I said was, I wasn't going to take that chance." CC glanced around the empty shop as if checking to see who might be listening. "I probably shouldn't be telling you this, but Ted loves guns. He has dozens of them. He spends a lot of time at the range. He even has practice bullets that fire wax. He loads them himself and shoots them at targets in the spare room. I'm not bothered by guns you understand; I grew up around them. They don't scare me—and I'm a pretty decent shot if I do say so myself."

"Whoa! He shoots guns in the house," Emily interjected. "How does that work? Don't the neighbours complain about the noise? My God! That has to be dangerous." Emily's mind reeled at the thought of Colm shooting his gun in the house. She couldn't conjure the image at all.

"No, it's not dangerous. The wax is soft, and the noise is no more than a cap pistol might make. I didn't approve you understand, but Ted actually let me shoot him with one, and all it did was leave a small red mark. He said it stung, but the pain was no worse than snapping an elastic band against your skin. What bothered me was the day he got fired, Ted flipped out. We had a cat, and he began shooting the poor thing in the butt with the wax bullets. He thought it was hilarious to watch the poor thing launch itself into the air whenever he hit it. It was cruel, and I told him so. I couldn't allow it to continue, so, without telling Ted, I re-homed it with one of my customers. She loves cats, and I know he is well cared for."

CC's eyes welled up with tears, "The next night he got blind drunk and threatened to shoot me for letting the cat out. That scared the hell out of me. I left and never went back. I hired a lawyer and sued for divorce. Instead, my lawyer applied for annulment, and it was granted. After that, I decided to stay here and used what savings I had to open this place. It's not Eaton's or The Bay, but I make a living. Everything was fine until about a month ago. I hadn't seen or heard from Ted since the annulment. Then, out of the blue, he shows up here. He won't leave me alone, and keeps saying he wants me back."

The tears were flowing now, and Emily knew she'd broken the dam. "If he's as dangerous as you say, you need a protective order."

CC shook her head. "No, no, you don't know him. A protective order would send him over the edge. I can't risk that. I can handle Ted, but crossing him is the wrong thing to do. I should have broken it off long before we were married"—she managed a wry smile—"I thought I could change him, but..." CC turned her face away. The tears soaked her cheeks, and her nose was running.

Emily searched her bag for some tissues and handed them to CC.

CC wiped mascara blackened eyes, looking at the mess on the tissue she said, "I must look frightful."

Emily gave her a sympathetic smile and nodded. "You might want to freshen up. I didn't mean to upset you, and I really should get going. You were going to say—but?"

CC nodded, blowing her nose, "But—he told me Harry Dalton would pay someday. I never knew what he meant by that, and I never asked. Now please, I've said too much. I have to get back to work."

As if on cue, the door beeped, but no one entered. CC looked to the rear of the shop. "It must be the back entrance," she said as she stood to check. CC returned a moment later struggling to muster a smile. "Must have been a false alarm."

"False alarm? Does that happen a lot?"

"Sometimes, the door is plainly marked, but people will open it out of curiosity," replied CC, edging her way to the front door. Emily followed, taking the hint.

CC held the door for Emily, "You know, it's been a slow day, and I'm a mess, I think I'll close early and go home. If there's nothing else?"

"I guess that's everything for now. I really am sorry. I didn't mean to upset you." Emily thanked her and assured CC she would be back, but next time it would be as a customer. The door beeped again as she left the shop. *Hmm, only one beep.*

G. A. PICKSTOCK

36

EMILY'S REPORT OF HER visit to Savage's ex-wife cemented Colm's suspicion that Savage was in this up to his neck. *And isn't that the problem? Savage is almost too obvious.* "And why would that be?" he asked himself out loud.

"Why would what be?" Kendra Jacobs poked her head through the doorway.

"Oh, just thinking out loud." Colm stood as Kendra entered the office.

"For heaven's sake, sit down. There's no need to stand in my presence." She sat across from him, indicating he should do likewise.

"You know that feeling you get when everything points in one direction, but your gut tells you something's missing, and even if you find the something, you're still not sure?"

"No, Colm, I don't. But then, I'm not a detective. I have two mysteries in my life right now. Where are my missing cops, and how do I program my DVR? Neither of which I have answers for. I'm not sure I can help, but go ahead, bounce it off me. Let's see what we come up with."

An hour and three coffees later, Kendra asked, "So what's your next move?"

"I'd like to bring Savage in for questioning, but I've got nothing on the guy. I can't convince myself that he's the killer, but I know he's connected. I can feel it—" he poked himself in the stomach— "in here."

"What about the ex, will she file a complaint?"

"No, according to Emily, she's too scared. The poor woman was beside herself when Emily left her. She told me the gun-crazy—"

Kendra saw the light flash in Colm's eyes. "What? You just thought of something, what is it?"

"I don't dare tell you, but if it works, I'll have him here this afternoon." Colm stood almost knocking his chair over in the bargain. Without waiting for Kendra to respond, he said, "Sorry! Gotta go, wish me luck."

* * *

Ted Savage paced around his apartment, holding his phone to his ear. Fed up with being kept on hold, he was reaching for his keys when Jim Roberts' voice came over the speaker.

"What is it, Ted? I'm busy."

"Busy! I'll give you busy. I need my money. Now! That stupid ex of mine is blabbing her mouth all over the place, and I want out. You promised me a payday, and I'm coming out there to collect. I'm telling you Jim, no excuses. I did what you wanted, now it's time to pay me. Have my money ready or else!"

"I can't raise that kind of cash in just five minutes, you know that. I haven't been paid myself, yet. I'm sorry, but you have to be patient."

Ted wasn't listening. "You don't understand. CC talked to the cops. She's spilling her guts to some broad who's working with them. All I want is my money, and then all you'll see of me is elbows and assholes. I'm outta here. Get me?"

"Can't do it, Ted. I don't have that kind of money available to me," said Jim.

"Find it! I'm not fucking around, Jim. Get me my money. Write a cheque on the company if you have to, but get me my dough. I'm on my way." Ted stabbed the end button cutting Jim's final response before he could hear it. He grabbed his keys just as the knock came to the door.

* * *

My turn, he thought as he stepped off the elevator leading to Savage's apartment. *This time I will find cause to detain you.* Colm led the way with two young constables close behind. One was tall and lanky with an elongated oval face, long chin and wide, thin lips. Colm figured him to be just on the right side of the minimum age range for the OPP recruitment parameters, a definite rookie. The other, a bit shorter than his partner and sporting a thirty-pound weight advantage, was round-faced with a bulbous nose, and perhaps, Colm thought, had few years under his belt. As he met them in the parking lot, he immediately labelled them *Ernie and Bert*. They were temporary replacements for the missing six-pack, and although that still left the detachment five men down, Colm was happy for the backup. As they approached Savage's door, he stopped short and listened to sounds emanating from within.

"Sounds like Mr. Savage is in a bad mood. Be ready, this guy probably won't want to cooperate. If he gets out of hand, all I want you to do is cuff him, stuff him into the cruiser and get his arse back to the detachment. Got it?"

The grins on their faces told Colm they understood, and he could only think that these two relished the possibility of a dust-up. Colm's heavy thumping on Savage's door reverberated down the hallway, causing the trio to glance around the corridor to see who might poke their noses out to investigate the noise. A moment later, the lock snicked, and the door opened.

"You again," said Savage holding the door ajar. "I told you I ain't talkin' to you without a lawyer."

"That's ok, Mr. Savage, we're here on a noise complaint." He stepped sideways to reveal his companions. "Were you going somewhere?" Colm took note of the keys in Savage's hand.

"As a matter of fact, I was just leaving," said Savage as he opened the door and stepped into the hallway, forcing Colm to move to the side. *Ernie and Bert* stood shoulder to shoulder, blocking Savage's passage toward the elevator.

"I'm afraid, Mr. Savage, we've received several complaints of gunshots emanating from inside your apartment, and we're here to check it out." Colm blocked Savage's way corralling him on three sides. Savage had no place to go except to retreat into his apartment.

"Gunfire? Bullshit! Yeah, I've got guns, so what?" Savage's face crimsoned. "Who says I've been shooting in here? Are you crazy? How the hell can I shoot a gun in a two-bedroom apartment? You guys are on glue."

"I'm sorry, Mr. Savage, but we have it on good authority that you habitually shoot wax bullets and that you shoot them at your cat." Colm grinned as Savage's eyes grew to twice their size. *Bullseye! He just figured out where I got my info.*

"What the actual fu— that bitch! That absolute bitch! I can't believe it. She did talk to the cops," Savage railed, pushing forward trying to get past the policemen. *Ernie and Bert* didn't budge, preventing Savage from moving.

"Am I under arrest?"

"No, sir, but we do have some questions for you," Colm said. "Now, if we could—"

Savage cut him off, "I know my rights. I don't have to talk to you, and if I'm not under arrest, you can't keep me here. So if you don't mind, get the hell out of my way. I have business to attend to."

Colm was adamant. "We need to see your firearms, Mr. Savage. We're concerned about the safety of the tenants in this building. Shooting your guns inside your apartment is a violation of the law. Now, are you going to let us in or not?"

Colm stood his ground. Savage's eyes darted from one to another and back again, gauging his chances with the three policemen. His shoulders slackened as he turned to unlock the door. "OK, fine c'm'in," he mumbled.

"I'm sorry, what?" asked Colm.

"Ok, fine, you can come in." The apartment door swung inward, revealing an untidy living room and a coffee table with three handguns on it. Realizing his mistake, Savage spun around too late to stop Colm. He was already deep into the room, along with his backup.

"Mr. Savage, these guns are improperly stored. Can you explain why?"

"I-I was cleaning them," Savage said, reaching to pick up one of the revolvers.

"Stop! Right there," Colm yelled, his hand instantly on the grip of his sidearm. Ernie and Bert already had their weapons drawn and aimed at Savage. "Step back, Mr. Savage, away from the table. Keep your hands where we can see them."

"Don't be stupid," Savage argued. "They aren't loaded, I was just—"

"All the same, Mr. Savage, we don't want any nasty accidents now, do we?"

Savage stepped away from the coffee table, his eyes transfixed on the two semi-automatic pistols, still pointing in his direction. Colm followed his gaze and said, "That's ok fellas, we're grand, I don't think Mr. Savage wants any trouble now. Do you, sir?"

Colm turned to *Bert* and said, "Let's detain Mr. Savage for the moment, so we can clear these firearms and make sure everything is safe."

Bert nodded, holstered his gun and pulled out a set of handcuffs. Taking Savage by the arm, he fastened the cuffs behind his back and told the man to have a seat.

"Am I under arrest?" Savage asked, flopping awkwardly into his couch.

"No," replied Colm. "We're just detaining you for your safety and ours until we can secure these weapons and satisfy ourselves that there are no threats."

Without any direction from Colm, the constables checked the apartment for occupants and any other unsecured weapons.

Ernie came back into the living room, holding a shotgun and a semi-automatic pistol. "Look what I found, Sarge," he said, grinning, making his mouth look even wider.

Savage spoke up. "Hey, you guys got a warrant for this? There's nothing in there that concerns any of you, and you don't have my permission to search."

Colm responded, "Well sir, you invited us in, and the evidence says otherwise. Look around you. We have unsecured firearms out in the open. You say you're cleaning them, yet there's no evidence of that on the table. Just before we knocked, we heard an argument coming from in here. You told us you were heading out on business, which leads me to believe those guns were going to remain unsecured. The place stinks of gunpowder and cordite. All of which tells me that the complaints about gunshots have merit. That gives me probable cause to search this premise."

It was a bluff, but one he had to play. None of it would hold up under testimony. However, he needed leverage. "Mr. Savage, the very least I could charge you with is unsafe storage of firearms, and judging by the evidence, I could get a warrant. A forensic team will undoubtedly find evidence of the discharge of those firearms, and as I'm sure you are aware, it is unlawful to discharge a firearm within the town limits."

Savage opened his mouth as if to speak then immediately closed it again. "You have something to say, Mr. Savage?"

Savage shook his head. "No comment."

"Right, let's get these guns secured, and take Mr. Savage to the detachment." He motioned to *Ernie and Bert* to gather the firearms. "We'll be taking these into custody, Mr. Savage. I guess we'll let the Crown decide whether or not you get them back."

* * *

"Let him go!" Colm couldn't believe what he was being told. "Let him go? You've got to be kidding?" The question was rhetorical, he didn't expect an answer, but the one he received blindsided him. He had Savage dead to rights on the gun storage charges and yet, here was the Crown Attorney saying, "Let him go."

"I've got him in an interview room sweating bullets over these firearms charges, and I don't care if you charge him or not, I want to know where he fits in with the murder of Harry Dalton. He's in it, I know he is. I just don't know how." Colm paced back and forth in front of Kendra's desk.

Newly appointed as the senior Crown Attorney for Clarksville, Gerry Lockheart sat stone-faced across from Kendra. He had almost twenty-five years in the Crown Attorney's office, and he'd watched this scene play out many times. It was the same old story, a young, ambitious cop had his man, or so he thought, had the evidence and because there were bigger fish to catch, he wanted to use the leverage that that created to go deep-sea fishing. The problem was, the evidence was tainted. Ted Savage had invoked his right to silence and was adamantly remaining so.

"Look at him," Lockheart said, pointing at the video monitor. "He doesn't look worried to me, he's calm and unemotional, and do you know why?"

Colm stared at the Crown Attorney in disbelief. "No, why don't you tell me."

"The man knows he's not in any trouble. He's got you beat." Lockheart shifted his three-hundred-pound carcass sideways to direct his remarks toward the still-pacing detective. The arms of the chair dug into his sides, making it uncomfortable to sit. "For God's sake, man, stand in one place. You're making me dizzy, and this effing chair doesn't flex easily."

Colm stopped pacing and took the last remaining seat. He turned to

Kendra. "Help me out here. I'm just after arresting the man on gun charges, and he wants me to let him go." Colm's eyes pleaded with his boss to step in.

Lockheart jumped in, "Are you going to charge him for Dalton's murder?"

Colm fixed his gaze on the Crown Attorney, and through clenched jaws, he muttered, "No, I can't do that. I'm not so sure he did it, but he's involved, I feel it in my gut."

"Your gut isn't good enough, and if you aren't going to charge him, you can't question him about it. You can, I suppose, but he doesn't have to answer, and I'm not prosecuting the firearms charges because they won't stick. He owns them legally, they were in his possession in their registered place of storage, and you can't prove he wasn't cleaning them as he says he was. He has a right to have them unsecured in his home, if for no other reason other than to admire them. As for the shooting indoors, unless you can produce a witness—you're screwed. And more to the point"—Lockheart pointed again at the screen—"he knows it; let him go."

The order was final, and as Lockheart pried himself out of his chair, he flashed a 'don't mess with me' look at Colm. "Get me something solid on this guy, and I'll back you to the hilt. But right now you've got nothing I can win with. I won't even try."

Finally, separating himself from the ill-fitting furniture, he straightened himself out and addressed Kendra Jacobs. "I'm sorry, Staff Sergeant, but my hands are tied. I'd like to help, but a gun charge like this is too weak. The man has rights, and I'm not so sure he's committed any crime. Hell, I have guns of my own and no, contrary to what many think, they don't have to be locked up all the time." He turned back to Colm, "Detective, why don't you try using sugar instead of shit to get what you want?"

G. A. PICKSTOCK

37

TED SAVAGE HADN'T SET foot in the Dalton factory since his termination. Nevertheless, he knew exactly where he was going, and not even Isobel with her silky blond hair, come hither smile, and bedroom eyes could deter him from marching straight into his cousin's office.

The door flew open, crashing into the adjacent wall with such force as to drive the doorknob through the drywall, causing the door to jam in place. Startled, Jim Roberts leapt from his seat, flipping his plush leather chair onto its side.

"What the hell—"

"Where's my goddam' money?" Savage demanded. "I've had enough bullshit for one day. I want my money, Jim, or so help me—"

"So, help you what?" Jim shot back, picking up his chair. "Shut the door and calm yourself down."

Savage pulled the door free from the wall and allowed it to close. Jim barely had time to blink, and Savage was on him. Face to face, his cousin demanded again, "Money, now. I've had enough, and I'm getting the hell out of here. I just spent the last two hours at the cop shop staring at four walls and a bunch of bogus gun charges. I'm done. Give me my money."

Ted's words shot through Jim Roberts with an icy sharpness. His cousin, until now a trusted ally, was suddenly a huge liability. If Ted started flapping his gums, he could mess up their whole deal. The chilling realization of the peril his mere existence presented forced Jim to think of an answer and fast.

"I said, sit down," Jim ordered, attempting to take control. "I told you, I haven't been paid yet either. I can't give you what I don't have."

Ted sat, grudgingly listening to his cousin. "I don't care. You can get the money, I know. Don't forget, I used to sit on your side of that desk. You have access to the company's chequebook. You can get money if you need it."

"You don't understand. That money was never coming from the company. Besides, with Harry dead, Anne Dalton is in control now, and she's no fool. If I start writing cheques, she's gonna want to know what's going on. I can't do it. Look, it won't be long now. The deal is still on, and the money will come, you have to be patient."

"Bullshit! Yeah, I guess Harry dying did change things, but don't try to bullshit me. Anne Dalton never gave a fiddler's fart about this place. It's my guess she still don't, and with the cops snooping around, I need to get out of Dodge, and for that, I need money now! What can you come up with?"

"Nothing, you're wrong about Anne. She's got this place tied up tight. I can't—no, I won't, I don't dare do anything that will attract attention. Not now."

Roberts fell silent, allowing the deadness in the air to permeate the room, while his own mind juggled and mixed his thoughts into a cohesive plan to assuage his cousin's ire. The answer came in a single moment of clarity. The solution made sense. Moments later, he said, "If you insist on leaving, I might be able to lay my hands on fifty."

"Fifty, fifty what—bananas?" Ted glowered at his cousin, "That's a damn-sight less than we talked about. What happened to six figures?"

Jim swivelled sideways in his chair and pointed to a map on the wall depicting the Dalton plant, and all the land surrounding it. Ted had seen the map before. It was, after all, his office before Jim took over. It was the same site plan that had hung on that wall when he ran the plant. Yet, there was something different about the cartography. It was the same image, but for some reason, it looked bigger.

"You see that?" Jim asked. "That is the future of this town. Take a close look at that map. That's where the money is, and until that happens"—Jim turned back to his cousin—"there ain't no money, not for me and not for you. What I can do is make a call. Maybe I can get you fifty-K. It's enough to get you out of town for a while. When this deal goes through, I'll send the rest."

"When do I get the money?"

"Midnight, I'll call and tell you where."

Fighting the urge to rip his cousin's arms off and beat him to death with the wet ends, Ted stood and made his way to the door. He cast his gaze back over his shoulder, "Fifty-K, I'll be there. If you screw me, you'll be sorry."

Jim followed Ted's departure on the video monitor. Convinced Ted had actually left the property, he lifted his phone and dialled the number. The line engaged, and without waiting, he said, "Savage is nervous, he wants money." Jim listened for a moment. "Fifty should do it, midnight—" he listened again—"I'll let him know."

* * *

The skiff slid through the still waters of Dangar Cove, a shallow body of water separating the tiny subdivision of Dangar Island from the north shore of the Clarksville River. Over the centuries, the river had receded drying up the land and forming a natural causeway connecting the island to the mainland. Dangar Island retained its name, and because it was situated behind Clarksville's first cemetery, the residents still enjoyed the benefit of hidden access to their island.

Ordinarily weed-encroached and lily pad laden, this time of year, the watery vegetation had all but died off, making access by water easy, and the small wooden vessel slipped silently onto the north bank. Like a ghost, the Ghillie suit stepped out and set off across the field.

The walk to the hide had its risk. Ninety metres of open ground, even at night, was ninety too many. The camouflaged suit did little to shield Shinkwinn's silhouette from the moonlight. Reaching the tree-line that surrounded the small cemetery, Shinkwinn settled in place. Eighty feet away, a gravel roadway encircled the graveyard looping back on itself near the entrance from the main road. A towering stone cross stood a few feet from the road. In daylight, one could see that it proclaimed to all who visited that this was the burial place of Sir William Clark, the founder and Laird of Clarksville. The old cross loomed large in the moonlight. Shadows from the trees danced in the wind and the lights from passing motorists strobed across the many headstones and monuments, each, in turn, briefly illuminating a solitary figure sitting on the stone foundation of the cross. Shinkwinn had watched for ten minutes as the man arrived on foot. He'd paced around the cross, as though searching for someone or something, coming to rest at last on its base.

Whenever a car passed, he would rise in expectation of the arrival of someone. But someone would never arrive. *Not this night, not ever.*

Settled and calm, the crisp night air drifted across Shinkwinn's nostrils bringing with it the unmistakable scent of grilled meat. Memories of the tasks flooded back, causing a slight wince of regret. Killing Nicole Saunders was unavoidable. All she had to do was sign the papers. She would have walked away with a couple of G's in her pocket and her life. Instead, she'd insisted she could save the property, believing that once the taxes were paid, she'd sell it for what it was really worth. When her attempt failed, and the land fell under the tax man's hammer, Nicole contacted Shinkwinn threatening to go public. Shinkwinn couldn't take that risk, and so, as the Ghillie suited figure lay in position, visions of the aftermath of that day were pushed aside as there was another job to do, and a clear mind was vital.

* * *

His instructions were simple. No cars, no cabs, no transportation other than his own two feet. He pulled his pickup truck to the side of the road and walked the last kilometre to the cemetery. Savage made a cursory inspection to ensure he was alone and sat. According to Jim, a vehicle would drive in and make the circuit, stopping once at a random grave, flash the headlights and drive off. Once out of sight, he would collect a package and leave.

The small voice in Savage's head told him something was wrong. The car had not arrived yet. Each set of headlights that came near sent his heart into palpitations. He would have left by now but for the money. He needed that to get away. And so he forced himself to be patient.

Aside from the wind and the coolness of the evening, it was a beautiful night, and Savage forced himself to think of better times to come. Fifty-thousand wasn't nearly enough, but it would do until Jim ponied up the rest. All he had to do was wait.

With the wind at his back, he heard noises coming from the island. Someone was barbecuing. *Midnight and some jackass is having a party. I bet the neighbours are impressed.* The thoughts floated through his mind as the aroma of grilled steak wafted its way into his nose. A dog barked, and he heard voices, muffled sounds he could not decipher. The aroma of the steak lingered, making him hungry.

The voices ceased, and the dog was now silent, leaving Savage alone with only his thoughts for company. Another sound, more familiar, came to his ears. He recognized the distinctive clack of steel sliding against steel— a rifle bolt closing on a breach.

"Oh, God—"

The realization hit him at the same instant the massive forty-five calibre round converted his head into a fine pink mist. The waning Hunter's moon hung high in the western sky, bathing the lifeless body of Ted Savage in its cold silvery light. The grass around the cross turned into a deep crimson carpet as the Ghillie suited ghost of Dangar Island slipped back into the river evaporating into the night.

G. A. PICKSTOCK

38

A LINE OF POLICE cars with their bubblegum lights flashing through the early morning fog blocked the entrance to the cemetery. The misty haze had cleared slightly, and from her vantage point, Emily could make out the forms and figures of police officers as they secured the area. Bob Gentry knelt over a dark figure lying prone alongside the large stone cross.

Crime scene tape encircling the area draped from one headstone to the next like a neon yellow crepe party streamer. The plastic tape was not at all festive, and judging by the look on Bob Gentry's face, this might prove a disturbing sight. *Maybe I should have stayed home.* She vacillated over whether to turn back when Colm pulled in behind her. *Too late to chicken out now.*

Gentry removed a long thin needle from the dead man's torso. A quick glance at the display caused him to frown. He gazed up at the couple as they approached.

"I'd stay back if I were you," said Gentry catching Emily's eye. "It's not pretty."

Colm opened his mouth to speak and caught himself. He recognized Ted Savage from the clothes he was wearing. The man wore the same peacoat and boots he'd worn on their last encounter.

"Damn! I know this guy," he said. "Ted Savage, Jaysus! I'm just after interrogating this guy. What the hell—?"

"Near as I can figure, he's been dead about nine or ten hours. Hard to tell for sure. It was cold last night—" He waved his arm around at all the fog— "the ground is warm, but the air is cold, which makes liver temp iffy. His liver temp is twenty-two point seven. Considering the ambient temp last night and the body temp, that's as close as I can come. If I had to guess, I'd say this happened between eight and ten last night, maybe a bit later. He's in full rigor, and that means at least six hours, maybe twelve."

Emily stood a few steps back, trying to keep her meagre breakfast down. No one had mentioned how Mr. Savage had died yet, and from what she saw, it wasn't an accident. Little remained of the poor man's face, and the back of his head was gone. He lay there on the ground, slightly tilted to his left as he must have fallen and twisted with the force of the projectile spinning him as it hit. There was little to identify the man from physical attributes, and Emily wondered how Colm could be so sure that this was, in fact, Ted Savage. She figured that the coroner would have to use forensic science to make a positive identification. Still, Colm seemed convinced.

Braving the scene before her, Emily stepped closer and sidled up to Colm. Placing her hand in the crook of his left arm, she asked, "Are you sure he's who you say he is?"

"Aye, as sure as I know my own name," Colm said. "See now, isn't that the same coat he was wearing just yesterday. Sure'n, I've seen him in it twice now. And there's no mistaking those boots. Still, to be sure—" he stooped to check the body— "is it ok for me to move him, Bob?"

"I can't see why not. I have all I need. The boys will be picking him up shortly. Forensics has all the pictures and such. The crew is searching the area to see where the shooter might have been, but I wouldn't hold out much hope. Whoever is doing this is a pro. Don't look for a bullet. You won't find one." Gentry pointed to a greyish mark at the point of entry. "We've seen that before."

Colm nodded. "Yeah, I noticed that already. I want his wallet. Need to confirm his ID." He spun Savage's corpse sideways. Reaching into his back pocket, he retrieved the man's wallet, sifting through the contents as he stood. "Not much here," he said. "Just a bank card, his health card, a coupon for a free car wash and his license. No money." He turned to show a wide-eyed Emily the driver's license with Savage's name on it. "What?"

The picture on the license was grainy and out of focus, but Emily knew precisely who she was looking at. "Oh, God, Colm. That's the guy who attacked Sammi."

* * *

Emily poured her third coffee of the morning. Raising her cup, she offered Colm a cup also. He shook his head and said, "When were you going to tell me this? Jaysus, Ted Savage attacked Sammi in the hospital. Why didn't you say something before this? I could have had him locked up."

"I didn't know it was him until you showed me his driver's license. All I'd ever heard was his name," Emily retorted. "There's something else I learned that I don't think you know."

Emily set her coffee on the table and sat across from Colm. She hadn't had time to tell him everything she'd learned from CC. Once he knew about the guns and his shooting indoors, he'd rushed off, leaving her on the verge of disclosing the vital information.

"Oh, and what would that be now?"

"I bet you don't know who the late Mr. Savage's cousin is?"

"It's a salesman, sure, at the tire plant," said Colm.

"Nope! It's none other than my favourite neighbour. It seems Mr. Roberts has been keeping a secret from us."

The words resounded in Colm's mind, turning and whirling throughout his thoughts. With his gaze transfixed on the wall opposite him, his mind's eye played the interview in Jim's office in fast-forward, then in reverse and forward again in slow motion. The man had deliberately lied to him, a lie of omission surely, but a lie, nonetheless. His mouth dried up, and for a moment, he saw nothing. Finally returning to the present, he said, "Why—" he reached across and took Emily's coffee from her, swallowing hard to wet his tongue— "didn't you tell me this earlier?"

"I was going to, but you bolted through the door so quickly that I couldn't. You were so intent on picking Savage up for the guns, you were gone before I had a chance to say anything."

"This opens up a whole new can of worms. Why would he lie to me? All he told me was that Savage's cousin worked at the plant."

Colm moved to the living room and peeked out the window. Jim's car was in his driveway. He checked the time on his watch and started for the door.

"Where you going?" Emily followed him, grabbing her jacket. "I'm coming too."

"Next door. Mr. Roberts has some 'splainin' to do."

* * *

Jim's front door gave way as Colm knocked. Jim Roberts' unit was a mirror image to Emily's except for a partition wall that he had constructed shortly after moving in. The wall created a short hallway forming a barrier to cold drafts entering the living space in the winter. They had been here before, and Colm remembered the gathering of suspects that had occupied the room at the time. Audri Seavers had sat in the big armchair, her shocked and frightened face imploring Colm to understand as he and Emily had walked in on what appeared to be an inquisition. This time the room was void of life, and an eerie silence filled the entire home. Dampness permeated the air as Colm, and Emily stepped further into the condo.

"I don't like this, Colm, I don't think anyone's home," Emily whispered.

"You might be right, funny though, his car is outside," said Colm. "Maybe he's in the backyard."

As they moved through to the kitchen, a tiny voice deep inside Colm nagged him to be on guard. The coppery scent of blood brought Colm to a halt. Standing in the doorway, he prayed he was wrong. He had not announced their arrival more out of caution than conspiracy. Emily nudged him, attempting to push past. Colm held his arm across her body, preventing her from moving further into the room. He took one more tentative step, and as they made the short turn into the kitchen, Emily gasped. Jim Roberts lay, lodged between the patio door and the doorframe. His head and shoulders rested across the threshold as his blood wicked its way from his shirt into the ever-darkening terracotta tile-work of the kitchen floor.

"Oh, God! Colm is he—"

"Stay here," Colm said as he sprang to the doorway. He pushed the door sideways, releasing the pressure holding Jim's body. Colm checked for a pulse.

"He's alive, Em, call 911."

Colm rolled Jim onto his back. Blood oozed from a mass of torn flesh in the man's shoulder. Colm snatched a towel from the table and jammed it into the wound. The unconscious man clung to life by a thread, but he'd lost a lot of blood. Still, his shallow breathing gave Colm faint hope that the man might pull through. He held tight to the towel as time stood still, and at last, they heard the sirens.

39

THE ATTENDING MEDICS TRANSPORTED Jim to the Clarksville trauma centre. Colm and Emily remained behind to secure what was now a crime scene. Little had changed since Emily's first visit to this house. Jim still kept an untidy home. No doubt, relying on his standby excuse that since his wife had passed away, he had lost any ambition to stay on top of the upkeep. Dishes remained in the sink, stacked precariously, threatening to crash down at the slightest vibration. Newspapers and magazines, along with his mail, covered the surface of Jim's kitchen table, all save for a small space reserved for his own use.

The couple searched the house. Satisfied that they were alone, they surveyed the scene. There was blood on the door. Colm stepped out onto the deck, careful not to contaminate the blood-soaked tiles where Jim had fallen. His blood had showered the glass just an inch or two higher than his shoulder.

"Jim must have been standing right here with the door closed behind him," said Colm. "He had to have seen his attacker, but at this range, why isn't the glass broken? A bullet passing through flesh at this distance should have shattered it. Yet, it's intact."

Emily looked up from the papers she was sifting through. "Why would that be?"

"Why, indeed?" said Colm. "Look at the blood pattern."

The blood spatter formed a starburst shape with streaks radiating in all directions on the window. An elongated streak formed an almost straight line down to the bottom of the door. Closer inspection revealed several small silver beads resting in the door's framework. Colm knew instantly what he was looking at. And then he knew why the door remained intact. The glass had been reinforced with security film. It would take a blow from a sledgehammer to even crack it, let alone break it. Judging by where Jim must have been standing, even at one-thousand feet per second, a mercury bullet passing through a heavy jacket, flesh and bone, would not have enough kinetic energy to break the security glass.

"I'm not sure you should be looking at those," Colm said, as he stepped inside. "Forensics will be here shortly, and we don't want to contaminate the scene any more than we already have."

"I'm wearing gloves," Emily replied, waving her hands in the air to show Colm the blue rubber gloves she'd pulled from her pocket. "There's something here you should see. I think I know why Jim didn't tell you about Ted Savage."

Colm stepped beside Emily. She held a blue three-ring folder, and as she flipped open the cover, Colm read the title page.

Blackmore/Dalton Holdings LLC - Urban Reclamation Proposal.

* * *

Three minutes north-east of the Macdonald-Cartier Freeway at interchange 394, the small firm of Llandeso Investments Limited occupied only one office in the building. Llandeso had one project in the works, the culmination of three years of planning. Three years of painstaking and meticulous manipulation of circumstances and events designed to put one man in the crosshairs of an enraged community, while creating millions in profits for Llandeso and its shareholders.

Llandeso was within minutes of success, but for one fatal event. Harrison Dalton was dead, a fact, that in and of itself, didn't bother Llandeso's CEO. Harrison Dalton was expendable. It was the timing of his demise that concerned the company director. As the CEO of Llandeso Investments sat fuming in her soft leather chair watching the traffic flow past her third-floor window, she vowed to find out who it was that leaked the information. Because someone had leaked it, and it wasn't Harrison Dalton. Of that, she was damned sure.

* * *

Emily rested the folder on the arm of her reading chair. She had read it twice from cover to cover as had Colm.

"I think we've found our motive," she said. "God, if news of this gets out, there will be hell to pay."

Colm agreed. The contents of the blue dossier held dire consequences for Clarksville and offered an ironclad motive for murdering Harry Dalton. The fact that Jim Roberts had it in his possession confused him.

"If Jim knew about this, then it fits that he has something to do with Harry's murder. I had Savage pegged as the shooter. Jim's hiding that they were cousins points to them being on it together, but Savage's death changes everything. If Jim's not involved in Harry's murder, why does he have this portfolio, and why is he lying in hospital with a gaping, great hole in his shoulder?" He reached for the dossier and flipped through it once again.

"Blackmore might be the key, and I think we need to talk to Anne Dalton again. Anne knew more than she let on when I spoke to her. Sure, I didn't like the way she reacted when I told her Harry was dead. It was like she expected it. I tell you what, if the two of them are in cahoots, let's not give them a chance to talk to each other. You do Blackmore, and I'll have another go at Anne Dalton. Only this time, I won't be so agreeable."

Emily nodded, standing, she reached for a sweater draped across the back of her chair and slipped it on. "Blackmore it is," she smiled. "Should I take a copy of this with me?" She picked up the folder and tucked it under her arm.

"No ma'am, that's evidence. No, we'll drop it at the detachment on the way. One thing, though," Colm's eyes became serious. "Whoever's out there pulling triggers is still out there. Our main suspect is dead, and his cousin has one foot in the grave. I'll have a guard put on him, and we need to be extra careful, understand?"

"I'll be careful. I promise I won't get into any more vans or let gravel-voiced strangers talk to me." She grinned as she slipped past him to open the door.

Colm was about to admonish her again but held his tongue. Nothing he could say would dissuade Emily from pushing forward with this, and he knew that she would not purposely put herself in danger. She could handle Blackmore, probably better than he could, and if nothing else, the old bastard might talk more to a bobby-dazzler than a scruffy bloke.

As Emily opened the door, the glare of the afternoon sun created a shimmering halo around her. Before she could step over the threshold, Colm spun her around and pulled her into him. He held Emily close for a long moment, feeling the warmth of her body, her heart pulsating against his chest as its cadence rose; he didn't want to let her go. They were one now, and embarking again into a world of uncertainty. What he thought he knew, he didn't, and now it was a whole new game. With three people dead, a fourth almost so, and a killer on the loose, he didn't want to release Emily to the darkness of the world. He wanted her home, safe and well, but it was a wish that would not be granted and armed with the information in the blue prospectus, Colm knew they were creeping closer to the edge. He didn't like it.

40

THE IVY-COVERED WALLS of the Blackmore building reminded Emily of an old brick farmhouse she'd seen every day of her young life as she made her way to school. The tapestry of vines intertwined and crept their way over the red brickwork of the old sawmill-come-furniture factory that now held the private offices of Blackmore Holdings and Property Solutions. The lush green foliage threatened to swallow the tiny, onyx-black sign engraved in gold-leaf informing visitors that this was indeed the Blackmore offices.

Grasping the large brass handle of the age-darkened oak door, Emily took a deep breath and pulled. The heavy wooden portal creaked on its ancient hinges as it swung open, and as she stepped through into the subtle lighting of the reception area, it was like she had stepped back into the nineteenth century. The sweet caramelized scent of maple filled the air as she surveyed the samples of Blackmore furniture from ages past. They stood, arrayed against the hand-hewn cherry panel walls of the tidy reception area. Four, time-worn oak armchairs sat back to back separated by a small side table of the same golden oak. Paintings of the old mill and later photographs of the furniture plant hung on the panelled walls of the room above the vintage cherry and maple tables and drop-front desks. Emily let out a short gasp as she recognized the bookcase she had seen at Angelo Pellini's house. She knew now with certainty that she had seen it before and now she remembered where.

As Emily ventured further into the chamber, she realized she was alone. There was no receptionist. There wasn't even a desk for a receptionist or secretary. She was about to sit when she spied an old black wall phone next to a door on the far side of the room. Painted in bold white letters, the word "SERVICE" was emblazoned on the backside of the handset.

Emily lifted the handset and was instantly greeted by a pleasant young voice on the other end of the line.

"Good afternoon, welcome to Blackmore Holdings. How may I help you?"

"Uhm-hi, I'd like to speak with Mr. Blackmore, please."

"Do you have an appointment?"

"No, please tell him my name is Emily James. I'm with the OPP."

Moments later, Emily was ushered into an iron-gated elevator and whisked away to the third floor of Blackmore Holdings. The ancient lift moved at a snail's pace giving Emily time to set the audio record app on her phone. As she slipped the phone back into its carrier on the side of her handbag, the elevator slowed. Barry Blackmore greeted her as the carriage bounced to a halt. The accordion gate slid open, and Blackmore held out his hand.

"I'm Barry Blackmore," he said, smiling. "And you are?"

"Emily James," she said, holding up her auxiliary constable badge careful to keep her thumb over the auxiliary designator. Slipping the badge back into her purse, she said, "Mr. Blackmore, your name has come up in connection to an incident we are investigating. Is there someplace we can speak in private?"

Blackmore led Emily down a long corridor into his office. The sound of rushing water filtered through the sliding door on the far wall of the dimly lit room. She could see a small balcony beyond and surmised that the noise originated from the waterfall, which, by her calculation, should be just outside the patio windows. Blackmore ushered her to a comfortable leather chair and took his position on the opposite side of his desk. She detected the aroma of cigar tobacco but could see no visible evidence of smoking in the room.

"You're wondering about the cigar smell, I can see it in your face," said Blackmore. "This used to be my dad's office. I moved in when he passed. He smoked cigars like fire logs. I'm afraid it's everywhere, the walls, the furniture, carpets. I could change it all I suppose"— he looked up at the ceiling and paused for a moment — "but I've come to expect it, it's as much a part of me as it was him and I guess the aroma of his tobacco keeps his memory close to me. So much has changed— I digress. How can I help you, Miss

James?"

Emily had heard much about this man. He was a shrewd businessman, and by all accounts, he'd been a tyrant in the furniture plant. Many who had worked for him despised him. His reputation for draining every ounce of effort from his employees was legend in the area. Yet, the persona of the man who sat before her belied this. He had kind eyes and a soft face, almost pudgy, but likeable, and his six-foot frame bulged over his belt when he sat indicating he'd had a bit of trouble passing the donut shop stationed just across the street. At that moment, Emily decided that she liked Barry Blackmore, but that could not dissuade her from asking some hard questions.

"Mr. Blackmore, my partner and I are investigating the murder of Harrison Dalton." Emily paused to let her words sink in. She studied Blackmore's face. He gave no expression at all, she might as well have been talking about the weather. "You did know Harry Dalton, didn't you?"

"Of course, I did. Harry and I did business together. The news of his death is tragic, but I fail to see what it has to do with me. We weren't partners. I'm sorry he's dead, but I had nothing to do with it."

"In that case, you won't mind telling me what business you did have with Harry Dalton."

"It was a long time ago. I helped him secure the original financing for the tire factory. When the original manufacturer wanted to close down operations, Harry went to bat for the employees. I guess he saw something his bosses didn't. He needed money to make it happen, and he needed concessions from the town. I helped him with all that."

"Why you?"

"What do you know about our business here, Miss James?" Blackmore rocked back in his oversized executive chair.

"I know this was once a well-known and respected furniture factory, and after that, you became active in land development, beyond that, not much more."

"Correct, we did make some money in the furniture game, but would it surprise you to learn that our history goes far beyond that? In fact, the Blackmore name dates way back to the time of the United Empire Loyalists. My ancestors arrived here after the Revolutionary War in the States and settled here on the North Shore of Lake Ontario, along with many other UEL. My family helped build this region, and at one time, we owned many tens of thousands of acres. This whole town used to belong to my family."

Blackmore rocked back a little harder in his chair. Emily thought he was dangerously close to falling backwards when he suddenly leaned forward, pointing at a painting on the wall behind her.

"See the man in that painting? He shared an office with our first Prime Minister. He was the Laird of Clarksville, Sir Robert Archibald Blackmore."

"I thought Sir William Clark was Laird and founder of this town."

"Yes, ma'am, William Clark was one of the original partners. He always fancied that title, so when he died, his family had it engraved on his monument. But Sir Robert built this town. He was the true Laird, and for many decades, over a century, the Blackmore family ran it. A lot of money was made right here in this office, and I still have a fair bit of influence. It was only natural that Harry Dalton seek my help."

"Would it be fair to say that without your help, Harry would not have succeeded in getting the factory?" asked Emily. She knew the answer, but she had Blackmore talking and wanted to keep it that way.

"That would indeed be a fair statement."

"So, have you had any other business deals with Harry?"

"Nothing of any consequence. I sold him some land outside of town. I think he built a house on it." He began rocking his chair again.

"I see, so nothing else? You weren't partners in the factory or anything like that?"

Blackmore shook his head, "No, Harry had his business, and I had mine. We'd see each other from time to time at various social functions, and I think we served together on a community project for the local Confederation Park, but that's about it."

"Then, can you tell me what or who the Blackmore/Dalton Holdings LLC - Urban Reclamation Proposal is?"

The question caught Blackmore on a backward stroke. His momentary loss of control caused the big man to lurch forward, reaching out to grasp the edge of his desk and regain his balance. His face flushed, his pupils dilated, obliterating almost all of his hazel-green irises. "What— I don't—how could you possibly know—"

The words sputtered forth as he slouched in his seat. The nerve had been hit. The man was contemplating his answer. She expected him to feed her a story, and after a long moment, Blackmore sat up, adjusted his posture, leaned forward, forearms resting on the desk, hands clasped together and said, "That never got off the ground."

* * *

Anne saw the dust trail long before Colm's Mini pulled into the driveway. *That was one thing Harry got right,* she thought as she watched the small black car make its way toward the house. Harry had bought the land and built in this location for a reason. Here, one could see for a thousand metres in all directions. He had created a home where no one could approach unobserved. Anne had never understood Harry's obsession with security. It was one thing to lock the doors and something else again to worry about anyone who might innocently drive by. Now she understood. The few seconds warning that the OPP Detective was approaching gave her a chance to prepare, and for that, she thanked her late husband.

Anne opened the door before Colm could knock. "Come in Detective, I've been expecting you."

"You have? That's strange, I didn't tell anyone I was coming here. How could you know?"

"Well, I saw the dust from your car, and I think you're the only one in this area that drives a motorized roller-skate. At least I've never seen another around here. That and the fact that you're overdue. I've been expecting another visit from you for a day or two. I'm sure you have a bunch of unanswered questions, as do I." She smiled and led Colm into the kitchen. "Coffee? I was just about to have one myself."

"That would be grand, black, one sugar, please," said Colm.

"Please, sit anywhere you like."

She indicated a large dining table at the far end of the black granite counter. Eight swivel armchairs with beige corduroy cushions surrounded the table. Colm chose one that allowed him a view out the patio window while also keeping his back to the wall. Scattered across the table were several magazines and periodicals. Colm fingered through the publications taking a mental note of the kind of reading material Anne Dalton seemed to enjoy. It was an eclectic mix of business and leisure journals with a couple of crossword puzzle books tossed in for good measure. The coffee maker made a final gurgle, and Anne Dalton set the steaming hot beverage down in front of him.

"You like crossword puzzles," said Colm.

Anne looked at the magazines Colm had been perusing. "Among other things. My sister and I love word games. Ever since we were kids, you know, Scrabble, Upwords, Wordplay, all kinds of crossword puzzles and such. It comes from travelling with my parents when we were kids. It was long before video games and Internet videos. Did you come here to talk about my reading habits, or do you have something to tell me?"

Colm blew on the hot liquid and touched his tongue to the coffee mug to test the temperature. He took a sip and said, "Yes, I suppose you do have questions, but that's not why I'm here." He looked up from his cup to see Anne staring back at him. "I have a few questions for you."

"What do you mean, you have questions? I have questions, like who killed my husband, and why?" Anne's voice rose half an octave. "I haven't even been able to recover his body. You still have it in the morgue for whatever reason, I can't imagine."

"Mrs. Dalton, please understand, this is an ongoing investigation. Your husband was murdered, and it seems he wasn't the only one. A young woman was killed within hours of your husband, and we believe, by the same killer. Do you know Nicole Saunders?"

The question took her off guard. Of course, she knew who Nicole Saunders was; she also knew she was dead. She'd read Harry's prospectus, and her conversation with Blackmore had revealed the woman's role in the land deal. The reason for her death was uncertain, but Anne had had nothing to do with it, and Blackmore denied any knowledge. Whoever killed her had a totally separate agenda. The land in question had fallen under the auctioneer's gavel, and Nicole Saunders had no part of it. Her death, while tragic, had nothing to do with the Blackmore deal, of this Anne was certain. However, she had to play it cool with the cop. He couldn't know about the deal, and she had to be careful not to let it slip.

"No—wait, yes, I think—yes, well, I didn't know her as such. I heard her name. Harry was talking to someone on the phone one night and he mentioned the name. I'm not sure who she is—er was."

"As it happens, Nicole Saunders owned some land adjacent to your husband's factory—I suppose it's your factory now."

Anne tried not to smile, but her facial muscles betrayed her. Money, indeed, was power, and the drug-like effect it had on her made her giddy. The fact that she owned the company had set tongues wagging all over the plant. It gave her some appreciation for the gratification Harry felt at having such power at his fingertips. She also knew what the future held, and she knew the truth of Harry's role in the deal with Blackmore. He would have made a lot of money. She wondered if Harry had intended to include her in any of his plans. With the kind of wealth, he stood to gain the man could have vanished forever, leaving her with nothing. She didn't care what had happened or who had done it.

"It's not entirely official, you understand. It won't be until you get your act together and close this case. Harry's will is still in probate. Hell, I haven't even buried him yet. That said, I'm running the show right now, and that has a lot of people upset."

"I'm a bit confused. I was led to understand that should something happen to Harry, the employees would take control."

Anne grinned at the detective's naivety. "The infamous ESA agreement, ha! Do you think for one second that I would allow that bunch of grease monkeys to run my plant? Not a chance. Roberts thought he had that sewn up, but I knew better. Harry owed me a lot of money. I have, a fortune wrapped up in that plant. I control it, and as soon as it's official, as far as the government is concerned, then I have plans—" Anne decided that was enough free info for the detective. It was his turn to talk— "So, do you have any idea who killed my husband?"

Colm withdrew a small black notepad from his inside pocket. Flipping it open, he said, "We have some leads, but nothing I can elaborate on just now. Why was Harry travelling to Toronto?"

Anne shook her head. She took a long sip of her coffee and lied, "I suppose it had something to do with the tire business. Harry didn't say why specifically. He seemed anxious to get going and was a bit—how can I put it—antsy, yes that's it, he was antsy about the trip, like he wanted to get going. He wasn't relaxed at all. I don't know anything more. I guess now we may never know." She took another sip of her coffee.

"So, you never knew the purpose of the trip. Did Harry have any enemies?"

"Looks like he did, doesn't it? After all, he's dead, right?" Anne couldn't help stating the obvious. *Is this guy for real? Calls himself a detective, duh, Harry's dead. Someone didn't like him.* The sardonic grin on her face showed her contempt for the question. "Of course, he had enemies.

Christ, you don't build up a multimillion-dollar business without stepping on a few toes. I'm guessing there's at least a dozen or more at the plant that won't shed any tears over Harry's death. I think you already know that. According to Jim Roberts, he gave you a list."

"So, you've talked to Jim."

"Of course, I've talked to him. He's the general manager. We have a business to run. Are you sure you're a detective?"

Colm chuckled, "Yes, Mrs. Dalton, I am a detective." He locked eyes with the woman and said, "And I am going to find out who killed your husband, Nicole Saunders and Ted Savage. And it's my guess it will be the same person who put Jim Roberts in hospital. He's in critical condition. Make no mistake, Mrs. Dalton, I will find whoever did this and why."

Anne never heard Colm's last sentence. His words trailed away like the distant sound of a fading movie credit. The world around her blurred and spun into a twisting maelstrom of colour and light. The coffee in her stomach reappeared, rising in her throat in waves, she tasted the bitter brew as it regurgitated forth. She swallowed hard, desperately aware of the small valve in her throat, designed to keep food from going down the wrong way. Now she needed it to work in the other direction. Holding it back with all the effort she could muster, the epiglottis did its job.

The detective's lips were moving, but there was no sound, no sound other than the steady whoosh, whoosh, whoosh of the blood pumping through her carotid arteries. Whoosh, whoosh, whoosh, the pink noise deafened her, obliterating all others. Anne suddenly realized she hadn't taken a breath in— *forever— I need to breathe.* She gulped in a lungful of air and slumped back into her chair. Somehow through the pounding in her ears, she heard a feeble voice that sounded like her own say, "Jim—in hospital— h-how?"

* * *

The question had taken him off-guard, and as Blackmore fidgeted in his chair, his mind scrambled for an answer. He had thirty years on this kid and the shock of how knowledgeable she was had thrown him. As far as he knew, only three parties knew about Harry's plan. Harry had insisted it be that way. However, it was a land deal, and issues such a zoning and land usage had to be addressed, and one couldn't do that without asking questions. Obtaining approvals for land development could not be done in the dark and Harry had to understand that fact. Not wanting to alert local officials to the potential changes, Blackmore made an enquiry through the Ontario Municipal Board. He was confident he could get the ball rolling without informing the Clarksville Town Council.

What he hadn't anticipated was the Saunders facet to all of this. The woman owned six acres of property that was vital to the success of Harry's plan. The trouble was, she owed taxes against the land, meaning she couldn't sell without raising questions. Gaining control over the property was the only way, and the best way to do that was with the heavy hand of government. Blackmore had set the wheels in motion to obtain the property, and that involved stepping on some toes.

"The deal never got off the ground," Blackmore lied. "I won't lie to you. Harry wanted to sell the plant. I think he was getting tired of it all. He wanted me to buy it. I guess he thought that since I had run the furniture factory, I might be interested in the tire company. I have to admit, I thought about it"— he paused for a moment swivelling his chair around to look out the window— "but I kinda like things the way they are."

"Let me get this straight, Harry wanted you to buy the plant."

Blackmore turned back to face her. "Yes, why? Is that so far-fetched? I do have a fair bit of experience in business, and if anyone could put together the cash, I could."

"With all due respect Mr. Blackmore, there is more to this than you are saying. We've seen the prospectus. From what we can gather, Harry was asking far more than the plant alone was worth. There must have been more to it," said Emily.

"Not that I'm aware of, Ms. James, but then, I never got to the bargaining stage with Harry. He approached me with a plan, I looked it over, but we never discussed money as I had no intention of buying."

"So, if I get this right, Harry Dalton came to you with an offer to sell the tire plant, you declined, and now he's dead."

"Yes, I guess that's about the size of it. I'm sorry about Harry, but it has nothing to do with me. Now, if there's nothing else, I must get back to work."

"One more thing, Mr. Blackmore, how well did you know Nicole Saunders?"

Blackmore rubbed his chin. This woman was getting on his last nerve. Where was she getting her information? Emily James was well informed, and that unsettled him.

"Saunders owned land out by the tire plant. That's *all* I know about her. I certainly didn't know her. Not the way you think."

"I see, and how about Ted Savage, how well did you know him?"

"Ted, who? What's the point of all this?"

"Oh, no point, I guess, Mr. Blackmore, only that they are all dead, and that they all had something to do with Blackmore/Dalton Holdings. Thank you for your time."

Emily stood and turned for the door. "Don't get up, I'll see myself out."

41

EMILY MET COLM AT the main entrance to the hospital. After comparing notes, they made their way down a long, curving passageway to the hospital's new intensive care unit. Constable Harold Papineau kept vigil at the door to Jim Roberts' room.

He'd done this duty before, and the memory of that night still haunted him. Only a few months earlier, he'd sat guarding this very room when a nurse entered under false pretenses. Harold's shift relief was due any moment, and the constant itch from an allergic rash had distracted him as, against his better judgement, he allowed the nurse to enter the room on the pretense that she was collecting blood samples. Ten minutes later, Harold was gone, and the nurse emerged, thanked the young officer who had replaced him, and then disappeared into the elevator. It wasn't until the morning shift came on duty to check on the patient in room 321 that all hell broke loose.

An autopsy proved the presence of Succinylcholine in the victim's blood. The prime suspect in multiple murders had herself been murdered in her hospital bed, and whoever had done it, had turned the victim's own weapon of choice against her. An investigation found no record of the nurse in any file. She was a ghost. Despite Colm's and Emily's suspicions, without clear evidence they could not move forward. The murder of Kallita Prewitt, considered to be the most hated woman in Clarksville, remained an open case, yet to be solved.

Harold spied the couple approaching the room and stood to greet them. Fighting the urge to yank at the collar of his shirt—the itch was driving him mad—Harold presented a clipboard to Colm.

"Sergeant, everyone must sign. It is the order of the commander, the Staff Sergeant Jacobs."

Colm's lips curled into a thin grin. He knew of Harold's history in this place and thought it somewhat ironic that he should be in this position again. "That's grand, Harold, Emily and I want to talk to Jim. Do you know if he's awake?" Colm signed the form and passed it to Emily.

"I 'aven't heard a sound from inside. The doctor, she was 'ere and then she was gone. She didn't said nothing."

Colm noted the time of the doctor's visit. They had missed her by only a few minutes. With a nod to Harold, he pushed the door to Jim's room open, and he and Emily stepped inside.

Jim Roberts lay in a semi-reclined position, pillows piled behind his back helped to support his injured shoulder. An IV drip of some clear solution hung beside the bed with a clear plastic tube running down and into a catheter on his right wrist. He had an oxygen line running under his nose, and a steady beep sounded from a large LED monitor displaying various vital sign graphs as they streamed across the screen. His heavily bandaged left arm and shoulder hung suspended from a triangular-shaped appliance resemblant of a giant coat hanger. Jim raised his head as the couple entered, and Emily sensed immediately that they were the last people he had wanted to see come through the door.

Emily moved to Jim's side and placed a gentle hand on his right arm. Colm followed, remaining a step behind. They had agreed that Emily would take the lead in questioning him.

"How are you feeling, Jim? You gave us quite a scare."

The tired eyes of a man subdued by painkillers and perhaps a realization that the world as he knew it was rapidly ending, stared back at her.

"The doctor says I'll live." He flashed a rueful smile and turned to look at his injured arm. "It's a long way from my heart," he said half-joking.

Colm eased his way closer to the bed as Emily said, "We were afraid you wouldn't make it. You are very lucky. If we hadn't found you, you might have died. Do you know who did this to you?"

Jim shook his head. "I—I didn't see anything. One second I was standing on my deck, and then a freight train hit me. I blacked out and the next thing I knew I woke up in here, strapped to this contraption"—Jim tried to move his shoulder, but the traction device barely moved—"I have no idea who did this. I suppose I should be thanking you—and your boyfriend." He looked over at Colm, who was edging his way to the opposite side of the bed.

"Jim, you must have some idea who did this. Who would want to kill you?"

"Nobody. The only one who could have anything against me is dead," Jim gave Emily a knowing glance. "As you well know."

Emily did know, and so did Colm. The irony was not lost on the couple. Jim Roberts now occupied the same hospital bed in which his one-time nemesis had expired. "Yes, well, we know it couldn't be her," Emily said. "Do you think it has anything to do with the plant and Harry's death?"

Jim's face turned ashen grey. The heart monitor beeped a rapid tempo, and a quick glance at the scale showed his heart rate was all over the place. He slumped into the pillows on his bed, and for just a moment, Emily had the impression of a man ready for death. The machine's beeping slowed, and the numbers and graph lines returned to normal almost instantly. However, it was plain to everyone in the room Jim Roberts was terrified of the possibility that Emily was right.

"Are you ok, Jim? We have more questions for you, but if you need a break, we can come back."

Roberts closed his eyes for a long moment, then opening them, he shook his head.

"No, I think I'd better tell you what's going on."

* * *

"I told you I wanted this to be a clean operation."

Shinkwinn had heard the distorted voice a few times and always struggled to discern its gender. The call was not unexpected, yet it was poorly timed. Although things were taking shape, not everything had gone to plan. Yes, Harry was dead, albeit too soon, and Nicole was a liability. Had the silly bitch not been so flaked out on drugs, it never would have happened. Ted's death was regrettable but necessary. The one fly in the ointment was Jim Roberts. He should have died, and would have, but for those two nosey neighbours.

"It is a clean operation," Shinkwinn retorted. "You always have to account for variables. I never promised total invisibility. I went to great lengths to ensure none of the tools could be traced. You need to relax. The loose ends will be tied up soon."

Shinkwinn heard what sounded like voices in the background. "Am I on speaker?"

The voice hesitated a moment then said, "N–no, not on speaker."

"Make sure it stays that way," said Shinkwinn.

"You have more to worry about than being on speaker," countered the voice. "I only ordered the main course, I'm not paying for the side dishes."

"You'll pay what I charge. You can bank on that. Don't call me again; I'll be in touch when the time comes."

* * *

The pain in Jim's shoulder paled in comparison to the fretfulness he suffered as he gazed upon his neighbours. He had a confession to make and yet he could not understand the anxiety he felt. He was embarrassed, that was for sure, but he couldn't see where he or his cousin had broken any laws. Still, here he was lying in a hospital bed, having just denied the reaper his due. It was time to show his side of the coin and let fate take its course.

"You'd better sit down," he said, making eye contact with Colm. "This might take a while."

Colm dragged a large vinyl-covered chair closer to Jim's bedside while Emily scooted up onto the foot of the bed.

"Perhaps," said Colm, "I should read you the caution. I wouldn't want to jeopardize anything we might want to use later."

Jim shook his head. "That won't be necessary, I know my rights, and I wave the caution. Besides, I've done nothing wrong, criminally, that is." Jim forced a smile despite the pain in his shoulder. The look on Colm's face was priceless. "You don't believe me, I can see that. You think I had something to do with Harry's murder, right?"

Colm leaned forward slightly. "Well, 'tis a bit of a mess you've got yourself into here. You've been holding out on me—ehm—us." The dagger Emily flashed at him did not go unnoticed.

"How so?" asked Jim.

"Why didn't you tell me Ted Savage was your cousin?"

"Yes, well, you'll understand the answer to that when I tell you the rest of the story."

Colm retrieved his cellphone from his pocket and opened the record app. "You don't mind if I record this conversation."

Jim shook his head and sighed. "It was about six weeks ago. Harry was out of the office, and Isobel forwarded a call to my phone. It was serendipitous really, she didn't know any better, and I would never have found out had Harry been available."

Emily shifted sideways to get more comfortable. "Why, what do you mean, found out?"

"About Harry selling the factory. The caller was Cal Jenkins, the town clerk. He wanted to know what was going on. I was flabbergasted. I knew nothing about it and told him so. I told him he was nuts, Harry wasn't selling the factory. I called him crazy."

Jim winced at the pain in his shoulder as he reached for a glass of water on his bedside tray. It was just out of reach, and Emily slipped off the bed to help him. "So, you knew about the sale all along," said Emily. "Why didn't you tell us before now?"

"It was all hush, hush. Harry didn't know that I knew. Fact is, I don't think he knew Jenkins was aware of it."

Colm interjected, "Jenkins knew because of the OMB. They were asking questions and required information."

Jim nodded as he sipped his water. "Right. Cal called me all in a flap over the sale, asking what was Harry thinking and getting all righteous about screwing over the town. I didn't know anything, least of all Harry screwing the town over. I finally got Cal to calm down long enough to tell me what was going on. I was pissed. Harry was going to sell, and well, that meant a lot of changes at the plant. And our guys don't react well to change."

"Selling the plant is no reason to kill the man," said Emily. "Surely, the plant would continue. If Harry wanted to take his money and retire or whatever, why should that be a problem?"

Jim shrugged and said, "I wouldn't know. There were more than a few who had a score to settle with Harry." He turned his gaze in Colm's direction. "I gave you a list, how did that pan out?"

"Not too well, as it happens," answered Colm. "Everyone on your list has moved away, retired or died."

Jim fell silent for a moment. Then he said, "There was one name on that list that—that shouldn't have been there."

Colm interjected, "Ted Savage, yeah?"

"Yeah, I kind of gave you a bum steer there. Ted had nothing to do with Harry's death. I promise you that."

Emily asked, "Why would you rat out your own cousin and back to the first question, why hide the fact?"

"Believe me, it was a stupid mistake on my part. The shock of Harry's death had me rattled, and I wasn't thinking."

From the look in the couple's eyes, Jim knew he wasn't explaining himself very well. He wanted to tell them his story but was having trouble getting the words out. In his heart, he didn't think he and Ted had done anything wrong. If anything, they'd acted in good faith. It was just bad luck that things went sour the way they did. Torn between fear and embarrassment, the truth finally spewed forth.

"All we did was try to make the best of a bad situation. When Cal told me about the sale and his fear that Harry was screwing the town over, I realized he was making sense. Applications had been made to rezone the plant and all the land around it. There was one small hiccup that was preventing the approvals, and that was the six acres abutting the northwest corner of the property," Jim said, pausing to take another drink.

"Go on," said Colm.

"That was the land that Nicole Saunders owned. Harry needed it to make the deal come through. I figured that Harry would pay dearly for that property. Cal told me that the land was up for tax auction. That's when I decided blood was thicker, so to speak, and called Ted. I figured if we could get Nicole to sell it to us first, then we could pay the taxes, Nicole would get a chunk of money for her trouble, and we would make out like bandits by selling the land to Harry. Win, win, win." Jim smiled and then frowned, "But Nicole wouldn't sell."

Colm stood up and stretched. "So what you're saying is, you and Ted tried to buy Nicole's land, she wouldn't sell so, what, you killed her?"

"Killed her! Hell, no!" Jim squirmed around to look Colm in the eye. "I never killed no-one, and neither did Ted. We're not killers. We're just a couple of guys caught up in a screwed-up mess. Once Nicole's land was off the table, we figured that was the end of it for us, but then I thought about what Cal Jenkins told me. The property the plant sits on is worth money, a lot of it. Maybe millions. Ted and I tried on our own to get the land at auction, but we were outbid. Some Italian guy from out of town bought it and he ain't selling for any price. I know, we tried. But then we thought something this big would need a local connection. There's only one guy I know in this town with that kind of weight behind him—"

"Barry Blackmore," Emily jumped in.

Jim nodded, thankful for the interruption. His mouth was still dry. "Right, I called Blackmore to find out if the plan to sell the factory was indeed true. He confirmed it, and when I told him this was too volatile to keep secret, that such a sale would be devastating to the town, he offered to buy my silence. He said if I kept everything under wraps, there was a quarter million in it for me. After all, as an employee, I was a stockholder in the company. If I kept my mouth shut, my shares at least, were worth money, if I talked, then nada. I told him I wasn't alone. Others knew of his involvement. He said that was my problem. If I wanted the money, I had to keep everything quiet." Jim raised his glass and drained the last of the water and continued.

"The night Harry died, Ted went to Nicole's house. She'd called me all liquored up saying she was going to blow the whole deal wide open, and why should she be the only loser in this deal? Ted went over to see her, but she wouldn't answer the door. When he heard the sirens, he got the hell out of there. Then, after the news about Harry, Ted went to the hospital to talk to Nicole," Jim turned back to Emily, "that's when you caught him in Sammi's room. Ted told me all about it. He was there looking for Nicole. We needed her to keep her mouth shut about our attempts to buy the land and to keep quiet about the deal altogether. We didn't want anyone at the plant getting wind of what was going on. I was scared shitless that they would all walk out and halt production. The shit would hit the fan in the media, and I could say bye-bye to everything, no job, no money, no quarter mil, nothing. Scared shitless, yep, that was me. I told Ted to get her to be quiet, and we'd make it worth her while. Then he saw you, Emily, and he panicked."

Jim reached for the pitcher on his tray. Emily helped, pouring the water for him as he held the glass. He took another long sip and continued, "Sorry, throat's parched, must be the drugs they have me on. Turns out, we didn't have to worry. Nicole was already dead by the time Ted got to the hospital." He cast his gaze down to the blanket covering his legs. "Goddam shame that. You have to believe me, we—Ted and I—we had nothing to do with that. I don't know who did it, but it wasn't us. All we did was try to buy the woman's land."

Colm spoke up, "Assuming I believe you, and I'm not sure I do, where does Jenkins fit into all this?"

"He doesn't," replied Jim. "Although I got the impression that he had his own agenda. For a while, I thought he was going to buy Nicole's property himself and cash in. But once Nicole's property sold, he was out. With Blackmore offering money for discretion, all we had to do was stay quiet. When Nicole turned up dead, I became nervous, but what could I do? I had nothing to do with it, and Ted definitely didn't. No, all we had to do was be patient. Anne Dalton hates the factory, and I know once she gets wind of this, assuming she hasn't already, she'll sell the factory in a heartbeat. Nope, all we had to do was keep quiet. We'd each get a tidy payday, and let the chips fall, so to speak, with the factory."

Jim fell silent again, trying to compile his next statement. "You know, had it not been for the Italian, Nicole might still be alive. He really screwed us." Jim shot a glance at Colm, "When you started poking around, Ted got nervous. He came to me just before this happened," Jim turned his head and nodded at his shoulder, "he wanted out. He was ready to break. I told him to hang on, but he was adamant, so I made a call—" he gazed up at the ceiling for a long moment— "anyway, Ted's long gone from here. I arranged to get him some money. He took the payday, and by now, he's on a beach somewhere."

"Not quite," said Colm. Standing beside the bed, he watched closely as Jim attempted to turn his body toward the detective. The traction pole swivelled, allowing Jim's arm to move slightly and as he shifted into position. "There's no easy way to say this, Jim, Ted's dead. His body was found lying in the cemetery on the edge of town. He'd been shot. We think by the same person who shot you. Do you have—"

Jim's face turned the colour of bread dough. For a brief moment, it appeared as though all the man's blood had left his body. His eyes rolled back in his head, machines beeped, and alarms rang. The door to the room flew open. A team of nurses and doctors stormed in, demanding that the couple leave at once. A nurse ushered Colm and Emily into the corridor, and they stood watching as the door to Jim's room closed with a muffled thud.

42

JIM'S REACTION WAS ENOUGH to tell Colm the man hadn't lied to him. Any sense that Jim was involved in the deaths of Harry and Nicole was gone now.

The couple stood with Constable Papineau and listened to the voices resonating through the door. The muffled sounds were indistinct and difficult to make out, but one word came through loud and clear.

"CLEAR," the command was followed by a thud and then more shuffling and bustling around. Another voice said, "sinus rhythm, BP 60 over 30, pulse thready." Then everything went silent.

Ten minutes later, the door swung open, and Dr. Awani stepped out. He motioned Colm aside to speak to him.

"He wishes to see you, he says he needs to tell you something. I told him, no, but he insists. I have no choice, but mark me now, only one of you may go in and only for a moment or two. Do not upset him." Awani's brow wrinkled, and his eyebrows drew closer together as he spoke. His professorial tone exuded an authority that Colm would not ignore.

"Will he live?" It was a stupid question to which there was no definitive answer. Colm was looking at the face of a worried man. Jim Roberts had once again cheated death, at least for now. Still, the man was holding on by a tenuous thread. A thread that might break under the slightest of pressure. Colm regarded the unblinking, brown beads set deep in the hollows that were the doctor's eyes. "I promise I won't upset him. I'll listen to him and won't say a word."

Dr. Awani nodded his agreement and said, "I'll wait here until you return."

* * *

Jim opened his eyes as he heard the door open. He crooked his fingers, beckoning Colm to sit. His voice was weak and subdued, and Colm had to listen hard to hear above the constant hiss of the oxygen ventilator and the steady beep, beep, beep of the machines monitoring Jim's current state of health. The man, who only moments before had appeared much healthier, now looked almost cadaver-like. His skin remained the colour of oatmeal and his once sparkling eyes, now clouded over with only a hint of life left in them. It was difficult to tell if the vacant look in Jim's eyes was due to the drugs or if indeed he was on the edge of death. He had cheated death twice in twenty-four hours. Colm guessed a third time would not be the charm. Following his promise to the doctor, he sat quietly as Jim rasped out what he needed to say.

Jim fixed his gaze on the light in the ceiling and confirmed, "Ted's dead?"

Colm nodded.

"Then I— was supposed to be next," said Jim. "He tried to shut us up. It's Blackmore. He's the only one who knew about Ted and the fifty-K…"

Jim's eyes closed, and he drifted off to sleep. Colm left the room, pulling the door shut behind him. He turned to Dr. Awani and said, "He's sleeping. At least I think he's asleep."

The doctor slipped past Colm and went inside to check his patient. He returned a moment later and confirmed that Jim was asleep. "Only time will tell us if he will have the hardiness to make a mighty recovery. For now, he must rest. I must insist on it."

* * *

In the early days of the factory, cargo ships laden with timber and coal transited the river to deliver the raw materials needed in the manufacture of Blackmore's world-renowned furniture. The ships would dock at the base of the waterfall only a short walk from the balcony where Barry Blackmore now stood looking across the Clarksville River. On the far side of the river, paralleling the bank, a paved pathway merged with the boardwalk that stretched from the waterfall westward to Clarksville's main street. The balcony rested atop the ancient waterwheel that had initially provided the power for the factory's machinery. The disused icon of yesteryear stood sentinel to the river as it flowed over the fixed-crest dam that created the waterfall. Many decades of erosion from the waterfall had laid claim to the riverbed preventing boats with even the shallowest of draughts from gaining access. Hence, the ships no longer plied their way this far upriver. Now, this stretch of the waterway was a fish sanctuary, and the spawning beds for walleye and salmon could be seen all along the riverbank.

Barry pulled his jacket closed, zipping it partway to block out the chilly air of the late October afternoon. He checked his watch. It was six o'clock, and as if to confirm the timepiece's accuracy, he checked the western horizon, ensuring that the sun was indeed about to set. Another forty minutes or so and the great golden orb would kiss the treetops, and all would be swallowed up in the gloom of the autumn night.

Barry had lived here all his life, but when the Dalton deal was done, he would move his family away. In his heart, he knew, none of his ancestors would approve of his part in what was to come. Punctuating that thought, a fine mist from the fountain assailed the back of his neck like spittle from an angry god. Shame on you, Barry Blackmore. Why are you doing this?

Why not, he thought? "Because this deal is mine," he answered himself out loud. Yet he was unsure. Tomorrow was Halloween. This will be the last Halloween here, he thought as he gazed across the river at a lone figure strolling along the boardwalk. The figure stopped every now and then to peer into the water. "Must be checking for fish," Barry said to himself. *Too late for the spawn, that was last month.*

He turned his attention to the east, facing the waterfall and the holding pond above it. The disapproving fountain geysered, and soon the lights would turn on, creating a shimmering tower of diamonds showering the water below. It was something he did every day. At this time of year, it was a fitting and brilliant way to cap off his day's work. Tonight, however, he felt no pride, no elation and no sense of accomplishment. Tonight, for the first time since this deal began, Barry Blackmore had doubts. His spirit would not settle. The words of his long-dead father came to him. *"Barry, son, if it doesn't feel right, it's not right."*

* * *

As Shinkwinn strolled along the boardwalk, the marksman-turned-sniper stopped periodically, gazed into the clear water and considered the wonder of the animal world. It was here that the fish began their lifelong journey, and it was in this location they returned every year to replenish the species, and in some cases, end their journeys. Most animals were creatures of habit. Animals tended to follow routines, and as an avid hunter, Shinkwinn had studied these habits extensively. Shinkwinn had tired of hunting animals. There was no profit in it, and for the most part, little satisfaction. The human animal was different. Some were unpredictable; most were not. Shinkwinn's current prey was indeed a creature of habit, and that would become Barry Blackmore's epitaph.

He crouched at the edge of the tree-line beside a wooden planter, swung the air-rifle into position, withdrew a projectile from the cold-pouch and loaded it into the rifle's breach. The bipod rested on the edge of the planter box, but Shinkwinn didn't need the platform to steady the shot. At this range, missing would be unthinkable. Time slowed with the sniper's heart rate, the finger caressed the trigger, and Shinkwinn counted the beat. *One breath in, one beat, breathe out, one beat, hold it, squeeze…*

The muffled thud of compressed air merged with the roaring rush of the waterfalls. The 350-grain projectile rocketed through the 34-inch bore of the rifle, exiting the muzzle at just under 1000 feet per second. Less than a tenth of a second later, Barry Blackmore leaned forward, flipped over the railing, bounced off the waterwheel into the river, and ended his journey.

Shinkwinn slipped silently into the dense cover of the tree-line. *No need to dial 911 for this loose end. It's tied up tight.*

43

RHONDA JEAN ROBERTSON WAS also a creature of habit. Every evening just before sunset, she would take Diesel, her German Shepherd mix, to Fallside Park and let him run. The park bordered the south-east edge of the river at the point where the river bent westward, forming the collecting pond above the falls. It was a place where Rhonda could shed the stress of the day. Here all she had to do was watch Diesel as he raced back and forth chasing squirrels who were too fast and could climb far higher than the dog could stretch or jump. Here, the world stayed away, Diesel would romp, and do his business, then stand and supervise as Rhonda dutifully picked up and disposed of the detritus.

She strolled along the fenced walkway above the falls with one eye on Diesel and the other on the rushing water as it blasted its way down-river.

It was a chilly evening, and the sun hovered above the distant tree-line. The river stretched before her following the curve of the riverbank, turning right and disappearing around the bend. A dark figure stooped beside a wooden planter backed by the thick underbrush of the tree-lined hillside. The figure held something in its hand, *a stick perhaps,* Rhonda thought. At that moment, a puff of mist sprang forth, and in the corner of her right eye, she saw the black silhouette of a man falling headfirst into the water. It was precisely at that moment that Diesel decided to bolt. As she watched her three-year-old Shepherd tear off down the walkway in the direction of the figure, Rhonda fumbled with her phone to call 911.

Running after the dog, she screamed breathlessly into the phone, "I just saw a man fall in the river.—No, I'm at the park near the falls, please hurry. I can't see him, he went under—the waterwheel, oh God I can see his legs, he's caught there—no I can't reach him, he's on the other side of the river by the factory. Oh God, where's Diesel, DIESEL! DIESEL COME!—yes, I'll wait. I have to get my dog—no, I won't hang up."

She waited for ten minutes before the police arrived, followed by a fire rescue crew. Diesel had disappeared into the bushes. Rhonda was torn as to whether to stay and wait or to look for the wayward mutt. Happily, he returned on his own, carrying a narrow black strap in his mouth, dragging a white pouch along the ground behind him. She took the belt out of the dog's mouth, picked up the bag and immediately dropped it again. Whatever was in the pouch was damn cold; Rhonda sucked her finger-tips to warm them up from the sudden bite of frost.

* * *

Bob Gentry wiped a muddy hand across his brow, leaving a dark streak of riverbed in its wake. Barry Blackmore's body lay at his feet covered in a greenish-brown slime from the ooze that coagulated near the base of the waterwheel. The slippery green algae seemed to stick to everything it touched. As Colm and Emily made their way to the river's edge, Gentry waved them off.

"It's Barry Blackmore. He's been shot, looks like he fell from his balcony and got jammed under the waterwheel. The rescue guys had a hell of a time getting him out. He's a mess, but otherwise, there's nothing to see here," he said. "He's just like the others. He's got a hole in his back, and it's my guess we'll find traces of mercury in the wound. Won't know that 'til I get him on the table. I'll let you know."

Gentry didn't wait for a reply. He climbed up the short embankment and walked to his car. Looking back at the bewildered couple, he shouted, "Sorry, gotta go. I told the wife I wouldn't be late for her party. Tomorrow's Halloween and she's having a party tonight." He checked his watch and frowned. "Looks like I lied," he said, forming a wry smile. "Oh, by the way, you might want to have a chat with that young lady over there"— he pointed toward the door to the Blackmore building— "seems as though she might have seen what happened and her dog found something interesting. I'm taking it to the lab if it's what I think it is—well, let's wait and see. I need to get it into a cold environment asap." Gentry slid into the driver's seat and drove away.

Colm looked at Emily and shrugged. "Wonder what's bugging him?"

"He did say he had to get home," said Emily as she scrambled back up the embankment. "We should check out Blackmore's office. Maybe we'll find something there."

"Yeah, we need to talk to the woman first," said Colm.

* * *

As Rhonda related her story to Emily, Colm searched for a way to gain access to Blackmore's main offices. The main entrance was unlocked, and although they were inside the reception area, it was after business hours, and there was no one inside to open the office door. Colm finally gave up and joined the two women. Emily was making a fuss over Diesel. She was rubbing his belly and talking to Rhonda at the same time. Whenever her attention strayed from her chore, Diesel would raise his head and gently nip at Emily's hand to remind her she wasn't done.

"He likes you," said Rhonda. "He's generally very protective of me and rarely lets others come near him." As if to prove her point, Diesel flipped over and stood to face Colm as he approached the women. His tail tucked between his legs, the dog bared his teeth and let out a low growl.

"That door is shut tight, sure, and I can't see any other way in. I guess I'll have to call a locksmith—" Colm eyed the dog and stopped short.

"Easy, Diesel," said Rhonda. "He's ok."

"Huh, what?" said Emily.

"We need a locksmith to open that door," said Colm, still watching the dog.

"Maybe I can help," said Rhonda. She stood and told Diesel to lie down, which he did, albeit with a low grumbling growl, his eyes still focused on Colm. Rhonda crossed the room and stopped at the door. She crouched down, studied the lockset for a moment then began rummaging through her purse. A moment later, she withdrew what looked like a credit card and slipped the plastic between the door edge and the frame. Rhonda jiggled the doorknob a few times, and a moment later, the door swung inward. Rising to her feet, she turned to face Colm and Emily. Her face beamed with satisfaction. "There you go," she said. "No charge."

Colm shook his head in disbelief. "How—"

"I worked for a locksmith for five years, picked up a few tricks along the way. It doesn't always work. A lot depends on the lock and how well the door fits. Luckily this door is a hundred years old or more, and it fits kinda loosely."

After a few more questions, Rhonda agreed to make a formal statement at the detachment the next day. They said goodbye and Rhonda and Diesel went home.

* * *

Thankfully, Blackmore's office was unlocked, and the couple wasted no time digging through the businessman's files. This was now a crime scene, and a warrant was unnecessary.

"What are we looking for?" asked Emily.

"I have no idea, but I'll know it when I see it," answered Colm. "There must be something here to incriminate Blackmore. Jim wasn't lying when he said Blackmore was the only one who knew Ted Savage was going to be in that cemetery."

"Do you think Blackmore killed him?"

"Not now. Now that Blackmore's dead and by the same method, I'd say whoever did Ted, did him. Probably to shut him up. The answer must be in this room."

Colm lifted Blackmore's phone and dialled *69. The automated voice relayed the number of the last person to call Blackmore. He compared that to the previous number Blackmore dialled, and they matched. Colm recognized the area code was one of three in the Toronto area. Whoever Blackmore was calling wasn't local, and he would need to obtain the phone records for a more complete history. That would take time, and time wasn't a luxury they had much of.

"Damn, we need to know who this guy was calling over the last day or so. It'll take ages to get the records."

"Maybe not," said Emily. She walked around the desk and sat in Blackmore's chair. "These phone systems have a memory. It's the same system they use at the call centre. I can access the phone log through the software." Emily tapped the keyboard on Blackmore's computer. The monitor lit up.

"Oh poop," she said. "I need a password."

They searched through the desk for half an hour. Everything that even remotely resembled a password failed. "Nothing, I've got nothing," Emily said, sitting back in the chair and rubbing her eyes to wipe away her frustration. When she opened her eyes, they lit upon the painting, Blackmore had pointed out during her visit. Blackmore's ancestor stood upon a rocky surface dressed in a long tailcoat, white waistcoat and black breeches that stopped at the knee. He had on brown leather shoes with pewter buckles and white leggings. An eighteenth-century gentleman if there ever was one. What was his name? Robert something—Robert Ar-Archibald Blackmore. "That's it! It has to be," said Emily.

Colm looked up from a stack of papers he'd been sifting through. "What's it?"

Emily typed "Archibald" into the computer. Nothing. She shook her head. "Poop, poop, poop, it's not working." She tried several variations, using capital letters, all lowercase, all uppercase, switching numbers for vowels, nothing worked. Emily banged the desk. "I know I'm on the right track, but I've tried everything." She sat back again, trying to think. Robert Archibald Blackmore, the Laird of Clarksville, no, it couldn't be? Emily leaned forward and stabbed the letters into the box on the screen. L A I R D. Instantly, the desktop opened. "I'm in!" She howled.

The phone log dated back for months. Hundreds of outgoing and incoming calls from all over the world had been securely squirrelled away in the deepest recesses of the phone system's memory. Colm scratched at the stubble on his cheek. It was beginning to itch, which meant Emily would soon be telling him to shave.

"We need to cross-reference these numbers with Blackmore's contact list. I don't suppose you can get access to that as well, can you?"

Emily clicked the contacts icon and prayed. This time her prayer was answered. Blackmore had obviously figured that he would be the only one using this computer.

"Easy," she said. "I'm in. What do you want to know?"

Colm referred to the number he'd written down earlier. "Let's start with this one. I'm curious to know who it belongs to."

Emily compared the number with the log. "This number comes up a lot over the past few months. It looks like Blackmore called it a dozen times in the past few days."

"Yes, but who does it belong to?"

Emily referenced the contact list. "Looks like it's a company, Llandeso Investments, Pickering," she said, looking up at Colm. "That's where Angelo Pellini lives. I wonder if…" her voice trailed off as the thoughts that ran through her mind overcame her. She'd had suspicions that Pellini wasn't exactly who he said he was. Still, her thoughts had not run to the possibility of danger.

The words on the computer spelled out Llandeso Investments, but all Emily saw was the image of Pellini sitting with Sammi beside him on a white leather sofa. With each breath she took, her chest tightened, butterflies took up residence in her stomach, and for the briefest of moments, Emily thought she might lose control of her insides. She had left her meeting with Pellini feeling sure that Sammi was in safe hands, but now, doubt had crept in. If Pellini was indeed wrapped up in this, then Sammi might still be in grave danger.

"Oh, Colm, I hope this isn't what I think it is. If Pellini is involved, then Sammi might be in trouble."

"Don't jump to conclusions. We don't know who Llandeso Investments is. There's nothing in the name to indicate he has any connection. We need to find out who owns the company."

Colm thought for a moment, checked his watch and decided it was too late to make the call. He would try in the morning. In the meantime, he would get Jen Stroud to gather some background on Llandeso and details about the phone numbers in the log.

"Are you able to get into Blackmore's email?"

Emily clicked another icon on the computer's desktop and was rewarded with Barry Blackmore's inbox. There were five emails from Llandeso Investments. One of them remained unopened.

Oct. 27 - 09:00 - Subject: Delay, BB, Sorry to hear about your sudden setback. I hope this does not interfere with our plans. **A.**

10:00 - Reply: A, - Not sure where we stand. Will get back to you ASAP. **BB.**

Oct. 28 - 14:00 - Subject: Moving On, BB, I understand AD is receptive to our offer. Please advise of any change of status. The situation is time-critical. **A.**

15:00 - Reply: A. - AD is on board. One obstacle remains. Pickering factor holds the keystone. **BB.**

Oct. 29 - 09:00 - Subject: Issue resolved. BB, Pickering resolved, keystone is ours. A.

Oct. 29 - Subject: Hiccup. A, We have an unexpected hiccup. TS & JR want to expedite their cut. Please arrange for fund transfer. **BB.**

15:30 - Reply: BB, - Leave hiccup to me. Local agent will deliver funds. Advise coordinates. **A.**

15:45 - Return Reply: A. - TS will meet at usual drop point. 24:00 hrs. BB.

15:50 - Return Reply: BB, - Consider it done. A.

Emily and Colm sat transfixed as they read the series of messages. They were short on detail, but from what the two detectives already knew, these messages filled in a few blanks. They turned their attention to the unopened email.

"This one's marked urgent," said Emily. "It came in only an hour ago. Blackmore never even knew it was here. Seems kind of eerie to think this is happening after he died. Kinda creepy almost." She clicked on the message. It read: Oct. 30 - 20:00 - Urgent! - BB, Contact with local agent lost. The consensus from this end is we must expedite paperwork immediately to bring to successful conclusion. We fear outside sources at work to block completion of our deal. We must meet tonight. Bring all documentation. Take extreme caution, trust no one. A.

Emily looked up from the screen. "He obviously never got the message, but what local agent could this email be referring to?"

"Too late for extreme caution," said Colm. "Blackmore was dead before this email was sent. Whoever A is, has no idea what has happened here." Colm's eyes widened. "If this email was sent just a short while ago, then maybe—" He snatched the phone from its cradle and dialled the number. The phone rang, and a voice answered.

"This is Detective Sergeant Colm O'Byrne of the Clarksville OPP. Who am I speaking to?"

"You're not Barry. How did you get this number?" A female voice asked.

"You're quite right. I am not Barry. Now please answer my question, who am I speaking to?"

The line went dead.

44

THE CALL FROM JEN Stroud came in the wee hours. Colm fumbled for his phone, knocking it to the floor. Dazed and only half awake, he switched on the lamp and searched for the wayward communicator. Finally, nabbing it from under the bed, he swiped to the right to accept the call and said, "This better be good."

"It's better than that even. How quick can you get back to Blackmore's office?"

Colm checked the time. "My God, girl, I'm just after goin' to bed. It's only ten past one in the morning."

"It's important. Bring Emily, I need to speak to her as well."

Colm glanced over at his sleeping partner and grimaced, "Wake up she who must be obeyed? Ok, it's on your head."

* * *

Emily parked directly opposite the front door to the building, and moments later, they entered Blackmore's private office. Colm was surprised to see *Ernie and Bert* systematically searching through every file and publication they could find. Jen Stroud sat at Blackmore's desk, leaning back in the plush leather chair swivelling from side to side.

Colm checked his watch for effect. "This better be good," he said as he stepped behind the desk. Emily followed, a little confused as to why she'd been summoned from her much-needed beauty rest. Nevertheless happy to be in the middle of it all.

Jen grinned, "I think I've cracked this case for you. I know who or what Llandeso Investments is, and I know who the chief director is."

"Oh really, and how would you be knowin' all this then?" said Colm.

"Easy. I did a search of the business registration database. You can find just about everything there is to know about corporations if you look hard enough. For instance, Llandeso Investments is a shell corporation. It has no assets at all, and from what I've been able to gather, it has no revenue. At least none that it has reported to the government. The company was formed about three months ago. It has one shareholder and one managing director." Jen clicked the mouse to bring up a document on the computer. "Care to guess who that might be?"

The grin on Jen Stroud's face was too much for Colm. "Why don't you enlighten us? It's late, and I miss my bed."

"Does the name Lonsdale hold any significance for you?"

Colm had to think. Somewhere in the reaches of his mind, there was a fuzzy memory of the name, but he couldn't place it. "It's familiar, but I'm not sure how."

"Well, look at it this way." Jen shifted her chair sideways to let Colm view the monitor.

It took a moment, and then it hit him, "Oh shite! It's a bloody anagram. Lonsdale is an anagram for Llandeso. And here I was thinking we were dealing with a Welsh company or at least one owned by a Welshman."

Jen's grin widened. "There's more. The director is none other than Amelia Lonsdale."

"And just who is Amelia Lonsdale when she's out walkin'?"

"Amelia Lonsdale is the sister of Anne Dalton."

"You mean?"

"Yep," said Jen with a smug grin on her face. "None other than the grieving widow's sister, and that, my dear Detective Sergeant, creates a lot of questions. Llandeso is owned by another corporation, a numbered company, and I haven't figured out its identity yet, but it's my guess Amelia Lonsdale is part of it. I'll stay on it. I've got all night."

"Uhm," Emily interrupted. "Why am I here? Jen, you insisted that I be here."

"Oh damn, sorry, I almost forgot. I need to talk to you"— she looked at Colm— "in private. Girl talk."

Colm was about to complain when his phone rang. "Jaysus, Mary, and Joseph, now who's this in the middle of the night?" He answered his phone and walked into the hallway.

Jen leaned across the desk and spoke quietly, "It's about that little matter you asked me to look into."

* * *

Emily waved goodbye as she watched Colm drive away. Amelia Lonsdale had just become a suspect, and Colm was determined to get to her before she could, as he put it, *"make like a tree and leave."* It was late, but the news Jen had given Emily invigorated her. So much so that she could no longer think of going back to bed. What Emily had learned had answered many questions. However, those answers raised even more questions. Answers that Colm might need before he talked to Amelia. After all, if Jen Stroud could get the skinny on Llandeso and connect it all back to Amelia Lonsdale, then maybe she could trace a few items of interest also.

Settling in her reading chair with her laptop and a cup of coffee, Emily logged onto the internet. An hour later, she picked up her phone and dialled Colm's number. He answered on the second ring.

"Where are you?"

"Just west of Brighton, why?"

"As soon as you can, pull over and call me back." Emily ended the call. Five minutes later, Colm called back.

"What's up, are you ok?"

"I'm fine, but there are things about Dalton Tire you need to know."

"Can it keep 'til I get back?"

"I don't think so. Harry Dalton was keeping a huge secret, and you need to know what it is before you talk to Amelia Lonsdale."

"Yes, Em, he was going to sell the business, we know that."

"Yes, that's right, but I just found out which one, and it wasn't Dalton Tire."

* * *

Worrying is not profitable, Amelia told herself. Still, she couldn't help it. The police were using Blackmore's phone to contact her. Calling her on a number reserved only for him and only for the purpose of their deal. She paced the small office, circling her desk, stopping briefly to glance out the window. The traffic on the 401 was a steady stream of white and red lights stretching like ribbons in both directions. *Why am I looking out this window? Even if Barry were coming, how could I tell in all that traffic?* She kept pacing, allowing her thoughts to be distracted only for a moment. *Where the hell is Barry? Why hasn't he called?* The only possibility she could envision caused a cold chill to crawl up her spine.

It had been hours since Amelia had sent the email. There was a read receipt in her inbox. *Is he on his way?* She checked the time. He'd read the message hours ago. *Maybe he is on his way.* It was a hopeful thought. She had to cling to it, if for no other reason than to maintain her sanity.

The thought buoyed her spirit, and she turned her mind to the other problem. A problem she feared that might become more expensive than initially anticipated.

"Action cures fear," she thought out loud. She picked up the phone and called a number she'd hoped she might never have to call again. By now he and his friends should be on the other side of the country, soon to be long gone. Long gone from her, long gone from Clarksville and, for that matter, long gone from the country. And once he was gone, he and his team of thugs were in for a huge surprise. The reward they were expecting would not be the payoff they deserved, and they would definitely get what they deserved. But for now, Amelia needed Kris Martin to answer his phone one last time before vanishing forever.

The phone rang four times before an angry voice answered, "What the actual fu—why are you calling? We agreed, you—"

"Shut up and listen," Amelia snapped back. "We've got a problem in Clarksville. I can't get in touch with Shinkwinn. People are dropping like flies. I think—"

"Shinkwinn's your problem," Martin snapped back. "You wanted him dealt with, I made it happen. Whatever goes on from there is your business, not mine."

"No," said Amelia. "If this gets screwed up for me, then it's screwed up for you too. Let me remind you, you've only received the down payment on what we'd agreed. Your final payment hinges on me getting mine. Fix this now!" Amelia slammed the phone back in its cradle just as Colm walked through the door.

* * *

"You'd be the sister," said Colm. "Anne Dalton's sister, yeah?"

Amelia's jaw dropped open, her eyes grew wide, surprised by the sudden appearance of the man in the dark blue suit and a handful of uniformed police officers standing behind him.

"Who—who are you? How did you... get in... here?" Amelia's words came in fragments of thought. *Had they heard her conversation with Martin? If so, how much? Had she said anything she shouldn't?* The man now standing directly opposite her on the other side of her desk was flashing a badge. She watched, half aware of what was happening as two constables bracketed her and held her arms. Their grips were firm but not painful; she heard words, although not clearly, as her mind raced. They seemed to be saying something about lawyers and remaining silent. *Silent about—what? Kris Martin? Barry?* "Yes, er, no—I don't know. What's all this about?"

"Ms. Lonsdale, we are investigating several incidents that have occurred in the Clarksville area. Your name has come up in connection with that investigation, and we believe you have vital information relevant to our inquiry. For that reason, we would like you to accompany us to the local detachment for an interview."

"I-I can't." Amelia's eyes darted around the office, now filled to capacity with policemen. They were searching through the file cabinet and opening drawers in her desk. "Say, y-you can't do that. That's private, it's mine. Stop it! You can't—"

Colm produced a folded three-page document stapled together in the corner. The first page read "Warrant to Search." He handed it to Amelia and said, "Yes, ma'am, we can. Now, about that interview."

Amelia shrugged her shoulders in an attempt to break free of the officers' grip. In a desperate show of defiance, she said, "I'm not going anywhere. I'm expecting a business associate here any minute. I don't know what you're looking for, but I can assure you, you won't find it here. Warrant or no warrant." She straightened up, pulled her shoulders back and looked Colm directly in the eyes. Taking the warrant from Colm, she gave it a cursory glance and tossed it on the desk. "Do what you have to and get out. I've got nothing to say to you."

"I'm afraid it doesn't work that way, Ms. Lonsdale. You see, you're not allowed to be here while we search. Oh, and just so you know—" he leaned forward and flipped the top page of the warrant over so she could read it— "this allows us to remove everything from this premise. Everything, right down to the carpet tacks if I want them."

"What! You can't, I told you, I'm expecting an associate here any minute," Amelia argued.

"That associate wouldn't be Barry Blackmore, would it?"

Amelia stiffened at the mention of Blackmore's name. Her heart fluttered and her face paled. "H-how do you know about Barry?"

Colm shook his head and signalled to the two constables guarding Amelia to back off. They moved away, giving her room to breathe. "I'm afraid Mr. Blackmore was murdered earlier, er that is to say—"he checked his watch as if to remind himself what day it was— "yesterday evening. I'm afraid he's made his final journey, at least in this life."

She collapsed into her chair, leaned forward, rested her elbows on the desk and buried her face in her hands. All activity in the room ceased as all eyes fell on the beleaguered woman. Colm cocked his head toward the door indicating the officers should step out. "Guys, give us a minute here," he said. "Sure, Ms. Lonsdale's not going anywhere, and I think she needs a minute in private." He turned to Amelia and said, "Was Mr. Blackmore special to you? I mean were you—"

Amelia looked up. Her eyes were tired and dark, but she hadn't been crying. They were worried eyes. Eyes that held a world of stress. Sad eyes, flat and lifeless. What Colm had perceived only moments before as determination and fire had vanished. Now he was looking at a woman whose life had suddenly and irrevocably been sucked into a vacuum.

She shook her head. "No, not like that, call off your dogs, Detective. Whatever you're looking for is probably on this computer." Her voice was tired and weak. Tears formed in the corners of her eyes. Amelia tried to wipe them, causing the salt to sting and irritate to the point where she couldn't keep them open. She pulled at her blouse, lifting the top to use as a tissue. Colm didn't carry a handkerchief and suddenly felt inadequate because of it.

"Somebody find me a tissue, bog roll something this lady can wipe her eyes with."

Seconds later, a constable appeared with a roll of toilet paper and handed it to Colm. Amelia wiped her eyes and was finally able to keep them open. She gazed across the desk at Colm and said, "Pull up a chair, I might as well tell you what you want to know."

G. A. PICKSTOCK

45

"BARRY AND I WERE business associates. Nothing more." Amelia's voice had returned to normal. "I met him at a conference in Toronto about a year ago. I'd heard the name before, and I knew about his family's furniture reputation. We happened to sit beside each other at a banquet we attended. One thing led to another, and we wound up doing a few land deals together."

Colm's eyebrows raised. "I'm sorry, Ms. Lonsdale, but we've checked. Llandeso hasn't done a dime's worth of business since its inception."

Amelia shook her head, "You're right, it hasn't. We set Llandeso up for one deal and one only. Any business I had with Barry, I did through my other company."

Colm checked his note pad. "Would that be your numbered company?" He read the numbers to her from his notes.

She nodded, "I'd have to check, but yes, that's right. I own several companies like that. Most of them are single-use entities."

Amelia noted the confusion in Colm's face. "It's not an uncommon practice. Many businesses do this, especially when dealing with large amounts of money. I suppose the most important reason is to limit personal liability. If something goes wrong and lawsuits ensue, then one must shield oneself."

"I think there might be another reason."

"Oh, and what might that be?"

"Secrecy, collusion, conspiracy, subterfuge, call it what you like. Listen, why don't we quit this little dance and get down to the details? I don't have time for a lecture on business 101. I've got four bodies lying in the morgue and the killings are all connecting back to you."

Amelia thought for a moment. *Perhaps there is a way to do this and drop it all in the lap of...* "I haven't done anything wrong, detective, here's what I know. Yes, I had a deal with Blackmore. You probably think that the deal was to buy Dalton Tire."

Colm nodded. "It would appear that way."

"What you don't know is Dalton Tire is worthless. It has no value beyond its receivables, and that money is encumbered." Amelia unfolded her arms and relaxed back into her chair. "Moreover, the profit from those receivables is negligible. By the time the bills are paid, there won't be enough left to buy coffee."

"How can that be? According to Jim Roberts, Dalton Tire was profitable."

Amelia laughed, "You're kidding, right? Dalton Tire is so far in the hole they'll never get out."

"How's that?"

"What do you know about factoring?"

"Enlighten me."

"Business 101, as you say. Factoring is when a business, such as Dalton Tire, borrows money against future earnings. Only in this case, it's not speculation for the lender. Repayment of the debt is guaranteed by the receivable. A bank or, more often, an investment company, will lend money against a bonafide purchase order. They will lend a percentage of the order's value so that the vendor can complete the job. The invoice is sent out to the customer and payment is directed to the lender in the company name. When payment is received, the factoring company takes a percentage of the gross sale and returns the rest to the company. When a substantial amount of the profit is eaten up in interest, little is left in the way of net profit, and in Dalton's case, it was leaving him operating in the red."

"How can you know this? Wait, don't tell me, I think I can guess. You and your investors are the ones financing Dalton's orders."

The smile that crossed Amelia's face could have been that of a proud professor after realizing that her student finally understood. "There you go."

"If Dalton Tire owned a thousand acres of land, why did he need your money? Surely that was enough to borrow against?" He glanced up at Amelia without lifting his head.

Amelia let out another chuckle, "First things first, Harry didn't know I was involved, but more to the point, Harry Dalton owned far more than that. Multiply your number by five. Harrison Dalton was smart, farmer smart, horse-trader smart. Do you know what I mean?"

Colm nodded, "I think so."

"Harry owned the land, but it had nothing to do with Dalton Tire. He had plans for that land and he had no intention of encumbering it. I don't think you've done your homework. Harrison Dalton owned a company called RealHard Holdings Inc. That company owns RealHard Manufacturing, RealHard Property and RealHard Leasing. Dalton Tire is owned by RealHard Manufacturing. Are you confused yet? I was when I first figured it out."

Colm rubbed at the stubble on his chin. The first glimmer of daylight distracted him for a moment. Another hour and the sun would be up. "Let's move this along, we don't have all day," he said. "You've got my attention. Go on."

Amelia continued, "Harry took advantage of my sister. Our parents left us a vast fortune. Millions, enough to last many lifetimes. After Anne and Harry got married, Anne and I fell out. She wouldn't speak to me, but the questions about her lending habits came to me through the trustee. I learned Harry was borrowing millions. I was worried about her, so I hired a firm to investigate. That's when I learned Harry had amassed over five thousand acres. When Barry and I met at the conference, it was only natural that we talked about Harry. He was, after all, becoming one of the largest landowners in the area. The fact that he was keeping it all on the down-low made us wonder why? Then it hit us. He was going to turn it into residential and make a fortune. Trouble is he didn't have the money. So, we decided to make him a huge offer, two-hundred-million for RealHard Holdings. It threw him, he didn't see it coming. Harry bit and bit hard. That was a lot of money. More than he could have imagined all at once."

"If Harry was borrowing so much money, how did he justify it, and how could he keep the land deals secret?"

"Easy, Anne was lending the money to Dalton Tire. Harry used that money to pay his overhead, which were, in fact, his own businesses. He was using us to factor the orders. The profit, if there was any, was being used in the same way. All the money funnelled up to RealHard Holdings."

Colm nodded as he finally understood how the man had done it. It was brilliant, and all entirely legal.

"So, over the years, Harrison Dalton had managed to keep everyone happy while wearing two faces. The employees prospered, the creditors made money, and most importantly, Harrison Dalton collected all the gold."

Amelia's professorial smile widened into a full-blown grin. "Now, you have it. It was a giant Ponzi scheme, and it would have continued had Anne not tied his hands. She'd cut him off. Without her backing, he panicked. He couldn't fix the tire business and couldn't afford the taxes on all the land he'd bought. When our deal came along, he jumped at it. There was one fly, however. Six little acres he'd never been able to get Nicole Saunders to sell to him. When it went under tax auction and he had no funds to make a qualified bid, it put him in a bad position. He needed that land as much as we did and for the same reason."

Amelia smiled at the thought as she relayed the story. "Happily, one of our investors made a successful bid."

"That would be Angelo Pellini?"

"Bingo! Got it in one, good for you! There's more to that, but I'll let that one keep for now."

She pushed back away from the desk and crossed her legs, leaned her head back and stretched her arms to get the kinks out. Amelia closed her eyes, reflecting for a moment on what she'd just told the detective. She was getting a massive weight off her chest, and thoughts of repercussions were drifting far from her mind. It was good to tell the story. She'd been holding it back for so long, even keeping her involvement from Anne while she helped her sister find a worthless document in Harry's shambles of an office. None of it mattered. In the end, the tire company was worthless. "Anne had no idea—I don't think she'd have seen it had Harry not died," she said softly, thinking out loud.

"What's that?"

"Huh, oh, my sister, she had no idea what Harry was up to. Anne doesn't know the corporate structure. Regardless of what happens here, the deal will still go through. All it's going to take is a signature. My sister will become very wealthy, and if I survive this, I will make five times what she will. There's a lot of money at stake, and there's no way you will stop it."

"Stop what?"

"The sale. I told you. The factory is owned by RealHard Manufacturing, which is owned by RealHard Holdings. Once we buy RealHard Holdings we will own it all. The factory will close. We have no interest in making tires."

Amelia sensed Colm still wasn't getting it. "Let me break it down this way. Dalton tire is owned by RealHard Manufacturing—"

"Yeah, I get that. But don't the employees own shares in the company? What happens to them?"

"No, you don't get it. All anyone owns are shares in Dalton Tire's profits. It's a profit-sharing group. Nothing more. The company is little more than a shell through which money comes in and money goes out. The company owns nothing. All the equipment is leased. The building is leased. Can you guess who the landlord is?"

"I'm guessing RealHard something."

"Right! Now you're on track. RealHard Leasing owns all the equipment right down to the paperclips and RealHard Property owns the building. It, in turn, leases the land it's built on from RealHard Holdings. And Harry owns, sorry, owned it all. Anne doesn't realize it, but now she owns it all. At least she will once your investigation is done."

"Two-hundred-million, that's a huge amount of money. How can it be worth that much?"

"Coffee money," said Amelia. "Developed properly, that land is worth billions. Over the past few months, we, Blackmore and I, along with our investors, have quietly been applying for rezoning permits. That's why we needed the Saunders property. All it would take to scuttle the whole deal would be one dissenter. One vote against rezoning to residential and we were done. Nicole would have sold, but she wanted more than Harry could pay. Harry gave up eventually."

"Is that when you tried to bribe Cal Jenkins to send the land to auction?"

"Who? Bribe? I have no idea what you're talking about. I don't know any Cal whatever his name is." Amelia looked Colm in the eye, "I don't bribe people to get things done. I authorized the purchase of that land. We were willing to pay dearly for it. Without it, we were dead in the water. There was no way we could let six paltry acres stand in the way of a multi-billion-dollar project."

"That sounds like motive to me. So, what, you killed Nicole for the land?"

Amelia's eyes turned to flint. Glaring at Colm, she snarled, "I buy land, I build on the land, I don't kill people. I would have paid a million dollars for her land. In fact, I put that much into an account for that very purpose. I lost a quarter of it before I was able to put a stop to it. Should have known better than to trust a cop. Especially since that land went to auction and yes, Angelo bought it. In the end, Saunders should have sold because Angelo paid nothing like what it was worth. Live and learn, I guess."

"But Nicole didn't live, did she?"

"I wasn't talking about her. I was talking about me. Never take on a cop as a partner, especially if that cop's name is Kris Martin."

Colm almost fell off his chair. "Kris Martin! How do you know Kris Martin? Do you know where he is? How—"

Amelia suddenly realized that as much as this detective thought he knew, in reality, he knew very little. She wondered how he'd come to tie her to all of this, and then it dawned on her. "Shinkwinn." The utterance left her lips before she could stop it. Reality drew down on her. She indeed was wrapped up in this. Firmly entangled in something she'd had no intention of creating. However, now it seemed that the detective would soon put it together, and in fact, as the realization hit her, Amelia could tell the detective was having an epiphany of his own.

"What did you say?"

Suddenly fearful that she'd said far too much, she said, "Oh, nothing. Just thinking out loud." *Time to call Sidney.*

* * *

The interview with Amelia had taken just under an hour. She had no idea that she was confirming what Emily had told him. It was all true. Harry Dalton had set it all up just as Amelia had described with one small but significant difference. Harry had, in fact, known of Llandeso's plan. They were going to shut the plant down and sell everything off. The plans for the new Clarksville Urban Reclamation Proposal were public knowledge, available through proper channels to anyone, if they knew what to look for.

Llandeso Investments was owned by a numbered company, which in turn had four registered partners. Emily had identified three of them as Blackmore Holdings, Llandeso Investments, and Pellini Land Development.

The fourth partner was an investment company known as Anon Dental Enterprises. Emily hadn't identified the owner yet, but Jen was working on it, and she might have an answer soon.

Emily's information was just what the doctor ordered. Colm knew from experience that people loved to talk, and if not about themselves, then about what they knew. *Gossip is a beautiful thing.* Some people revelled in their ability to prove to others just how smart they were. *What is it people say, open mouth, insert foot?* Amelia had done just that, but she'd gone a step or two further. She'd dropped Kris Martin's name, and that was why she was now cooling her jets in an eight-by-ten cell at the Pickering detachment. He had twenty-four hours to decide whether or not to charge her. Colm could charge her for colluding in the disappearance of the six-pack. It was thin, and he might not get a conviction, but maybe by then, he'd have enough to charge her in connection with the murders.

Something nagged at him. He couldn't get the word out of his mind. He'd heard it before, and as the miles flew past as he raced home to Clarksville, he repeated it in his mind. *Shinkwinn, Shinkwinn, Shinkwinn, where the hell have I heard that before?*

Colm's second call came from the detachment commander in Pickering. After consulting with her lawyer, Amelia Lonsdale had more to say. She also wanted a deal.

46

THE FIRE WASN'T OUT yet. The embers needed little more than a quick stir with a stick, sending hundreds of small sparks skyward, rising on the hot air, curling and spinning in a turbulent spiral until ultimately emitting one last brilliant glow, and vanishing into the blackness. Kris dropped a few small sticks onto the coals. They ignited immediately, bathing the area around the campfire in a soft orange glow. Six apprehensive faces peered back at him through the flickering light of the fire.

"What do you mean, we have a problem?" Only one voice spoke, but Kris could see the question in each man's eyes.

"Shinkwinn's gone ballistic. Shit's getting real back home, and it needs to be fixed."

Another voice chimed in, "I knew it! That guy was a mistake from the get-go. Shoulda dealt with him before we left. So, now what?"

A third voice spoke, "So what! He's not our problem anymore. Let Miss High 'n Mighty deal with him."

Martin wanted to agree with his crew. They'd dragged their families across the country. They were all tired and fed up with living on wheels, and the finish line was just on the other side of the mountains. The trip had been arduous despite the comfort of the motor homes. Travelling with wives and kids to an unknown future was a challenge neither of these men had ever anticipated. They'd stayed under the radar, sometimes in convoy and sometimes independently, but never out of touch and never more than an hour's drive apart, but now it appeared that there was one more roadblock.

They'd decided that their last night on the road would be an early one, allowing them to rest for the final push into Vancouver. Amelia's call had changed all that. They were less than three hours from their final destination. Three hours to freedom, but that freedom came at a price, and the money was not yet in the bank. They had risked everything to get this far. There was no way he would let some little twerp Irishman screw it up now.

"I shouldn't have to remind you, there's a lot of money in this deal for all of us. More than any of us will ever need. We only get paid if Lonsdale stays healthy. The way it looks right now that loony Irish bastard is going to kill this deal. One of us has to deal with Shinkwinn, or we've done all this for nothing." From the expressions on the faces of his crew, Kris Martin knew he'd be the one.

* * *

Four hours later, Kris and his six-pack arrived at the Port of Vancouver. Kris Martin kissed his wife goodbye and assured her he would join them in Hawaii in a few days. The lies had spewed forth so easily he almost believed them himself. A trial date had been moved forward, and his testimony was vital. *"I know, this was supposed to be a family vacation of a lifetime, but it's police business, and I have to testify,"* he'd told her. It was a weak excuse, one that could easily be verified, but Kris hoped that the excitement of the cruise ship, and the distractions that that offered, was enough to allay any concerns his wife had. After all, it must be vital that he get back if the OPP was springing for a private jet to get him home.

* * *

The Gulfstream G4 touched down on the runway and taxied to the private business terminal. Kris Martin disembarked, hailed a taxi and settled in the back seat for the short ride back to Clarksville. *With any luck, I might make it back to Vancouver before the boat sails.*

He'd thought it through on the flight. With the time difference, he might be able to make it back in time for the boat, and he could easily justify the change in plan. The Gulfstream jet was expensive, but if this worked out, it would be worth it.

Shinkwinn had served his purpose. All he needed to do now was keep his head down. Instead, he'd become a liability, and Martin could not fathom why. At this point, it no longer mattered. Shinkwinn had to go.

* * *

It was serendipity that Shinkwinn would find himself in this place on the eve of All Saints Day. Halloween was a day like any other, yet, he knew the history of All Hallows Eve; a time when people prayed for the release of the souls in purgatory. The release he had in mind would save many, not from purgatory, but from hell.

Anne Dalton would die for her betrayal just the way Harry did. She'd had her chance to change things, but greed was more important. She didn't care how it affected the employees. Indeed, the whole town would suffer. Selling the plant was just the beginning. Thousands of acres of fertile farmland would be devastated, offered up, on the altars of brick and mortar in solemn sacrifice to the asphalt gods.

And for what? Shopping plazas and housing, for who? Not Clarksville's citizenry. It would die without the plant. Dalton's plan would transform Clarksville into a refuge for retirees. Big city big-shots, from Toronto, Vancouver, and any other major cities, would sell up, making millions on their properties. They would take their pensions and migrate to God's country where the cost of living is lower, and their newfound wealth would last a lifetime. A once robust and proud heritage of industry and productivity would fall to a swarm of golf crazy, entitled parasites. And all because a handful of avaricious, grasping predators, seized upon a plan to line their own pockets and vanish, abandoning Shinkwinn's beloved Clarksville forever.

The plant was the key, the source of all Clarksville's prosperity. Harry knew that, but then, he'd become one of them. Selling was wrong, and now, Anne was going to complete the deal. Shinkwinn would not allow it to happen.

Her hands tied behind her back, Anne's torso rocked sideways as the van bounced along the uneven terrain. With one hand, Shinkwinn turned the wheel sharply to the left, and Anne's shoulder smashed against the doorpost, her head slamming into the window, instantly rebounding back. Restrained only by the shoulder strap of the van's seatbelt, she slumped forward, unconscious, chin pressed hard against the top of her breastbone. He looked over at the woman slouched in the seat beside him.

"Don't die on me yet, bitch, I've got plans for you."

* * *

They'd decided that Emily should give Anne Dalton another visit. Colm needed to return to Pickering to interview Amelia. He was barely ten minutes out when Emily called.

"She's not here!" The urgency in Emily's voice bordered on panic. "Colm, the front door has been bashed in, and it looks like there's been a terrific fight in here."

Colm eased the car over onto the shoulder. "Have you checked inside?"

"Yes, I haven't touched anything, there's no one here," said Emily, regaining her composure. "She's definitely not here, but her car is."

The words had barely escaped her lips when she heard the roar of an engine being revved up. The noise came from behind the house, and as Emily dashed around the side of the property, she saw it. A dirty black van bounced its way across the back lawn of the Dalton homestead. It lurched forward, fishtailing across the vast expanse of snow-covered grass, finally reaching the tree-line at the far side of the property. The van followed the trees for a short distance, made a left-hand turn, and disappeared into the forest.

Breathless, Emily gasped into the phone, "It's the van, the black van. It ran off into the woods behind Dalton's house." Within seconds the van streaked past the front of the house. "Oh Jesus, Colm, it's heading into town. What if they've got Anne? I'm going after them."

It was too late for Colm to argue. Emily had hung up. He punched the throttle and headed for the nearest U-turn.

47

COLM RACED EASTWARD, WEAVING in and out of traffic, his eyes constantly scanning the blur of vehicles as he dodged around them. In the distance, approaching at an agonizingly slow rate, the Clarksville interchange loomed into view. He had no idea where Emily was or where she was going. Wherever it was, the black van had become synonymous with danger as far as she was concerned, and now Colm feared she was careening headlong toward it.

Efforts to identify the van and its owner had failed. Emily had tried to read the plate number, but it was so dirty and faded that she could make out only the last digit, and even it was obscure. She couldn't decide if it was a 1 or an I. The first four letters of the plate had been faded by time and covered by dirt. This, in itself, was enough to warrant a ticket. Cops generally overlooked this minor infraction, choosing instead to issue a warning and only in cases where they had pulled a vehicle over for more serious reasons. Emily had thought that the fourth letter might be an X or possibly a K. It was so obscured, she couldn't be sure, and she'd been so shaken by the ordeal as to doubt her own memory.

Colm had left that part of the investigation to his new Detective Constable, Jen Stroud. He and Jen had formed a pseudo partnership long before her promotion. As the acting commander of the detachment, Colm had relied heavily on Jen to help him keep things running smoothly. Now that she had become a permanent member of the investigative team, she'd proven herself to be a valuable asset. It's worth another try, Colm thought as he pressed the home button on his phone. "Siri, call Jen."

"Hey, boss, what's up?" Jen Stroud's voice came through loud and clear as Colm approached the exit into Clarksville.

"Are we any further along on identifying that old black van?"

"I don't have much to go on. I mean, an X that might be a K and a 1 that could be an I, You realize there are thousands of registrations with those numbers. I narrowed the search to vehicles within fifty kilometres of here, but I can't find any vans with that description. I was checking on one idea just as you called, hang on."

Colm heard Jen thrashing away at the keyboard of her computer. "There is one thing, I have a plate here that reads, Sierra, Hotel, November, Kilo, One, oh, wait, it's invalid, no longer registered."

"What was that?".

"S H N K - 1," she spelled it out for him.

"Shink one!"

"Yeah, I guess you could say it that way," said Jen.

"Jaysus, I never put it together until now. It's been bothering me all night."

"What has?"

"Shinkwinn," said Colm. "You say it's deregistered. Who was it registered to?"

"Just a sec." Jen tapped away at the keyboard. "Oh, Christ! Colm you're not going to believe this—"

"Don't tell me," Colm cut her off. "My guess is it's Cal Jenkins. Go ahead, tell me I'm wrong."

"How could you know that?" said Jen. "Yes, he's had that plate for years. He let it expire three years ago. Something about it being too faded to use. Oh, shit! Colm, the plate is registered to an '89 Ford Econoline E150."

"Yeah and I'm betting it's black," said Colm. "Put a BOLO out on that van. Bring him in for questioning. If he resists, arrest him."

"What's the charge?"

"Kidnapping and murder."

"Wait, how did you know it was Jenkins?"

"I'll tell you later, I have to find Emily." *God, I hope she doesn't catch up with him.*

* * *

The first snow of the season continued to fall. The fluffy cotton-ball flakes drifted lazily to the ground forming a velvet carpet of white. Jenkins faltered as he dragged Anne Dalton down the embankment toward the river's edge. Slipping on a loose stone, he fell, almost landing in the water. The river ran high this time of year, and the water was swift near the bank. Regaining his footing, he held tight to the air rifle and stared back at the top of the hill. Their trail was easy to spot. It was too late to change now. All he could hope for was more snow to cover their tracks. Just a little further, and he would win. Anne Dalton would soon join her partner in the watery grave, and control of the plant would revert to the ESA. *I'll be a hero. Hell, they might even erect a statue of me.*

Jenkins turned, pushing Anne further down the bank. "Move, bitch, I need you over there." He pointed to a small outcropping of land where the river water bubbled and churned around its edges. "You're going for a swim," he sneered, lifting his rifle.

Jenkins jabbed the muzzle of the gun into Anne's back, shoving her forward. She stumbled, collapsing to her knees onto the mud-encrusted rocks. The icy spray from the windswept waterfalls stabbed at her exposed skin. Semi-frozen mud soaked through her jeans, numbing the pain in her kneecaps. With her hands bound behind her, Anne could not feel her fingers as she fought to keep her torso upright.

Masked by the sound of the river rushing past, Anne thought she heard something off to her left. Stalling for time, she stayed down, refusing to move. A twig snapped, and then another, followed by a frightened yelp. Captor and captive turned to see the flailing image of a young woman tumble into the trunk of a bush halfway up the embankment. They watched as Emily grabbed at the branches of a large juniper bush, her feet scraping at the snow-covered ground in a desperate attempt to gain her footing.

* * *

Emily's insistence that they buy new cellphones after her abduction was bearing fruit. Colm had resisted at first, but now, the new phone's tracking feature made him thankful he'd acquiesced. He'd tracked Emily's phone to a familiar neighbourhood. Only months before, he'd made an important arrest on this street, and now, here he was back again. In fact, Emily's Mustang was parked in front of the very house where Colm had made the arrest. He recognized the woman standing in her driveway behind the now infamous black van, waving him in, pointing toward the backyard.

"What the hell is going on?" gasped Mary Taylor. "I saw a man with a woman, he forced her out—" she pulled Colm's arm, pushing him past the van and up the driveway— "they ran through the bushes. Emily chased them through there. Be careful, he has a gun."

Colm followed the snowy footprints into an alcove formed by a stunted forest of sumac and juniper, mixed with baby maples and just enough prickly ash to make life miserable. The low-hanging boughs bit hard at his face as he raced through the narrow passage. Breaking through the tangle of brambles and branches, he halted. Ten feet below, through the underbrush and forest of saplings and small bushes, Emily struggled to maintain her balance. Holding fast to the trunk of a thick juniper bush, her feet flailed at the wet, slippery ground in a frantic attempt to get a foothold.

Colm saw the muddy slide Jenkins and his hostage had left behind. As the river roiled and splashed over the side of the embankment, he watched as Jenkins stood over the kneeling, mud-caked figure of Anne Dalton. The muzzle of his rifle pressed between her shoulder blades.

Colm dropped to one knee, drawing his pistol. The rush of the wind and the roar of the river faded as he concentrated on the torso of Clarksville's town clerk. With both eyes open in a marksman's stance, Colm raised his firearm, pulling the front sight into view. His dominant eye took control of the sight while his left eye allowed him an unobstructed depth of field. With robotic precision, the rear sight moved into position. The white dot of the front blade sight centred in the gap of the rear V-notch. Cal Jenkins was a heartbeat away from his final breath.

"Drop your weapon and show me your hands," Colm yelled over the roar of the river. "Don't move, Cal, or I will shoot."

But Jenkins moved. He pushed Anne Dalton to the ground, face down, and with just one step, he put himself in a position Colm had prayed he would not. Jenkins crouched; pulling the air rifle to his shoulder, a frosty vapour enveloped the breach of the powerful rifle. He had the advantage. The move placed Emily directly between Colm and Jenkins. Despite the onset of cold weather, the cornucopia of vegetation retained much of its canopy, and through the leafy growth, Colm could barely make out the form of Jenkins' left shoulder. He had a shot, but not without risking Emily's life. A scene flashed in his memory. Déjà vu. He'd been here before, but this time there was no taking the shot and Emily could not see him.

Jenkins' lips curled into a cold sneer. His ace in the hole stood a mere thirty feet away, obliterating any thought of Colm using his weapon. Emily James meant nothing to him. He could kill her without a second thought and would do so if necessary. Nothing would prevent him from finishing his task, not even the auburn-haired beauty clinging desperately to the bushes and certainly not some smug Irish cop who'd only lived here a year.

"You drop your gun," Jenkins yelled back, drawing a bead on Emily's chest. She had managed to wedge her left foot against the base of the juniper's trunk, her right foot still resting on unstable ground. "I will kill her. You know, I will."

"I can't do that," Colm yelled back as he searched for a better vantage point.

There wasn't one, the brush was too thick. The only way down was the path before him, and in his street shoes, he didn't fancy his chances. Colm had to get Emily out of the line of fire.

He was sweating, but it wasn't the adrenaline coursing through his veins; he realized the snow had stopped falling. The thin carpet of white had almost vanished, melting away as the mid-morning temperature became practically spring-like. Early snowfalls rarely lasted, and Colm recognized an opening. Time itself had suddenly become his ally, and he knew now exactly how to use it.

"Emily, love, hang on, try not to move. I'll get you out of there." Colm called loud enough to be heard over the river noise. "Cal, be reasonable. It's all over. You have no place to go. Killing anyone else won't change things. You need to put your gun down and let these ladies go. Sure, you can see, I'm right."

Jenkins shook his head, "I'm in control. I make the rules now. You don't know what they have planned. You have no idea." His grip tightened around the rifle's pistol grip, raising the muzzle a bit higher, bringing the crosshairs of the scope dead centre of Emily's chest.

Grand, talk away boyo, keep it up. "You're right, I don't know. Tell me why? Why kill all these people; why do you want to kill Anne Dalton?"

"Why? Why do you think? To save the plant, that's why. To save Clarksville. They—they're going to sell it." Colm took a tentative step and leaned forward, straining to see what Jenkins was doing. "First, Harry, then this—this bitch. She never cared about the place. Harry's dead. All she wants is money. They're nothing but a greedy bunch of bastards, all of them. Saunders, Blackmore, Harry, and this bitch and her sister. They were gonna screw this town, and I saved it, or I will once she's dead. I'm doing this town a favour. You all should thank me."

Without a clean shot, Colm had no choice but to delay. He had to keep Jenkins talking long enough for his theory to work. Through the tangled twigs and branches of the underbrush, Jenkins was little more than a dark blur, and Emily blocked most of Colm's view.

"Why, Cal? You have nothing to do with the plant." *You're a fekkin' bureaucrat for God's sake.* "How could selling the plant possibly hurt you?"

The redness in Jenkins' face deepened. "You don't get it, do you? That plant is this town. Everything about it affects everything else, and they want to sell it. All those people, my dad, they count on their pensions from that plant. They're going to kill that. I can't let that happen."

Colm delayed his response. His tactic was working, and if his theory were correct, another minute was all he'd need. He paused a little longer and was about to speak when Jenkins stood, presenting Colm with a clean shot.

"I've had enough," Jenkins said. "I don't care what happens to me." Raising his rifle, he swung the muzzle back to Anne Dalton. "Time to end this now." He pulled the rifle butt into his shoulder and placed his finger into the trigger guard.

"No, Cal, don't!" Colm leapt from his perch. His right shoe slid forward, knocking his balance askew. Twisting to his right side, his left foot caught a root sending him into a pirouette, ending in a groin-wrenching split as his hamstrings stretched beyond their ability. An agonizing wail belched forth. He landed hard on his right side. Headfirst, he slid toward the river. A branch caught his right hand, sending his pistol skidding into the muddy mess below. As his body slid ever closer to the river's edge, he watched in abject impotence as his firearm preceded him, finally tumbling into the water.

Wet and mud-soaked, Colm came to rest inches away from his surprised and bewildered adversary. Fighting the carbonizing pain in his inner thighs, Colm struggled to his knees. Attempting to stand, his tortured muscles could not take his weight.

Reaching out with one hand, he said, "Cal, don't do it, mate. It's not as bad as you think. Don't make this any worse than it is. Anne Dalton doesn't need to die. Nobody does. You didn't have to kill all those people."

Jenkins turned his gun on Colm. "Stay down Irish, or you and your girlfriend won't live out the day."

* * *

Anne Dalton saw her opportunity. Lying in the cold, she had formulated a plan. Her escape route lay directly ahead. The pathway back to the main street was only a few metres away, and if she ran fast enough, she could disappear into the bushes and run for help.

As Jenkins made his turn, she rolled to her side. Scrambling to her feet, she darted forward. Her left knee buckled, sending searing pain into her thigh. Swinging his rifle back toward her, Jenkins drew aim at her back and pulled the trigger.

It wasn't the sharp crack he'd expected to hear. Instead, the air rifle emitted what sounded more like a muffled fart as it discharged. A fine mist exploded from the muzzle spraying forward in a shimmering shower covering Anne Dalton's back and hair in a metallic sheen reminiscent of a can of silver spray-paint. The impact from the shot knocked the wind out of Anne, she fell after only a few feet, forcing her to once again become one with the ground. She lay there, weeping, waiting for the finishing shot.

* * *

Colm willed his legs to move, but the pain won, causing him to fall forward, coming to rest on all fours. Jenkins had already reloaded and was levelling the rifle at him. Colm's theory was right, but now he was in the crosshairs with a fresh round in place. The first round had thawed in the chamber and subsequently was not as effective as intended. Cal Jenkins had made one error. Colm couldn't count on him to make it again. He scanned the scene. Emily, clinging to the bushes for dear life, had not uttered a word. Anne Dalton lay prone, face down, dead perhaps, injured maybe, Colm could not tell. He turned his face up to his would-be executioner.

"Cal, don't do this. It's no use. Whatever you think this will accomplish, it won't."

"No more talk, you're done. If you know any prayers, you should have said them by now." He raised the scope to his eyes and squeezed the trigger.

Emily's scream paralyzed time itself as she hit Cal Jenkins. For less than a second, the world froze as one hundred and ten pounds of fury hit Jenkins harder than a linebacker. It was all she needed. Smashing high into his shoulders, Emily knocked the rifle out of his hands as it fired, launching three-hundred-and-fifty grains of frozen mercury into the raging water. The force of the impact drove her and Jenkins into the river. Wiping her hair away from her eyes, Emily stood knee-deep in the gravel-bottomed river. Cal Jenkins flailed about on his back, thrashing at the water.

"I—I can't swim!" he cried.

Emily wanted to laugh at the man, but the sight of Colm lying prone on the bank made her angrier. She sloshed her way to Colm. "Are you ok?"

"Find my gun," said Colm. "It's just there—" he pointed— "I can see it just under the water two feet in front of you."

Jenkins continued to thrash about crying for help. Emily retrieved the pistol and pointed it at Jenkins. "As my man here, would say. Try standing up. Eejit."

48

JENKINS ROSE FROM THE riverbed and stood facing Emily. "You're not going to shoot me," he sneered. "You're just a dumb busybody who can't keep her nose out of other people's business."

The gravel in Jenkins' voice caused Emily's blood to run cold. The chill running up her spine wasn't the result of the frigid river water. She recognized that voice. Emily had become familiar with its tone and timbre. She flipped the pistol's safety to the fire position. Glancing over at Colm, Emily caught his eyes as he sat rubbing at his inner thighs. Emily's wet hair clung to her face in auburn streaks, her eyes were black and hollow with black streams of mascara running down her cheeks, and as she turned back to Jenkins, the sneer on her lips turned into an evil smile. Colm shook his head and flashed a "don't do it" look at her.

"Move," Emily commanded, waving the gun in the direction she wanted him to go.

Jenkins remained defiant. "I'm going nowhere," he said. "If you know what's good for you, you'll leave and get the hell out of here."

"You seem to forget, we're the law, I have the gun," Emily countered.

Colm jumped in, "Ah fer godsake, just shoot the bastard and have done, sure nobody'll miss his arse."

Jenkins' eyes bulged as Emily complied and fired a round in Jenkins' direction. The bullet torpedoed its way through the water mere inches from Jenkins' leg. Cal Jenkins danced out of the river and fell to his knees on the riverbank. He didn't need to be told to put his hands behind his back.

Colm tossed Emily a pair of handcuffs and said, "Jaysus, Emily! I wasn't serious."

Emily turned to Colm. "He pissed me off," she said. "Besides, he had it coming. My shoulder still hurts."

"You should check on Anne. She's been down a long time, and I'm not going to be walking anytime soon," said Colm.

Emily handed Colm his gun and cuffed Jenkins. She turned her attention to Anne Dalton. Kneeling beside her, she asked, "Anne, can you hear me? Are you ok?"

Anne turned her head and rolled to her side. "Is it over? Did you get him? Is he dead?"

"See for yourself," said Emily as she helped Anne to her feet. "Turn around, I'll untie you."

Anne rubbed at her wrists as the circulation slowly returned. She glared at her kidnapper and snarled, "You're a goddamned mental case. Where did you ever get the idea the factory was going to close? You idiot!"

* * *

The faint wail of sirens reached their ears, and as they waited for reinforcements to arrive, Colm pondered his next move. Climbing back up the hill in his condition was out of the question, and Anne Dalton didn't appear to be in much better shape. She had a cut on her knee from when she'd fallen and was having difficulty walking. Emily would not be able to herd all three of them up the hill, and the walkway to the main street was at least a half a kilometre trek. He doubted he would be able to do it. Emily certainly could, but there was no way he was going to let her take custody of Jenkins alone. The irony of it hit him as he gazed across the river. Barely forty metres away was the Blackmore building and the service road where only hours ago they'd pulled Barry Blackmore out of the water. Dead, undoubtedly killed by the same man that now sat handcuffed and sullen in the same cold, muddy place as the rest of them. Jenkins had a lot to answer for, and many questions still remained. Colm needed to get the man into custody and fast. He was about to send Emily to get help when he heard voices coming from the top of the hill.

"Hey Sarge, are you ok?"

Colm looked up through the bush to see *Ernie and Bert* standing in the very spot from which he'd fallen. "We'll live, but we need help. Get fire and rescue down here. I can't walk, and we've got one more who's cut badly.

She needs a medic." Colm turned to face Jenkins. "Sure, you're lucky you don't need one," he said.

* * *

Colm wasn't the only one with a fancy new phone. When he left town and headed for parts unknown, Kris Martin had bought one also. His new Smart Phone had a police scanner app on it that allowed him to monitor police frequencies. It was a no-brainer for him to set up the app to monitor the OPP radio calls. This little piece of technology had kept his six-pack in the loop as they travelled across the country. Whenever they were the subject of police chatter, Kris and his crew knew precisely which areas to avoid. So when he got back to town following the activities of his old boss had been a cake-walk. All the chatter about black vans and kidnapped women had brought him to this place.

As he crouched behind a thick stand of dogwoods, Martin observed the activity being played out before him. Across the river a man, Martin recognized as Cal Jenkins held a woman at gunpoint. Jenkins was yelling up the hill at someone. Martin couldn't make out who it was, but then, he saw the second woman desperately clinging to a stand of bushes. Martin heard the frantic scream as Colm came sliding down the hill, and he watched expectantly as Jenkins held his rifle on the detective.

Shoot, dammit, shoot that Irish bastard, and save me the trouble. Martin's arms vibrated, and his legs tensed, ready to spring forth as though he could telepathically induce the action to the would-be killer. He'd come a long way to see this. He hadn't anticipated it, but now that it was before him, he waited in abject expectation for the final act to be complete. Kris Martin's patience reached its peak when suddenly from nowhere, the woman on the ground ran. The rest happened so quickly he barely saw it, and now he was faced with the task of finishing the job. Not only did Jenkins have to go, but the intrepid Colm O'Byrne and his luscious sidekick had to be neutralized as well.

It had all come down to this. A twenty-five-year career with the OPP had started off as most do. He'd wanted to help people, to serve and protect as the motto goes, but he'd learned relatively quickly that criminals could evade justice, and that the system was rigged in their favour. His frustration with the system grew as he watched the scenario play out over and over. They'd bring the perps in, charge them, and watch impotently as some hotshot lawyer or inept Crown Attorney would blow the whole case.

The line they walked as policemen was a thin one, and the temptation from the wrong side was strong. Better cops than he had fallen to its charms, and it wasn't long before Kris realized just how profitable life on the edge could be. He and his crew had racked up a fair chunk of change over the years, but it wasn't enough. Then Kris learned about Harrison Dalton and his plans to sell the factory. Finding the land prospectus in Lonsdale's car was a fluke, and Kris was not about to allow one of the best opportunities he'd ever encountered slide through his fingers. He wanted in, and Lonsdale was in no position to argue.

Now, he was in, up to his neck, as it were. Martin had walked that thin line long enough to bump elbows and rub shoulders with a lot of influential people. Most of whom were squeaky clean, but not all. So, when the need for a cleaner arose, Kris knew how to go about finding one. His end of the deal was a significant share of thirty-million dollars, tax-free.

Forty metres was all that stood between him and a vast fortune. All he had to do was pull the trigger. The thing was, there were four targets grouped closely together. It was a long shot for a .40 calibre pistol, a percentage shot at best. *Can I get four rounds on target fast enough?* He might hit his intended target, he might not. Decision made, Kris stood away from the bushes where he'd been hiding, aimed his pistol, and had Jenkins in his sights when Colm turned to shout at someone at the top of the hill.

Shit! Reinforcements, damn. They'll be on me in seconds. Kris lowered his gun and stepped back into the bushes. Time was running out. If he was to make it back in time to board the cruise ship, then he had to act now.

* * *

The first round smashed into the ground just above Colm's head. A millisecond later, the second one took Cal Jenkins in the shoulder, two more rounds missed Emily's feet by inches, sending mud splattering in all directions. Anne Dalton let out an ear-piercing scream as a fifth shot hit her. She fell to the ground, holding her side as blood oozed between her fingers.

Colm spun his head in the direction of the shots, levelled his pistol at a dark figure standing directly across from him. He fired twice, as a hail of gunfire erupted from behind him. Mud and stones flew everywhere as the rounds from *Ernie and Bert's* firearms hit all around the shooter on the opposite side of the river. Colm fired a third time, hitting the gunman in the upper thigh. The figure fell to the ground and crawled behind some bushes.

"After him!" yelled Colm. "Don't let him get away." He cast his eyes over at Emily. "Are you hit?"

"No, I'm ok," she said. "Are you ok?"

"Yeah, he missed me, but not by much, we've got to get out of here." Colm looked past Emily to see four firemen, with stretchers, running down the boardwalk toward them. He kept his pistol trained on the bushes across the river. Moments later, *Ernie and Bert* slid down the embankment, guns drawn, watching as the red and blue lights of a police cruiser flashed through the bushes, and stopped at the spot where the shooter had taken refuge. Two constables searched the area and reported on the radio.

"He's gone, but he shouldn't be too hard to find. Looks like he's losing a lot of blood."

G. A. PICKSTOCK

49

"WE TRACKED THE BLOOD-TRAIL to the street, then nothing," said the constable. "The shooter must have had a ride waiting for him."

Colm listened to the reports through a fog. The doctor had given him something for the pain, and it was making him drowsy and light-headed. He looked up at the constable.

"I can't swear to it, but I think the shooter was Kris Martin," said Colm. "I hit him, I know I did."

"Oh, you hit him all right," said the constable. "My bet is you hit something important, a vein maybe or an artery. Whatever it was, he's bleeding bad."

"If that's the case, then he'll need medical attention. Spread the word, check all the hospitals within a hundred kilometres of here."

The constable nodded and said, "It's been done. If he surfaces, we'll find him."

"How's Anne Dalton? Is she badly hurt? There was a lot of blood."

"Don't worry about Anne Dalton, she'll be fine. You have to rest and take care of that leg."

"What about Jenkins, where is he?"

"Both of them are in ICU. Papineau is standing guard over Jenkins. In fact, he's sitting right beside his bed with orders not to move. Oh, and by the way, Kendra will be in to see you in a while. She says, well done."

"Well done, no way we aren't done—there are too many loose ends here—Jenkins is good for the murders, but there's more to this, and I'm not sure we have all the guilty parties…"

The pain killers were taking full effect, and Colm was fading fast. His eyelids fluttered as he forced himself to stay awake, "Don't let…" Colm passed out before he could finish.

* * *

It wasn't going according to plan. Throughout the flight back to Clarksville, Kris Martin had plotted his moves carefully. With the time differences, it could work. He would take a taxi from the airport to his uncle's cottage. There was an old pickup there. He'd borrowed it many times over the years. This time of year, the place would be unoccupied, and therefore, it was the logical choice. Kris had it planned to the last second. Get the truck, find Jenkins, which shouldn't be too hard since the man was a creature of habit, and would, at this time of day, be in his office. He would call him and arrange to meet, put out that little fire, and be in the air with time to spare.

That part hadn't gone so well. Jenkins was unreachable, and it wasn't until he heard all the commotion on the scanner that he realized Colm had done him a favour. They were all down at the river, and he knew exactly where to find them.

When he saw the pandemonium at the river, Kris had hoped that Colm would take Jenkins out. But Colm wasn't wired that way. He wouldn't shoot unless necessary, so, it had fallen back to him.

Getting shot wasn't part of the plan, but the bullet hole in his leg had changed all that. Now he had to get away, far away, where he could get medical attention, and hospitals and emergency rooms were out of the question.

There was an old friend who lived about an hour north of town, a nurse who would tend his wound, and keep it to herself. All he had to do was stay awake long enough to get there. Kris stared down at his blood-soaked jeans. The belt he'd used as a tourniquet wasn't holding. He watched in horror as he fought to tighten the tourniquet. His left hand, slippery with his own blood, struggled with the belt in a panicked effort to stem the flow. His life was ebbing away, and with every heartbeat, the patch got wetter and wetter. His vision blurred, and his mind drifted. The distant, urgent blast of a horn drowned out his thinking as he turned his attention back to the road. It was too late, he never saw the eighteen-wheeler that plowed into the side of his truck.

* * *

"Amelia Lonsdale is being transported down here," said Kendra, as she took up residence in the big vinyl easy-chair beside Colm's bed. "She'll be at the detachment in the morning. Mr. Jenkins is singing like a canary, although, for the life of me, I can't figure the man's reasoning."

Colm pressed the button on the side-rail to raise up into a sitting position. Emily sat on his right with Kendra on his left. He was alone in a semi-private hospital room. Through the open door, Colm saw a constable standing watch in the corridor. He turned to face Kendra.

"Do I need protection?"

Kendra smiled. "No, he drove me over here, when we're done, he'll drive me back. Now, how's the leg?"

"Sore as hell, I've got a torn hamstring. It will heal, but for the next few weeks—" he nodded toward a set of aluminum crutches leaning against the wall— "I guess I'm a peg-leg. They tell me they'll have me up and walking later today. Still, the doctor says it could have been worse. Sure, I could be stretched out on one of Gentry's tables. I felt that bullet pass over me." Colm shuddered at the thought and turned to Emily, his eyes welled up, "It could have been a whole lot worse."

For a long moment, no one uttered a sound. Kendra finally spoke, "One bit of news for you. Kris Martin is dead. Instead of you down on Gentry's table, he's lying there now."

Colm snapped his head around and locked eyes with his boss. "Did I—"

"We don't know yet. Bob Gentry hasn't done his magic yet. You hit him in the leg, but we don't know if he was dead before or after the semi hit him. Either way, he's dead. The good news is, we know where the rest of his crew is and right about now, the RCMP is busy rounding them up. You gotta love smart-phone technology."

"And Anne Dalton, how's she doing?"

"Anne was hit in the side. Nothing serious, the bullet passed through without hitting anything important. She's sore and won't be running any marathons, but she'll live. She gets discharged—" Emily checked her watch— "right about now; actually, she could probably leave anytime."

Colm lurched forward, causing his leg to tighten up, sending a searing shock of pain up through his inner thigh and into his groin. He flopped back instantly, "Don't let her go," he gasped. "She needs to be questioned. I don't want her leaving town." He turned to Kendra. "Send himself—" he waved toward the cop outside the door— "stop her from leaving, she's in this up to her arse, I know it. Don't let her leave."

Kendra bolted for the door shouting instructions to the constable. The pair of them raced down the hall toward Anne Dalton's room. Moments later, Kendra reappeared in the doorway. The frown on her face told Colm all he needed to know.

"She's gone," said Kendra. "We put a BOLO out on her. Don't worry, Colm, she'll not have gone far. We'll find her."

* * *

The doctors were true to their word. They had him up and walking in no time. It had taken a few attempts, but Colm finally found his rhythm with the crutches. He knocked on Kendra's door and walked in.

"Colm, my God, what are you doing out of the hospital? You shouldn't be here. You need to rest."

"You tell him, Kendra, he won't listen to me," said Emily as she followed Colm through the door. "He's being stubborn. He seems to think he needs to be here."

With a white-knuckled grip on the crutch handles, Colm's left eye closed, and he bit his lower lip as he moved deeper into the office. "I'm grand, so I am. I need to be here. There's work to be done. Every minute we delay takes us further from learning the truth."

He eyed the monitor on Kendra's desk. The display was divided into four squares, each showing the image of a different room. Two of the rooms were occupied. Amelia Lonsdale sat with her lawyer in the first room, and her sister, Anne, occupied the second.

"Jenkins?" Colm asked. "Where is he?"

"He'll be along shortly," replied Kendra. "The doctors wanted to be sure the wound to his shoulder would not reopen. Constable Papineau and two others will put him in room three when they get here."

"Right, well, no time to waste. Let's get to it." Colm headed for the door. "I want to talk to Amelia first."

50

AMELIA LONSDALE SAT SLUMPED forward across the tabletop, her head resting in the crook of her arm. A middle-aged man with a white goatee and moustache gave her a nudge as Colm entered the room. He was completely bald and had the pinkest skin Colm had ever seen. The lawyer wore a crisp, grey, pinstripe suit, an immaculately white dress shirt, burgundy necktie and gold cufflinks. The Rolex on his left wrist told Colm this guy's hourly rate probably outpaced his weekly wages. Amelia Lonsdale might appear done in, but she'd brought a power hitter with her, and Colm reckoned he was in for a bit of a battle. He had to admit the attorney intimidated him just a bit. *Let the games begin.*

"Morning, Ms. Lonsdale, I understand you've been cautioned again," Colm placed a document on the table as he maneuvered his crutches around so he could sit. "This is a statement of the acknowledgment of that fact. Please sign it."

The lawyer gave it a once over and nodded. Amelia stretched her arms out wide and rubbed her eyes. She took the pen that was offered and signed.

"Grand," said Colm. "Now, I'm told you want to make some kind of deal. Is that true?"

"I don't know why I should," said Amelia, "I haven't done anything wrong."

Colm remained silent for a moment, then cast his gaze at the lawyer and said, "In that case, Mr.— I don't think I got your name."

"Hastings," said the lawyer holding out his hand. "Sidney Hastings."

Colm let the man's hand hang in the air. "Well, Mr. Hastings, I'm sorry, but you'll have to step outside."

Hastings' face and scalp turned almost crimson. "I, er, I well—you can't ask—"

"Oh yes, I can, Mr. Hastings. I intend to interrogate your client, and since she's had ample time to seek your guidance on this matter, it's time for you to leave."

"Wait, what?" Amelia jumped in. "I have the right to have my lawyer present."

Colm smiled and turned his attention back to his suspect. "Sure, that might be true if we were about a hundred kilometres south of here."

"Huh, what?"

Colm turned to Hastings, cocked his head back toward his suspect and said, "You tell her."

"He's right," said Hastings. "We're not in the States. Here, in Canada, lawyers can't sit in on interrogations." He turned to Colm. "Could I have a moment alone to explain it to her in more depth?"

"Right," said Colm. "But as you can plainly see, it's difficult for me to get around. If you make me move, I'm not going to be in a very receptive mood when I get back." He shifted his chair as a pretense to standing up.

"Wait," said Amelia. "What kind of deal?"

"That depends on what it is you'll be tellin' me, so it will."

Amelia let out a sigh. "He stays, or I don't talk."

"Agreed," said Colm. "But understand this, Mr. Hastings has no input, and everything you say is considered voluntary, and can and will be used against you."

Amelia nodded.

"I need you to say it—for the video." Colm pointed to the camera in the corner.

"Yes, I understand."

"I thought you might see it that way."

Colm leaned his elbows on the table and placed another paper out in front of her. It was upside down and only showed one paragraph. Amelia had to strain to read it — Sworn Statement of Confession — Subject: Calvin

Kieran Jenkins. Charge: Murder in the first degree. 4 Counts. Attempted Murder - 3 counts - Kidnapping - 2 counts - Assault - 1 count.

The list carried over to the next page, which Colm did not show them. "I have enough here to put you away for the murder of Harry Dalton. What you tell me will determine whether or not I proceed and recommend that the Crown prosecute you for murder or whether I decide to charge you with conspiracy to commit an indictable offence. Mr. Jenkins is in the next room, and he's been talking volumes."

It was a lie. Jenkins wasn't even in the building yet, and although he'd been spilling his guts to Constable Papineau, he hadn't been cautioned. Still, that didn't prevent Colm from enacting his ruse on Amelia.

Hastings pulled Amelia aside into the corner of the room. They spoke for a few minutes, and finally, Amelia nodded, and they sat down.

"I don't know this Jenkins character," she said. "I don't know what you think you've got on me, but you're barking up the wrong tree."

Amelia threw her shoulders back, crossed her arms, and raised her chin in defiance. Her tired eyes brightened as she glanced at Hastings and smiled. Remaining silent, Hastings too, sat, arms crossed and gave her a nod. Colm allowed her to have a moment of triumph.

It was short-lived, and when Colm said, "Perhaps the name Shinkwinn holds more meaning for you?"

Amelia grabbed Hastings by the arm, her fingers digging into his jacket sleeve, causing him to wince.

She began to sputter, "H-how do you know—"

"Oh, we know a lot more than you think," said Colm. "Would it surprise you to learn that Mr. Jenkins and Shinkwinn are indeed one and the same? Now maybe you'd like to do yourself some good and start talking."

"What do you want to know?"

"You've already told me about the business end of this deal, I'm sure there's more to it, but for now, I want to know about your relationship with Mr. Jenkins," said Colm. "How do you know Shinkwinn?"

Amelia looked over at her lawyer. Hastings remained stoic and unreadable. "He can't help you," said Colm.

"I don't know him, I never met him, I've only spoken with him three times. You have to believe me, I had nothing to do with the killings. That was all on him."

"You did nothing to stop it."

"How could I? I had no idea what he was up to. H-he wasn't supposed to kill anyone. He was just supposed to create an accident that put Harry out of commission long enough for—for—"

"For what?"

"For Anne to take power of attorney. It wasn't supposed to happen until after Harry signed the deal. The stupid ass fouled up everything."

"So, your sister is in this too," said Colm.

"Huh—no, Anne had no idea what was going on. Where Harry was concerned, she was totally oblivious. Harry was supposed to sign the deal, have an accident, and Anne would take over his affairs. He wasn't supposed to die."

"Causing an accident like that, that's a pretty big risk to take. How did you expect to do it without the risk someone might die?"

"I never thought of it that way. Kris said he could make it happen."

"You mentioned him before. How does Kris Martin fit into all this?"

"He's an asshole. Do you guys know what he does when he's out on patrol? One thing good will come out of this," said Amelia. "That sonofabitch will get his. He extorted thousands from me, but then he learned about our deal with Blackmore and decided he wanted more. He told me that he knew someone who could create a car accident, he'd get the call to respond and see to it that Harry was in no condition to walk by the time it was over. We never discussed killing anyone. It wasn't until Harry died on the highway that he realized there was a problem with Shinkwinn. That's when Kris decided his end of the deal was worth a much larger share. Millions, in fact, thirty to be precise."

"Thirty million, and where was that supposed to come from?"

"From the profits of our land deal. I paid Kris five million up front with the balance due when the deal was ratified. He assured me that they would take care of any obstacles that came our way. You know, planning permits, zoning, et cetera."

"They, they who?"

"Kris said he had a crew, and between them, they could ensure everything would work out in our favour. I don't know how he planned to do it, but obviously, something went wrong, because he split along with his friends, and Shinkwinn or Jenkins, whatever he calls himself, went totally offside."

"And you're telling me Anne Dalton had nothing to do with any of this. I find that hard to believe."

"Believe it. My sister is as dumb as a stump. Anne let that sorry excuse of a man run her life. I took over and when I'm finished—and regardless of what happens to me, I will finish it—Sidney has my full power of attorney should I become indisposed, so to speak, Anne will, by inheritance, become mega-wealthy."

"How so?" asked Colm.

"We intend to build a retirement community. Four-thousand homes in total. High end homes, very expensive and very exclusive. There are many affluent people out there. People with bags of money all looking for a little piece of heaven and this area is just that. We intend to build a community that will be the envy of the most popular places in Canada. We'll have a tournament class golf course, swimming and boating only minutes away. You know yourself, some of the best fishing and water-sports already exist in this region. To top it off, we're only two hours from three international airports. It's an absolutely perfect location for this kind of project. The total project should gross somewhere in the order of fifteen to twenty billion."

Colm raised his eyebrows.

"Yes, I said billion, with a B. The net profits for the company should be in the order of twenty-five to thirty percent. It would have been split four ways, but now I'm not sure. Blackmore's widow may opt-out. Shinkwinn hasn't done anyone any favours. Asshole!"

"Yeah, four ways, that reminds me, we know who the partners are, um, were. What we don't know is who is behind Anon Dental, your fourth partner. Care to shed some light on that one?"

Amelia shook her head. "Can't tell you. The truth is, none of us is sure who's behind Anon. Anon approached us through a lawyer in Toronto. We had the company's assets checked out, and it seems they had enough capital to invest. Each of us was to put up fifty-million, either in cash or letter of credit. That was Harry's end of the deal. He was going to get two hundred million for the whole works. I told you this already."

"Yeah, we got that much. We just need to know who the principals are in this deal. There may be more charges to lay. You might not be the only one that's in this up to your arse."

"Well, sir, that's where my cooperation ends. I can't help you, and even if I could, Anon had no knowledge of what was going on here. Pellini only knew about the Saunders land. He wouldn't have gotten involved with that; only he said he had a personal interest in it. So, who was I to argue? I let him get on with it. As it happens, it all turned out to our favour. Blackmore's dead, not that he had anything to do with this. He's a victim, not a suspect."

"So, you're falling on your sword as it were. Exonerating your partners, that's mighty noble."

"What good would it do to point fingers. All it would achieve is to kill the project completely. Nothing points to any guilt on their parts because Kris Martin was my problem and mine alone. Nobody knew about him or the shit he put me through."

Colm had all he needed. He still had doubts about Anne Dalton, but Amelia's insistence that Anne was oblivious to these events rang true. However, there was something else that niggled at him when it came to the widow Dalton. If Emily's theory was correct, he'd have his answer.

Colm pushed his chair back and grabbed his crutches. "I'm recommending that you be charged with conspiracy to commit an indictable offence. I'll leave it up to the crown as to whether he prosecutes or not. Unfortunately, the Kris Martin aspect of all this can't be verified."

"And why not?" asked Hastings. "He's one of yours, is he not?"

"True," said Colm. "I'll even go so far as to agree with Ms. Lonsdale, Kris Martin was a first-class asshole."

"Was?'

"Yeah, he's dead."

* * *

Emily had a score to settle with Cal Jenkins, but sitting in on the interrogation was out of the question. Instead, she had to share Jenkins' confession with Kendra Jacobs and Jen Stroud. The trio of women watched on the big screen located in the conference room.

"Harold Papineau has given his statement in writing," said Kendra. "Let's see if Mr. Jenkins comes anywhere close to Harold's interpretation."

"Did anyone bring popcorn?" quipped Jen. "This is kinda like a triple feature. We really should be charging admission for this."

"No," said Emily. "I think we're in for a quadruple feature, look there, bottom quarter, that's—oh, shit! That's Angelo!"

Kendra focused on the bottom left quadrant of the screen. "Yes," she said. "We issued a warrant for him yesterday. Conspiracy to commit, he's here on his own recognizance. We gave him twenty-four hours to turn himself in." She checked her watch. "He's right on time. Sit back, girls, let's watch the show."

Emily couldn't sit. She had to stand. Angelo's involvement in murder did not register. Her mind could not accept that possibility. Emily paced back and forth behind her comrades. Wringing her fingers in her hands and wishing she could be someplace else. She glanced over at the monitor periodically, absorbing the images, shaking her head in disbelief. *Cal Jenkins, okay, that makes sense. Amelia, maybe, the woman has motive. Her sister also has a reason. It might be possible that she's that dumb. But Angelo? No way!*

Jen had done the background work. Emily needed to be the one to question him. Authority or not, she was determined to confront Angelo Pellini, and she would do it today.

G. A. PICKSTOCK

51

THE MEDS WEREN'T DOING anything to ease Cal Jenkins' discomfort, and his mind could not process the fact that resting his weight on his arm only added to his misery. Beads of sweat formed on his forehead, yet the room was almost Dickensian cold. It was as if Scrooge himself was paying the heating bill.

Jenkins had had the benefit of the duty counsel's advice to remain silent, and like Amelia Lonsdale, he was surprised to learn that the lawyer could not be present in the room while he was being questioned.

"What, how will I know whether or not to answer any questions?" He stared at the lawyer with disbelieving eyes. "I have a right to a lawyer," he said.

"Yes, you do," said the duty counsel. "And I've told you to keep your mouth shut. All you need to remember are two words—no comment."

"But I've already told them everything. How can I say no comment now?"

"Had they cautioned you before you talked to them?"

"I—I don't remember. I was in a lot of pain," said Jenkins. "All I know is, there was a cop in my room, and I told him everything."

The lawyer thought for a moment. "I don't know how to help you, but I do know this. Keep your mouth shut. Your only response to any question should be, no comment. Can you do that?"

Jenkins nodded his head in the affirmative and the lawyer left the room. Cal Jenkins was prepared to follow the lawyer's advice, and then Colm walked in. The detective set his crutches against the table and sat across from Jenkins.

"Well, Cal old son, sure'n you're in a heap of trouble here." Colm sifted through the warrants for his arrest. "Four murders, attempted murder, assault, kidnapping, this list is endless. You're going away for a very long time."

"No comment."

Jenkins sat silent, trying through the pain in his shoulder to take it all in. His mind wandered in and out, hearing some of what Colm had to say. He knew he should follow the lawyer's advice, but he'd already said a lot to the cop that had guarded him. *So what's the point in shutting up now? When all this hits the news, I'll be a hero. They'll understand I was right. No jury will convict me.*

"Come on, Cal, or do you prefer Shinkwinn?"

Jenkins snapped his head up. Suddenly the pain in his shoulder was the least of his worries. It might have been the meds finally kicking in, but it was more the realization this cop knew about his Celtic ancestry. How in God's name could he know about Shinkwinn?

When they'd ushered him into the room and told him to have a seat, the pain in his shoulder was all he had on his mind. He hadn't noticed nor cared about anything in the dreary little room. Now it smelled like old gym socks and the air was cold and clammy. The table took up most of the space, and the old steel chairs were designed more for torture than comfort. Jenkins had failed to notice the camera pointing in his direction, but he was aware of it now. Painfully so, and no matter what he'd been telling himself, he knew this cop had more information than was good for him. Colm had Jenkins cold turkey at the river, but could the cop really pin anything else on him? He had to know.

Colm could almost hear the gears grinding in the town clerk's head. He let the silence in the room speak volumes to the man, and after a long enough pause, Colm said, "You almost got away with it. You know when you messed up, don't you?"

"No comment."

"Oh, I know you think that's going to save you in court, but you're wrong. And that failure of a lawyer who told you to keep your mouth shut is wrong. He gave you bad advice."

"No comment."

"Look, Cal, we've got you dead to rights, man. Can't you see that?" said Colm. "We've got your gun, we've got your prints on the gun, we've got your ammo, and your prints are all over the ammo bag."

"What ammo?" Jenkins asked. "You've got no ammo." A smug grin crossed his lips as he thought about the choices he'd made. Any ammunition the cops might have would have disintegrated by now. His bullets would have melted within minutes of being fired. Anything they might have found wouldn't last long enough to save intact. No, this cop was bluffing. He'd chosen mercury bullets for this very reason. No ballistics anywhere, and the rifle, well, it was purchased legally, no crime in owning an air rifle. Okay, they had him at the river. That would be tough to fight, but he had money, and a good lawyer might just get him off.

"No comment." Jenkins settled back and crossed his arms, once again reminded of the wound to his shoulder as he did so.

"Oh, come on, Cal, you can't think we're that incompetent. We know about Bannister and his bullet making artistry. We know you killed Blackmore. Remember the dog that chased you that night? Remember how the mutt snatched your fanny-pack away and ran off with it? That pack had your bullets in it. It was good of you to keep them in liquid nitrogen for us. And don't you worry mate, all three of those little beauties are safe and sound in our lab, frozen stiff, just the way you like them."

Colm paused to let his words sink in. The smug smile on Jenkin's face slowly faded, his chin dropped, and his complexion paled. It was precisely the effect Colm had wanted to elicit.

Colm continued, "What I don't understand is why did you kill him? I know about Harry Dalton, but even there, I don't understand why?"

Just as Colm was about to press the man harder, Jenkins breathed a huge sigh and said, "You're right. What does it matter now? I did it because they were going to kill this town. I had to stop them. Don't you see? If Dalton sells the factory, then it closes. If the factory closes, then the whole town dies. I watched it happen when Blackmore closed the furniture plant. I couldn't let that happen again."

"What makes you think the factory would close if Dalton sold it? Surely, whoever bought it would keep it running."

Jenkins shook his head. "You know, for a detective, you sure are stupid. I did my homework. Don't forget, I'm the town clerk. Everything that happens in this town crosses my desk at some point. They tried to hide it. They thought by going around me to the OMB, I wouldn't find out. They thought their plan would remain secret. But I figured it out, and when Martin contacted Shinkwinn, he had no idea what he was really doing. What I can't figure is how you made the connection."

Colm smiled and said, "Ah, now boyo, 'twas the leprechauns, so it was."

Jenkins shot him a quizzical look.

"You forget, I'm Irish. I speak Irish, not the way you think, with an accent, but real Irish. Mharaigh tú Harry Dalton, Cén fáth? Translated, you killed Harry Dalton. Why? Shinkwinn is Irish for Jenkins. All I had to do was search the web to find that out. So, go on, tell me the rest."

"Dalton was buying up land like crazy. The OMB was asking a lot of questions, and I had rezoning forms coming at me from all sides. Then I found out about Llandeso Investments. I knew which company actually owned all the land. They were going to buy it all, and cancel the leases on the property, and because of the way Harry Dalton structured everything, Llandeso would have absolute control. It wasn't until I saw the rezoning application for the plant that I knew for sure."

The picture came into focus, and Colm finally understood the mind of the man across the table from him. "Where does Shinkwinn fit in all of this?"

"Shinkwinn is a phantom," replied Jenkins. "Kris Martin knew that I'm an avid target shooter. We met one day at the gun range. Martin was there for training, and I was out there sighting in my new rifle. I guess he was impressed with my shooting skills, and later, in the clubhouse, we got to talking. He asked me if I could hit a moving target. I told him I'd shot more than a few deer on the run. It depends on the firearm, of course, but it's not hard. Then he asked me a strange question. Was there such a thing as a disappearing bullet? Had I ever heard of one? I told him I had never seen one, but that got me thinking, and I knew if I asked Jeremiah Bannister, he would know. Not long after that, Martin asked me if I wanted to earn some good money. I was joking when I said, who do I have to kill? I mean he's a cop, right? Then he tells me no one, just shoot out a tire. Make a car flip over, and he'd do the rest. I told him no, then he said, take the money and do it, or else. I gotta tell you, he scared the shit outta me. I agreed to do it on one condition:

he keep my identity a secret. We agreed to use a name my grandfather had used many years ago. Shinkwinn." Jenkins paused. "I need a drink, can I have a glass of water?"

Colm nodded and cast a glance over toward the camera. "Someone will bring a bottle in for you." A minute later, a constable knocked and walked in with two bottles of water. He set them down on the table and left the room. Colm opened one and handed it to Jenkins. "Carry on. So, what happened next?"

"I got that bank statement, you know, the one you found. A quarter of a million in a Cayman account. I even had the password. It was mine. All I had to do was shoot out one tire. I decided to take the shot. It wasn't supposed to happen until after the deal was signed, but when I found out what would happen if Harry sold the plant, well, I couldn't let that happen. I would be okay, but what about everyone else. This town relies on that plant, my parents rely on their pension from that factory, and it was all going away if Dalton sold out. I took the money and moved it to another account, then I decided Harry had to go, and it had to happen before he signed any contracts. I had the bullets made, and I took that rat bastard out with one shot."

"What about Nicole Saunders? What did she ever do to you?"

Jenkins' eyes almost looked sad at the mention of Nicole. "I had tried to get Nicole to sell me the property, but too many had become interested in it. She'd smelled a big payday coming and was hesitating, waiting for the best deal. When the land went to auction, and she lost out completely, Nicole went ballistic and threatened to go public with everything. I couldn't let that happen. The woman wouldn't listen to reason. Then you and your girlfriend got involved. You know the rest."

Colm didn't know the rest. "That's not all, is it? Why did you kill Ted Savage and try to kill Jim Roberts?"

"A woman called me, asking for Shinkwinn. She told me there was a package out at the farm. I confirmed it with my monitoring company."

"So, the farm belongs to you?" Colm interjected.

"I guess it does, although it's still in my grandfather's name. I never had the heart to transfer the deed. Anyway, I went out there, and sure enough, there was an envelope with fifty-thousand in it along with instructions to take it to the cemetery and drop it by a grave. When I found out who it was for, I decided to keep it. I was in this up to my neck by now. So, I decided what's one or two more. Take them out, keep the cash."

"And Blackmore and Anne Dalton, why them?"

"They were going to do what Harry had set out to do. Can't you see? I'm trying to save this town. Why can't you understand that? I thought with Harry dead, Anne Dalton would take over the plant, but no, she decides to finish the deal, and Blackmore was in it up to his ass. He deserved to die. That sonofabitch had already screwed this town over once, and now he was going to do it again. So, I shot that arrogant bastard and watched him fall into the river. That stupid dog chased me up the hillside and grabbed on to my belt. I had to let it go, or he'd have had me. It wasn't until later, when I watched you all cleaning up the mess, that I realized Anne Dalton had to go. She was the lynchpin, after all. Without her and the land, no deal could happen. But ain't that the way of it? There's always one more domino that has to fall."

Jenkins resigned himself to the inevitable. There would be no deal for him, no fairy godmother to swoop in and save him. There was no magic for Cal Jenkins, only a concrete cell and a lifetime of what-ifs. He'd tried to do the noble thing. His sacrifice was fruitless. Still, there was money in a Cayman account no one could touch. His wife and family would be looked after, and with that knowledge, he finally shut up.

52

UPON ARRIVING AT THE detachment office, Anne had been met by a young female officer and ushered into a pillbox they called an interrogation room. Shivering from the cold, she tried to control her temper as she waited for the detective to enter the room. She wanted to break something, pound on the door, anything to get attention. She'd been in this icebox so long, she needed to pee. *If someone doesn't come in here soon, I'm going to wet myself. And if that happens, I'll sue these assholes for all I can get.*

Anne glared at the surveillance camera. "I need the restroom now!" She yelled at the empty room. "What the hell is going on? It's been over an hour. I know someone is watching so you better get in here now or I'll—"

The door opened, and Kendra Jacobs entered the room. "I'm sorry, Mrs. Dalton, I'll show you to the washroom. Those bozos should never have left you like this."

"I haven't even been told why I'm here. Only that the detective needs to question me about Harry's death," said Anne, as she walked down the hallway to the washroom. "What's going on?"

Kendra opened the door to the washroom for her, "We just need to clarify some things about your husband's death, I'm sorry you've been inconvenienced, believe me, heads will roll. I'll wait here until you're finished."

Moments later, Kendra ushered Anne back into the room. "Brrr, it is cold in here. Let me see what I can do about getting some heat in here for you. Detective Sergeant O'Byrne will be in shortly, please, take a seat."

Colm walked in just as Kendra was leaving. They exchanged a knowing glance as he hobbled on his crutches to the table and sat across from Anne.

"I apologize for all this," said Colm. "Believe me, I didn't know you were going to be treated that way. I'm sorry. How are you feeling? Is your wound healing properly?"

"I'm fine," said Anne. "And sorry don't feed the bulldog, I have a good mind to call my lawyer and sue you bastards for false arrest. You had me locked in here. Why am I here? Am I under arrest?"

Colm smiled and asked, "Have you done something you should be arrested for?"

"What the hell kind of question is that? Of course, I haven't done anything wrong. What the hell's going on here? You ask me to come down here, lock me in this igloo of a room, and forget about me to the point where I damn near pissed my pants. I'm being treated like a goddamned criminal. Do I need a lawyer?"

"You're not under arrest, Mrs. Dalton, you're free to leave at any time. However, I do have some questions about the events of the past few days. We need to clear some things up, and I need a statement from you regarding the shooting at the river."

"Ask your questions and let me get the hell out of here. And turn up the heat, I'm freezing."

From the first time he'd met her, Colm had suspected this woman was no pushover. She just pretended to be easy going, but beneath it all, this was a lady who had her finger on more than one pulse, and Colm was about to find out just how many.

"Staff Sergeant Jacobs is working on the heating issue. I'm sure she'll get it sorted shortly. Right now, I need to know what you know about Llandeso Investments."

"Everything," she said. "What would you like to know?" Anne didn't wait for the next question. She knew exactly where this was going, and she had some surprises for the detective. "I knew what Harry was doing. He thought he had me fooled. He borrowed millions from me, but there was no way he needed that much to run the company. So, I decided to shadow him. I hired a company to investigate all of the financials of Dalton Tire. I've known for years that he's been buying land around here. Then I learned about my sister and her nefarious plan to take advantage of Harry and make a bundle. All this while Harry was keeping it from me. Let me ask you this, have you figured out who the fourth partner is yet?"

Colm smiled and rubbed his chin. He flipped open a folder he'd brought with him into the room. "I have to admit, at first it had me baffled, so it did." He grinned. "My last visit to you gave me the clue, although it really didn't dawn on me until the night Blackmore was killed. We deciphered your sister's connection to Llandeso. Llandeso is an anagram for Lonsdale. Anon Dental sounds like a dental practice of some kind, but in fact, it, too, is just an anagram for Anne Dalton. You girls do like your word games, don't you?"

Anne had to hand it to the detective, up until now no one had made the connection. She had couched her identity under a half-dozen umbrella companies, all of which were headed by what she called paper people. Friends whom Anne trusted and paid a generous stipend for nothing more than the use of their names. Her own sister hadn't made the connection, but then all she cared about was whether or not Anon Dental had the financial clout needed to invest in Llandeso.

"Good for you, detective, I'm impressed. My sister thinks I don't know what's going on, and I'm betting you haven't told her that you solved this part of the mystery."

Colm nodded. "True, Mrs. Dalton, I haven't revealed your part in this to her. What I need to know is whether you're a victim or a suspect."

"Suspect! Are you on glue? You were there. That maniac tried to kill me. Hell, he tried to kill you and your girlfriend. Suspect? Give your head a shake."

"You need to understand, Cal Jenkins killed all those people, and it all started with your sister conspiring to take out Harry. I just need to know, because Llandeso Investments is in this up to the brim. Anyone associated with the company is under suspicion."

"Well, you can take it from me, I know nothing about any of this. Jesus, even my sister, didn't know who was behind Anon Dental, and believe me, had she known, she would have ended it tout suite. No, detective, I'm sorry about all this, but I had nothing to do with any of these deaths. I was ready to consummate the deal with Blackmore and Llandeso. I wanted to see the look on Amelia's face when she realized I had bamboozled her out of fifty million, and that I stood to make a whole lot more than she would."

Anne could see the lights flick on in Colm's mind. The young detective was figuring it out at last. "Yes, sir, if Harry had sold, he would have received two hundred million for RealHard Holdings. I made the same deal with Blackmore. However, unbeknownst to anyone, I also had a vested interest in Llandeso. So, in reality, I was getting a hundred and fifty-million from my partners while still retaining a quarter interest in the property, and in turn, a quarter share of all future profits. I get my cake, and I get to eat it."

"So, what happens now? Jenkins did all this because he's deluded. He thinks the plant will close, and the whole town will be ruined."

Anne shook her head. "That was Amelia's plan. Once Llandeso got control of RealHard Holdings, Amelia would have controlling interest in the tire plant. She planned to liquidate everything, shut down operations and lay everyone off. It would have happened, but for my involvement. I didn't want the plant to close."

"But you don't care about the tire company, isn't that so?"

"I don't want to run it, but it is viable. It's just that for the past five years, Harry wasn't focusing on the plant. He was too busy buying land. I've been the one keeping it afloat."

"I don't get it, you said the plant was failing and that Harry was using your money for other purposes."

"Yes, he was, but the orders were still coming in. Jim Roberts had to go outside the company to finance them. Who do you think has been doing that?"

"You?"

"That's right, one of my shell companies has been factoring Dalton Tire's invoices for almost two years and making a tidy little profit. Harry had no idea. He was building his empire, and I knew it. When the opportunity arose to take advantage of all his efforts, I formed Anon Dental and wormed my way into the fold, as it were. I'm going to walk away from all this with a very healthy bank account, and my sister has no idea it's coming. As for the plant, well, I'm sorry Blackmore is dead, but that only opens up the door for me to get a larger share."

Colm didn't respond right away. He sat, contemplating what Anne had just told him. After a long pause, he said, "You say you were factoring Harry's work, but Amelia claims it was she who provided the cash for those jobs."

"Amelia's got so many shell companies she doesn't know what she owns. Together we inherited an immense fortune, but neither of us is without limits. Amelia spread herself pretty thin, and with her plan to oust Harry out of his company, she needed investors. So, I invested. I funded her factoring business. She bought the debt from Harry, and I bought the debt from her. Hell, mortgage companies have been doing this for years. Remember the banking crisis of '08? That all happened because the banks bought debt that had no chance of ever being repaid. The difference here is, I knew where the money was coming from. Amelia was little more than a pawn." Anne sat back and smiled, "She thought she had me fooled, helping me to find Harry's will. Shit, I knew where it was all along. I just needed to gain her trust, is all."

"Well, Mrs. Dalton, I think that's enough for now. If your story checks out, then I guess that will put an end to it. However, it still doesn't answer the question of what happens to the plant."

Anne stood to leave. She walked around the table to the doorway, turned back to Colm and said, "Things have changed. I don't know what will happen to our development project now. One thing is certain, the plant will survive. I take it, I'm free to go?"

"For now," said Colm. "I may need to speak with you again. If I do, I know where to find you."

Colm exited the interrogation room in time to watch Chrysti McNeil escort Anne to the door. Kendra Jacobs approached him from behind and whispered, "What do you think?"

Colm turned and said, "Who's next?"

"Pellini is in room four."

"Ok then, no rest for the weary. One thing, though, I need you to do something for me."

* * *

Looking every bit the businessman he was, Angelo stood as Colm entered the room. With a broad smile, he held out his hand to Colm and said, "Good morning, detective, I'm Angelo Pellini, please call me Angelo."

Colm shook the man's hand and took a seat across from him. "I'm Detective Sergeant Colm O'Byrne. Before we get started, I should caution you."

"That won't be necessary. I have nothing to hide."

"As you wish. Just so you know, everything in this room is video and audio recorded. I want you to know you are not under arrest. The door is unlocked, and you are free to leave at any time."

Pellini shot Colm a quizzical look. "I understand, Detective. How can I help you?"

"Tell me about your connection to Llandeso Investments."

Angelo spent the next few minutes reiterating what Colm already knew about the Blackmore/Dalton deal. Either he didn't know or was conveniently omitting any knowledge of Shinkwinn and his killing spree.

"The way I understand it, Llandeso hasn't closed the deal yet."

"That's right. I was hoping to get it done today. All the parties are in agreement."

Colm leaned back in his seat. "I guess you haven't heard, Angelo."

"Heard what?"

"Your deal is probably dead. You're here because five people connected to your project are dead, four of them murdered and the fifth shot in the attempt to murder me and three others. Two more have been seriously wounded, and one, someone who happens to be very close to me, has been assaulted and kidnapped. The charges are heaping up, and you are smack in the middle of it. I think your project might be as dead as the victims in this case."

Angelo slumped in his seat, his smile vanished, and although the man sported a fabulous tan, Colm saw the blood drain from his face. He couldn't speak. Colm let the news sink in before continuing.

After a long moment, Angelo asked, "You said four people, I only know of Harry Dalton and Nicole. There's more?"

"Yes, I'm afraid so. Barry Blackmore was killed two days ago, and before that, a man named Ted Savage was murdered. We have the murderer in custody, but there are still many questions to be answered. What we don't know is how deep this conspiracy goes into your organization."

"Our organization? Why would you think we had anything to do with this?"

"Come on now, everything points back to your organization. We know what the killer's true motives were, but the fact remains, this wouldn't have happened had your partner not engaged this man to interfere in the first place."

"My partner? Which partner? I have three, only one of whom I've met."

"I know that," said Colm. "And one who is quite dead, we've charged Amelia Lonsdale with conspiracy, and we've interviewed your third partner. As far as we can tell, she is in the clear."

"She, she who?" asked Angelo. "How did you find out—"

"Suffice to say, we did our homework. My job is to determine the level of your involvement."

"Do you have any evidence that points to me?"

"I admit, apart from your partnership in the company, I have nothing that connects you directly with these murders. Still, you had a connection to Nicole Saunders, and you could have had motive to kill her."

"I didn't kill her, and you know it. Don't play that game with me."

"No, you didn't kill her, Jenkins did that. She wouldn't cooperate with him, and he saw her as a threat," said Colm, shaking his head. "The man is delusional. It's sad really, and you're right, I have nothing that points directly at you. I just needed to look you in the eye to see for myself."

"So, are you going to tell me who the other partner is?"

"I imagine this will come as a shock to you. Anon Dental is owned by Anne Dalton."

* * *

Anne and Angelo formed a new partnership. Blackmore's widow had been offered a share, but she declined. Mrs. Blackmore had had enough of the controversy surrounding the Blackmore name and planned to move away. Amelia was out of the picture. The tire plant would survive. Dalton and Pellini had agreed to gift one-hundred acres to the plant along with all fixtures and equipment. Controlling interest of the business was turned over to the ESA. The new company retained forty-nine percent and held a line of credit sufficient to meet the needs of the operation. At a competitive interest rate, of course.

Cal Jenkins remained in custody awaiting trial. Colm doubted the man would serve any prison time. He was obviously mentally unbalanced, and pending a psychiatric evaluation, he might or might not be found guilty. At the very least, Cal Jenkins was delusional, but something still niggled at Colm's neck. There was one piece of the puzzle that hadn't dropped into place.

53

THEY TALKED FOR ANOTHER hour before Colm released Angelo. Once he recovered from the shock of Anne Dalton becoming his new partner, they discussed the future of the development project. Angelo was unsure, not having spoken with Anne, as to what direction things might take. Nevertheless, he had faith that they might be able to do something good for the community. The two men shook hands, and Colm followed Angelo into the hallway.

"I'm glad that's over," said Angelo. "I can't imagine what it would be like to be locked up in a room like that for an extended period."

"That's not entirely true, is it, Mr. Pellini?" Emily stood, blocking Angelo's way.

"Excuse me, what?" said Angelo.

"Or should I call you, Mr. James?" Emily had waited for this moment. She wanted to see the look on her brother's face when she confronted him. She wanted to know what kind of man would abandon his own family, to disappear and never return.

"You are Gary James, are you not?" Emily said, fighting back her tears. "You are my brother. Right?"

"H-how did you—how could you know—"

"Don't try to deny it. I have proof. Get back in that room, we're not done yet."

The three of them moved back into the small cubical. A bewildered Colm O'Byrne sat silently, wondering what was happening. He glanced over at Emily, opened his mouth to speak and promptly closed it again.

"I'll take it from here," said Emily. She locked eyes with Angelo. "You asked how? I wasn't sure until my friend Jen did some digging for me, but it was the bookcase in your living room."

Thanks to Jen Stroud, Emily had learned of Mr. Pellini's true identity. It was her father who had clued her in, but it was the bookcase that solidified it for her. The bookcase, one of only a hundred in existence, had sat in her living room in Blind River for as long as she could remember. Then one day, years after her brother had vanished, it wasn't there anymore. She hadn't missed it, hadn't noticed its absence until she went to find a book she wanted to read, and it was gone. Yet, her parents wouldn't say what had happened to it, just that they had given it away. She'd recognized that bookcase in Angelo's house. There was a small nick in the woodwork where Emily had banged her tricycle against it when she was little. Jen had done her magic, and now she knew. Angelo Pellini was, in fact, Gary Albert James, long lost brother and felon, turned real-estate developer.

Her father hadn't told her the whole story about what happened to Gary, and why they kept it secret all those years. The truth was that Gary had been accused and convicted of sexual assault on a young girl. He was sentenced to fifteen years and served three of those years in a correctional facility just south of Clarksville. It wasn't until after the girl retracted her statement and DNA evidence proved that Gary was innocent, that he received complete exoneration of the crime. However, the damage to the family name had been done, and Gary James had to disappear forever. Gary had sued the Ministry of Justice and won a massive settlement. He changed his name, and as far as Emily's father knew, Gary was living somewhere in Southern Ontario. Her brother had made one visit home after being released. He stayed long enough to retrieve some personal items and one or two pieces of furniture, the bookcase being one of them. Beyond that, he knew little else other than Gary was working in the construction industry.

"Admit it," said Emily, tears flowing freely down her face. "You are Gary, I know it. You've changed your hair, and you're older, but it's you. Why?"

Angelo stood, moved to Emily's side of the table, lifted her out of the chair and burst into tears. "I've missed you so much. Please forgive me. I didn't know what to do. I didn't think anyone wanted me to come home."

Emily fell into her brother's arms and kissed his cheek. She held him tightly and buried her tear-filled face in his shoulder.

Colm pulled himself to his feet and said, "I'll give you some privacy. Emily, are you okay?"

She nodded, and through her tears, she said, "Yes, I'll be okay."

* * *

Officially, Colm was still on sick leave, and with Christmas just around the corner, he thought it might be a good time for Emily to meet his parents. He wanted to take Emily to Ireland, and so, they stopped into a travel agency to inquire about flights. Emily saw the sign that read CC's Footwear & Leather Boutique and pointed it out to Colm.

"That reminds me," he said. "I want to talk to this CC. She has a bit more explaining to do."

"Ok, and I can show you the bag I like. I was thinking, maybe, if I'm a good girl, Santa Colm will buy it for me." She led Colm down the long, crowded passage into CC's shop.

Unlike her first visit, the shop was busy. Caroline sat at her desk with a short line of customers waiting to complete their purchases. She acknowledged them as they appeared from the hallway. "I'll be with you directly," she said. "Please feel free to look around."

The couple browsed the displays, finally arriving back at the small desk where Emily had seen the bag. Caroline looked up. "How can I help you?"

"I wanted to express my condolences on Ted's passing," said Emily.

"You mean his murder, don't you?"

"Yes," said Colm. He looked around the shop. One or two customers were browsing, but for the moment, the rush seemed to have died down. "I have a couple of questions for you concerning Ted. Can we talk for a few minutes?"

Caroline pushed back from her desk, moving her chair away. "I-I don't know anything. All I know is Ted's dead. What more can I possibly tell you?"

"You can tell us about Shinkwinn," said Colm as he pulled out his badge.

"Shinkwinn? I don't know any Shinkwinn."

"Don't lie to us," said Emily. "I think you know very well who Shinkwinn is. Now tell the truth, how do you know him?"

"I don't know what you're talking about."

The volume of their conversation had reached a level where the customers were beginning to take notice. Emily took advantage. "Ok, we can do this here or at the detachment, you choose. Either way, you're going to answer the question."

CC glanced at the inquisitive faces and relented. "Ok, I'll tell you. Ted and Jenkins—Ted always called him Shinkwinn—used to do a lot of shooting together. They would spend days at the range. They were always messing around with experimental firearms and ammunition. They got it in their heads one day to make an invisible bullet or some such thing. We were long since separated so I didn't care. Then one day, a woman called here looking for Shinkwinn. I told her there was no Shinkwinn here. She insisted that she'd been given this number and that I could put her in touch with him. So, I gave her Jenkins' mobile number."

"And the woman's name?" Colm saw the reluctance in her eyes. "Here or uptown, your choice."

"Anne Dalton, Harry Dalton's wife."

* * *

"I don't understand," said Emily. "Anne Dalton stood to make billions. All she had to do was ride it out. Why would she kill her husband?"

Colm reached under the Christmas tree and lifted a present. "This one has your name on it," he said, handing it to Emily.

"Don't try to change the subject. Tell me why."

"Because she didn't want to share. If she rode it out, as you put it, Anne would have to split the profits with Harry. There was no love in that marriage. She told me as much. No, she wanted him out of the picture, and simply putting him in the hospital wasn't enough. It's ironic that both sisters relied on the same shooter to do the job. Cal Jenkins must have thought he'd won the lottery, getting paid twice for the same work. And then taking out the one man who could identify him as Shinkwinn. Killing Savage wasn't an act of greed, it was self-preservation. Anyway, your brother is in control of the company. That must make you feel good."

The smile on Emily's face could have lit up the room. This was the first time in many years she could actually have a full family Christmas, and to top it off, she had two nieces she could spoil to her heart's delight. "I'm in heaven," she said as she tore open her gift.

Emily opened the box to reveal the golden leather handbag she'd admired at CC's shop. "Oh! I must have been a good girl."

"Look inside," said Colm grinning.

Emily opened the bag and reached inside to pull out an envelope. She opened the flap. Two first-class round-trip tickets to Ireland fell out. "Really! We're going to Ireland?" Emily threw herself at Colm and kissed him.

"I think there's something else in there," he said as they parted.

"What! There's more!"

Emily reached further into the bag and withdrew a small white velour-covered box. "Is this…"

* * *

There had been three snowstorms in the weeks leading up to Christmas, none of which remained on the ground for very long. The temperature had been unseasonably high, with more rain falling than snow. Colm looked across a field where bulldozers and excavators ploughed away at the soggy earth. Daylight was upon them, and the machines worked away at a feverish pace. They had progressed a fair distance with the building project. One whole street of basements was finished with the framework of multi-million-dollar homes sprouting out of the ground like matchstick models. Colm estimated there would be thirty or forty new homes ready for occupancy by the time summer rolled around. The new PelTon Retirement Community was well on its way to becoming a reality.

Christmas was over, but Santa Colm still had his naughty list, and one little girl hadn't been nice at all. It had been a collaborative decision, arrived at by studying and analyzing the evidence. Everything pointed in that direction and it all made sense. There was motive, opportunity, means and money. And it all fit. Everyone involved stood to profit, but she, most of all, had the most to lose if she failed.

Kendra Jacobs had obtained a warrant for the phone records Colm had requested. The conclusion was logical, and they had enough with the phone records and GPS data to prove their theory. Jenkins was the key. Much to Colm's surprise, he'd been found competent to stand trial and was desperate for a deal. With his testimony, a conviction was assured.

Colm pulled the Mini-Cooper into the driveway, and two more OPP cruisers followed behind him. He stepped up and pounded on the front door. A tired-eyed and bedraggled grey-haired woman rubbed her eyes as she opened the door.

"Anne Dalton, you are under arrest for conspiracy to commit murder, do you understand? You have the right to retain and instruct counsel without delay. We will provide you with a toll-free telephone lawyer referral service if you do not have your own lawyer. Anything you do say can and will be used in court as evidence. Do you understand? Would you like to speak to a lawyer?"

About the Author

With thirty years in the corporate world as a security consultant and locksmith, and as a former outdoor columnist for a local newspaper, G. A. Pickstock had many opportunities to work with law enforcement; fuelling his fascination for mysteries. Since retiring in 2013 he has turned his talents to the world of fiction and has written many short stories and novels. He is the author of two novels in the River's Edge Mysteries series. The second in the series, Edge of Death, is due for release in the summer of 2020, and book three will debut in the late fall of the same year.

Thank You

Thank you for reading Edge of Death. If you enjoyed the book, I would appreciate it if you would consider leaving a review. I can't stress how helpful this is in helping other readers decide if they should invest their time. Reviews from readers like you are the best recommendation a book can have. Without reviews, an author's books are virtually invisible on the retail sites. It also lets me know what you liked. You can leave a review by visiting the book's page. I would greatly appreciate it. It only takes a couple of seconds.

* * *

Thank you for buying Edge of Death. I like to build a relationship with my readers. It is one of the best things about writing. I occasionally send out a newsletter with details on new releases and subscriber only special offers. For instance, with each new release of a book, you will be alerted to it at a subscriber only discounted rate.

Hard Reprisal

By

G. A. Pickstock

G. A. PICKSTOCK

Chapter 1

WEEKENDS TIED TO THE CONFEDERATION Park dock generally meant relaxation, good conversation, good music, a few wobble pops in the cooler, T-bones sizzling on the grill and with luck, the company of some soft and willing personnel. With a single shout for help, all Walt's Tapin's plans were shot to hell.

He was tying up the stern line of his charter boat when the kid, fishing under the bridge, hollered. Climbing back aboard, he stepped onto the starboard swim platform to get a better look at the teenager heaving on his fishing line. His rod bent into a question-mark with each pull, then straightened out as he dropped it to reel in the slack. It was working. Judging by the action of the boy's rod, whatever he'd hooked was heavy, and Walt guessed right away, it was no fish.

Walt had seen the lad hauling on the line as he pulled the boat up to the dock. He'd been at it a while. Veins popped out in the boy's arms as he struggled with each mighty pull on the graphite rod. His catch inched closer and closer. A fluorescent flash of orange and green appeared at the surface, then vanished in the murky water. Line screamed off the reel as the river's current caught hold of his catch dragging it under. The teenager's struggle drew a crowd, and the know-it-alls offered their two cents.

"Whatever he's got there is huge."

"Keep the tip up, or you'll lose it."

"You're reeling in too quick, easy does it."

"Kids, you can't tell 'em nothin'."

"Probably a snag, that river's full of crap."

Walt kept one eye on the young angler and another on the crowd. The rubberneckers packed the dock, getting too close to his craft. A couple of them had the gall to use the gunwales as lawn chairs, taking a front-row seat to the action.

"I didn't buy this boat so you could set your fat asses on it," said Walt. "Step away, or you're gonna get wet."

"Take a pill, mister. We're not hurtin' your precious b—"

The rubbernecker stopped short as a collective gasp rose through the crowd when the young angler yelled, "Someone call 911."

Walt snapped his head around in time to see the lure one more time, the treble hooks embedded in the fabric of a pair of blue jeans. The only problem was, the owner was still wearing them.

***

The interlopers vacated their spots as Walt stepped back into the cockpit of the cabin cruiser. He took a towel out of a locker and wiped the spot where they'd been sitting. The crowd had grown to almost thirty or more as the teenager held firm to his catch. A couple of *'experts'* tried to assist the kid, but he was adamant that he could handle the task. A woman screeched and everyone jumped when they heard the siren. The sudden blast startled Walt as well. The sea of onlookers parted as a black and white Chevy Tahoe rolled to a stop only a few feet from the dock.

Walt's stomach did a figure-eight at the sight of the two Ontario Provincial Police officers as they exited the SUV. He recognized Gavin Harker right away. There was no mistaking the four-inch scar across the big constable's right cheek. At six-feet, two-hundred and twenty pounds, the cop didn't need the added bulk of his Kevlar vest and heavy leather gun belt to command authority. The scar alone said, "Don't fuck with me or you'll regret it." He wasn't afraid to mix it up, and his partner, Tanya Janosa, also had a mean streak.

In fact, Walt thought, she could be more sadistic than her partner. It was like she had something to prove. Janosa wasn't a pretty woman. She had a boyish frame, although that could be belied by the vest and the rest of the hardware, she donned every day. Her short, blonde hair was more masculine than feminine. She had what Walt could only describe as a face that resembled the south end of a northbound horse.

Walt had his reasons for wanting to keep his distance with this pair. He didn't trust them; he'd seen them in action. He was at home when the duo apprehended a man suspected of assaulting his wife. The couple lived next door to him, and from the privacy of his backyard deck, Walt had watched.

His neighbours had been at it for hours, arguing and screaming at each other. By the time the police arrived, the woman had a black eye, and so, Harker cuffed the husband, and when his back was turned, Janosa grabbed the man by the scrotum and squeezed. Even from a distance, Walt had winced in sympathetic pain at the ferocity in which Janosa administered her own brand of justice.

The body in the river had nothing to do with him. Nevertheless, Walt could not afford to be seen anywhere near these two cops. He suddenly wished he'd chosen another place to park for the weekend. Going below was an option, but doing so left his pride and joy at the mercy of the crowd now uncomfortably close to his boat. Some of the idiots were in danger of being knocked into the water and if it hadn't been for his boat being where it was, they might well have had a few Olympic hopefuls already. He turned away from the action. He took up residence in his captain's chair and busied himself at the helm. There was cover here in the shade of the canopy. He could keep his back to the crowd while keeping a weather-eye out for any who might try to take advantage of his deck-space. The boat was another matter. As one of the biggest boats on the river, it was easily recognizable. All he could do was keep his head down and bide his time.

"You folks want to give some room here," Harker commanded, as he stepped out of the Tahoe.

Walt cast his gaze backward. Harker pushed through the crowd. "I said, step back!"

Janosa approached the teenager and said, "Jeremy, right? Can't you reel it in?"

The boy nodded. "I didn't know if I should. I had it up to the shore almost, then the current dragged it away again. I was afraid I'd lose it. All these people around—I didn't know what to do."

From his captain's chair Walt angled himself to watch the action.

Jeremy had been fighting the current for almost an hour, his white-knuckle grip on the fishing rod never relenting for even a second. Walt wondered if he, himself, would have the stamina to hold on for so long.

As if the boy had read his mind, Jeremy said, "I need help here. It's heavy, and I'm getting tired."

Harker reached down and took the rod from Jeremy. The lad scrambled to his feet, flexing his right arm, stretching his cramped muscles.

"I got it." Harker looked at Janosa and grinned. "Looks like you're getting wet," he said. "I don't dare let go of this rod."

She wasn't happy and Walt grinned as he watched her trudge back to the Tahoe to unburden herself of all her gear. *Oh shit! She actually does have a frame under all that armour. Who knew?* Walt vacated his chair, pulled his hat low over his forehead, and risked venturing out onto the deck of the cockpit.

With her gear safely stowed away, Janosa, barefoot, trousers rolled up to the knee, fired daggers at her partner. She took a tentative step into the river. The water rose above her knees, soaking her uniform.

"Careful," said Jeremy. "No telling what's down there. Oh, and there's about a ten—" Janosa reached for the waistband and promptly disappeared under the water, popping up again about fifteen feet further downstream— "foot drop-off right about there."

Walt chuckled and hopped over the side and pushed his way through the bystanders crowding the dock. It was time to get out of Dodge. He found the cleat where his bowline was fastened and fumbled with the lines. Another boater had used the same cleat and, in true land-lubber fashion, had captured Walt's line in such a way as to force him to undo both lines to free his own. By the time he returned to let go his stern line, the constables had pulled the corpse onto the dock, leaving it precisely as it landed.

For a moment, his desire to leave was interrupted by all the commotion. After all, a body in the drink wasn't something one encountered every day. Like the crowd around him, he watched with morbid interest as the cops pulled the corpse out of the river. Janosa stood beside the boat, dripping wet. Walt froze as she locked eyes with him. Momentarily stunned, he grabbed the towel he'd used on the gunnel and handed it to her. Each held the towel slightly longer than necessary as they made eye contact. She gave a slight nod and turned away.

Harker keyed his mike, "6Juliet508, code 750, roll the Duty Sergeant to this location, and we're gonna need an ambulance and the coroner."

Getting at his stern-line now was impossible. The cleat he'd tied up to was right beside the spot where the cops had dumped the body.

***

Walt's nerves had almost settled when the detective and his girlfriend showed up. A few in the crowd had dispersed, returning to their boats and their beer to gab about the events of the evening. As the couple approached, he recognized Colm and his girlfriend. The butterflies were back, and they were threatening to take control of every one of Walt's bodily functions. As they walked across the grass, the woman immediately busied herself, wandering through the remaining crowd asking innocuous questions. *Jesus, it's like a goddam reunion. They're the last two I need to see right now.*

He toyed with the idea of going below deck, hiding away in the cabin until the hubbub died down. But then the girl spotted him. She looked right at him and headed in his direction. Hiding below would not be an option. *I shoulda left when that kid started yippin'.*

Walt scanned the area looking for a way out when someone called her name, distracting her long enough for him to grab a knife and cut his stern line free. The boat drifted away from the dock. Without a sound, the bow thruster nosed the boat toward the centre of the river, and before the nosey girl in the flowery skirt and the white tank top could react, Walt tapped the throttle. The triple Yamaha 425s came to life, powering the cruiser down the Clarksville River, emitting little more than a quiet hiss. By the time the girl looked back, he was too far away. Walt let out a deep satisfied sigh, "Damn, that was close."

G. A. PICKSTOCK

Chapter 2

DR. BOB GENTRY WIPED the perspiration from his forehead as Colm and Emily approached.

"What have we got here, Bob?" Colm asked.

"Not sure yet," said Gentry, shaking his head. "Looks like a drowning. He's got a laceration on the side of his head just above the temple. He might have hit something when he went into the water. I won't know until I get him on the table."

"Foul play?"

"Possible," said Gentry, nodding. "The knock, on his head, could be from anything. He's been picked clean; no watch, jewelry, keys, nothing. It's possible, he's been robbed."

Colm nodded and stooped beside the body. "Can I move him?"

Gentry nodded as he pulled off a pair of latex gloves. "Sure, but like I said, there's nothing there. Let me get him on the table. I should have some answers as to COD in the morning."

The man appeared to be in his mid-forties, he had brown hair and no visible scars except for the cut on the side of his head. The detective rolled the man onto his side and searched for a wallet. Just as Gentry had said, there wasn't one.

He surveyed the area. The gawkers persisted despite the presence of emergency vehicles dominating the space. Fire department EMTs were busy setting up to remove the body. An ambulance waited to transport the victim to the morgue. Colm counted fifteen boats tied up the dock; filling it to capacity.

7

It was summertime, and the weekend activities in the park always attracted the boaters. They would spend the weekend visiting and partying. The largest boat in the group was tied up only a few feet away from where the body now rested. Its owner busied himself at the helm and it looked to Colm as if he was preparing to leave. Constables Janosa and Harker stood gawking at the whole works as though they'd never been to a crime scene before.

Janosa was trying to dry off in the darkening heat of the evening. Harker, however, seemed disinterested and detached from the whole scene.

"Who found the body?" said Colm.

Harker motioned over toward Jeremy and said, "That young fella over there found him. He hooked him with a fishing line. Janosa pulled him in."

"Then what?"

"Then we called in a 750 and waited for the troops to arrive," said Harker.

"Did you bother to interview any of the bystanders? Maybe ask a few questions? Maybe someone saw something, maybe someone knows who this guy is," said Colm.

Harker's face flushed. He rubbed the back of his neck and stammered, "Well—I —that is—I was helping—"

"Never mind," snapped Colm. "Get yer large self, moving and take a statement from the young lad. Then help yer partner wrap this lot up."

Colm shook his head as Harker turned away while poking around in his pocket for his notebook.

"Hey, you, Jeremy, I need to get a statement…"

Harker and Janosa had only been with the detachment for six months, and this lack of professionalism had just put the constables on Colm's radar.

***

Colm leaned against the Mini-Cooper as Emily approached. "Did you learn anything from the lookie-loos?"

"No, nothing of value," said Emily. "There was a boat at the dock, and I was going to speak with the owner, but he took off before I could get to him."

"I saw that boat," said Colm. "Nice bit of kit. Must have set that bloke back a few bucks. The kid, Jeremy, said he pulled up just before he hooked the body. I doubt he had anything to offer. I wouldn't worry about him."

"There was something about the way he looked at me," said Emily. "We made eye contact. He knew I was heading his way. We were barely ten feet apart. I feel like he was in a hurry to get out of there; that he didn't want to speak to anyone."

Colm grinned, "I don't know. I watched him. People were using his boat as a park bench. He was pushing the crowd away. Sure, I think he took off because he didn't want the rubberneckers damaging his pride and joy."

"Maybe, but he cut the stern-line to get free. Seems awful fishy to me. Believe me, those lines aren't cheap. I know, my dad's a charter captain. Something's not right there—"she shrugged—"So now what?"

"I have to go and check out the restaurant across the river. See if anyone there might have seen anything. I guess you can go home, and I'll be along shortly. We won't know anything until Gentry has completed his examination and the forensics team has nothing to do here. They'll pack up in a bit. Janosa and Harker are taking statements which they should have been doing all along. You can be sure, I'll have a few choice words for them when we get back to the office."

***

The sign on the restaurant entrance said, 'Closed for Renovations.' It had been closed for over a week and would not reopen for another two weeks. Colm turned his attention to the scene across the river. In the waning light of the evening, the tumult of the discovery had died down. The medics were gone, the body whisked away to the morgue for Bob Gentry to perform his magic, the crowd had dispersed, and Janosa and Harker looked to be wrapping things up. The weekend boaters had returned to their boats and the festivities of normalcy had begun.

Colm cast his eyes around the parking lot. On the far side of the vacant space, a solitary van sat in the shadow of the bridge. Its dark colour made it almost invisible in the fading light, and the streetlamps, from the roadway above, cast an even deeper shadow over the spot. As he set off toward the vehicle an ear-splitting howl made him jump. Startled by the pain-filled wail, Colm looked down in time to catch a glimpse of a tabby cat racing away from him, tail in the air as the cat hurtled back toward the van. The tabby vanished under the truck. Concerned about the moggy's welfare, Colm walked over to see if the cat was injured.

He approached the back of the vehicle and traversed to the driver's side in time to see the animal jump through the open window into the van.

"Excuse me," said Colm as he approached the window. There was no answer. He peeked inside. The tabby hunched down on the driver's seat, ears laid back, mouth open revealing four bayonet-like fangs. The cat's whiskers bristled. The hair on his neck stood straight up. His eyes wide and focused, the feline glared at Colm and hissed his warning letting out a low mournful growl. The muscles in his legs tensed, ready to spring forth, launching a surprise attack on any who dared to enter. Colm backed away.

From his vantage point, Colm saw the keys to the van dangling from the ignition, and a burst of realization hit him. *This van might belong to the corpse in the river.* He backed away and called in the registration.

"It belongs to one Haydn Francis Hard, Sarge," the voice from the phone stated. "I have an address. I'll text it to you."

"Do that," said Colm. "And send animal control to get this cat. I'd take him myself, but he's not very friendly. I'll wait 'til they get here."

"Will do, Sarge. Anything else?"

"No, not just yet. That'll do for now."

***

The animal control officer gathered the cat without much fuss and stowed him away in the back of his pickup truck.

"What will happen to him?" asked Colm.

"We'll keep him for two weeks. If no one comes to collect him then he'll be offered for adoption, and if, in a month, he's still with us, then we'll try to find a foster home until he is adopted. Failing that,"—the control officer grimaced and shrugged—"I'm afraid it's the long sleep for him."

"That seems drastic," Colm said.

"We don't have the space or the resources to keep them any longer. You have no idea how many strays we have turned in to us. There's only so much we can do."

Colm dug into his pocket and produced a business card. He wrote on the back of the card and handed it to the control officer.

"That's my personal cell number. I want you to call me in two weeks if he isn't claimed."

The animal control officer shrugged and shook his head. "I have nothing to do with placement. I just pick 'em up. I'll give this to Cindy back at the office, but I can't promise anything."

Colm rubbed his chin, "Sure, this cat is vital to my investigation and if anything happens to him without informing the OPP there will be consequences. Don't lose that card."

Hard Reprisal

WILL BE AVAILABLE ON AMAZON IN THE FALL OF 2020

Printed in Great Britain
by Amazon